Praise for

CARTWHEEL

"DuBois hits [the] larger sadness just right and dispenses with all the salacious details you can readily find elsewhere.... [*Cartwheel*'s] portraiture hits delightfully and necessarily close to home."
—*The New York Times Book Review* (Editor's Choice)

"[A] gripping, gorgeously written novel."
—*Entertainment Weekly* (The Must List)

"[A] page-turner of a novel... The power of *Cartwheel* resides in duBois's talent for understanding how the foreign world can illuminate the most deeply held secrets we keep from others, and ourselves."
—*Chicago Tribune* (Editor's Choice)

"Sure-footed and psychologically calibrated ... Reviewers of duBois's first novel, *A Partial History of Lost Causes,* called it brainy and beautiful, a verdict that fits this successor.... As the pages fly, the reader hardly notices that duBois has stretched the genre of the criminal procedural. The limberness is welcome, indeed."   —*Newsday*

"From the first page, duBois's intelligent, penetrating writing makes this sad story captivating, delivering it from the realm of scuttlebutt and into that of art.... What else can we learn from these events? The answer is plenty, as duBois explores grief and love, youth and aging, and Americans abroad through a set of distinctive characters bound by calamity."   —*The Dallas Morning News*

"[A] thrilling book... What influences our perception of reality— morality, faith, sexuality, privilege—and what happens when we realize those perceptions aren't infallible?"   —*BuzzFeed*

"Perhaps the twenty-four-hour news cycle's headline splashing, surface-grazing details of international murder cases involving youth and beauty are driven by the allure of discovering the elusive psychological meanderings of a case's central characters. This is precisely the

bet Jennifer duBois places—and wins handily—in her sophomore novel. . . . Burrowing into the psyche of the full-blooded cast of characters, duBois writes complex, shifting points of view and gripping revelations of plot points."
—*The Austin Chronicle*

"[Jennifer duBois is] heir to some of the great novelists of the past, writers who caught the inner lives of their characters and rendered them on the page in beautiful, studied prose. . . . She aims to observe the thoughts that intrude at the most inappropriate times, to capture memories and intricate emotions, and to make penetrating comments about living today. In *Cartwheel*, she accomplishes this with acrobatic precision."
—*Pittsburgh Post-Gazette*

"A convincing, compelling tale . . . The story plays out in all its well-told complexity."
—New York *Daily News*

"Jennifer duBois is destined for great things."
—*Cosmopolitan*

"Stunning . . . gripping . . . It's a novel that a reader will be eager, perhaps even desperate, to discuss with other readers."
—*BookPage*

"Masterful . . . [a] compelling, carefully crafted, and, most importantly, satisfying novel."
—*Bustle*

"[DuBois] does an excellent job of creating and maintaining a pervasive feeling of foreboding and suspense. . . . An acute psychological study of character that rises to the level of the philosophical . . . *Cartwheel* is very much its own individual work of the author's creative imagination."
—*Booklist* (starred review)

"*Cartwheel* is at once a philosophical and discursive novel, but also an addictive, challenging read. . . . Astonishing, breathtaking, and harrowing."
—*New York Journal of Books*

"Scalpel-like . . . DuBois is a brilliant young writer with an ironic wit and mastery of the complexity of human character. . . . It's mesmerising on the foibles of an ordinary middle-class family trapped in a nightmare of public suspicion and distortion it can't control."
—*Sydney Morning Herald*

"DuBois boldly turns scandal and gossip into intelligent, psychological literature." —*Dominion Post Weekend* (Wellington, New Zealand)

"A bold literary novel ... [suffused with] dark humour while never downplaying the seriousness of the event at its core.... DuBois has wisely dispensed with callow exploitation to tell a story that's challenging and engrossing." —*Big Issue Australia*

"*Cartwheel* is so gripping, so fantastically evocative, that I could not, would not, put it down. Jennifer duBois is a writer of thrilling psychological precision. She dares to pause a moment, digging into the mess of crime and accusation, culture and personality, the known and unknown, and coming up with a sensational novel of profound depth."
—JUSTIN TORRES, *New York Times* bestselling
author of *We the Animals*

"Jennifer duBois's *Cartwheel* seized my attention and held it in a white-knuckled grip until I found myself reluctantly and compulsively turning its final pages very late at night. It's an addictive book that made me miss train stops and wouldn't let me go to sleep until I'd read just one more chapter. And it's so much more than just a ravenous page-turner—it's a rumination on the bloodthirsty rubbernecking of the twenty-four-hour news cycle and the bewitching powers of social media, and a scalpel-sharp dissection of innocence abroad, a book charged with a refreshing anger, but always empathic. Jennifer duBois has captured the sleazy leer of lurid crime and somehow twisted it into a work of art."
—BENJAMIN HALE, author of *The Evolution of Bruno Littlemore*

"Like its namesake, *Cartwheel* will upend you; rarely does a novel this engaging ring so true. Inscribed with the emotional intimacy of memory, this is one story you will not soon forget."
—T. GERONIMO JOHNSON, author of *Hold It 'Til It Hurts*

By Jennifer duBois

Cartwheel
A Partial History of Lost Causes

CARTWHEEL

CARTWHEEL

A NOVEL

RANDOM HOUSE TRADE PAPERBACKS · NEW YORK

JENNIFER duBOIS

Published in the United States by Random House Trade Paperbacks,
an imprint of Random House, a division of Random House LLC,
a Penguin Random House Company, New York.

RANDOM HOUSE and the HOUSE colophon are registered
trademarks of Random House LLC.
RANDOM HOUSE READER'S CIRCLE & Design is a registered
trademark of Random House LLC.

Originally published in hardcover in the United States by Random House,
an imprint and division of Random House LLC, in 2013.

Library of Congress Cataloging-in-Publication Data
duBois, Jennifer
Cartwheel: a novel/Jennifer duBois
pages cm
ISBN 978-0-8129-8582-5
eBook ISBN 978-0-8129-9587-9

1. Women college students—Fiction. 2. Americans—Argentina—Fiction.
3. Murder—Investigation—Fiction. 4. Psychological fiction. I. Title.
PS3604.U258C37 2013
813'.6—dc23
2013016952

Printed in the United States of America on acid-free paper

www.randomhousereaderscircle.com

9 8 7 6 5 4 3 2 1

Book Design by Liz Cosgrove

Although the themes of this book were loosely inspired by the story of Amanda Knox, this is entirely a work of fiction. None of the characters are real. None of the events ever happened. Nothing in the book should be read as a factual statement about real-life events or people.

To Justin

I was the shadow of the waxwing slain
By the false azure in the windowpane

—*Pale Fire,* Vladimir Nabokov

PART I

CHAPTER ONE

February

Andrew's plane landed at EZE, as promised, at seven a.m. local time. Outside the window, the sun was a hideous orb, bleeding orange light through wavering heat. Andrew was still woozy from his two Valiums and two glasses of wine, the bare minimum that he needed to fly these days—to anywhere, for anything, though especially for here, for this. The irony of being a professor of international relations who was terrified of international travel was not lost on him (no irony was lost on him, ever), but it could not be helped. Neither could it be mitigated by the knowledge—always understood but now finally believed—that the things that go wrong are rarely the things you've thought to worry about.

Andrew patted Anna on the shoulder and she roused herself. He watched her forget and then remember what was happening. He was glad he didn't have to remind her. She pulled her iPod headphones out of her ears, and Andrew caught snatches of some ambient, low-key music—the music of the day was so bloodless, he often thought: Didn't these kids *want* anything, and weren't they *mad* at anybody?—before she thumbed it quiet. Anna had endured the trip reasonably well—her sensible hair was limp in a ponytail; her nautical stripes, so favored by his students these days, were barely creased. She wore her competence lightly. She didn't know how terrifying it was to him.

"Dad," she said. "You need to blink."

Andrew blinked, painfully.

"Does your corneal abrasion hurt?" she said.

"No," he said. It always hurt. He had poked himself in the eye during class one day—while making a particularly vigorous point about Russian cyber-terrorism in Estonia—and he'd had to go to the ER for a local eyeball anesthetic. Now his eye hurt every morning, every flight, every time he was tired or stressed, which he always would be, now, for the foreseeable future.

"Will we see Lily today?" said Anna.

Andrew licked his lips. His eyeballs were so dry that he thought they might tear. The Argentina flights from the East Coast went only once a day, and only from D.C., and it was impossible to get to D.C. in less than seven hours, no matter how you looked at it. Andrew could not, he reminded himself, have gotten here any earlier. "Probably not today," he said.

"Will Mom see her when she comes?"

"Hopefully." Andrew's voice cracked, and Anna looked at him, alarmed. "Hopefully," he said again, to show her that the crack had been fatigue, not emotion.

Outside, it was summer, as Andrew had known—but secretly not entirely believed—that it would be. Anna shimmied out of her jacket, her nose crinkling at the smell of gasoline. Inside the airport, the terminal thrummed with travelers. Andrew offered to buy Anna a soda, then rescinded this offer when he spotted the newspaper outside the kiosk—he didn't have much Spanish beyond what one absorbed through cultural osmosis and a general familiarity with Latinate words, but it was uncomfortably easy to get the gist of the headlines, whether he wanted to or not. Andrew wished desperately to keep Anna away from the newspapers. She knew the contours of the accusation, of course, but Andrew had managed—or thought he'd managed—to protect her from the worst of it. The coverage was only just beginning to leak over to the United States, anyway, and Andrew had spent long hours on the Internet looking for the stories: the depictions of Lily as hypersexual, unstable, amoral; the lurid intimations about her romantic jealousy and rage; the accounts of her smug and towering atheism. The fact that she hadn't cried—not after Katy was killed and not during the interrogations, either (the Internet had harped on this so much that Andrew had found himself shouting *"She's not a crier! She's just not a fucking crier!"* into the computer). And finally, the worst, most militantly misunderstood information of all: the fact that a delivery truck driver had seen Lily running from the house with blood on her face the day after the murder. No matter that she'd been the one to find Katy; no matter that she'd been the one to kneel over her and try to administer brave and futile CPR. The news reporters weren't bothering with that information, and Andrew didn't expect them to start. He was beginning to understand what story they were trying to tell.

Announcing that the sodas would be better outside the airport, Andrew maneuvered Anna (rather deftly, he thought) toward baggage claim, where they waited for fifteen minutes in silence. In wrestling the suitcase off the conveyer belt, Andrew accidentally stomped on the foot of an androgynous teenager.

"Permiso," he muttered to the teenager, who was wearing a T-shirt that said SORRY FOR PARTYING. Beside him, Andrew could feel Anna stiffen; Andrew liked to at least know how to apologize wherever he went, but Anna hated it when he tried to speak any language other than English. Two summers ago, in a different lifetime, Andrew had spent three months doing research in Bratislava—his area was emerging post-Soviet democracies, though his job got a little less interesting the more fully the democracies emerged—and afterward the girls had met him in Prague for a week of castles and bridges and beer. Anna had flinched every time he opened his mouth to deploy some phrase he remembered from his three semesters of college Czech. "Dad," she'd said. "They speak English." "Well, I speak Czech." "No. You don't." "It's polite to address people in the local language." "No. It's not." And so on. Lily, on the other hand, had made him teach her as much Czech as he could, and had then thrown it around willy-nilly—mispronounced, absurd, chirping informal greetings at storekeepers who tended to smile at her, even though she was basically insulting them, because she was so obviously well-intentioned. Andrew used to imagine that Lily's general goodwill, the buoyancy with which she addressed her life, was easily detectable by all people of the world, and that it would protect her. It seemed now that this was not the case.

In the taxi, Andrew and Anna passed fruit stands, dingy-looking bars, backfiring motorcycles. Through the hazy heat, Andrew saw barrios with squat, intersecting systems of housing; clotheslines shimmering with brightly colored clothes; the occasional corrugated tin roof winking astral-bright in the sun. The roads were medium-good; the infrastructure in general seemed decent. Out the window, Andrew saw satellite dishes wedged improbably between houses, looking like the detritus of abandoned spaceships. He saw a large compound, walled and razor-wired, manned by two security guards with walkie-talkies. He craned his neck to see if it was the prison, but it turned out to only be a housing development.

"Nothing's open," said Anna. She was looking out her own window and did not turn around.

"It's Sunday," said Andrew. "Very Catholic country."

"It's too bad that Latin America isn't your area."

Andrew stared at the back of Anna's head. She had lately taken to making inscrutable declarative statements in studied neutral tones. Andrew desperately hoped that this was not the onset of irony.

"You might get some work done, I mean," she said.

"I don't know about that." Andrew was suddenly nauseous, awash with their strange new calamity. There was, of course, no possibility that Lily had actually been involved in any of this; Andrew's confidence on that point was part of what had made the situation seem, initially, not catastrophic. The accusation was so ghastly and so wild and so patently, transparently, ludicrous that he'd nearly laughed when he first heard of it. Not that there weren't a few things he could imagine Lily getting justly arrested for. Before she had left, he and Maureen had had a series of sober conversations with her—about the harshness of Latin American drug laws, mostly, as well as the laxity of Latin American sexual safety standards. They'd sent her off with an enormous box of Trojans—industrial-sized, Andrew thought, issued for health clinics or music festivals, no doubt; a box that size could not possibly be intended for the use of a single human being. Andrew reeled to think of how much sex his daughter would have to have to run through all of them. Nevertheless, he had bravely and maturely had the conversation, alongside Maureen (such was their commitment to pragmatism! such was their commitment to co-parenting!), and then bravely and maturely sent Lily off with the box. And Andrew had worried about Lily constantly—he worried about her being kidnapped, trafficked, impregnated, sexually assaulted, afflicted with some horrible STD, arrested for marijuana use, converted to Catholicism, wooed by a long-lashed man with a Vespa. He worried she'd make too few friends, then he worried she'd make too many. He worried that her GPA would suffer. He worried about her bug bites. He worried so much that when there came a call from Maureen—on his work phone in the middle of the day, her voicemail left in a strangled half whisper—Andrew could taste metal in his mouth, so certain was he that something life altering had happened. And when he heard Lily was in jail, his mind flooded with grim visions of drug use and anti-Americanism and political points to be scored. He could imagine how she'd look to everyone (naïve, and entitled, no doubt), and he could easily imagine the incentive for punishing her harshly.

So when the accusation turned out not to be drugs—not drugs, or fare jumping on the metro (did Buenos Aires even have a metro?), or trespassing through someone's field while looking at the stars, or any one of the countless thoughtless crimes that he could believe his daughter might have committed—Andrew was mostly relieved. An accusation of murder was outrageous to the point of being comic, and thus was no great threat.

Andrew had tried to communicate some of this feeling to Lily on the telephone, when she'd finally, finally, been allowed to call. "Don't worry," he had said, over the terrible connection. It seemed absolutely vital that Lily know she did not have to tell them she had not done it; her innocence and eventual acquittal must be the unspoken premises of all their interactions—to be referenced in passing, perhaps, but never formally declared. "I know," he'd said. "We all know." Mordantly, from a great distance, she'd said, "Know what?"

But now, in the overheated taxicab, with fragments of Buenos Aires flashing through the window, Andrew was beginning to wonder. He was beginning to wonder if this was indeed a catastrophe on the order of the others; he was beginning to wonder if it might join them, making a triad that would hold up his life like Roman columns. First—most importantly, most irreducibly—there was the death of Janie, their first daughter, at two and a half, from aplastic anemia. This was the tragedy that made all other tragedies pale, the template onto which all other grief was mapped. The divorce, comparatively, was a minor hiccup. Nobody had been surprised—not even he and Maureen had been surprised—though they had been disappointed, certainly, in their own lack of originality. And now there was this. It was all, Andrew thought, a little much for one lifetime—though he had to weigh it against his socioeconomic privilege, health, maleness, whiteness, heterosexuality, American citizenship, etc., etc.; he'd been in academia long enough to know how far the scales were tipped in his favor, and how strenuously he must try at all times to acknowledge this, and how earnestly he must attempt to make his life an apology for its central accidents—and yet, and yet.

"Look," said Anna. She pointed to a mansion—enormous, drowning in its own decadence, already receding behind them. "Is that where *he* lives, do you think?"

Andrew was not quite sure who *he* was—the rich boy with whom Lily had conducted a five-week-long romance, presumably—but he was resolved to answer firmly anyway. "No," he said, tapping Anna's shoulder and frowning at its boniness. He tapped his own for comparison. "How are you holding up, Old Sport?" he said. He'd started calling Anna "Old Sport" sometime during her adolescence, when it became quietly clear to him that she was his least favorite daughter.

"Okay," she said dully. "I'm tired."

"You can conk out at the hotel."

"I have to run at the hotel."

"Oh. Right."

Anna was on the cross-country team at Colby—she wasn't a star, but was known for her diligence—and she'd gone running every day for two years straight, even on holidays, even with the flu. There had been a local newspaper article about it. She had almost cried—and it was the only time she'd almost cried—when Andrew had told her that there was no fucking way she was going to be allowed to run outside on their trip. "Your sister is locked up for life, and you're worried about getting your exercise? Priorities, please." He had shouted it. It had been a terrible day with Peter Sulzicki, the lawyer. "You think you're going to run through the streets of that city? You'll be kidnapped in five seconds flat. I don't need another daughter arrested or dead." Andrew wished immediately that he had not said this. To make it up to Anna, he had promised to find a hotel with a gym. But Andrew knew that this trip would break her streak, one way or another.

Poor Anna. She loved Lily, but she must have had the sense that Lily was always the one to be involved in spectacles, that Lily was the one for whom the rules were always bent. It was all the more unfair, then, that Andrew loved Lily more. Not much more—but no difference could be truly negligible when it came to the love of your children, since what it really meant was that he loved Anna less. This was only because Anna had such tough competition: Janie, precious Janie, was a tragedy, and Lily, cherished Lily, was a miracle. Anna, to her enduring misfortune, had only ever been a child.

Still, Andrew was filled with a lunge of tenderness for her now. "Hey," he said, pulling at her ponytail.

"Dad, stop it."

"I'll order us some room service for when you get back. Something special. What's the thing here? Steak?"

Anna gave him a flat stare. How could Andrew have produced a child whose face was unreadable to him? He'd *made* that face. "Well," she said. "Since we're going to be flying back and forth between here and home like every week for who knows how long, maybe you should be trying to save your money?"

She wasn't wrong. Andrew tried not to think about how long all of the trouble with Lily might last, but he wasn't kidding himself—even under the best of circumstances, it was probably going to last a very, very long time, and Andrew would no doubt be burning through his retirement fund to finance it. Though it was true he'd never particularly looked forward to retirement, especially now that he was alone: He imagined himself scraping along, scrambling eggs in his undershirt (he'd never learned to cook, and now he realized what an optimistic thing that was—it meant that he'd secretly believed he'd always be too busy to bother), watching the BBC at all hours of the day and night. This, exactly this, was what a life of the mind got you, give or take a 401(k) and some unnatural disasters.

At least Andrew could be grateful that he and Maureen had already spoken, and that they had agreed on so much. They had agreed that they would alert the State Department and contact the media; they had agreed that they would start a website and accept donations of frequent flier miles and, if it came to it, money. They had agreed to remortgage the house, though they had also agreed that they would most likely need to sell it eventually. (They had been keeping it ostensibly to minimize the disruptions in the lives of Anna and Lily, but for reasons both dreadful and benign this was a ship that had, decidedly,

sailed.) They had also agreed that only one of them should go to Buenos Aires first: They both wanted to be there, of course, but it was wise
to plan for the long term, and if they switched off weeks, Lily could
always have a visitor. Andrew had insisted on going first because he
knew that if Maureen did, Lily would want her to stay and stay. Maureen, in an act of extreme kindness, had agreed. The unspoken concession on Andrew's part had been bringing Anna along. It was these
sorts of small, practical generosities that had made the final eight be-
numbing years of their marriage endurable—when they'd soldiered
on, producing Lily and Anna in rapid succession, insisting on each
other's survival. Their marriage had run on the inertia that keeps a
moving object in motion, at least until the girls were in school. Then
came a sense of sputtering, of hopeless decline, and Andrew had had
the image—inapt, but recurring and intrusive—of a headless chicken
that runs around for a bit before falling down dead.

Andrew swallowed and tried to smile at Anna. "I think we can
spring for it just this once, Old Sport," he said.

At the hotel, Anna took a shower and went off to run with wet hair.
Andrew lay on the bed for seven minutes—he counted—and then sat
up, opened his laptop, and began looking again through the photos
Lily had sent him before all of this began. She'd taken a lot of pictures
of fruit: guavas and bananas and weird melons that looked like hedge-
hogs. There was a picture of Lily standing in front of a church, and
Andrew grimaced again at what she was wearing: a low-cut top, one of
those cheap, flimsy things she bought at deep-discount clothes ware-
houses. All the women around her were dressed conservatively. Had
she really not noticed? There was also a picture of Lily and the dead
girl, Katy, who was as strikingly lovely here as everywhere—she was
extraordinary, really, with ash blond hair and strangely depthless eyes.
Her beauty was, of course, terrible news. ("This does not help," Peter
Sulzicki had said, tapping Katy's face in the photograph. "This does not
help at all.") In the picture, Katy and Lily are laughing, drinking beers

at a bar somewhere. They look friendly enough. But Andrew cringed when he thought of Lily's emails and the things she'd written in them about Katy. *"Katy thinks that punning is the highest form of humor." "Everything about Katy is perfectly average, except her teeth." "Can we talk about her name? Katy Kellers. What were her parents thinking? Was their dearest ambition that their daughter grow up to be a local TV anchorwoman?"* The emails were already out there, of course—they'd been published in the local tabloids and helpfully reposted by what seemed like every blogger in the universe—and Andrew knew how bad they sounded. The dismissiveness and condescension wasn't even the worst of it—the worst was the implied assertion that Lily must not be average if she could muster such disdain for the average. The irony of that was that Lily was indeed average, more or less—bright, of course, and curious, and a bit reckless, and possessed of an annoying tendency to try to bring philosophy to bear on daily life in rather purist and militant ways—but all that this added up to, essentially, was average for a decent young student at a decent New England college. Lily bounced through life with the sense she was discovering everything that existed for the first time—Nietzsche, or sex, or the possibility of a godless universe, or the entire continent of South America—and all that was *fine,* of course: She was twenty-one; she was allowed. It was maddening, then, the narrative that Lily somehow deviated so egregiously from the norm. She was typical, she was aggressively typical—all the more so if she didn't quite know it yet.

In one photo, Lily licks salt from her hand; in the next, she sucks on a lime. In another, she has climbed a hill somewhere and is making a gesture of mock victory. The next picture is of a three-legged dog. The next is a terrible shot of the dome of a cathedral, from straight below: White rays lace through the architecture; the cupola is ablaze with light. How could a twenty-one-year-old girl *not* take this photo? All of these photos. Andrew's heart broke on their banality.

He closed the computer and thought about what he needed to do next. Maureen would be calling soon. Tomorrow was the first meeting with the new lawyers. And at some point, Andrew wanted to go talk to

Lily's rich friend—Andrew recoiled from his own use of the term "friend" here. It was a euphemism borrowed from Maureen: She had insisted on introducing one of Lily's unfortunate college boyfriends as her "friend," over and over, until Lily finally flounced dramatically and said, right in front of a dinner party, "Mom, he's my *lover.*" The guy here was named Sebastien LeCompte, which sounded to Andrew like the name of a high-end suit store—though he knew he shouldn't complain: If the name hadn't been exotic Lily would never have written it out in its entirety. And silly name or not, Sebastien LeCompte was the single most important person in the universe: He was the person Lily had been with on the night Katy Kellers was killed. Andrew needed to know exactly what he was planning on saying about that. Sebastien LeCompte himself had not been arrested—though perhaps he might still be, of course—and Maureen and Andrew careened around this fact obsessively, with little sense of how they should regard it. In various lights, it could appear promising (if Lily had been with this guy and the police weren't even bothering to arrest him, perhaps they knew that the case was weak?) or terrifying (what might have he told the cops in order to avoid arrest?) or patently good (no sense in two innocent kids being thrown in jail?) or baldly unfair (if one innocent kid had to be thrown in jail, why the hell wasn't it this asshole instead of their daughter?). Andrew needed the answers to these questions, and he needed them as soon as possible, and he was going to go find Sebastien LeCompte and get them.

Andrew did not plan on mentioning any of this to Peter Sulzicki, the lawyer—although, to be technical, the only people he had specifically prohibited Andrew from contacting were the Kellerses. On this point, Peter Sulzicki had been emphatic. This was painful for Andrew, because he understood what the Kellerses were going through; he knew that losing a child was the single worst experience that life had to offer. Andrew did not know, of course, which way was harder—whether it was worse to lose a child when she was far away and you were sleeping, or when you were cupping her tiny head and feeling her delicate pulse go quiet. Not that Andrew had ever given up on working through the hierarchies of pain, teasing out the taxonomies of grief; he scorned people who were untouched by death, and he *loathed* people who shared experiences about their dying parents when he spoke of Janie (*Who cares?* he wanted to shout. *This is the way of things!*). The only people he truly respected were the ones whose pain was objectively, empirically, worse than his. There was a man in Connecticut, for example, who'd lost his entire family—wife and two daughters—in a home invasion. They were raped and set on fire. Andrew felt sorry for this man.

And the Kellerses: Despite the details, their loss was, fundamentally, his. It pained him not to send a card, at the very least. And not reaching out to them would be even harder on Maureen, he knew; she had always been very into sending sympathy cards. *It's the ritual,* she was always saying, swirling her cursive into a note destined for some barely known neighbor or long-forgotten aunt. *It's the acknowledgment. Love is expressed through pragmatism. It may be just a card, but it's also the objective correlative of their loss.*

The objective correlative? Andrew would say. Maureen taught high school English. *I thought we said not to take work home.*

The phone rang and Andrew put the computer on the floor. "Hey," he said.

"You made it," said Maureen.

"So it would seem."

"How's Anna?"

"Running."

"Outside?"

"Of course not."

"Good."

Talking to Maureen tended to lift Andrew's spirits—this was not the typical experience of men speaking to their ex-wives, he realized, but then theirs had not been a typical divorce. In a way, Andrew often thought, the divorce had actually been deeply optimistic. Right after Janie died, all they'd cared about was stanching the hemorrhaging hole in the center of their lives; romantic love, or any of its shadowy iterations, was no longer a concern. So the fact that they realized, almost a decade on, that they *weren't* dead to the world, that their sexual selves still existed, that the notion of an adult relationship that wasn't irredeemably destroyed actually held appeal for both of them—well, this was a sign of progress, in a way. It was probably the most hopeful thing they'd done since having Lily; it gestured toward the idea that things could be better for them both. Though it was true that nobody else saw it that way, and that all of their mutual friends tended to treat Andrew like Oedipus with his eyes clawed out—his situation no less distressing just because fate had ordained it.

"So," said Maureen. "I have some not great news."

"Oh, Christ," said Andrew. Maureen was notoriously understated.

"It looks like they were maybe sleeping with the same man." Maureen inhaled; it sounded like she was breathing through her teeth. "And that maybe they had a fight about it."

"What?" Andrew stood up. "Who? That Sebastien character?"

"It seems so."

Andrew walked into the bathroom and turned on the light. In the mirror, he looked abominable—flyaway hair, leaking red eyes. Coffee on his collar, though he couldn't remember when he'd last had any. It seemed to Andrew that his eyes were sinking into his face; receding, somehow, like his hairline. Was this normal? His eye sockets were twin apses now, overshadowed by the dome of his forehead. "And they fought about it?" he said.

Maureen coughed. "Yes," she said. "Or anyway, they fought about something."

"How did they, ah, establish this?"

"The fight? They've got half a dozen witnesses. It happened at that bar she worked at."

"And the other thing?"

"Emails."

"Of course." Andrew's eyeball was throbbing. He took a tissue and dabbed at it. He didn't know why his eyes were seeping quite so much; maybe he was having an allergic response to some South American tree, the relentless fecundity of this awful city. He wasn't crying. Like his daughters, he was not a crier. "Was there anyone else?"

"Down there, you mean?"

"Yes. Or, I mean, at home, too. How many total, do you think?"

"You're asking me how many men did our daughter sleep with?"

"Trust me. It will be relevant."

"Andrew. I don't know."

"You really don't know?"

"I really do not know. You know how Lily is. I mean, there was this guy, obviously."

"Yes." Andrew approached the mirror and put his eye right up against it. Up close his eye was comical and a bit spooky, with cirrus strands of bloodshot threading out from the pupil. He could see no clear evidence of damage. He could not believe that something invisible could hurt so much.

"And the economist from Middlebury, of course."

"The economist?"

"Andrew. You met him."

"Did I?" Andrew turned on the faucet and ran his hands under the water. He splashed his face. He slapped himself on the cheeks, lightly.

"They dated for months. We had lunch at the Impudent Oyster. What are you *doing* over there?"

"The *Impotent* Oyster? What a name for a restaurant."

"Impudent. Andrew. Don't you remember? It was tremendously awkward for all of us."

A vague, repressed memory came to Andrew. Maureen had insisted on arguing with no one about IMF loans to Peru; she had jabbed her fork in the air to make a point. What lifetime was this, when they had all met prospective suitors together for lunch? When the biggest challenge was presenting a sufficiently united front? "Okay," said Andrew. "Okay. So that's two. And anyone else?"

Andrew could hear Maureen thinking for a moment. "I imagine there were a few others," she said finally.

"I see."

"I mean, nothing outrageous, I'm sure."

"What's outrageous?"

"I just mean, she's, you know. She's of her generation. They have different ideas about sex."

"I thought our generation invented all the different ideas about sex," said Andrew. He didn't know if he really thought this, but it sounded like the kind of thing he might once have thought.

"Well, sure," said Maureen. "I just mean, you know. The girls now are like the boys. They sleep around. They expect not to be judged. I'm not saying I think it's the right thing for her. I'm just saying it's normal now."

"Right." Andrew flipped off the bathroom light.

"Not that the norm is what matters. I mean she could sleep with a hundred guys and it doesn't mean she did this, right?"

"Right." Andrew walked to the bedroom and drew the curtains. He sat heavily on the bed.

"Not that she slept with a hundred guys."

"What—fifty?"

"Andrew!"

"What?"

"Don't be absurd."

"I have absolutely no idea what's absurd."

"No. No. Of course not, no. Like, ten maybe. Like ten would be a very, very liberal estimate."

"I see." Andrew sighed. "Didn't you ever talk to her about this stuff?"

"About sex? What do you mean? We both did."

"Well, I mean. About, I don't know. About not having quite so much of it."

There was a dark pause. "Would you have talked to a son about that?"

"No," said Andrew reasonably. "Realistically, no. But then it matters more for her, doesn't it? It doesn't help our case."

"Well, yeah, her entire personality doesn't help our case. It doesn't mean I wish she didn't have one."

Andrew closed his eyes. He didn't understand why he couldn't see it, the wound: why it didn't appear against the backdrop of his swollen eyelid, lightning shaped, blood colored. "I really cannot believe this," he said. He kept his eyes closed, afraid that if he opened them, he'd somehow see Maureen's face. "Can you?"

"Yes, actually," said Maureen. All of a sudden, she sounded old. "You know, I'm not sure anything could ever really surprise me again."

Andrew spent the first full day in Buenos Aires learning that he could not see Lily until Thursday. On this, everyone—the police, the lawyer, the Internet—was firm. He could not see her until Thursday, and there was nothing to be done, even when Andrew snarled at the diplomatic representative from the U.S. embassy over the phone.

"I need to see her today," he said. He felt that if he spoke very slowly and clearly, this would be believed. He understood faintly that this was making him sound nearly sarcastic, but he did not care. Anna was taking a shower. She had spent the first twenty-four hours in Argentina showering, or running, or stretching mutely before that car-sized television, her face bruise colored and alien in its light. Andrew was trying to have all the worst phone conversations while she was gone.

"I do understand, sir," said the woman on the phone. She was professionally trained not to hear hostility. She also sounded about fourteen—Andrew pictured braces, he pictured a unicorn sweatshirt—and yet it was she, not Andrew, who had already visited Lily and was likely to visit her once more within the week. "But there's nothing I can do."

"*You* personally, maybe. Sure. Maybe there's nothing you personally can do." Andrew was picturing an international embargo, a land invasion. He was picturing a coup d'état.

"There is nothing more that the embassy can do, at this juncture," said the woman. She was professionally trained to be firm. In theory, she was saying, the embassy was supposed to have been notified when Lily was detained, but in practice they often weren't notified until the detainee was transferred to a prison. In this case, they'd been notified when Mr. Hayes's wife—his ex-wife? excuse me, ex-wife—had called, the moment their offices opened, the morning after Lily's arrest. The woman assured Andrew that nothing had been lost in this delay. Andrew thought he could detect a slight lisp in her speech, something a little messy around the sibilants; she had a voice, at any rate, that was altogether too sweetly girlish to be relaying such information. Lily was still in the police holding cell, the woman was explaining. The protocol was to move a detainee after forty-eight hours, but in practice detainees often stayed in the holding cells for months. The prisons were sometimes too crowded for a timely transfer, as was now the case.

"How does she seem?" Andrew said.

"She's well." The woman sounded careful. "Quite well."

Instead of yelling that "well" was a fucking relative term, Andrew let the woman explain to him that it usually took six to fourteen months for a trial to be arranged. Andrew had had this number quoted at him before, but he knew from Janie that getting mired in statistics, in averages, was the fastest way to despair. He also knew that there were plenty of slower ways.

"She's seen a lawyer?" said Andrew.

"We understand that she declined public representation."

"She *what*?"

The representative, accustomed to rhetorical questions, said nothing. Andrew felt a compression in his chest that he feared might be clinical. In the shower, he heard Anna drop the shampoo.

"You're sure she was offered one?" he said. Maybe she wasn't, and maybe that was the best of all possible news. Or the worst. It was very hard to say.

"We are told that she was," said the woman. He thought she might be chewing gum. He was going to file some kind of formal complaint if she was chewing gum.

"Told by whom?"

"The police."

"This is unbelievable. It is fucking unbelievable." Andrew paused to try to catch the woman in her gum chewing, but heard nothing—only the low-grade bureaucratic snufflings of some terrible office. "Did they offer her a lawyer in English?"

"That I don't know, sir, though they usually have to bring in external translators. You've hired a private penal specialist, I understand?"

"Yes."

"The public legal representatives are generally quite good."

"We're hiring a private representative." The shower turned off, and Andrew could hear the wet slap of Anna's inelegant distance-runner feet against the linoleum. Something was occurring to him, something so obvious that he was almost embarrassed to let himself think it for the very first time. "Did they interrogate her in Spanish?"

"She addressed them in Spanish."

Andrew closed his eyes. Lily was vain—obnoxious, really—about her Spanish; you simply could not take the child to a Mexican restaurant. But it was college Spanish, suitable for verb conjugation quizzes, nothing worse. "I see," he said. "Without a lawyer?"

The representative, unwilling to repeat herself, said nothing.

That afternoon, out of desperation, Andrew took Anna sightseeing. Buenos Aires, they both immediately agreed, was overrated; it had the sprawl and grunge of a major city, but none of the European charm he'd been promised nor—frankly—any of the high-spiritedness he'd imagined. Andrew had thought it might be like Barcelona—parties in the streets all night long, big tree-lined boulevards tumbling to the sea, generic Latin fun on every corner—but it was mostly just hot, and dusty, and people sweated through their synthetic fibers, and always looked like they were on their way to work.

At La Recoleta Cemetery, Andrew and Anna walked desultorily among the tombs. They stared at Eva Perón's grave, with its chintzy flowers, its interminable fleurs-de-lis, dizzying in the broad daylight. Nearby, bleached angels held eternally theatrical poses. Anna snapped some pictures. Off in the distance were small trees, stark and terrible as crosses, but Anna didn't take pictures of those.

Afterward they sat at an outdoor café and drank beers, even though it was only three o'clock. Andrew read aloud from Eva Perón's *Wikipedia* entry, which he'd printed out and brought along, for edification.

"She was born out of wedlock in the village of Los Toldos in rural Buenos Aires in 1919, the fourth of five children," he said.

Anna stared dourly into her beer and did not speak.

"In 1951," Andrew announced, "Eva Perón renounced the Peronist nomination for the office of Vice President of Argentina."

"Dad," said Anna. She touched him lightly on the hand. "You don't need to do that."

Andrew folded up the pages and put them under his empty plate. They hadn't ordered any food. "How are you doing, Old Sport?" he said. He kept forgetting to ask. "Are you hanging in there?"

Anna shrugged. "I'm tired. I'm hot."

"How are you doing, you know, emotionally?" Anna had a tendency to respond to queries about her well-being in only the most literal terms. Try as he might to dig into her inner life, she usually only offered him reports about new records broken, or shin splints suffered, or exams taken—as though this would tell him all he needed to know.

"I want to see Lily." Anna squeezed her lemon into her beer, even though she'd already drunk most of it, and then stared at it, blinking. "What do you think it's like there?"

"It's probably not so bad, Old Sport," said Andrew, which he hoped was reasonably true. Lily's holding cell wasn't really equipped for long-term detention—there was no exercise yard, Lily had told Maureen, and no separate quarters for women, and the guards could see her when she peed (she apparently returned to this issue frequently)—but then this wasn't going to be a long-term detention. And a little compromised privacy was a worthy trade, Andrew felt, considering what he'd read about the prisons—about the open sewage, the meningitis, the tendency of prisoners to burn themselves in order to get medical attention. "I mean, it's probably not the Ritz or anything," said Andrew. "Not a five-star hotel situation. But probably not so bad."

The reason Andrew did not know more was that he had spoken to Lily only once on the phone. She was allowed to make fifteen-minute calls once a day with her own phone card, and someone—some guy, Andrew figured—had brought her a whole bunch. Still, she had called Andrew only once, thirty-six hours after her arrest and twelve hours before his flight. Every other time, she had called Maureen.

"Lily said it was okay on the phone," said Andrew. "She said it was manageable." What she'd actually said was "endurable," but "manageable" seemed to convey the same thought without the troubling connotation. Andrew did not mind his child managing, not really. After all, everyone had to manage.

"Dad." Anna was shaking her head, looking amazed at Andrew's stupidity. Her lemon was a little yellow buoy in her beer. "Don't you know that she'll say anything?"

They left the café, and Andrew, not ready to return to the hotel, cajoled Anna into going to the modern art museum, where they walked with joyless thoroughness—Anna squinting gravely at the art, Andrew squinting gravely at Anna. He couldn't understand any of the art. He was too old for all of this; everything challenging was for the young. He sat down on a bench in the middle of the room. He could see the bobbing of Anna's scapula through her T-shirt when she adjusted her purse; running had made her wiry in a feral cat kind of way. What, he wondered, would this moment come to mean to Anna? Maybe it would become merely one episode in her crazy sister's crazy life—something to talk about in bars, on dates, or to tell Lily's wide-eyed, ruddy-haired children one day ("Your mother," she might say, "was *wild*"). Maybe this hour at the modern art museum would be merely one of the narrative's many surreal asterisks, something decorative that did not appear in every single telling. Or maybe, Andrew thought, this moment would become something else. Maybe Anna would remember it as the very last second that they were still trying to pretend that their whole lives hadn't gone fully to shit. Maybe she would talk about it in therapy one day—recalling how they'd gone through the sad little self-conscious motions of enjoying the city, as though they were on fucking vacation, and how this was the *exact* kind of pathological WASP repression that had motored them all through everything, always. Which story were they in right now? Andrew was not sure he wanted to know.

On the taxi ride back to the hotel, Andrew and Anna gazed out separate windows and did not speak. Every few blocks, they passed graffiti in support of Cristina Fernández—newly beloved in the wake of her husband's death, newly forgiven for raising the taxes on soybeans—and Andrew experienced a minor stab of satisfaction. Encountering something in the world that confirmed what he'd learned of it always gave him a nice solid sense of existing in an actual universe—a reassuring feeling, and one that had been slipping away from him, faster and faster, in recent years. Even before Lily's arrest, Andrew had felt untethered—like his life had come undone in big sloppy pieces, and nothing had held together long enough to really count. Sometimes it seemed to Andrew that the meaning of his existence had been like a rare gas in a bottle he'd mistakenly uncorked—it was still out there somewhere, presumably, but was now so diffuse as to be undetectable.

Andrew had not slept with anyone since Maureen. He rarely put it in a sentence like that, but there it was. Of course, there had been chances—graduate students: ambitious and/or working out father issues and/or bored and drunk—but he had never taken any of them. The closest call had been an ABD named Karen, who had sleek hair and a creamy avian face and glasses that offset her unruffled beauty in a way that made her look like a porn star playing a librarian—there was no way, there was just *no way*, that those things actually had corrective lenses in them. Her area was Central Asian republics, and she'd spent an entire summer in Almaty trying to quiz Kazakhs on their feelings, their actual feelings, about Nursultan Nazarbayev. And there'd been one night when she and Andrew had had too much wine and too much high-spirited talk about whether the revolution in Egypt was best compared to the Eastern bloc countries in 1989 or to Iran in 1979 or to Iran in 2009, which had gotten them onto the CIA's overthrow of Mossadegh in 1953, and this had led them into dark cynical snorting about U.S. involvement in Afghanistan in the '80s, and then the assassination of Ahmed Shah Massoud two days before September 11th, and then they'd gotten onto rogue intelligence services generally, and conspiracy theories they'd never articulate in the classroom—he spoke of the ISI and Benazir Bhutto, she spoke of the FSB and Lech Kaczyński's death in that weird plane crash, which, Andrew had to admit, was admirably, almost sexily, audacious. And maybe there was a moment when he'd looked at her mouth—not something you usually do, he realized, unless you've got some ideas—but then he'd backed away, and scratched his neck, and went off to get some cheese cut into cubes which, as Karen pointed out, was not really the best way to maximize the surface area of cheese.

Andrew did not know what Karen had wanted from him. There was nothing he could really do for her, he didn't think, besides write her the glowing recommendation she was already going to get. But there must be something—some power he had that he hadn't yet unpacked—because there was no way she'd be talking to him if it weren't strategic. She was a student of Kissinger, after all, a believer in realpolitik. And though there might be permanent interests, there were no permanent allies.

In the taxi, Anna was still staring out the window. "Hey," said Andrew. He pulled on her ponytail and she shook it away from him. "What do you think of the city?"

"I don't like it," said Anna, still looking out the window. Outside, the midafternoon light was coming down in great golden bars, like some kind of ancient currency.

"Do you think you'd like it here if this weren't happening?" said Andrew.

"I don't know," said Anna. There was a long pause, and then she said, "No."

On Tuesday, Andrew left Anna at the hotel and went to Tribunales to meet with the lawyers. There were only two of them—Franco Ojeda and Leo Velazquez—but Andrew couldn't help but think of them as a phalanx; they were mercenaries, it seemed to him, come to fight for pay. The conference room where Andrew met them was wood paneled and high ceilinged; it reminded Andrew of 1987, a terrible year. Ojeda was very fat and Velazquez was very bald; the overhead light caught his pate in a complicated, adamantine shine. Ojeda offered water, which Andrew declined, and Velazquez pulled down the blinds, which Andrew did not understand. And then, with the help of audiovisual supplements, the lawyers laid out the criminal case against Andrew's oldest living daughter.

"First," said Ojeda. His English was only very lightly accented; Andrew cringed at how much this surprised him. "The emails."

The emails—which the lawyers had helpfully printed out, color coded by date and arranged in a binder—had emerged almost immediately after Lily's arrest; Andrew could only assume Lily had accidentally left herself logged in on one of the school computers, which was the kind of thing she would do. Andrew had read them over and over already, and they never sounded any less damning; this time, he closed one eye and half-skimmed, not wanting to look at them straight. Lily really could sound awful if you didn't know her.

"Second," said Velazquez, opening a new binder. "The love triangle."

The lawyers had produced pictures of all three of them, somehow—Andrew recognized Lily's picture from her Facebook page—and with their images all lined up like that, Andrew saw something important that the lawyers were not saying. Lily's looks did not help. She was pretty, but it was a sloppy sort of prettiness, suggesting carelessness,

sensuality, unearned privilege. Her breasts were, to her eternal chagrin, her mother's. "I have the breasts of a medieval peasant!" she'd
shouted as a teenager once. Andrew had been waiting in the foyer to
pick the girls up for the weekend; he'd gazed at the ceiling and pretended not to hear. "What the hell do I need them for?"

"You'll like them one day," he'd heard Maureen say.

"I won't," said Lily miserably. "I got a 2300 on the SAT. I am never
going to like them."

"You got a 2280," said Maureen.

Lily dressed them with varying degrees of success; in the heat, she
tended to dress them very inadequately indeed. In the Facebook picture, she was wearing something ridiculous—some spaghetti strap
thing, Andrew didn't know what to call it—and they (the breasts) were
simply not battened down in any serious way at all. Andrew blamed
Maureen for this, somehow; some important, delicate conversation
had been missed, somewhere along the line, and now here they all
were, staring at this photo, which contrasted so starkly with Katy's neat
hair and sparkling teeth and compact body—all of it somehow vir-
ginal, somehow the particular beauty of an innocent.

Between Lily and Katy was a picture of Sebastien LeCompte—that
name! In the photo, he appeared young, foppish, with overlong hair
that reminded Andrew of some kind of ornithological plumage. The
idea of this boy inspiring murderous lust was absolutely comic. Andrew was going to actually laugh about it, in fact, just as soon as he got
out of this office.

"I'm sorry, but this guy?" Andrew tapped the photo. "Really? You're
expecting me to believe those two girls were fighting over this guy?"

"We're not expecting you to believe anything," said Ojeda. "But it's
what the prosecution will assert, and we have to assume that the panel
will believe it."

"Why?"

"There is some evidence," said Velazquez. "A few emails the deceased wrote, indicating a new romance that she needed to hide from
your daughter. And Carlos Carrizo—that's the host family father—"

"I know," said Andrew.

"—Has grudgingly admitted to seeing the deceased return from LeCompte's house late one evening. But in terms of the trial, what your daughter believed to be the case is more important than what was actually the case, as I'm sure you understand. And your daughter believed that the deceased and Sebastien LeCompte were romantically involved. She said as much in her initial interrogation."

"Are these really the concerns of law enforcement, though?" Andrew sat back heavily in his chair. "I mean, it all seems a little—tawdry. And, frankly, trivial."

Ojeda blinked, impassive. "Your daughter's emails characterize her relationship with the deceased as fraught, at best," he said. "The love triangle element establishes a motive. And then there's the question of your daughter's behavior on the day of the murder."

"You mean, trying to administer CPR to a dead body and then calling the police?" said Andrew. "You mean, doing exactly what she was supposed to do?"

"We're not as concerned about the blood the truck driver saw on Lily's face," said Ojeda. "Lily found the body of the deceased, as you say, and we have every confidence that the DNA report will support that story. What's somewhat more worrying for our case, actually, are the reports from the initial interrogation of your daughter's rather . . . subdued . . . reaction to Katy's death. And in conjunction with the cartwheel, of course, that looks a little strange."

Andrew felt his tongue freeze momentarily in his mouth. "What cartwheel?" he said.

The lawyers exchanged another glance. "You didn't know about the cartwheel?" said Velazquez.

"She did a cartwheel?"

"During the interrogation."

"*During* the interrogation?"

"Afterward. Right after the first interrogation, when they left her alone."

"Okay," said Andrew, his tongue unfreezing. "Well. That's odd, I suppose. But I don't really know what it has to do with anything. I mean, maybe she just wanted to stretch? Maybe she hadn't moved in a while? At any rate, I just don't see how it matters at all."

But he did, and the lawyers could see that he did, and that they did not need to explain.

"Finally," said Ojeda apologetically. "There's this." He clicked a remote at the TV, summoning a black-and-white image of Lily and Sebastien LeCompte, who appeared to be shopping at some kind of Walmart-type store.

"What is this?" said Andrew.

"Security footage. From the day of the murder."

"Why are we watching this?"

"You'll see."

On the screen, Lily and Sebastien were grainy and grim, moving in that strange halting way—disappearing and suddenly rematerializing three feet away—that was particular to people on security tapes. Andrew leaned forward. They looked guilty, and why was that? He realized it was because you only ever saw people on security footage when they were suspected of a crime; the way they dropped out of sight and then popped back up began to seem intentional, furtive. On the screen, Lily and Sebastien looked ghostly and very young. They moved through the store picking out basic, sensible things—a toothbrush, some toothpaste, the necessities for a person locked out of a house. At the end of one aisle, Lily lingered and, incredibly, produced a pack of cigarettes from her pocket. She put one in her mouth without lighting it. Andrew felt a muted, faraway surprise that he knew, under any other circumstances, would be much larger—he had never known his daughter to smoke. On the screen, Lily turned to look at Sebastien and nodded toward the shelf behind her—which, Andrew could see now, was lined entirely with condoms. She raised an eyebrow and Ojeda paused the tape, freezing Lily's face into an expression of strange, nearly vulpine suggestiveness.

"That," said Velazquez, pointing, "is what they're going to play."

"Who?"

"The television."

"What?"

"That she gave him this provocative look with the condoms."

"I wouldn't really say it's provocative," said Andrew, even though he knew it didn't matter. He was beginning to see how this was going to go. "I mean, it's not like she bought them, right? It's just kind of silly, I think."

"You have to understand, this is five hours after she's learned of Katy's death," said Velazquez.

"She's just making a joke," said Andrew.

And Velazquez looked at Andrew blankly and said that that's exactly what he meant.

On Thursday, Andrew and Anna took a taxi to Lomas de Zamora police station.

"Aren't you hot?" said Andrew. He had told Anna to wear something modest, and now she was wearing a high-necked sweater and he worried she was hot. He was hot.

"No," said Anna. She was resting her head on the window. Andrew managed not to comment on this, though he flinched every time they hit a bump. He had to figure that she'd quit it if she wanted to quit it.

From the outside, the police station looked normal enough—like a place you might voluntarily go, certainly, if you were in some kind of trouble. Andrew reminded himself for the hundredth time that this wasn't Russia: This was a country where you were encouraged, on balance, to find the police if you had a problem. Inside, Andrew and Anna were conducted through a multi-phased entrance; they relinquished their documents to a man in a lucent box and were ushered into a small waiting room. Andrew was again relieved: The walls were papered with flyers for social service programs, and there wasn't a single festering wound or homicidal gang in sight. The huge light on the ceiling was spackled with the desiccated bodies of a few electrocuted flies, some of them still twitching; in the corner of the room lurked an enormous spindly-legged bug, as grand and improbable looking as a lob-ster; the smell of cloying disinfectant half-obscured the smell of something heavily organic. But in general, the room looked okay—like a place where petty obligations were fulfilled. A DMV, perhaps. Though Andrew saw how this place's innocuousness could be dangerous; maybe it was why Lily had not realized the threat she was under—letting things go on in Spanish, failing to ask for a lawyer. He could scarcely believe it about the lawyer. Hadn't she watched enough TV growing up to know to reflexively demand one, no matter what? Per-haps she actually hadn't—they'd been stingy with TV, allowing only the most tedious and high-minded of programming, protecting their daughters from exposure to the mind-coarsening and the lurid. How funny that the most important thing Lily would wind up needing to know would be, essentially, a cliché, a little beat of verisimilitude in the preordained rhythm of a crime drama. How darkly hilarious, that this would turn out to be what they'd most needed to teach her. But instead they had raised an unworldly daughter; a child so confident in her language skills (a 5 on the AP exam, after all!), and so proud of the sophistication of her reasoning abilities (those papers on Quine!), and so assured of the infallibility of her innocence (!) that she assumed, wrongly and bravely, that her rational goodness could prevent disaster—even though the thesis of all of their lives had been that this was not so. How strangely funny that was. Andrew was going to laugh about that. Andrew was going to laugh about all of it, just as soon as he got out of this jail.

"Okay," said the man in the box. "You can come in now."

Andrew squeezed Anna's shoulder, and they walked through an-other set of metal detectors and down a long hall of blue doors. The light was dimmer here, and Andrew had trouble telling if the clots of darkness in the corners were dirt or only shadows. The blue doors ended and a glass-walled room began and there, sitting at a table, fin-gers spread out before her with an odd, unsettling sort of precision, was Lily.

Her head was bent forward. Her hair, Andrew could see, was very dirty. He couldn't remember the last time Lily's hair had been really dirty—maybe that time she'd had pneumonia for ten days when she was seven. She looked sallow, bony—a little Third World, Andrew couldn't help thinking, though this was no longer a relevant term, post–Cold War. He could feel Anna startle against him, and he pressed his hand to her wrist. It was very important that neither of them seem startled.

The guard fumbled with his keys, rattling them. Lily still did not look up, and Andrew realized she couldn't hear them. But she knew they were coming; shouldn't she have been waiting, head raised, face expectant? The fact that she wasn't seemed another bad sign, alongside the hair and that awful thing she was doing with her fingers.

The guard opened the door, and Lily finally looked up. The skin underneath her eyes was dark and dingy; her lips were very dry. Andrew flashed to an image of Janie—unconscious, intubated, her little macerated mouth a gaudy red, too gaudy for a two-year-old. The paleness of Lily's skin now reminded him of the paleness of Janie's skin then: It was the color of absence or impending departure. Andrew had expected Lily to stand, maybe even jump up, but she didn't—she just smiled a sickly smile and waited for them to come to her.

"Dad," she said. Andrew went to her and hugged her, taking some basic inventory as he did so. Up close she seemed about the right size, he supposed, like the same essentially sturdy child she'd always been (he remembered a picture of her on her fifth birthday, wearing some goofy little red jumper that Maureen had bought and that Anna wore later, her calf muscles straining as she stood on tiptoe to give a kiss to a man in an enormous Winnie-the-Pooh suit whom Maureen had hired for the occasion). Andrew grazed his hand along Lily's forehead—her temperature seemed normal—and he squeezed her fingertips—like her mother, her circulation sucked, and her extremities were always getting too cold—but they seemed okay, just chilly, not frozen. He cupped the back of her head with his hand, a gesture that he knew was self-consciously maternal, that he knew he was copying from Maureen. It occurred to him briefly that it had been years since Lily would have allowed him such familiarities; since college began she'd become physically curt, a giver of hugs that seemed to communicate her general displeasure with the overall project of hugging. Andrew lingered for a moment with his hand on Lily's head, just because he could. Then he stepped away so Anna could hug her—fiercely but swiftly, pulling away after a moment to stare at her feet.

Andrew sat. He left his hand in the center of the table, in case Lily wanted to hold it at any point. "Sweetheart," he said. "How are you doing?"

Lily blinked, and Andrew could see shivering blue capillaries on her eyelids. Were they always like that? They were probably always like that. "When's Mom coming?" she said.

"Next week," said Andrew. "She'll be here for your next visit. On Thursday."

"Why isn't she here now?"

"We're going to trade off weeks, sweetheart." Andrew was going to have to stop saying "sweetheart" with such frequency, he knew. Lily was not likely to tolerate it for long, and he did not want to know what it would mean if she did. "So you'll always have a visitor. Every Thursday." Lily's innocence was implicit. It was implicit. Andrew would ask questions that reflected that. "How are you being treated?" he said, in the same moment as Anna leaned forward and said, urgently, "Lily. Are you okay?"

Andrew saw a momentary sardonic flash in Lily's eyes—encouraging because it was so characteristic—but then it went away and Lily said, "I'm okay." And Andrew knew then that she was protecting them, and he was afraid.

Lily stood up. "Dad," she said. There was a wavering note of hysteria in her voice. She began to pace. "I have to tell you what happened."

Andrew had never seen anyone pace before, and it was distressing. She really did look like one of those caged animals—her body seemed to register, at the edge of each cycle, that there was no place left to go; and she was doing something with her head that looked nearly equine—and he said, "Lily, do you want to sit down?"

"No," she said. Andrew could hear something toddleresque in the dismissal—in the jejune thrill at having something to reject—and he realized that this was a small thing they could give her.

"Okay," he said soothingly. "You don't have to sit down."

"Dad, I have to tell you." Lily's gaze was narrowing, and Andrew felt that she was on the verge of some kind of change in pitch.

"Lily," he said quickly. "You don't need to tell us anything."

"I do."

Andrew leaned forward and gestured to the ceiling. "Lily. You understand, right? You don't need to tell us anything, if you don't think you should."

Lily looked at Andrew then with the most open and wrecked expression he had ever seen; it was an expression that was shattered, that was nearly autopsied. "Dad," she said, close to sobbing. "Of course I should. What the hell do you think? Of *course* I should."

"Okay, okay."

Anna was silent: hands folded, face terrified.

"I was staying over at Sebastien's," said Lily.

Andrew nodded. "Sebastien is your boyfriend?"

Lily looked at him dimly. There was a time when she would have quibbled with this formulation; she would have said "lover" or maybe even "paramour," or told him not to be so conventional, or asked him to remind her what century this was. Now she just shook her head and said, "No, I don't think so."

"Okay," said Andrew, "but so, you were staying over there."

"The Carrizos were gone for the weekend. That's why I was staying over."

"What did you do there?"

"Dad."

"Okay." Andrew hadn't meant to ask any questions, but he did not know what he would say if he didn't. "When did you get back?"

"Like, maybe, eleven? I went to the bathroom to shower. Someone hadn't flushed the toilet, which I thought was weird. It wasn't like Katy. She's a very neat girl."

Andrew could hear Lily struggling to manage her mouth here—the juggling act of teeth and tongue and saliva seemed to be eluding her, and there was a faint breathiness in her voice.

"There was," she said. "There was also. I can't see."

"Put your head between your knees," said Anna.

"Yeah," said Lily, and did. She stayed there for thirty seconds, then carefully brought her head back up. "There was also some blood on the floor."

"Some blood?" said Andrew casually. "Like, how much?" He wanted to stop with the questions, but he could not. At any rate, Lily seemed to be used to them.

"Like, not very much," said Lily. "I thought maybe she'd cut herself. Or had her period and bled coming out of the shower or something. It wasn't like her not to notice, though."

"But you didn't see her?"

"The door was closed. I thought she was still asleep. I went and got some cheese from the fridge and sat on the couch for a few hours watching some game show. I was pretty hungover, to be honest. I fell asleep for a while. When I woke up, it was much later—like maybe almost four. Excuse me." She put her head down again. Andrew went to her and tried to wrap his arm awkwardly around her shoulder, but she shook him off. Anna tried, and Lily accepted this.

"I just keep thinking about her lying there, while I was napping on the couch."

"Don't think about it," said Anna.

"You try it," said Lily. She sounded like herself, almost. She sat up. "So I got up. I felt really weird. Like, massively thirsty, but also weirdly emotionally, like, fragile. It wasn't getting dark at all yet, but I just felt this kind of permanent emptiness in the house. I don't know. I went down to the bedroom. I wanted to find Katy. I wanted to see if she wanted to go for a walk or something. Get out of that house. The door was still closed. And outside the door, there was a blood footprint. It seemed enormous, like it was from some kind of monster. And it was so detailed on the white carpet. Like, you could see each ridge on the sole of the sneaker. I screamed and ran into the room. She was lying in the middle of the floor with a towel over her head. I think I knew she was dead. I went over to her and pulled the towel off. Her face was turned to the side. Her lips were blue. I tried to give her CPR for like one second and her lips were so cold and I got her blood on my face."

Lily was shaking so hard that she was moving Anna's arm along with her shoulders. Andrew tried putting his arm around her again, and this time, she allowed it.

"I was totally bawling by this point. I ran out of there and over to Sebastien's and then we called the police. Then the cops came and we were locked out of the house. The Carrizos couldn't get a flight until the next day. I called Mom. Sebastien took me to buy a toothbrush. He was going to let me stay with him. I spent the whole night puking, I don't know why. And then the next day they came for me and brought me here."

Outside the door, the guard was telling them two minutes, which was unbelievable. Andrew hadn't done anything yet, and he especially hadn't done the most crucial thing.

"Lily." He grabbed her hands so hard that he could feel the slight accordioning of her bones. What he wanted to say was *Wait a minute. Just wait one goddamn minute here.* As though the issue was only that things were going too fast. As though he could manage it, no problem, if he just had thirty seconds to sit still and really think about it. "How are they treating you?"

"I don't know if I should say."

"Tell me."

"I have to pee in front of the guards."

"I know."

"There's no trash can. There's no running water except the shower. There's no fork. The toothpaste doesn't work."

"It doesn't *work*?" said Andrew.

"We'll get you real toothpaste," said Anna.

"Can you get me real tampons?"

"*Real* tampons?" said Andrew.

The guard had entered the room and was standing, with quiet obtrusiveness, in the corner.

"Yes," said Anna, emphatically.

"What are real tampons?"

"Dad."

"The shower is freezing," said Lily. "I mean, *freezing*. I swear they're doing it on purpose."

The guard was upon her, and he stood her up—not roughly, but in a way that left no ambiguity as to what she was going to do. Andrew wanted to punch the guy in the face. He wanted to hold Lily and Anna and let them weep into his shoulders and tell them he would protect them always. But he knew he couldn't. And he knew that a scene like that would terrify all of them. It would feel like a goodbye, which this certainly was not. They would see Lily very soon. Hysteria invited hysteria. There was nothing to be gained from it.

"We'll see you in seven days," said Andrew. He gave Lily a hug that was warm, but without any undertones of apocalyptic clinging. "Your mother will be here."

"I love you," she said.

"We love you," they said.

They walked out into the hallway, leaving Lily behind them. When Andrew turned back to look at her, her head was down again, her long greasy hair obscuring her face. And she didn't look back up at them, even though they waved to her all the way down the hall.

CHAPTER TWO

February

Eduardo Campos was not sure until he saw the pictures. Later, people would ask him—informally, socially—when he knew. Be honest with us, they'd say. We won't tell. We knew when we heard about her Facebook page. We knew when we heard about her cartwheel. We knew when we saw the footage of her with the condoms—that cold, seductive look she gave the boy, and only hours after that poor other girl was knifed to death. That's when we knew Lily Hayes was guilty. When did you know? And Eduardo would laugh and say that of course he never knew, that he still didn't know. His job was just to make the case for the state, and the state's case, one had to admit, was ironclad. But the truth was he did know, and he had first known when the judicial police brought him Lily Hayes's camera.

The crime scene had not surprised him. Nothing surprised him, really, though there was certainly an incongruity between the upscale neighborhood and the well-kept house and the young American woman dead in a vast swamp of her own blood. It had taken Eduardo years to get used to how much blood one body could produce. But he was used to it now, and he studied the scene with his practiced dissociative attitude, reminding himself that the best way to help this young woman now was to pay very close attention.

She was lying on her stomach with her face to the side, hunched in the characteristic awkwardness of the dead. There was substantial bruising along her inner thighs. It was overwhelmingly likely that she had been sexually assaulted.

Eduardo followed the police with his notepad. He did not touch anything. In the kitchen, they found a knife, which was collected. In the victim's drawer, they found a half-empty packet of Skin Skin condoms, which was also collected. In the bathroom, they found three discrete spots of blood and an unflushed toilet, all of which were photographed, then sampled. In the garden, they found Lily Hayes, who had discovered the body (according to her) moments before running across the lawn with blood on her face (according to the driver who was now shakily smoking a cigarette in front of his delivery truck). Lily Hayes was white, late teens or early twenties, with a squarish jaw and auburn hair and high, vaguely witchy eyebrows; she appeared to have already washed all of the blood off her face. She was standing morosely next to a very young man in suspenders. Behind them, the bald double pates of San Telmo Pedro gleamed in the distance. Lily Hayes was not crying. She was pale, but perhaps she was always pale. She kissed the boy once, somewhat chastely, and then again, a little less chastely. She looked, Eduardo decided, harassed. Inconvenienced. If she looked anything at all. There was a stillness to her face that would probably seem perverse under any circumstances, but especially these circumstances, and which could only be intentional. Eduardo let himself think the thought, and then he let it pass. He'd been at this long enough to know that you couldn't scour yourself entirely clean of hunches and biases and premonitions; lurking suspicions; kneejerk reactions. You couldn't help but know some things without knowing why you knew them.

But at that point he did not know; he was not sure. He wasn't sure that afternoon, when he went home to drink two tumblers of whiskey and take ibuprofen for his costochondritis (an inflamed chest wall, his doctor had told him, though he knew that it was actually the somatic manifestation of loneliness, that his heart was finally quitting in protest). He wasn't sure that night, when he was still awake past three, walking heel to toe through his living room, the apartment so empty around him that he could hear the sonic groans of his own intestines, like whale song. And he wasn't sure the next day, when the police brought him the transcript of their initial conversation with Lily Hayes.

There were a lot of transcripts—the police's first talks with the neighbors, the vendors, the traumatized American study-abroad students, the family who'd been hosting both girls, the improbably named boy who had been kissing Lily Hayes in the garden. But the conversation with Lily Hayes stood out, and not only because there was no sign of a break-in and she was the only person in a hundred kilometers who'd had a house key. Eduardo read the transcript in his apartment with the shades drawn, while the sky outside his window stayed maddeningly light well past eight o'clock. In the transcript, of course, it was difficult to ascertain exactly what Lily Hayes's tone had been as she answered questions about Katy Kellers's short life and violent death. But Eduardo detected a cold current, a psychological dislocation, that made him read and reread the interview—though, for obvious reasons, Lily Hayes was not likely to have been the sole perpetrator of the crime.

"You say you saw some blood in the bathroom," said the interviewing officer.

"Yes," said Lily.

"How much blood was there, exactly?"

"Not much," she said—and Eduardo could feel the pause there, the implied flippancy. At one point, the transcript remarked flatly that Lily Hayes, left briefly alone but for the watchful gaze of the security camera, had done a cartwheel. Eduardo turned this image over in his mind.

He regarded it without judgment. He was surer, but he was not yet sure. And it was very important to be sure, because once he was sure, he was never wrong.

The next morning, Eduardo arose before dawn to run through the darkness. He was sweating by the end of the block; he was, as usual, overdressed for the weather. He could never believe that the world outside was so much warmer than it looked.

The running was new, though the general ritualized masochism was not. Whenever Eduardo felt it coming back again, he commenced a series of steps, a sequence arrived at through guessing and testing and the emergence of a grim, white-knuckled will. First, he assessed all the things in life that would make him feel worse. You won't feel any better if you get fat, he'd tell himself, while jogging. You won't feel any better if you get gingivitis, he'd tell himself, while flossing. The corollary—which was intrusive and unarticulated and omnipresent—was that he wouldn't feel any better either way. It never worked, of course. But it did make Eduardo feel as though he had tried. If Eduardo did anything, it was try. And, after all, it had been only two months since Maria left.

Maria—Eduardo would be the first to admit—had crashed into his existence, unearned, unwarranted. They'd been married for three years, and during that time Eduardo had never entirely gotten used to the idea. So when she left him—for a Brazilian opera singer, he'd heard—who was Eduardo to say she was not making the right decision? He had felt, somewhere in his devastation, that the universe was actually righting itself, and that resenting this was irrational. And if Eduardo was anything, it was rational.

Around him, Belgrano's streets were rain-slicked and silver. Eduardo tried to breathe evenly. He thought about all the cigarettes he hadn't smoked in the fifteen years since he'd quit. Could he feel the difference in his breathing? He was not sure. Sun split the clouds, startling a flock of birds off their telephone line. Eduardo could not feel a difference, he decided. But he did feel a little stab of virtue every time he wanted and did not allow himself a cigarette, which was still a few times a day, every day, even now. Sometimes it seemed to Eduardo that his whole life was only a collection of small impulses denied. The birds flew over his head, casting chevrons of shadow on the concrete.

At least, Eduardo knew, his work would not suffer. In the very precise triage system he'd set up within his life, work was the most critical priority. And on his better depressed days, Eduardo didn't so much as snap out of his sadness as sink into it—it contracted in his chest like a heart, giving him some propulsive force as he moved through an investigation. This compulsion to work could sometimes feel congenital, genetic—though, in fact, Eduardo had not originally wanted to be a lawyer. He had studied piano as a teenager and had hoped to continue in college, right up until the day he watched Julio César Strassera deliver closing remarks in the Trial of the Juntas. It was 1985 and Eduardo was sixteen. He'd been practicing Mozart's Sonata in F Major for a school recital that would later be canceled due to bomb threats, and his time with the school's piano was limited, but still he went to the cervecería across the street to watch. Never again, said Strassera. The television cut to footage of the Mothers, testifying. The bar around Eduardo smelled sour, and a man next to him was crying. One of the Mothers looked straight into the camera. "What has happened cannot be fixed," she said. "It can only be told." On her face was an expression of righteous sadness, a grief well beyond weeping. And suddenly Eduardo understood—with shocking and fatal clarity—that she was not trying to get her child back. This thought had never really occurred to him before. "They have to be dead," the woman was saying, "but they are only truly desaparecido if we turn away. They are only really gone once we stop looking for them."

Standing before the television, Mozart's allegro still throbbing in his fingertips, Eduardo had felt himself rising to a grave and difficult understanding. Perhaps this was only because he'd been looking for one—he was, after all, sixteen. But whatever the reason, he'd known that he was seeing something he could not forget: He was learning that goodness could not be goodness if it was dimensionless and passive; he was beginning to believe that there was a compassion beyond compassion. Eduardo looked at the Mother's face, and he saw that forgiveness without justice was not Christ's forgiveness, or any other kind worth extending. He walked out into the blazing sun and did not return to the piano that day, though he could not now remember where he went.

Eduardo, it turned out, was suited to studying law. He had always been diligent and high scoring, but he did not have that easygoing sheen that made people want to think well or expect much of him; he had never managed to effortlessly inspire confidence or lust. There was something about him that was too solicitous—it was subtle as a pheromone and just as permanent; it made people understand that they could ignore him and get away with it. Eduardo's freakishly good memory did not help matters. Growing up, he had often surprised peers he barely knew by revealing his shockingly accurate retention of any scrap of information they'd volunteered the first time they'd met him, which occasion they invariably could not recall. Children reacted to this party trick with some bemusement, since their worldviews were not really at odds with the notion that everyone around them might somehow know who they were. As he grew older, however, Eduardo learned that mature narcissism responded with more suspicion: People tended to assume that Eduardo's attention was particular to them, and he watched as their eyes narrowed and they wondered, visibly unnerved, just what exactly he might be after.

Still, Eduardo excelled in the clean realms—standardized testing, blind admissions, paper applications—where personality was scoured away; where memory was a strength, not a weakness. And it was these successes that delivered him to the University of Buenos Aires School of Law, where he finally learned—not in the classroom, but the bars— how to effectively wield his memory. Women, he learned, could be made to feel that Eduardo had a depth and singularity of feeling for them, whether he did or not. Men, as long as Eduardo used the right tone, could be made to feel quietly flattered and impressive. No matter how people felt about Eduardo, they usually left Eduardo's company feeling faintly good about themselves. And Eduardo quickly saw that this was what mattered—that that slight untraceable rosy glow was the important emotional takeaway, even if it had nothing to do with Eduardo at all. He would never be particularly attractive or charismatic or possessed of the kind of authority that commanded attention. But he could make anybody he met feel that *they* were. And this, Eduardo saw, could leverage a power that was subtler and, depending on the situation, more potent than what was lost.

After graduation, Eduardo began clerking in Córdoba. Around him, Kirchner was repaying the IMF loan; privatization was peeling away every expectation the people had ever had for anything beyond themselves in this world. Shared Dreams was investigated for corruption and the economy exploded overnight. Forgiveness was work, Eduardo told victims' families—but so, then, was love, and deciding what was right, and defending it. Recusing yourself from judgment so you won't be tainted by the aggressor's sin is the same as turning away from empathy so you won't be touched by the victim's pain. And God did not shrink from either task, Eduardo often thought—though he didn't say this to anyone. Eduardo would never have been fool enough to try to persuade anybody of the existence of God, just as he would never have been fool enough to try to persuade anybody of the existence of his own consciousness. No one can ever really prove their sentience externally—there's no argument or syllogism that gets you there: The systems of measurement are too fatally implicated in the thing they're trying to measure—and God, Eduardo thought, presented the same sort of mess. It was, at heart, a kind of epistemological Heisenberg uncertainty principle problem. But Eduardo's morality did not require a belief in God. If anything, man's compassionate justice was even more necessary in a secular universe. Because if not now, after all, then when? If not for this, after all, then for what?

After a few years, Eduardo was appointed the fiscal de cámara for Buenos Aires Province. Forgiveness is admirable, he told the judicial panels, but not when it is automatic; not when it is done because it's the easy way to stay shallowly blameless. Eduardo developed instincts of great accuracy and precision about suspects, and these instincts led him to a streak of notable and just convictions. Standing outside the courtroom after one of them, he posed a question to the assembled press: What does it mean for a killer to deserve our empathy if a victim does not? It just means that we are lazy. It just means we want to be left alone.

But Eduardo did not want to be left alone; instead, he wanted to work, and to try. Trying was a modest thing to have at the center of one's life. Nevertheless, it was going to save him. He wanted to try, and he wanted to keep trying—even now, with Maria gone. This meant he was not suicidal. He knew because he had looked it up.

Eduardo turned back toward his apartment building. He could still see it, all those blocks down the street, looking hazy and insubstantial in the mist. A mile away, Eduardo figured, the rain must be starting again.

That day, the emails were subpoenaed.

Lily Hayes and Katy Kellers were, it turned out, voluminous correspondents—they both kept track of the minute contours of their emotional lives, and this careful accounting produced several salient facts. First, it seemed that Lily had not much cared for Katy—in two emails and one Facebook message, all sent in early January, she had gone to some lengths to support her thesis that Katy was a "bore." Second, it seemed that Katy and Lily had had a fight, or possibly several fights, toward the middle or at the end of February. This fact was not mentioned in Lily's exchanges, but was described by Katy in a Google Chat exchange with one friend from home (who, alas, seemed already familiar with the situation, rendering the narrative fairly sketchy) and possibly referenced in a conversation with another (Sara Perkins-Lieberman: How are things with the roomie?? Katy Kellers: Uggggggggh : /). Finally, the third and most interesting piece of information revealed in the emails was that Katy, apparently, had been in a relationship. In an email written to that same Sara Perkins-Lieberman, she'd said: *I've met someone. It feels kind of crazy.* . . . *We're sort of sneaking around because I don't think Lily would like it very much (she's kind of histrionic), though maybe partly it just makes things more fun? I don't know. I didn't think I was really ready for anything yet, but now I sort of wonder.* This revelation, of course, explained the condoms. And it seemed that Katy had indeed kept the relationship from Lily: In all of her extensive narrative journalism about their lives in Buenos Aires (which continued to cover Katy throughout the rest of February, though in increasingly fond terms), Lily never mentioned it. Katy's relationship, apparently, really had stayed a secret. At least for a while.

In the afternoon, over coffee, Eduardo Googled "Lily Hayes." It was a common name in the United States, it turned out, though it struck Eduardo as fussy and prim, an odd moniker for Me Generation parents to give to a child. Nonetheless, "Lily Hayes+Middlebury" yielded several hits. There was Lily Hayes dressed up as a green pepper for some children's theater troupe, and there was Lily Hayes raving about the generosity of alumni donations in the school magazine, and there was Lily Hayes arguing in the Middlebury *Campus*—with a blend of self-righteousness and world vision totally unsullied by reality—for an immediate withdrawal of U.S. troops from Afghanistan. Next, Eduardo found Lily on Facebook: a Molière quote, a variety of subsexual poses, a loving catalog of reasonably challenging fiction. He scrolled down. He saw stern admonishments to sign petitions, flirtations with bearded and bespectacled young men, birthday wishes sent and received. It was certainly not the kind of trail that most of Eduardo's suspects left in their wake. Eduardo did not believe that crime—murder, in particular— was ever inevitable. But with most defendants, you could track the way each misfortune had impelled the next; you could look at their lives and nearly reach out to trace the filigreed twists and turns that had deposited them, with shaking hands, before their victims and their fates. Most defendants Eduardo saw were broken. Lily Hayes—if she was guilty—had never been whole.

Eduardo scrolled down further. A few months back, Lily Hayes had posted a link to a blog. "I wrote a piece for my Intermediate Creative Writing class, imagining a crime," she wrote, and fourteen people had "Liked" this statement, for reasons Eduardo could not fathom. He clicked on the link, which took him to what looked to be a mostly abandoned blog—*Reveries,* it was called, and underneath it were the words "feminist," "artist," "dreamer," and "explorer"—and the top post was her imagined crime, creatively written, apparently, for a college course. The piece seemed to revolve around a jilted lover who goes back into the house of the woman who has betrayed him to steal an expensive necklace he has given her. Eduardo read with keen attention, feeling that he was watching a thing in the distance assume its shape. Underneath the florid writing, the girlish overreliance on adverbs, there was something troubling and emotionally askew—the same thing, he was almost sure, that he'd detected in the transcript from her interview. He read the piece's ending. Then he read it again.

In my ire and haste, I have tripped the alarm. I must move with alacrity now. I grab the necklace swiftly. It is so beautiful. Its varicolored hues glitter dazzlingly in the light. I look at her sleeping peacefully there. I admire her swanlike neck of ivory. It is so innocent, so unsuspecting. I raise my knife in murderous wrath, but do not strike.

Eduardo printed out the story with the benumbed feeling of encountering astonishing good luck. It was significantly less than a written confession, of course, though it was hard to think of anything much closer.

But still, he was not sure.

Thursday was the judicial interrogation, to which Lily Hayes had submitted without a lawyer. Her father would be coming, apparently, and a U.S. consultant to the Argentine defense team and various private defense attorneys were being hired; these people, it was clear, had some money. Eduardo did not know why Lily had rejected the offers of a state-appointed lawyer. Perhaps it was due to a low opinion of the quality of Argentine state defenders, or a foolish calculation that this would make her look innocent, or an unusual though by no means unheard-of indifference to her own fate. Eduardo felt some sympathy for her. But he wasn't going to talk her out of making her own strategic mistakes, if she wanted to make them.

In the interrogation room, Lily Hayes looked even paler than the day Eduardo first saw her; her fingers were spread out on the table in a gesture of bald terror, and her hair did not appear to be entirely clean. She did seem very young—but Katy Kellers had been young, too, and Eduardo's empathy for her was not contingent on age. Neither was it contingent on her guilt or innocence. He was going to be as clear and kind as the situation allowed. This was only humane. He sat down.

"Quien es usted?" she said.

"*Eduardo Campos,*" he said. He did not extend his hand, because he didn't want to be patronizing. For the same reason, he did not switch to English. "I'm the fiscal de cámara, a representative of the investigative magistrate. My job is to help decide whether there's enough evidence against you to bring you to a criminal trial. I have ten days to make that determination, starting from today. I'll make my assessment and issue a recommendation to the instructor judge as to whether we should continue our case against you. In the eventuality that your case is brought before the criminal court, I'll argue the state's case alongside the instructor judge. It will be heard by a panel of three judges, who will determine your guilt or innocence. Has all of this been explained to you?"

He saw her pause, unsure whether to admit she had no idea what was going on.

"Yes," she said carefully.

"This is your judicial interrogation. You understand that you don't have to talk to me?"

"Yes," she said, more confidently. Eduardo flashed to an image of the unthinkable cartwheel this girl had done during her initial questioning; he saw her starfishing her way across the interrogation room under the cold light of the camera. "Why can't my dad bail me out?" she said.

"Bail has to do with the seriousness of the crime, not the evidence against the accused. Do you have any other questions for me?"

She did not, but Eduardo had a few for her. He spent the first twenty minutes asking for factual information he already knew—Lily Hayes's full name, her date of birth, her reason for being in Buenos Aires. ("I thought it would be an interesting place to study abroad," she'd said. "And has it been?" She'd laughed a harsh, unbecoming laugh.) These were the equivalent of lie tests on a psych battery or polygraph. He asked her to go through the day of the murder minute by minute, in order to catch deviations from the account she gave to police; he then asked her to repeat it four more times, in order to catch variations between accounts. Certain variations were suspicious, of course, but then so was no variation at all. Lily Hayes was chewing a strand of hair, he noted, which was intriguing. It was a strange, careless thing to do—it was vulgar, really, and he wasn't sure he could remember seeing anybody over the age of about seven do it—and it was interesting to him that she felt comfortable engaging in such an activity in this, one of the most important formal conversations of her life. At the forty-five-minute mark, Eduardo began asking the real questions.

"So," he said. "I understand you felt that Katy was insipid."

At this, Lily looked green and appalled. "Where did you hear that?"

Some prosecutors wouldn't tell her, in order to make her wonder who among her friends might not be on her side. They'd want to make her understand that the days when she could expect answers were over; that avenues to comprehension were charities now, to be dispensed or withheld at their whim. These kinds of prosecutors would want to build up the breathy edginess of paranoia, that bewildered lost-in-the-woods-at-night disorientation that makes someone look for any sort of beacon or semaphore. Paranoia in a defendant was a great asset for a prosecutor, it was generally thought. But Eduardo did not like to withhold answers. Partly, it offended his sense of fair play.

And partly, he disagreed with the strategy. He felt that giving defendants a false sense of marginal competence—a slight idea of where they stood in relation to the world—made them relax just enough to make a mistake, if there were any mistakes to be made (which, of course, he never assumed that there were).

"An email you wrote," he said.

"I see."

"Do you remember who you wrote that email to?"

"No."

"So it could have been any number of people, then?"

Lily said nothing. Eduardo pretended to look at his notes. "When you said she was insipid," said Eduardo, "did you mean she was 'lacking in qualities that interest, stimulate, or challenge'?"

"I mean—yes, I suppose so. Yeah."

"Was there anything in particular you found especially insipid about the victim?"

There was really no need to refer to Katy as the "victim" just now—though it was how Eduardo would refer to her in court, of course, to remind the three judges (over and over and over) that the dead girl, in stark contrast to the living girl in front of them, was dead. But it was best to get in the habit early.

"I don't know," said Lily.

"Her reading tastes, perhaps? Her vocabulary?"

"I guess so."

"Do you consider yourself a smart woman?" said Eduardo. This language, too, was intentional. In public, in the courts, Eduardo would refer to Katy as a "girl" and Lily as a "woman," whenever he wasn't referring to them as "victim" and "defendant," even though Lily was, in fact, three and a half months younger than Katy had been when she died. This was, again, just good sense. You could subtly direct the judges toward the truth through small adornments and pressures and omissions; Eduardo would never deviate from the facts, of course, but there was nothing wrong with using words with slightly different connotations in order to illuminate the reality of a situation. Who could deny that the differing designations reflected an emotional veracity, if not a biological one? You looked at Lily—leaving aside questions of guilt or innocence—and you saw her callousness, and her emotional remoteness, and her sexual experience, and you knew you were dealing with an adult. And then there was the small matter that Lily would grow up, in prison or out, and Katy would always be a girl and would always be dead.

"What?"

"It's a simple question."

"I don't understand what you're asking."

"Is it fair to say you thought were you smarter than the victim?"

"Is it fair to say you think you're smarter than me?"

Eduardo put down his notepad and raised his eyebrows. Lily's face was flushed; he could tell that she was slightly surprised, but also slightly pleased, at what she had said.

"I would not presume that," he said firmly, and lifted his notepad again. "Insipidness aside, there were a lot of other things you didn't like about Katy Kellers."

"That's not true."

"Let me remind you of some of the things you didn't like about her, according to emails you sent during the month of January alone: her hair, her name, her teeth—"

"I loved her teeth!"

" 'They were not the teeth of a serious person,' according to a Facebook message you wrote to your friend Callie Meyers on January seventeenth, 2011."

"I liked her teeth. I wanted teeth like that."

"Do you think Katy ever had to have braces?"

"I don't know."

"She never had braces. They were just naturally straight."

Lily stared at him.

"You had to have braces, didn't you?" said Eduardo. "I understand you had them into college. I understand you had to visit home on weekends for orthodontic follow-up."

"I don't see what this has to do with anything."

"We'll move on. Tell me about your relationship with Sebastien LeCompte."

"We were friends."

"You had a sexual relationship?"

Lily turned her face to the side. "Briefly."

"Were you aware that the victim was also having a sexual relationship with Sebastien LeCompte?" This query contained a bluff, as well as a fairly obvious supposition—but, being a question, it was not exactly a lie. And at any rate, the reality of Sebastien LeCompte's involvement with Katy Kellers did not matter half as much as whatever Lily had believed that reality to be.

"I wouldn't necessarily have called it a relationship."

"You were aware of it, though?"

"I mean, I certainly wondered."

"What made you wonder?"

"I'm not stupid."

Eduardo pretended to make a note of this, though he wasn't really writing anything.

Lily shifted in her seat. "I just mean, I could tell. They weren't as careful as they thought they were."

"And how did you feel about it?"

"Not much."

"Really? You weren't angry?"

"Not really. We weren't in love or anything."

During his seventh week with Maria, Eduardo had whispered into her ear while she was sleeping: "Tell me who you are, because I love you already and I want to know who I love."

"I mean," said Lily, uncertain about what to do with his silence. "Sebastien and I weren't, like, a couple."

"But you were sleeping together."

Lily looked pensive; the light through the bars made long tapering wicks on her face. "I don't think I want to talk to you anymore today," she said.

Eduardo nodded. "That's your right," he said. He snapped his notebook shut in order to convey a sense of finality, of satisfaction. "This has been a good conversation. You can go have your medical exam now."

Though he would never let it matter, it was true that something about Lily Hayes reminded Eduardo of Maria. What was it, exactly? The breeziness of a person to whom nothing was ever denied? But in Maria this quality had been charming and elfin, and in Lily it was, assuredly, only obnoxious. And at any rate, Eduardo knew that there was something sinister about Lily that went well beyond impulsivity.

Take, for example, the cartwheel. Eduardo had worked enough high-profile cases to know how the cartwheel would play, what binary of accusation and defense would grow in its wake. For the prosecution, by way of the media, an argument would be made that the cartwheel was callous, flippant, reflective of the same kind of bottomless disregard that could, given the right circumstances and drugs, disregard another human life. The counterargument, obviously, would assert that the cartwheel was whimsical and guileless; an exuberant outburst that was now being willfully misunderstood by the old and the humorless and the agenda having. Indeed, the defense might say, if the cartwheel was evidence of anything it was evidence of innocence: How could someone guilty, someone who wanted to look *not* guilty, do something like that? Only a person who knew that she was innocent and was too young to know that this might not matter would ever, ever do a cartwheel in an interrogation room.

But Eduardo knew better, because he had spent years studying an impulsive woman. Maria sometimes did things that were crazy or ill-advised, Eduardo would be the first to admit—though more commonly she did things that were merely strange: He'd once found her in the living room at three a.m. staring at a red umbrella she'd lit up with a flashlight, and more than once he'd passed by the closed bathroom door and heard her murmuring to herself in the claw-footed tub. One time she'd hung up a paper moon in a tree, where it shone through the branches like an illuminated coin.

"It's beautiful," he'd said, assuming Maria had wanted to do something beautiful.

"Oh, is it?" she'd said distractedly, as he wrapped his arms around her.

"I just wanted it to be interesting."

"It is," said Eduardo. He could hear the sticky note of pleading in his own voice. He so wanted to see whatever it was she wanted him to see.

"No," said Maria, looking at him calmly. "Nothing beautiful is really interesting." She'd torn it down then, though not angrily—just methodically, thoroughly, as though correcting a mistake she now saw that she'd made.

There were difficulties, too, of course. Maria had a tendency to internalize free-floating stress from the universe, though her life was not, as far as Eduardo could discern, at all stressful. This knotty, inaccessible melancholy of hers was so different from his own; whatever went on with Maria was always some strange iteration away from sense. She'd fall into black spells, growing monosyllabic and morose, speaking in a kind of halting iambic pentameter. She'd disappear into the bathroom to sob (and how she sobbed—these choking, wretched sobs that somehow came at exactly even intervals, so that they seemed almost like some kind of biological or geologic process). One winter she even went a little bald; Eduardo came upon a collapsed black octopus of hair in the shower drain, looking like the remnant of a massacre.

And there were times—rarely, but memorably—when she could be cruel. The first time he'd really seen it was the night he'd been appointed fiscal de cámara. Maria had organized a celebration for him at a restaurant, though he realized later that every night with Maria was a kind of complicated, triple-edged celebration—like the wedding of an old lover, or the birthday party of an old enemy. There was always a manic sheen of strenuously sought and hard-won fun and an underlying sense of deep and growing trouble. The night of the promotion, Eduardo had felt humble and serene and pleased with himself for the first time in he didn't know how long. Their friends were laughing and drinking and having a great time until Maria clinked her glass for a toast. Everybody stopped speaking and stared at her happily, and Eduardo felt grateful and honored—because she was so beautiful, because he was so lucky— as he waited to hear what she would say about him.

"Eduardo," said Maria. She was smiling. She was radiant. "I always knew you'd excel at this job. You were born for it, weren't you? You were born to be a prosecutor. Or maybe a prison guard."

Eduardo could feel his smile freeze. "I don't know what you mean," he'd said, trying to keep the bleakness out of his voice. Truth be told, he rarely knew exactly what she meant.

"Oh, Eduardo," said Maria, and the strangest thing was how much genuine affection was still in her face, her voice. "The reason you're a genius at your job is because you love to punish people. You love to make sure everyone's having as little fun as you are."

People never actually put down their forks when these things get said in public. They gather themselves further into the small tasks of eating; they busy themselves with spoons. Eduardo tilted his head back and laughed. This was what he'd learned to do whenever Maria said something like this; everyone was long accustomed to understanding nothing of the romantic relationships of others, and so they could accept anything as a sort of baffling in-joke, if that's how Eduardo treated it.

"I'm having fun." Eduardo laughed again. "I am having fun."

After Maria left, it had been occasionally suggested to Eduardo that she might have been a bit selfish. It had been once proposed that she might, in fact, have had a diagnosable narcissistic personality disorder. "Garden-variety crazy," his friends had said, "just your typical crazy-woman crazy," but Eduardo could never agree. Maria was crazy, perhaps, but she was not typical; her lunacy was the blue electricity running through a more finely wired system. And though it might be a kind of madness, it was also a kind of rare brilliance, a rare honesty.

And so Eduardo could easily imagine Maria cartwheeling from joy in any number of odd places, and in any number of inappropriate situations, where others might prefer that she not. But it was the joy that was the key; nobody cartwheels when they're paralyzed with grief. And so Lily's cartwheel wasn't damning because it was quirky, as a small but self-righteous vanguard of quirkiness defenders the world over seemed to believe. Lily's cartwheel was damning because it was, like Lily herself, indifferent. Lily's cartwheel could not tell you that she was guilty. It could only tell you that—during that interrogation, not twenty hours after her roommate's death—she had not been sad.

Nevertheless, of course, Eduardo was not sure.

On Tuesday, Eduardo met with Beatriz Carrizo.

"I'm so sorry for what you've been through," he said, pouring her a glass of water.

They were sitting in his office with the shades drawn. Beatriz Carrizo's hair was heavy and shiny; she wore a stretchy shirt with a pattern of beige-and-red florets. A gold cross glittered between her breasts. "Why can't my husband be here?" she said.

"I need to interview you separately," said Eduardo. Beatriz's eyes widened. "I don't mean to alarm you. You're not suspects." This was true. They'd been away that weekend, at a nephew's baptism in the north. "But I am interested in hearing your independent impressions of Lily Hayes. Separately."

Beatriz nodded. "Now." Eduardo shuffled his papers, to create an aura of shifting gears. "What can you tell me about her?"

Beatriz Carrizo shook her head. "I don't know," she said. "I really didn't know her very long."

"Just your overall impressions would be helpful."

Beatriz took a long gulp of water, then stared out the window with a queasy, unresolved expression. "Well," she said finally. "She was an odd girl, I'll say that."

"Odd, how?"

"She was cold. A little deceptive, maybe. She hung around with that boy next door at all hours of the day and night." Beatriz pursed her lips momentarily as if wanting to stop herself, then unpursed them and went on. "I know she stayed over there when we were out of the house. Also, she was arrogant. She was always telling us things she'd learned about the city, as if we didn't already know them. It was nice she was interested, I suppose. But it was also so silly. She just didn't think about other people, that's all."

Eduardo nodded. This was his impression, too, though, of course, he would not say so. "And what was Katy like?" he said.

"She was a sweet girl. Quiet. We didn't know her that well, either. It's absolutely horrific, what happened to her. Is that your wife?" Beatriz was looking at the picture of Maria on Eduardo's desk—one of the two framed ones he'd allowed himself to keep. It was taken four years ago, at a beach, and she was doing a handstand. Her hair was whipping around her face and she was smiling, her mouth like a peony. She was the only adult Eduardo had ever known who could do a handstand.

"Yes," he said, because he always said yes.

"She's beautiful."

He looked up at Beatriz quickly. "Did you have any difficulties with Lily?"

"Difficulties?"

"She was obedient? She was respectful? She followed the rules?"

"Difficulties. Well. I suppose there were a few."

"Yes?"

"Well, I caught her going through our papers."

"When was this?"

"Maybe two weeks," said Beatriz. "I mean, maybe two weeks before."

Eduardo nodded. "And you confronted her?"

"Yes."

"And how did she react?"

"Well, she was not sorry, I'll tell you that. She didn't even pretend to be sorry."

Eduardo made a note on his pad. "And what else?"

"And then she took that awful job at the club, meeting God knows what sorts of people. She started coming back even later. I'd lie awake waiting to hear her come in. I was so afraid of having to call her parents and say that something had happened to her. Funny, I never worried about anything happening to Katy." A little fork of wrinkles appeared on Beatriz's chin. "And then she got fired from her job and lied about it."

"She did?"

Beatriz nodded and bit her lip. The fork on her chin deepened.

"Do you know why she was fired?" said Eduardo.

"No, but I also can't imagine why they hired her in the first place. She could barely find the kitchen sink at our house."

"That's very helpful," said Eduardo, making a note on his pad. "Was there anything else?"

Beatriz covered her mouth and nodded.

"What happened?" said Eduardo. Between them, the air felt heavy, salt rimmed; Eduardo could smell the cilantro edge of her sweat, the tang of an insistent perfume. He should not be attracted to her, of course, given his role and hers. What was troubling was that he actually wasn't.

"She—laughed—at my husband's depression," said Beatriz finally.

"She laughed at it?" Eduardo did not blink. His own depression was a thing with claws and teeth and eyes, its own set of tics and preoccupations and prejudices, its own entire integrated personality. The trick to not killing yourself was to convince yourself, every single day, that your departure from the world would have a devastating effect on absolutely everyone around you, despite consistent evidence to the contrary.

"Yes. She'd seen my husband in a state of extreme—depression—"

Beatriz looked at her lap. "He was drunk, I mean. And when I spoke to Lily about it, she laughed."

Eduardo nodded again. "Nervously, perhaps?"

"That was another thing about her. She was never nervous. She was oddly flat. Her—what?"

"Her affect?"

"Right. Her affect was flat."

Eduardo leaned forward. "This next question I'm going to ask you is not the most important question," he said. "Even though I'm asking it last."

"Okay."

"Did you ever think she could do something like this?"

Beatriz frowned. "Well, no," she said finally. "I have to say no. I didn't."

"Thank you, Señora," said Eduardo. "This has been very helpful."

Beatriz looked up, and Eduardo saw that she was tearful. "Should we move?" she said.

"I'm sorry?"

"How long are the police going to need the house?"

Eduardo poured her another glass of water. "You'd want to ask the police about that. Quite a while, I should think."

"People drive by and honk at all hours of the night. It's awful. I don't know how we're going to live there again."

"Maybe you can't."

"But we'll never be able to sell it."

Eduardo pressed his thumb against his glass. "This case is probably going to get quite a bit of attention, you know," he said. "If Lily Hayes is formally charged. That will help with the sale."

Beatriz gaped. "You mean, you think someone is going to want to buy the house *because* of what happened?"

Eduardo looked at her wearily. "I have seen it happen before, Señora."

Beatriz shook her head. Behind her, the light coming through the window was hemorrhagic. The little gold cross on her chest winked in the sun. "I can't imagine anyone would be horrible enough to do that," she said.

And Eduardo told her that, in his professional experience, there was someone horrible enough to do almost anything.

On Friday, the police brought in Lily Hayes's camera. And finally, Eduardo was sure.

Everything he really needed to know was in the pictures. In the pictures, the ease with which Lily Hayes floated through the universe was ruinously apparent; there simply was not a frisson of friction between her desires and their arrival. *Arise, world!* she seemed to say. *Part, seas! Reveal yourself, Buenos Aires, and let me take your picture!* On the camera was a picture of a woman with a blood-colored lesion on her face, clearly taken on the sly. There was a picture of a tiny pantsless boy. There was a picture of Lily Hayes herself, giving an exaggerated thumbs-up as she points to her bug bites. Here, Eduardo saw, was a person without humility. And Eduardo believed that humility, more than anything, was the basis for morality. Goodness begins when the Buberian I/it shifts to the ethically accountable I/thou; it begins with the belief that you do not have a monopoly on consciousness—that you are not, in fact, the only person who exists. And here is Lily Hayes, standing in front of the Basílica Nuestra Señora de Luján, her prodigious bosom spilling out over a too-tight tank top. She is nearly aglow with the light of her narcissism. Does she notice that all the other women are modestly dressed, that their heads are covered? She either does not notice, or she does not care. A person who does not notice is silly. A person who does not care is dangerous. And when Eduardo looked at Lily Hayes's photos, he could see which kind of person she was. For whatever other qualities she had, Lily Hayes was not unobservant. She noticed everything; the pictures attested to this. Here she is noticing the wings of a dragonfly, and here she is noticing the dew on a guava fruit, and here she is noticing the hilarious discrepancy between an enormous sign advertising COMIDA VEGETARIANA alongside the butchered hide of some unfortunate ungulate, glistening in the sun. What Lily Hayes noticed was gratingly predictable, perhaps, but she did notice. So Eduardo had to conclude—tentatively, of course—that what she didn't do was care.

That afternoon, Eduardo submitted his request to schedule the hearing before the instructor judge. He felt he had enough to say.

CHAPTER THREE

January

Lily had lately come to two conclusions: one, we will all be dead one day; and two, we are not dead yet.

It was possible she had always known the first thing. In Lily's family, the winter—all winter, every winter, even these twenty-four years later—was hallowed, depressive ground, everyone tiptoeing around the memory of Janie, the daughter who had died in the winter two years before Lily was born. In the photo on the mantel, Janie was square jawed and sensible faced, like Lily and Anna; you could tell she would have grown up passably pretty if she'd ever learned not to look so severe. But in the picture Janie is only two years old, and riding a rocking horse is taking all of her attention, and anyway she will be dead in a year so you can't blame the kid for not having a sense of humor. Lily had looked at that picture countless times, and more than wishing that Janie had lived—though she wished that, too, of course she wished that—she wished that Janie had been a boy, or that she herself had been a boy, because losing that first daughter had really ruined her parents for daughters.

Lily's childhood had been, accordingly, criminally tedious: all happiness scrupulously prescreened, all sorrow decidedly offstage. She and Anna had coasted along, passively reactive to the most benign of benign stimuli—roller-skating parties, two trips to Disney World, craft projects at their school (which was a public school but was in a terrific neighborhood and thus tremendously well resourced). Visits to Janie's grave were firmly linked to holidays, primarily oriented around all of the objects involved (the selection of flowers, the placement of balloons, the clearing away of dead grass), and always felt about as scripted and dispassionate as a congressional filibuster. Perhaps not coincidentally, Andrew and Maureen's divorce, when it finally came, achieved what must have been a level of truly world-record-shattering tepidness: After years of existing in a collective state of medicated and vacant life-tolerance, they merely drifted off into separate ethers, and that was that. They were, essentially, zombies. Both Anna and Lily agreed on this—though Anna tended to think their zombie state was forgivable and understandable and Lily tended to think that life was short and that, yes, a terrible thing had happened, but that terrible thing had happened long, long ago and one day everyone would be dead and nobody would get any extra points for having hated life so much. Because Andrew and Maureen did hate life, really: They were just always very polite to it.

So yes, Lily was familiar with the concept of mortality. What was newer, maybe, was this acute sense of awareness, of aliveness, of gratitude. It was Argentina that had given it to her. The feeling had started on the airplane, when the rust-colored light wheeled through the windows, illuminating the blond hairs on the arm of the flight attendant as she poured the wine, and Lily felt her life beginning to open. She'd grinned idiotically right through losing money at a criminal exchange rate at EZE, right through a startlingly pungent Subte ride, and right through the first day and a half with the host family, the Carrizos. The Carrizos were perfect: Carlos was in real estate and Beatriz stayed at home, though she dressed well and always seemed busy, and they were both charming and, crucially, gently incurious about Lily's whereabouts. They understood English, but Beatriz pretended not to, so Lily got to practice her Spanish whenever they spoke, which she loved. She loved, as it happened, almost everything. She loved her room, which was small and sunny, even though it was in the basement, and had a bunk bed with bright green sheets. She loved the huge, sagging house next door, which just had to be haunted. She loved the chorizo sandwich—with its smoky-tasting egg and salty, seeping cheese—that you could buy and eat on the street. She loved her academic schedule— a Wednesday morning political philosophy seminar, a creative writing independent study project, and a midday Spanish-language class that was widely viewed as optional. And most of all, maybe, she loved how close the Carrizos lived to Avenida Cabildo, where you could catch a bus to anywhere in the city. Already, Lily could feel herself expanding to fill the new space the world had afforded her; already, Middlebury was turning back into the collection of catalog snapshots it once had been—explosively autumnal trees, international relations textbooks, laughing groups of friends of improbable and, as it turned out, wholly unrepresentative racial compositions. Everything about Lily's life there—Harold the economist, and those awful Hawaiian parties thrown by the coed social houses, and the hissing of the radiator in her formal logic class, and her articulate, bespectacled women's studies classmates, doomed to eternally debate gender versus equity feminism—began to seem less real. All of that was the detritus of a shallow, conscripted life; all of that had merely been preparation for this: getting off a plane in a new country, in a new hemisphere, and emerging from the chrysalis of academia to fly off into the bald, stunning sky of reality. For a day and a half, Lily was thrilled. For a day and a half, Lily was free. And then Katy arrived.

Katy was Katy Kellers, the roommate. The informational email Lily had received from the program in December had revealed only that Katy attended UCLA and studied international finance, and this second fact, in particular, had left Lily unprepared for how distressingly beautiful Katy would be. Katy Kellers, it turned out, had dusky blond hair and preposterously even teeth and eyes that seemed somehow more dimensional than was normal. The day she arrived she wore a tight-fitting brown turtleneck—the kind of thing that could only flatter someone who ran very long distances recreationally (Lily had gone shopping with Anna often enough to know)—and, even after fourteen hours on a plane, did not appear to be the slightest bit tired.

"You're Katy?" said Lily, holding out her hand.

Katy's hand felt exactly like it looked. "And you're Lily," she said, and smiled. Those teeth! Lily was going to have a hard time getting over those teeth. Lily's own mangled teeth had been hammered into relative normalcy by a series of truly gruesome procedures during high school (this was why she'd experimented sexually so much early in college, she'd explained to Anna once—because her teeth had been so bad for so long that her self-esteem had taken a while to iron itself out). Lily's teeth were fine now, but not like Katy's. Katy's teeth were like the Platonic ideal of teeth.

Katy bent to unzip her suitcase and began rifling through a polychrome array of sweaters. The most feminine muscles Lily had ever seen toggled in her arms.

"So," said Lily, climbing to the top of the bunk bed. "What brings you here?"

"Here?"

Lily swung her legs out over the side. "To Buenos Aires."

Katy shrugged. "I wanted to go to Barcelona—actually, I was supposed to go with my boyfriend, we were supposed to go together, but then—"

"You broke up?"

Katy bit her lip—actually bit her lip! "We broke up, right, and so I decided to go somewhere else."

"And by then all the other programs were full."

"Well," said Katy. "Not exactly. I could have gone to Senegal."

"Oh," said Lily.

Katy brushed her bangs with her fingers, even though they didn't really need brushing.

"Yeah," said Lily. "I mean, I think that's why it's hard to really commit to one person at our age. I was seeing a couple of people last semester, but nothing really serious, so I was sort of free to do whatever I wanted."

Lily had made a philosophical decision during sophomore year to refer to her dates in gender-neutral pronouns as much as possible, in solidarity with the gay rights movement. As it happened, all of her sexual partners (four to eight, depending on how conventionally one was defining the act) had thus far been male, but she wasn't narrow-minded. She'd always imagined she might kiss a girl before college was out. She knew it was cliché, but one couldn't always avoid being cliché. She was twenty, she was a double major in philosophy and women's studies, and this much she'd learned the hard way.

"Right," said Katy vaguely.

"Well, one person, mostly," said Lily. "His name was Harold. He studied economics. I can't believe I dated someone named Harold. I had sexual *intercourse* with someone named Harold. He's twenty-one years old, can you imagine?" Katy's eyes were flattening, maybe, a little. She zipped her suitcase back up, even though she hadn't finished unpacking. "What was your boyfriend's name?" said Lily.

"Anton."

"Anton, see?" Lily sat on the bed. "Now that's a name."

"I really loved him." Katy breathed in quickly, and Lily was afraid, for a brief, harrowing moment, that she might cry. It was too soon, it was far too soon, for this conversation.

"Well, sure," said Lily soothingly. She swung her feet back onto the bed and tucked them under herself. "Are you guys still friends?"

"No," said Katy uncomprehendingly. "We'll never be friends."

"No?" This was a matter of some interest to Lily; when she and Harold had broken up, they had solemnly vowed to stay friends. And why wouldn't they? They were both young and resilient and had had their hearts broken two or three times already. But soon he'd taken up with a new girl—an accounting major, please!—who'd forbidden him ever to speak to Lily again. This she found crushing; she had very much wanted to stay friends with him, partly because being friends with ex-lovers seemed sophisticated and mature and continental, and partly because it seemed humane, and partly because she harbored a catastrophic fear of losing touch with anyone. It reminded her of death, and she was too easily reminded of death already. Then again, she knew that she had a more acute sense of the passage of time in general—and the swiftness of life, in particular—because of her dead sister, or almost-sister, or whatever. So she'd learned to forgive people their shortsightedness, and be happy for them that they'd lived the kinds of lives that would allow it.

"He cheated on me at a substance-free house party," said Katy.

"Oh geez." Lily whistled. "That's bad. You definitely want substances involved in infidelity."

Katy looked stricken. "I don't know," she said doubtfully. "I'm not sure that really matters."

Lily tried to backpedal. "No, of course," she said. "But I mean, I don't know. I don't really think monogamy is natural for people our age, do you?"

Katy scratched her nose. Somehow this, even this, looked delicate, preordained. "Well," she said. "I think maybe you can decide it is."

Overall, Lily knew, the roommate situation could have been a whole lot worse. Katy was neat and polite and she quickly acquired a collection of reasonable girl friends with flatironed hair—none of whom were as beautiful as she was, but all of whom seemed about as nice—and went out with them almost every afternoon. Still, Lily couldn't shake a feeling of deflating uneasiness—a kind of awkwardness, but with harder edges—whenever she was around Katy. Lily spent hours after classes ended drinking wine in cafés and reading Borges in Span-

ish, circling all the words she didn't know, and when she returned to
the Carrizos' house at night—unhinged and awestruck, rapturous over
the scope and beauty of the world—she'd sit down at the dinner table
and Katy would say something like, "Lily, you have wine on your teeth."
And that would be that.

Still, Lily loved Buenos Aires; she loved to think of the vast meat of
the world—ocean and Amazon and rain forests and drug wars—that
separated her from everyone she had ever known. She couldn't help
but feel a little sorry for all of them, now that she was so happy. In her
psychology class at Middlebury, Lily had once been assigned to write
about birth order in her family and how she felt that she did or did not
conform to the postulated birth order personality types discussed in
class. Lily had written about how she was technically the oldest, and in
some ways she felt like the oldest—she was maybe more adventurous
than Anna—but in other ways, she felt like the middle child, because
she certainly was lost in the shuffle between the needy poles of Anna
(the baby) and dead Janie (also, perpetually, the baby), but in *other*
ways, absent Janie only reconfirmed Lily's status as oldest, because no
first-time parents could be as paranoid or restrictive or dictatorial as
second-time parents who'd lost their first. And Lily, of course, had had
to break them down, remind them that not all colds were terminal illnesses, and not all broken curfews were catastrophes, and not all boys
were rapists—you're welcome, Anna!—and eventually they'd come to
some mutual uncomfortable agreement that they were willing to let
Lily have something like a life, though they didn't have to like it.

She'd gotten an A on the paper.

But in Buenos Aires, for the first time, Lily felt herself stepping out
of those roles; she felt herself finally filling out the template of her own
autonomous selfhood that she now knew she'd been mapping—in secret, on her own time—for her entire life. Each day after classes—
which were academically comical, everybody dead-eyed and hungover,
the teachers bored, the classrooms too hot, the city shimmering right
outside the window—Lily went wandering out into the enormous af-

ternoons. She took epic, dusty walks around the city, to San Telmo and La Boca and Palermo, hopping in cabs to skirt the bad streets. She spent an afternoon trying to photograph a certain beam of light on the obelisk. She spent a day taking the train out to the basilica in Luján to try to see what all the Catholic fuss was about. She sat in bars drinking Quilmes and trying to look mysterious; she sat in cafés eating alfajors and licking powdered sugar off her fingers and not minding that she looked silly.

She would be dead one day, but she was not dead yet.

Around her, the air was humid, languid; it made all the other air she had ever known feel thin. Something about the lushness of the city made Lily think of prehistoric times—she half-expected to see a dinosaur with mossy teeth emerge from a swamp. The mosquito bites gave her enormous welts because she wasn't used to Argentinean mosquitoes; they rose and grew and burst, volcanically, horrifyingly, and then healed into thumb-sized dust-colored scars. Lily documented this entire process on her camera, using American coins for scale. The bugs here were ridiculous, but everything here was ridiculous. The exchange rate was ridiculous. The fruit was ridiculous. Lily took pictures of the bugs and the fruit. She took pictures of the people, too, and sent them back to Anna.

"Do people mind you taking pictures of them?" said Katy.

"I don't know," said Lily. "I didn't ask."

For the most part, Lily loved the Carrizos, too. She got along very well with Carlos: The two of them drank the most at dinner, and got into good-natured rollicking screeds about George W. Bush during which they congratulated each other on a series of ever-more-implausible theories and opinions. Beatriz was sweet, in a no-nonsense sort of way—and, though she was possessed of a clear preference for Katy, Lily did not like Beatriz any less just because she liked Katy better. It was fine to have each host parent prefer a different study-abroad student. It made them all feel like a convincing temporary family.

On Sundays, Lily and Katy attended church with the Carrizos. Though Lily scorned church with her own family—Maureen attended a milquetoast Unitarian institution where all possible modes of being were enthusiastically and cloyingly *affirmed*—she felt that church in a foreign country was a different matter altogether, more along the lines of an anthropological investigation, even if it was uncomfortably situated, broadly, within her own abandoned tradition. After all, she wouldn't *not* go to the Blue Mosque in Istanbul, she wouldn't *not* go to the Wailing Wall in Jerusalem, just because she didn't believe these sites were actually sacred. In church, of course, she didn't cross herself and didn't take Communion, but this was, in fact, a reflection of her profound respect for the religious beliefs of others. Lily tried to explain all of this to Katy on their second Sunday in Buenos Aires.

"I'm just saying," said Katy. "A bite of toast, a swallow of wine, and they're happy. Who cares?"

They were standing over the sink in the bathroom, and Lily was trying to somehow pluck her eyebrows without seeing Katy's image in the mirror next to hers. Lily and Katy didn't usually wash up together, but it was the first night they were alone in the house—Carlos was out with his friends, and Beatriz was visiting her sister—and a temporary, lukewarm camaraderie seemed to have grown between them.

"But do you believe that stuff?" said Lily.

Katy made a face and spat a mass of mint toothpaste into the sink. Somehow she did this, as all things, daintily. Lily could not get used to the way Katy seemed to move through the physical world while remaining utterly untouched by it: her hair never discernibly disturbed by wind, her lips never discernibly stained by wine, her clothes never discernibly wrinkled by any amount of movement or exertion. "That's not even the point," Katy said. "It costs you nothing."

"I think it's really despicable to pretend to believe in it if you don't."

"But if you don't believe it, why do you care? If there is no God, it's not like He's gonna know."

"But *you're* gonna know," said Lily. She rapped her tweezers against the sink conclusively and then went to stand at the window. All the windows in the basement looked out at ground level, which made Lily feel like she lived in the steerage section of a ship. She looked up and across the yard. Next door, all the lights in the mansion were out. "Do you know who lives over there?"

"A young guy. Our age." Katy joined Lily at the window. Lily could smell her citrus shampoo. "Haven't you seen him?"

"No." Lily squinted. "His lights are never on, are they?"

"You'd think he could afford lights. Beatriz says he's very rich."

Lily was about to ask *how* rich, exactly, when a spectacular crash— echoing, multidimensional, seeming to involve many kinds of different materials—issued from somewhere upstairs.

"Jesus," said Katy.

"Is it a robbery?"

"Did you lock the door when you came in?"

"Shit."

"Did you?"

"We should go up there."

They crept upstairs, their cell phones casting neon squares of light onto the stairs. Lily tapped Katy on the shoulder and pointed questioningly to the light switch; Katy shook her head. When they reached the top of the stairs, Lily flung the door open, ready to scream. But in the living room, it was only Carlos, and he was, it seemed, only drunk: He was staggering about, his center of gravity askew, pantomiming the kind of exaggerated inebriation that would be comic in a movie but was somehow frightening—then sad, then frightening once more—in real life. In the corner of the room, one of Beatriz's potted plants had been knocked over, leaving an escarpment of dirt on the rug.

"Girls," said Carlos, issuing a bipolar laugh that turned into the first fragment of a sob. He grabbed at the wall, and one of the framed photographs—of Beatriz in a graduation gown—fell to the ground and shattered. "Girls."

"What should we do?" hissed Katy.

"What do you mean, 'do'?" said Lily.

"Should we call someone?"

"Call someone, please. We should go back to our room."

"What if he hits his head or something?"

"He's not going to."

"What are we going to tell Beatriz?"

"We're not going to tell her anything."

"What about the picture?"

"What about it?"

"Should we try to fix it, or what?"

"Just leave it."

They went back downstairs, the crashing continuing above them. Lily felt a minor, untraceable thrill with every bang, but Katy seemed not to want to listen. Instead, she pulled out her iPod and sanctimoniously turned up the volume until the bass lines began rattling around the room, like the skeletons of songs. Lily, who could never bear to tell anyone to turn down music, said nothing.

After a while, the sounds stopped, and Katy got up and produced some Neutrogena from her bag, even though Lily could have sworn she'd already washed her face. "You need to remember to lock that door," she said on her way out of the room. Lily stared at her: She was standing in a bedroom doorway, holding a domestic object, and issuing a directive. Did she not realize how weirdly old, how fussily maternal, she seemed?

"It was only Carlos!" said Lily. "He lives here!"

The next day over breakfast, Carlos was swollen-eyed and chagrined; Katy chattered about her classes, her voice a half an octave higher than normal, until he went to work early. Beatriz had not emerged by the time Lily left for class. But when Lily came back to the house at lunch, she was standing in the kitchen, as though she'd been lying in wait.

"Lily," said Beatriz. She looked serious, but then she always looked serious. "I want to talk to you about last night."

"It's okay." Lily laughed—an indulgent, knowing sort of chuckle—to show Beatriz that it was not a big deal. "Don't worry about it at all."

"Lily," said Beatriz. She wasn't smiling. "Do you understand the word 'depressed'?"

Lily felt a sliver of cold in her sternum. She was doing the wrong thing, the exact wrong thing, by laughing. "Oh. Yes," she said. "I'm sorry. Yes."

"Do you understand?"

"I'm sorry. I do understand. Yes."

Beatriz nodded as though an agreement had been reached, then bent and began unloading the dishwasher. "We'd like to have a dinner Friday night," she said. "To welcome you girls properly. We thought maybe you'd like to invite the boy next door? Katy was asking about him."

"Oh," said Lily. "I suppose so, sure."

Beatriz frowned. "We've been meaning to ask him around since we moved here. But it'll be more fun for him, anyway, now that we've got young people around."

Later, in the bunk beds, Lily asked Katy if she thought the dinner offer was an attempt to get them not to tell the program about Carlos's drunkenness. Katy was reading some punishing textbook by flashlight; outside, Lily could hear people laughing on the street. They were probably headed out to dinner. It was only eleven o'clock.

"Like a bribe," said Lily. "Maybe."

"No," said Katy. "I think they're probably just trying to be nice."

"It's odd timing, though, don't you think?"

"You're so conspiracy minded."

A bar of weak light flashed up the wall and onto Lily's comforter. She could hear the whisk of Katy's pages, the efficient squeak of her pen.

"I had no idea this was going on with Carlos," said Lily a little while later. "I mean, they seemed so happy. Their lives seemed really perfect."

"Well," said Katy. "I guess we don't really know that much about them."

Lily went over to the mansion the next afternoon, right after classes ended. The path to the house was overgrown with some kind of scrubby grass that looked potentially poisonous. The knocker was heavy and shaped like the head of a mythical beast that Lily couldn't identify. She stood back a few feet away from the door and waited for the rich boy, he of the perpetual darkness, to emerge.

The door opened, and an implausibly young-looking person appeared. His eyes were beautiful in an obnoxious sort of way, and he had freckles, which made him seem tremendously unserious.

"Hi," said Lily in Spanish. "I'm Lily. I'm staying next door with the Carrizos, and I'm supposed to invite you over for dinner."

"Are you?" The boy answered in English. It was flat, American English, not the vaguely British kind that most people who learned English as a second language seemed to sport (as if it weren't enough to speak a second language fluently, you had to speak the classier version, too). "Well, go ahead then."

"You're invited for dinner," said Lily dumbly.

"What a delightful surprise."

Those eyes! You got annoyed at him just for having them. Lily knew that it was technically her turn to speak again. "I didn't know anyone lived here," she said.

"Well, someone does. After a fashion."

In addition to being beautiful, the boy's eyes were extremely, outlandishly tired. Lily was not sure she'd ever seen a young person look as exhausted as this boy; everything he said seemed all the more impressive because he appeared to be on the verge of narcolepsy or coma. Lily wanted to be rude to him, a little, just to wake him up. "How old are you?" she demanded.

"One never asks a lady her age. How old are you?"

"Twenty. You live here by yourself?"

He mimed looking around. "It would seem so."

"How long have you lived here?"

"Excuse me, how long have *you* lived here?"

"You speak English very well."

"Yours is tolerable."

Suddenly, Lily felt exhausted, too; you couldn't talk to someone who wanted to win every single piece of dialogue. Maybe that's why he looked that way; the horrendous drain of being the funniest person in the room, in every room, in this enormous horrifying house. "Seven o'clock, tomorrow," she said. "If you want."

CHAPTER FOUR

January

The house next door had been dark like Sebastien's until the Carrizos moved in. They came in March, during his second year alone, though he tried never to think about those years in term of years. When the Carrizos came, the evenings got brighter, and Sebastien sat watching their yellow kitchen lights and the soft blinkered hysteria of their television; the house was ablaze, like a forest fire on a hill. People don't think about how much you can see through a window at night in a house that's very well lit—this was not why Sebastien kept his so dark, though it was certainly an auxiliary benefit. He tried not to stare at the Carrizos' house once they moved in. But it was impossible sometimes not to gaze a little longingly at all that light.

Sometimes he imagined that they could see him, too. This fantasy kept him busy and decent, dressed, up at reasonable hours, engaged in activities that were arguably fruitful. He had employed a similar strategy toward his parents, back when they were recently dead and he was first learning how to live this way. He'd imagined that they were watching him—stern, censorious, though not entirely without sympathy for his plight—and this had saved him, he was sure, to the extent that he could be said to have been saved at all. He realized he was inventing gods for himself—false gods, at that—but he also knew he was not above it. Though he hoped to take the secret to his grave, he really was a pragmatist at heart. And it could be argued that pretend-believing in the occasional surveillance of the neighbors—the indubitably literal neighbors, with their gleaming car and their showy appliances and their honorable recycling habits—was marginally healthier than pretend-believing in the constant surveillance of ghosts. At any rate, it seemed to have some of the same salutary effects. In the backyard, Sebastien grew flowers, effeminate hobby though it was. On the Internet, he watched his investments go up and down; he followed every twitch and flutter of the New York Stock Exchange, and London, and Tokyo; he was a compulsive reader of the news. It was not impossible, after all, to still be witness to the world. He played online poker, too, which would be a vice, he knew, for a person with less money and time. As it was, both money and time were abstract curses, and Sebastien could not reproach himself much for a habit that squandered either of them.

He thought often of selling the things. The house was overrun with expensive and oppressive objects—his mother's jewelry, his father's antique weapons, all manner of treasures plundered from all corners of the globe—and it would not have been hard to get rid of them. He could have sold them online—Sebastien vacillated between an intense solitude-compounded agoraphobia and a loneliness so clawing and vast that it was like vertigo—and he could have donated the proceeds, of course. (He could not bear the thought of acquiring any more money; he'd never live long enough, or have enough of a populated life, to spend what he had already, and this felt like a particular brand of bitter reproach in a newly capitalist society.) But somehow he never got around to it, just like he never got around to going over to the Carrizos' house and introducing himself. The objects kept sitting there, accruing talismanic qualities and dust, and Sebastien himself kept sitting there, accruing only dust.

In spite of his close observation of the Carrizos, the arrival of Katy and Lily was a surprise—and perhaps it was the fact of the surprise that moved Sebastien more than the girls themselves, at first. Though he'd barely met the Carrizos, he had not expected them to make any sudden moves; he'd known when they were going to buy the new car, for example, and he had not been shocked when the rumors emerged of Carlos's shady business dealings (you had to only look at the man's leisurely hours and unlikely acquisition of exponentially more expensive household goods to know that something was amiss). But the girls—one light haired and delicate, as lovingly formed as a deer, the other pale and inquisitive looking in a way Sebastien rather liked— were a mystery. Were they far-flung—and hopefully wayward—young cousins? But then, they looked too different to be related, and their closeness in age could not be entirely coincidental. They were foreigners, it was clear, though they were both lacking the slouchy sexuality of the European girls he had known; they were attractive, but there was a frankness and—he thought at first, before he knew them both and before he loved one of them—a kind of dumbness to their beauty: It was so sincere, so unreconstructed, so unapologetic. It was being subverted by nothing. It was just there, flapping about in the wind, like a flag.

Basic questioning of the women at Pan y Vino bodega revealed that the girls were Katy Kellers and Lily Hayes—what a fussy, old-fashioned, Edith Whartonish name that was!—and that they were study-abroad students from the States. Sebastien watched them for a few days—their comings and goings, their outings, and occasionally, though not often, their evenings—against the shining backdrop of their breathtakingly well-lit house. He found himself continuing to like Lily the better of the two, though not for her appearance, particularly. She was pretty enough—with reddish hair and high-arched eyebrows that made her look *extremely* wide-awake—but pretty girls were like flowers: astonishing and utterly common, both. Instead, what drew him to Lily was what appeared, at least from a distance, to be her strange solitude—a solitude much less complete but, he had to assume, far more elective, than his own.

It had been a long time since Sebastien had had a crush on an actual girl. He watched a lot of pornography, though he didn't really like things quite so mechanized and denuded; there was something about the clinical insertions and withdrawals that always reminded him a bit of the dentist. He was aesthetically though not ethically opposed to prostitution. There were women at Pan y Vino, where he went to buy his toilet paper and cereal and shittiest wine (almost everything else was ordered from online gourmet shops, though he bought mostly condiments and liqueurs and actually, he realized, ate very little by modern standards). But those women were purely no-nonsense (how he longed for some nonsense!), and rough with him in a way that suggested vast reservoirs of matronly concern. They often stuck extra candies in his bag, as though he needed them. As though, really, he needed anything.

He could hardly believe it, then, the day that Lily showed up at his doorstep. Nobody ever came to his door anymore; even the Jehovah's Witnesses were sick of him, having learned long ago that he'd do absolutely anything to detain them (he told himself that this was due to high-minded social experimentation, and not grave and crushing loneliness). So when Sebastien heard a knock at his door he initially thought he was hallucinating. But then it came again—stubborn and, he thought, just the tiniest bit harassed. He could still hope for a snake-oil salesman, he supposed; he could hope for some scam designed to bleed him dry on behalf of a fictional broken-down child or old person or car. He was up for it, he thought, as he walked to the door. He was up for anything. He peered out through the huge, baroque keyhole. There, framed by its jagged silhouette, was the unmistakable Lily Hayes from next door, her face like the sunny pistil in some strange-petaled flower. Sebastien opened the door.

"Hi," she said, extending her hand. "I'm Lily. I'm staying next door with the Carrizos, and I'm supposed to invite you over for dinner."

"Are you?" he said. "Well, go ahead then."

As it happened, he had no other plans. The night of the dinner, he was ready by six-thirty, wilting in his suit, one of his father's better clarets— a 1996 Château Lafite Rothschild Pauillac—liberated from the cellar and cradled in his arms like a doll. At seven of seven he began the walk across the yard and down to the Carrizos', taking stock for the first time in a long time of what his house might look like through the eyes of another person. The weeds were scabby and tall and vaguely lethal looking. He should get them taken care of, he knew; he had no excuse not to; he could certainly afford it. Why had he never bothered? Maybe he'd liked the idea of the weeds conveying some kind of desperation and disorder within; maybe, he realized with a flicker of self-disgust, they were meant to be a kind of cry for help. He comforted himself briefly with the thought that nobody would notice such a gesture, even if he were inclined to make one. But then he looked at the well-lit house at the end of the path, and he wondered grimly if perhaps some-body already had.

He reached the Carrizos' porch at 6:56, then had to decide whether it was worse to be early or to stand creepily on the porch for no reason. After a moment or two of what he hoped was semi-plausible fiddling with his hair and tie, he rang the doorbell. It was 6:57.

Beatriz Carrizo appeared at the door, her décolletage glimmering with tan and sweat and good health, her black hair pulled back into a heavy braid. "Oh! Hello!" she said. She sounded surprised, although he did not know why she would be surprised. "You must be Sebastien!"

His initial reaction—*Must I be?*—ran through his head, before he reminded himself to try, really try, not to be maddening.

"Guilty as charged, I'm afraid." He flashed a smile that he hoped was winning. He'd been thought winning once, in some misty past—

he'd been considered precocious, and charming, and all the young female teachers at Andover had touched their hair a lot when they called on him in class. But those days were over, and now he could only meekly hope that he was vaguely fit for the company of normal people. "You must be Señora Carrizo," he said.

She smiled warmly. "Come in."

In the modern light of the well-appointed kitchen, Sebastien felt ridiculous. Around him, the monstrous refrigerator buzzed and all the surfaces gleamed brutally white. Everything was new and shiny and unobtrusive, and Sebastien was ancient and absurd. Why had he worn a suit? He looked like he was dressed for a costume party.

Panicked, Sebastien handed Beatriz the wine. "I brought this," he said. It was far too expensive, of course, and the wrong thing entirely, and Sebastien was struck by the realization, like a physical convulsion, that the evening was going to go very badly.

"I'll open it," said Beatriz, getting a corkscrew. Sebastien wanted to tell her she didn't have to open it now—that she could save it for a better and worthier occasion—but that seemed potentially obnoxious, and Sebastien only liked being obnoxious deliberately. Mercifully, it was clear that Beatriz had no idea how expensive the wine was; she opened it and spilled a little on the linoleum and poured five glasses and took a sip of hers without even letting it breathe. Sebastien was relieved that this particular mistake of his had not been noticed. Others certainly would be. He was far too warm in his suit, and he began to feel feverish and anxious. He tried to remember the last time he'd worn it. It must have been in his final year of Andover, not long before the plane crash, when he was visiting Boston for an accepted students' dinner at Harvard. He remembered being hot in it then, too—it had been unseasonably warm for May in New England, and the subways were coughing up that particular smell of theirs, that strange blend of steam and chalk—but there'd also been a lightness all around him, and a sense of life unfolding satisfyingly along its intended trajectory. Now, in Beatriz Carrizo's terrifyingly clean kitchen, Sebastien almost thought that if he buried his head into his overdressed arm he might smell Boston, and his father's borrowed cologne, and his own youthful sweat, full of frightened happiness.

Beatriz was looking at him with concern. "Are you all right?" she said.

He flashed another diamond smile. "I simply could not fathom being any better."

"Would you like to sit down?" said Beatriz.

Sebastien swallowed. "Sitting down is one of my favorite things to do, if you can believe it."

In the dining room, Lily was already at the table and Sebastien gave her a courtly, overstated nod. She was pale in the bluish wash of the evening light; her dark eyebrows were slender isthmuses against the milky sea of her forehead. Next to her sat Katy Kellers: beech-colored hair; marble, nearly kaleidoscopic eyes; small, symmetrical features etched with what seemed like obsessive fineness. Lily watched Sebastien watching Katy and gave him an appraising look.

"You made it," she said flatly, and shot him a dubious smile that somehow employed exactly one-half of her mouth. Her eyebrows, it seemed, were eternally convex, giving her an expectant sort of look that could seem intelligent or erotic—or both, Sebastien figured— depending on your prejudices.

"Last-minute cancellation," he said. "Though the commute was atrocious." Sebastien waited to be introduced to Katy. When nobody ventured to do this, he introduced himself.

"Hello," he said, reaching his hand across the table and being careful not to disturb the butter dish. "I don't believe we've met."

Katy nodded. "Katy Kellers," she said. Sebastien wasn't used to women who said only their names by way of introduction—but then, he reminded himself, he wasn't used to women in general, or people in general, for that matter, anymore.

"Sebastien LeCompte," he said.

Katy nodded. "I've heard."

Silence ballooned between the three of them then, punctuated only by the sounds of Beatriz bustling in the kitchen. Sebastien was tempted to remark on the bustling—how the sound of high-quality bustling was really the *capstone* achievement in the domestic arts, or something—but he forced himself to stay quiet. The tense energy between Lily and Katy felt like some kind of subverbal bristling; Sebastien did not flatter himself that he was the cause of whatever this was, but he did ruefully see that neither Lily nor Katy was interested in making the evening any easier on anyone. It was apparent, then, that Sebastien was going to have to be the one to break the silence. Since he wanted to say something to Lily, he decided to speak to Katy. "Katy Kellers," he said. "Where are you from?"

She waited a beat too long to answer, as though she'd had trouble registering that he was actually talking to her. "Los Angeles," she said.

Sebastien glanced at Lily. She was looking out the window, and he felt a throb of bittersweet attraction. She did not look back.

"I wouldn't have thought," he said to Katy.

"Nobody ever thinks."

This line of conversation was mercifully euthanized by the appearance of Carlos in the doorway.

"Good evening, girls," he said, and looked at Sebastien, who felt suddenly overwhelmed by the tedium of having to keep reconfirming his own identity. "You must be Sebastien."

Yes, he thought, a thousand times yes! "Yes," he said.

The evening disintegrated predictably from there. Over dinner, Sebastien forced himself to ask questions for which he already had all the answers—how long have you lived here, how long have you been married, and what did you do, and when precisely did the lovely young ladies arrive? He ran out of pretend questions halfway through dessert. Then the questions started coming at him from all quarters—though not, notably, from Lily's.

"Where are you from originally, Sebastien?" said Beatriz, stealthily trying to foist a second piece of cake onto his plate.

"Here. Oh, no, thank you, I simply couldn't. It's been so long since I had such a fine meal. I fear another bite would put me in the hospital."

"Buenos Aires?" said Carlos.

"Here, precisely." Sebastien pointed out the window and across the lawn, toward his moldering house. "There. Since I was four, anyway. And I'm told that before that I wasn't terribly interesting."

"You were born in the States?" said Beatriz kindly.

"In the awful state of Virginia, according to my biographers."

"And you went to school there, too?"

Sebastien shifted in his seat. "Prep school," he said lightly. "In Massachusetts."

"Did it prepare you?" said Lily, rousing herself momentarily.

"It did. For unemployment, principally, and drinking during the day." Sebastien kept his eyes on Lily in the hope that she'd say something in response, but instead she busied herself with pouring a grotesque amount of milk into her instant coffee.

"When were you there for school?" said Beatriz.

Sebastien squinted. "It's very hard to say," he said. Could it really have been five years ago? That was simultaneously preposterously long ago and bafflingly recent; no amount of linear time, small or vast, could properly capture the experience of moving from then to now. It was a lateral skitter across the universe, a drop into a rabbit hole or acid trip or nightmare. Talking about time, in a conventional sense, was really not relevant in this case. "I mean," he said. "It just seems like a very long time ago now."

Lily's face, Sebastien noticed, was squinched into a sour contraction of disapproval, and everyone else was looking nonplussed. Sebastien would, he knew, have to try to be more normal. He was just about to begin, but Beatriz immediately followed up by asking him if he'd liked living in the States—and this, it turned out, was another very difficult question. It often seemed to Sebastien that the entirety of his actual existence had already taken place, and he was now living in a dull and fitful afterlife—that he had not been damned so much as completely forgotten. The time in the States had belonged to his life, and so it was wholly incomparable to anything afterward—it was a qualitative, not quantitative difference—and this made it impossible to talk about the AP classes and the cocaine in the dorm bathrooms and the sleeplessness and the way the snow caught red streetlights when he was up late and lonely, and certainly it made it impossible to talk about the political implications of living in a capitalist and corrupt society, an empire reaching the edge of itself, whatever. It had been reality, merely, and as such it was both more complicated and vastly simpler than anything language could capture. There was no way to properly answer this question; he could only answer it improperly. This was why he was so often insufferable, he knew: The real answers were unutterable and strange and upsetting, so he had no choice but to give fake ones. He issued a jaunty smile.

"As much as one can be expected to like anything, I suppose," he said.

"Well," said Beatriz brightly. "Let me wrap up some leftovers for you."

Moments later—after giving Lily a painfully abstruse hug and passing her his business card, both of which moves had seemed like better ideas in his head—Sebastien stood on the Carrizos' porch and tried to get his bearings. The night had been, quite obviously, a disaster. The only question was whether this spoke to the overarching futility of ever interacting with other people again, or whether the trouble was specific to these people. To Lily, more precisely. The smell of smoke billowed suddenly from behind him.

"Is that you, Satan, come for me at last?" said Sebastien, turning around. But it was only Katy, pinching a cigarette between her forefinger and thumb. The moonlight caught the flat edge of her bare shoulder.

"Well, you were very rude," she said.

Sebastien was clinically incapable of taking any real offense at anything, and he usually staved off the strangeness of this by often feigning vague offense at everything. But tonight, he found he could not summon the energy. "I didn't know you smoked," he said wearily.

"Why would you know I smoked?"

"I wasn't being rude," he said. "That's just how I talk."

"Well, how you talk is rude." Katy ashed her cigarette off the porch. "Have you ever considered that?"

"I am almost wholly unsocialized."

"That is quite obviously untrue. You are socialized half out of your mind."

Sebastien wished Katy would offer him a cigarette so that he could grandly decline it, but she did not. "It was a lovely dinner," he said, nodding to the house. "Is that a pretty typical meal?"

"What?"

"They manage to feed you two well, in spite of their troubles?"

"What are you talking about?"

"Nothing, nothing. Neighborhood gossip, that's all. I'm afraid I can't repeat it. Rumors of a lawsuit or some such. It would be wrong of me to spread them."

Katy rolled her eyes, then shook her head. "You like Lily," she said sternly.

"What an accusation." Normally, he would have said more—something about the insubstantiality of affection, the transience of love, *et al.*, *ad infinitum*—but his mouth felt cottony and he was suddenly exhausted. He did not want to talk any more tonight.

"She's young, you know," said Katy.

"She's your age."

"Obviously that's irrelevant."

Sebastien had to concede it was; time, he knew better than anyone, was a myth. "Well," he said. "I'm not plotting anything."

"But she is."

Sebastien could not bring himself to summon the depths of banality that were required here; to fearfully ask in a halting, tremulous voice, *Has she—has she said something about me?* The wine eddied around his head; Katy's cigarette smelled rich and sapid. Sebastien shrugged and pointed to it. "Won't they smell that out here?"

Katy looked back at him blankly. "I don't think it's really some big secret."

Halfway across the lawn, Sebastien turned to look back at the Carrizos'. Behind him, their house was like an enormous ship at sea, flooded with light. Did they know that they were shadow puppets in there? Did they know how vividly the details of their lives were conveyed? It was like staring into a stained-glass window; it was like staring into a Fabergé egg. What invincibility one must feel to offer oneself up to the night like that. Sebastien shuddered to think about their electricity bills. One of these days, he thought, jimmying his key savagely into the lock, those people were going to get robbed.

In the living room, Sebastien lit a candle. The smell of smoke always made his house feel churchlike and consecrated; he thought often of the Catholic cathedrals in western Europe that he'd visited with his parents on various trips. It had been a good life they had given him, if a brief one. One of the most consoling thoughts Sebastien could produce—and, during those first few months when he was alone in the house, pinioned by grief, it was nearly the only one—was that his parents must have thought very highly of him in order to have left him the way they did. At some point in the course of his childhood, they must have turned to each other and agreed that he could afford to lose them. They must have decided that he was strong and brave enough to endure it. And even though he knew now that they had misjudged him, he took a certain pride in their mistake.

Sebastien went to the mantel, to the picture of him and his father with the downed tapir. He'd been fifteen when it was taken, hunting for the first time at some awful Brazilian big-game preserve that his father had frequented. In the picture, Sebastien is wearing a wobbly, cross-stitched smile. He remembered that day and how scared he'd been. He remembered the strange elated revulsion of standing so close to a dead animal.

"This is something you need to know," his father had said, pointing to the tapir. Sebastien still didn't know what he'd meant by that. Maybe, in that sentence, his father had been lamenting all the things he could not tell his son. But maybe not. Maybe, after all, that moment with the tapir really *was* all there was to say, and see: white belly bleeding out, blood black as an inkblot, eyes blanking from one kind of indifference to another.

"Dad," Sebastien said to the picture. "I think I met a girl."

He'd just begun summer orientation when the plane had crashed. His French aunt Madeleine called him at four in the morning. It was the middle of a heat wave; even the wood floor of his dorm room had been warm. He stood listening in the dark and then threw up into the fireplace. The smell of vomit mixed with the smell of dead ash from fabulous parties long ago.

Sebastien had known what his parents did for as long as he'd thought to be interested, which was admittedly not that long. It was probably sometime during his early adolescence that the long-standing patterns of their lives—the house, the vague explanations about his parents' work, the suddenness of their move to Buenos Aires in 1994, right after the Jewish community center bombing—resolved into some kind of understanding. By then he'd been embarrassed to acknowledge he'd ever not known (and indeed, on some level, he surely always had). So the realization itself was layered under other information that was new and, at the time, more compelling—mostly about sex, of course. And, like sex, his parents' work became a topic that was unmentionable among sophisticated people, among whose number Sebastien had counted himself back then.

Now he kept the secret for reasons both practical and personal. As a practical matter, Sebastien felt protective toward those Argentine nationals with whom his parents had had dealings. Naturally, he had no idea who any of them were, and naturally the fact of his parents' death meant that somebody else—somebody important enough to crash a plane—already did. Nevertheless, Sebastien didn't want the neighborhood knowing, if they didn't already, and he didn't want life to be any harder for the people who his parents had worked with, assuming any of them were still alive.

Underneath this, though, was something far less explicable: the sense that keeping a secret for the dead was a way of keeping a promise to the dead, and that keeping a promise to the dead meant allowing them to assert a claim on you, and that anything that came with obligations of that sort was still a kind of relationship. Somehow, Sebastien felt that his parents were a little less dead every time he was coy to a stranger in conversation.

"A girl, huh?" he imagined his father saying. "Well, what's she like?"

"She's really something," he imagined saying back. "She's really something."

Was she, though? It was a reasonable question. Sebastien felt his broken and rococo heart crawling out to Lily Hayes, throwing itself around her in joy and relief, but why? She was, after all, only a parochial sort of beauty (curious-faced, slightly snub-nosed, pale almost to translucence), and she could veer in a sentence from beautiful to practical—bordering on plain, really, compared with the impeccable girls Sebastien had known at Andover, with their sleek hair and bubblegum-colored fingernails and outlandishly perfect bodies (the kind of perfect bodies that, forget genetics, could really come only with narcissism and money). You looked at those girls and felt that it was entirely possible to do everything in life very, very well. You looked at those girls and felt that there was plenty of time to get it all right. But nevertheless, Sebastien was still thinking of Lily Hayes: her angular expression, the way she'd looked out the window every time he spoke. The way she made it seem as though she had better things to be thinking about, and the way he was almost—almost—inclined to believe her.

Sebastien went to the computer and logged on to Facebook. He had a lot of Facebook friends somehow—almost all from Andover, almost all now off living on the distant planets of Ivy League education or corporate law indentured servitude or trophy wifedom—and every year on Sebastien's birthday they enthusiastically wished him well. This was the weird prolonged false intimacy that the Internet created: These people—who mostly did not know that his parents had died and that he'd never gone to Harvard and that he'd retreated back to Buenos Aires to live in a falling-down mansion, and that there were termites

coming through the floors and sapphire earrings rotting in the upstairs bedroom—these people (bless them!) all pretended to have actually remembered his birthday.

But then, the Internet was good for a lot of things. He typed in "Lily
Hayes." There were, predictably, hundreds of Lily Hayeses, almost all
white and middle- to upper-middle-class, their lives lovingly Insta-
grammed. But he finally found her, his Lily Hayes: Her picture was of
sun-flecked feet in strappy sandals, her profile was set to the insubstantial privacy settings characteristic of very young people of goodwill. This girl, thought Sebastien. He could write to her right now.
Phenomenal. He hovered his mouse over the message box, came to his
senses, closed it. He got up to fix himself a drink.

When he sat back down, to keep himself from logging back into
Facebook, he went to vagrantorscenester.com. This was a dull website,
briefly popular in the mid-aughts, where players were invited to judge
pictures of people snapped anonymously on the street. Sebastien hated
this game, and the reason he hated it so much was that he'd actually
invented it, back when he was in the ninth grade at Andover. He'd
arrived there scrawny, young, and—having skipped a year—already
living under a cloud of presumed academic earnestness. All of this had
required Sebastien to pioneer brand-new methods of social cruelty
in order to survive; his primary tactic—then and now—was to make
remarks that sounded cutting but that nobody could ever be totally
sure they understood. Adolescent Sebastien had never bothered with
mocking his peers for the usual reasons (you were fat, you were or
seemed unattractively sincere or striving, you were or seemed gay).
Those were the vulnerabilities that children knew they had and had
properly strategized for. Instead, Sebastien invented entirely new categories of social evaluation, and soon found that by referring to these
categories, he could actually erect them. (He remembered this now
through the prism of Hannah Arendt's observation about totalitarian-
ism: Convincing people things are true is much more difficult than
simply behaving as though they are.) Young Sebastien could crack his
classmates open like lobsters, it turned out, revealing new areas of self-

loathing they didn't even know they had yet. The sociopathic Vagrant or Scenester game was part of all of this, though back then it was called Cool or Crazy (by the other kids—even as a child, Sebastien had found alliteration tiresome). Sebastien had invented it during his first term at Andover. He'd usually played it with CJ Kimball and Byron "The Box" Buford on Saturday outings to Harvard Square, chaperoned by noticeably resentful intern teachers, in those first few yellow, surreal, cinematic weeks after September 11th. U.S. flags were everywhere, even in Cambridge; at home, Sebastien's parents told him, everything was in economic and political chaos—inflation was in the double digits, there was a looming default on some important loan. All of it was terribly dry to Sebastien then—and anyway, he was usually too busy to talk for long, run ragged, as he was, by the demands of mocking Harvard students and homeless people in a judicious 1:1 ratio. That's how he'd actually thought of it then: as equal opportunity derision. As though he were extending some important leveling force. As though he were animated by the spirit of blindfolded lady justice. If he'd been left unmolested on the trajectory he was on then, Sebastien saw now, he probably would have wound up heading straight for the editorial page of some conservative college newspaper to write portentous, bloviating opinion articles he could never disown because they would live forever on the Internet. Maybe it was just as well, then, that he'd never gone to college. Sebastien laughed and took another sip of his drink.

The way CJ and Byron played Cool or Crazy was straightforwardly, unimaginatively sarcastic: guessing Cool for a muttering, emaciated woman with meth-brown teeth, Crazy for a college boy with expensive jeans and exquisitely mussed hair. But Sebastien had never played that way; instead, he'd always picked less obvious targets and designations. A middle-aged woman in a gray sweatshirt drinking straight from a two-liter bottle of Mountain Dew was deemed Cool, a well-muscled young man wearing a Puka shell necklace was pronounced Crazy. Sebastien never tired of how nervous these pronouncements made CJ and The Box; when they asked for explanations, Sebastien always told them that the game was an art, not a science, and that he had the soul of an artist, and that that's why he always won.

And now here was his beautiful, idiot game, all grown up and online. Sebastien liked to check on it sometimes, in much the same way he liked to check on the Facebook profiles of half-remembered classmates from grade school; he liked to know that it was basically doing okay. It was, after all, his brainchild—in a more reductive and palatable form, admittedly, though was this not the universal fate of the ideas of great thinkers? Truly, Sebastien had always had his finger on the pulse of the zeitgeist. He laughed again and hiccupped and got up to pour himself another drink. When he sat back down at the computer he found that he was once again, somehow, on Lily Hayes's Facebook page.

Sebastien stared at her sandals, her toes. This girl. What would become of her? He hovered his mouse again over the message box. This girl. Were people really this open? Were their lives really this lucky? He opened the message box. He hesitated. But then: really. What did he have to lose? He had literally nothing to lose. Few people experienced the pure liberation of having absolutely nothing to lose, but Sebastien had the particular blessing and curse of this kind of freedom—he had zero claims on the attention of anyone, anywhere; he had the totally unsullied indifference of the universe. He could crawl into the bathtub and slit his wrists and nobody would care. He could torch this entire house and all of its treasures and nobody would care. He could certainly message this girl and confidently expect that nobody would care about that, either.

"Gilded Lily," he began.

CHAPTER FIVE

January

The day after the dinner, a message from Sebastien LeCompte popped up in Lily's in-box. "Gilded Lily," it began, and things went downhill from there.

Lily was surprised. Sebastien LeCompte was not the kind of boy— Lily could not think of him as a "man," really, and certainly not as a garden-variety "guy"—who usually liked her. Over dinner, it had become clear that Sebastien had lived in that mansion for most of his life, that his parents had been American diplomats (this explained the accent) who died in a plane crash when he was seventeen, and that he was fabulously wealthy. He didn't say this last part, but it was apparent: There were references to playing polo, attending Harvard, summering in the Alps—things that Lily had never fully realized that actual people actually did out in the actual world. If Sebastien was going to like anyone, Lily figured it would have been Katy. He'd spent several minutes talking to her on the porch after dinner, when he'd only passed

Lily a business card—an actual business card!—that read SEBASTIEN LECOMPTE, SLOTH, in both English and Spanish.

"Are you going to write him back?" said Katy, while Lily was brushing her barely adequate teeth.

"Maybe."

"Even though he lives next door?"

"Maybe. Do you think his parents really were diplomats?"

"Sure," said Katy. "Why not?" There was a minty bubble at the corner of her mouth, which somehow made Lily feel inordinately relieved.

"I don't know," said Lily. "The plane crash sort of makes you wonder."

"What?"

"If they were CIA."

"You're *so* conspiracy minded."

"I get it from my dad," said Lily. "Anyway, I have never in my life even heard of a real person playing polo. Shouldn't he be at Oxford by now, or something?"

"Well," said Katy, sounding doubtful. "I guess you would sort of think."

Lily waited three days to write back. When she did, she tried to ape Sebastien's tone and style: employing absurdly inflated language she never used in real life, invoking belabored extended metaphors. Sebastien responded by inserting random French phrases into his emails, so Lily started doing the same—though he had to know that this did not count as sophistication, since, of course, you could Google anything you wanted to say. He moved on to Italian; she saw his Italian, and raised him Hungarian—the one phrase she actually did know: *Nem beszelek magyarul,* I do not speak Hungarian—but this, it seemed, was enough. He asked her to dinner.

"You have a date already?" said Katy.

"What do you mean, 'already'?" Lily was wearing a ruched floral shirt that she'd decided communicated a sense of general fun, and plastering makeup on her face with both hands. She was afraid that her emails might have given Sebastien the wrong idea.

"Well," said Katy. "I just mean, we just got here."

"We've been here two weeks."

"I just wonder if it's going to be a problem with Carlos and Beatriz."

"It's a host family, not a juvenile detention center."

"They're conservative, I think."

Lily leaned toward the mirror and embarked on the project of eyeliner. "I don't think we can assume that. Carlos seems to know how to have a good time, at least."

"There are crosses everywhere."

"It's dinner. Does the Vatican have a policy on dinner?"

"Don't be sarcastic."

"No, I am actually asking. I mean, they actually really might, for all I know."

Katy climbed into her bed then and began to read. She'd managed to enroll in the only rigorous class on offer—something about economics in the post-Peronist era—and it seemed to require a vast amount of studying and note-taking and highlighting with markers in three different colors.

"I think it's so cool that you're taking a real class here," said Lily, to apologize. "Everyone else has basically just dropped out of school for the semester."

Katy studied her for a moment to see if she was serious, then seemed to decide she was. "I just think it makes sense to learn a little bit about the country we're in, you know?"

Lily nodded vigorously. "Totally."

Katy smiled. "You look nice. Don't be nervous."

"Thanks," said Lily. "I'm not."

At five past eight Lily once again walked up the winding path to Sebastien LeCompte's mansion, which, in the falling light, suddenly looked dilapidated and underwhelming. Lily had told Katy she wasn't nervous. But she was. For one thing, she was nervously wondering if she should have brought a condom. She didn't know if that would have projected some kind of unsexy premeditation, or else some kind of unattractive feminine wiliness, or else some kind of massively inflated sense of her own charms. She then remembered that she wasn't supposed to care. Her parents had given her an enormous box of Trojans before she came here, alongside an earnest discussion about *making smart choices.* Poor old Andrew had blinked compulsively throughout the entire conversation; he'd poked himself in the eye (actually poked himself in the eye!) once, and his eyeball, he reminded everyone all the time, had simply never been the same. The condom box they'd given Lily was appalling, mortifying, industrial-sized—for cults, maybe, or university women's centers. Lily was vaguely flattered, and then vaguely insulted, when she thought of how much sex her parents must think she was having. She was then vaguely disgusted to think that her parents thought about this at all.

Suddenly, Lily was on the porch. She knocked the weird knocker (what the hell was that thing, anyway?), and Sebastien answered immediately, as though he'd been standing there, right on the other side of the door, waiting for her—which, for all she knew, he had. He was wearing a jacket, even though it was about a thousand degrees out, and probably even warmer inside.

"Dearest Lily," he said. "Do come in."

"Hi," said Lily. "How's it going?" She knew she wasn't going to be able to keep up the email tone in person, and he might as well know it now. She followed Sebastien into the house. Inside, the living room was dusty and ornate, dominated by an enormous grandfather clock and some kind of ancient painted cloth on the wall. At the center of the room stood a grand piano that Lily felt sure was woefully out of tune.

"Pretty piano," she said. "Do you play?"

"Only 'Chopsticks,'" said Sebastien. "Would you care for a glass of wine?" He handed her one before she could answer. SORBONNE 1967 was etched, in flamboyant swirls, on the glass.

"Oh, thanks," said Lily. "I can't drink out of anything from a state school." With the first sip of wine pain flooded her mandible. She swallowed hard. On the mantel, there was a picture of Sebastien and an older man with a smallish hoofed animal that looked like a first draft of a zebra. She pointed.

"You killed that?"

"I had to, sadly." Sebastien stood behind her. "It owed me money."

Lily looked more closely at the picture. The man Sebastien was standing with looked exactly like him; he had greenish eyes and wavy brown hair and a jauntily cocked head. The animal's neck appeared broken; it was twisted at an odd angle that made it seem as though more violence had been done to it than was strictly necessary. Its belly was white and looked soft. "Where was that?" she said.

"A resort in Brazil. You pay to enjoy your dominion over the beasts."

Lily wondered what it would have felt like to kill that thing. As a child, she and her good friend Leah had once murdered a banana slug. They had found it in the tree house—Andrew had built Lily and Anna a tree house because Janie had died, which was also why their parents had sent them to art camp, and given them music lessons, and allowed them to be far too present and assertive at adult dinner parties—and she and Leah (who had grown up to be a lesbian at NYU, and who even as a kid had always wanted to play the boy) had taken a fist-sized piece of basalt to it just to see what would happen. They'd been learning about the scientific process together in the second grade—about making observations, and recording data, and making hypotheses, and forming theories—and Lily had convinced Leah, or Leah had convinced Lily, that this was science. There'd been an underwhelming squish; the slug had oozed, relinquished a yellow substance that neither Leah nor Lily could identify, and then died, silently. And Lily had felt something odd then, a guilty but nearly gleeful sort of power—an edginess, somewhere between nausea and euphoria—and of course she'd gone to her mother later, and of course she'd cried, but it had been a complicated sort of cry.

She turned to Sebastien. "Why do you have a French name?"

"*Pourquoi pas?*"

"How many languages do you speak?"

"I don't remember."

"You're boring, you know."

He raised his eyebrows. "Am I?"

"You are."

"Say a little more about that," he said, refilling her glass.

Lily took another sip. "You're boring because I know exactly how you're going to react to every single thing I say. You're going to look for the least sincere response possible, every time. You're like an algorithm." Sebastien gave her a look of incredulous amusement. "So all I would suggest—if you're open to suggestions—"

"Please. Humility is a virtue."

"I would suggest that you mix it up a little. You should occasionally say things that have an unexpected relationship to reality. You could even throw in some things you mean, from time to time. Nobody's going to know. It will make you more interesting."

Sebastien's eyebrows were still raised. He did have beautiful eyes— so green and humane and, weirdly, so expressive. He'd get far with those eyes, she thought. Then she told him so. Then he kissed her.

His kiss was more vigorous than Lily would have expected—not that she'd expected him to kiss her, necessarily, though then again here she was, drinking wine, in his house, so really, what did she think? She was grateful for the swiftness of his approach; she thought with chagrin of many an awkward windup, staggeringly embarrassing advance-and-retreats, faces too close to do anything else, and then not quite, and then finally the clink of tooth on tooth, the tepid warmth of another person's mouth. Awful. She felt confident enough once the whole business was under way, but the first kiss gave her pause. It was just so odd, when you really thought about it.

Sebastien pulled back and looked at her gravely. "Thank you for the suggestions," he said.

"See?" said Lily. "You're doing it. I have no idea what you mean. You're more interesting already." She'd meant it teasingly, but it came out a little flat, a little mean, she thought, though Sebastien didn't seem to care. He smiled.

"That roommate of yours," he said.

"Yes?"

"She's quite pretty."

"Yeah." Lily giggled, then hiccupped. "She has a face you sort of want to keep looking at. I think she's really insipid, though."

"Insipid?"

"Yes," said Lily severely.

"But she's your friend, isn't she?"

"My friend? My friend. Well, sure."

Sebastien kissed her again. "You're a wicked woman."

And because she wasn't wicked—because she wasn't wicked at all, in fact, she didn't think—but it was terrific to make someone wonder, she said, "Maybe so. Maybe so."

Sebastien hurried along the aisles of Pan y Vino bodega. From behind the checkout, the cashier eyed him with amusement; it was obvious that she suspected from what he was buying that he was going to try to *cook,* and he understood why such a prospect might seem hilarious. As it happened, he was *not* going to try to cook. He was going to try to order Ethiopian takeout and then arrange the spices from the store in such a way that it looked like he had cooked. He wasn't going to pretend he'd cooked, necessarily. But he did want to present the *feeling* of having cooked; he wanted to fill up the house with a sense of domesticity and competence; he wanted to give the impression of being someone who lived an actual life—with ups and downs and commitments, with a vocation and an avocation or two, and a population, and some kind of a cosmic deadline. And all of this was because Lily Hayes was, somehow, coming over for dinner tonight. Again.

Sebastien was surprised she was willing to repeat the experiment; their first evening together had not gone entirely smoothly. An hour before she'd been due to arrive, Sebastien had made the fatal mistake of idly considering what his house might look like to a stranger, and the deeply vexing results of this exercise had thrown him into a panicked despair. He was already bewildered that Lily was coming at all. It was scarcely believable that—through some arbitrary and uncharacteristi-' cally magnanimous intervention of the deities—she hadn't been terri- fied by his original message, or by the epistolary theatrics that followed; that she'd been willing to treat familiarity with idioms in a variety of languages as some kind of sophistication—even though, after the In- ternet, familiarity with anything at all could be faked and did not really count; that she'd put up with a week of this nonsense before Sebastien could find the courage to ask her over and had actually said yes when he did. All of it, all of it, was astonishingly good luck.

But an hour before the appointed time, Sebastien saw that his luck had run out: The house would never, never do. Suddenly he could see how odd and empty it looked; how loneliness seemed to clutter around the corners of the rooms, how desperation was a thing you could al- most smell. The house was a monstrosity. The house was a horror. And Lily Hayes, he'd realized with startling and growing anguish, was going to see it in an hour.

He was going to have to torch the place, he'd decided. He was going to have to make it look like arson. But no, no. He'd looked at the clock sorrowfully. He had no time for that. Instead, he was going to have to try to clean it. Sebastien never really cleaned in earnest (though nei- ther did he engage in the activities that necessitated the most cleaning— cooking, child rearing, hosting other human beings). Nevertheless, he'd spent an anxious and sickening twenty minutes making ill-advised attempts at tidying. He'd swiped limply at the tables and mantel; he'd found some candles in a cupboard in the kitchen. Lighting them, he'd hoped, would make the place look romantic and European—tragic in the way of widowers and heirs to mysterious fortunes, and not in the way of serial killers or animal hoarders or the mentally touched. He'd wasted a quarter of an hour considering the picture of the felled tapir. His parents had put up the picture—maybe, he thought now, because he and his father looked so very much alike in it—and Sebastien had never really thought about what having it on display might say about his character (to whom? being the salient question, of course). But suddenly Sebastien saw that a stranger would think he'd selected the photo with solemn care—as the representative image of his time with his parents (bad) or else the proudest triumph of his short and underwhelming life (worse). He'd considered hiding it, but he worried about the time, as well as what unspeakable horrors he might find behind the picture if he moved it. Instead, he'd reached behind the grandfather clock and dislodged a nest of dark gray dust. He did not know why he was doing this; he did not think Lily was likely to inspect behind the clock. Perhaps he had seen the overarching futility of the project and was willfully undermining himself. It wouldn't be the first time, he'd thought, as he went to light the candles.

She'd shown up right on time, dressed in some kind of straightforward floral getup that was exactly the outfit Sebastien himself would have picked if he'd been told to dress up as an American girl for a costume party. In the frantic cleaning, Sebastien had forgotten that he'd planned to elaborately hand Lily an already poured glass of wine; instead, he'd had to grab the first glass that was handy, which turned out, horribly, to have SORBONNE 1967 etched into it. It wasn't long after that that Lily had accused Sebastien of being boring. This was not an assessment that Sebastien necessarily disagreed with; nevertheless, he'd felt that the best approach was to treat it as an accusation so ludicrous that he could react only with benign and divested curiosity—which meant, of course, that he'd wound up sounding more boring still. To keep himself from talking, Sebastien had then kissed Lily. It had been a long time since he'd kissed anyone—years, in fact: long enough for him to have nearly forgotten the strange alchemy that brought one pair of lips to another. But in the moment, he wasn't thinking of that; he was thinking only of the endless and undeniable whorls of Lily's mouth. She had the most utterly perfect mouth he had ever encountered, of that he was sure; an entire planetarium moved through his head as they kissed. When he pulled back, however, he saw that it had not been the same for her; he saw that she had been oblivious—and this, childishly, had made him want to be cruel in a way that would make him seem oblivious, too. He'd groped madly for some kind of blunt object and landed on a remark about Katy's attractiveness, which had prompted Lily to observe that Katy was "insipid," which had led Sebastien to reflexively counterobserve that he'd thought she and Katy were friends. In fact, he'd had no opinion on the matter—surely modern relations weren't mapped by such metrics?—and he'd been sure that Lily would see how desperate this was. Instead, she'd seemed to take the question seriously; her face darkened, and Sebastien could see the lengthening shadows of New England guilt, the heartrending consideration of the most middle-class of values and virtues. "My friend," she'd said. "Well, sure."

Sebastien had kissed her again then. "You're a wicked woman," he'd said. He did not mean it. He did not mean anything, ever, and especially, maybe, he did not mean this.

He had not expected to see her again after that. And yet, *mirabile dictu,* she had texted the next day, and come back again a day after that, and now he'd seen her a half dozen times, perhaps, in ten nights. That morning, for the first time, she had actually called him.

"Do you know who this is?" she'd said. She had a certain quality to her voice—it was a bit raspy, a bit out of breath—that made her always sound like she'd just come from doing something wholesome and outdoorsy.

"I know who I hope it is," he'd said.

"It's not Beatriz Carrizo."

"*Hélas.*"

"What are you doing tonight?"

Sebastien swallowed. "It so happens that my schedule just cleared."

And now, racing up and down the aisles of Pan y Vino, Sebastien felt a sense of quickening, enlivening. He should not, he knew, be allowing himself to get quite so worked up about things. He should not be thinking of his and Lily's as some kind of world-historical romance; it was not, he realized, even a terribly original one. The evenings they had spent together so far had all been the same: French kissing, Italian cinema, talk of the most sophomoric and navel-gazing variety before retiring to the bed to paw at each other up to a point of stasis. Sebastien wasn't sure of Lily's history in this realm, though it was a pretty safe bet that she was overestimating his own. The bulk of Sebastien's sexual experience came from one drunken evening with an anorexic premed during his Harvard accepted students' weekend; her arms had been covered in silken hair, and their union had been perfunctory and unmemorable. Despite this early adventure, the years of solitude since had contributed to a sense of renewed virginity. Sex belonged to the world, to the living, if anything did, and Sebastien never felt this more acutely than on his nights in bed with Lily, when matters escalated to a certain pitch and then some decision—not discussed, and not mutual—was made, and she rolled over and thrust the cupola of her ass into his thighs and Sebastien, mute with cathectic longing, abandoned her to her even breathing and faraway thoughts.

And yet in a fundamental way it seemed to Sebastien that Lily had dragged him, just a little, back into the world with her. Isolation and proximity to mortality had made his life feel oddly timeless; it stretched out before him, flat and featureless as the African savannah. But tonight Lily was coming over, and Sebastien had to buy these things now to have them ready. There was a satisfying urgency to this—even if it was, as he realized, truly the most basic contour of a typical life. Tonight, he would try to find a tablecloth. He would bring up one of the better wines from the cellar. And he would also, he'd decided, try to give Lily a bracelet.

Sebastien was not sure how this was going to go. He did not want it to seem grasping or desperate or, far more devastatingly, like some sort of bribe. And yet he had so many things he could not use, so many things he would very much like to give to her. He had spent the afternoon going through his mother's jewelry—touching her emerald brooch, holding her sapphire necklace up to the light and letting it splash cerulean on the floor. He tried to imagine the parties where she must have worn these things. As a child, Sebastien had been patient with his questions, certain that all the answers would someday be forthcoming. And now he was grown up, and he looked back and found all the questions right there where he'd left them: gathering dust, perhaps, but remarkably well preserved. The questions were more durable than anything, really—the questions and the objects. Everything else trended toward annihilation. Sitting on the floor, Sebastien had fingered his mother's diamond bracelet; the opal ring that she'd always been superstitious about wearing, though he'd never known why. He imagined all of them transformed by proximity to Lily, and to life.

That night, Lily didn't show up until nine, a bit later than she'd said she'd be.

"Hey," she said, when Sebastien opened the door. She was wearing long and overly involved earrings. Her hair was slightly damp and brushed back behind her ears.

"Dear Lily," said Sebastien, and kissed her. He could smell the implausible scent of her down-market perfume—freesia, wisteria, cyanide, whatever—that she'd probably bought at a pharmacy somewhere. When he pulled away, he saw that she was looking at him patiently. He glanced over at the table, where an oily epidermis was growing across the top of the mauve casserole and bleeding out onto the paper plates. He had set the food out too early.

"Sit down," he said. The words came out too soft: Somewhere during the kiss his voice had dissipated along his sternum, it seemed, and become a kind of effervescent fizz. "Sit down," he said, more loudly. "I have something for you."

"You do?" She sat.

"Here," said Sebastien, producing the bracelet from behind a lamp and dangling it before her. It was heavier than it looked. He had not wrapped it because he did not want Lily to feel that she could not decline it. "Do you want this?" There was more Sebastien might have said, but he had vowed to talk less.

"What is it?" said Lily. Her eyes widened, so he knew she already knew.

"A bracelet." Sebastien's mouth was so dry that he was sure Lily would be able to hear something wrong in the way he was talking, but she didn't seem to notice.

"I see that. Is it real?"

At this, Sebastien felt something within him collapse; something fragile that was holding back a floodgate. She was being crass. She was being, he thought grimly, American. Did she think he would try to give her some sort of toy jewelry? How little she must think of him. How little she must think he thought of her. He cocked his head to the side and laughed. "Oh, I don't know," he said. "Is anything?"

"Where did you get it?"

"It was my mother's, if you really want to know."

"You can't give me something of your mother's."

"She hasn't registered any protest, actually." Sebastien's despair was a rhizomatic root now, digging its stems into his heart. He would manage not to show it. He would manage to keep his gaze even.

"You can't," said Lily. "I won't take it. I'm sorry, thank you, but you can't."

"All right," said Sebastien. He took it back. What did she think he was going to do—beg her to accept an heirloom? Even his devotion had its limits. "All right. I've got all kinds of this stuff lying around. And it doesn't look like much on me—my wrists just aren't delicate enough. But all right."

Lily looked stricken and sorry, which Sebastien loathed. He had a vertiginous sense of observing this tableau from the outside in, and he could imagine how pitiful it would look.

"You don't have anyone else to give it to?" said Lily.

"Apparently not," said Sebastien. "I mean, there are elderly aunts off *en France* somewhere, but I wouldn't want to give them heart attacks. I suppose there's always eBay."

"No one helped you clean out the house? No one came for you when they died?"

Sebastien took a deep breath. He did not deserve to be angry that this had not occurred to her already. She did not owe him this kind of consideration. She did not owe him, in the end, anything at all.

Carefully, lightly, he said, "Who would possibly have come?"

Somehow, when Lily wasn't looking, Buenos Aires had become ugly.

The change had been gradual but unmistakable, she decided, as she walked back across the lawn from Sebastien's house. The city's light, previously so luxurious and elevating, had become brittle and harsh. Her bug bites had healed but had not disappeared, and she was beginning to fear she might be scarred for life. The wine made her sluggish; she struggled to stay awake in classes, she dragged her feet through ever-longer afternoons. So many thoughts in her head these days were "I feel" statements—actually phrased that way, *I feel tired, I feel lonely, I feel dusty,* little declarative sentences, like her own consciousness was some kind of barely mastered second language.

And this night with Sebastien—with that awful, incomprehensible offer of the bracelet—seemed to confirm Lily's worst suspicions somehow. Over the past couple of weeks, Sebastien had developed an interest in Lily that was sustained and unlikely and, entirely possibly, completely faked. He texted her almost every night now to invite her over for "nightcaps"; about half the time she went, and they'd banter twitchily on the couch for a bit before making out in the dark. It was always dark in that house, no matter the time of day. The living room had French windows overlooking a mangy overgrown garden, but what little light came through them was somehow always dusty; the clock and collectibles cast strange shadows, even during the afternoons. Sebastien LeCompte, it seemed, had a very tenuous relationship with lightbulbs. *I feel sorry,* Lily thought. She could hear the dry grass snap underneath her feet. *I feel bored.*

She was back at the Carrizos' at five past midnight, which was, she thought, a depressingly reasonable hour to be home on a Friday night. But when Lily walked into the kitchen, she found Beatriz sitting at the counter, reading a women's magazine and looking annoyed. Katy was already downstairs—studying beatifically before a wholesome eight-hour sleep, no doubt—and Lily knew, with a vestigial childhood certainty, that she was in trouble.

"No more of this, okay, Lily?" Beatriz sounded tired, even though she was still dressed. Lily remembered how early Beatriz got up—around five, to make Carlos breakfast before he commuted to the City Porteña—and Lily realized she'd been waiting up for her, and she was sorry. Still, Lily wished that it were Carlos, not Beatriz, who was waiting up. He'd probably wink at her about the late return. Beatriz was not the winking type. "You don't know that boy very well," she said.

"He's my friend."

"He's your friend? You've known him two weeks. We brought him over here two weeks ago, exactly."

"I think he's lonely." Lily said it as an excuse but realized immediately that of course it must be very true.

"Well, sometimes people are lonely for a reason," said Beatriz. "And anyway, I can't imagine your parents would like to think of you sneaking out nights to spend time with a boy."

"They wouldn't mind. My parents respect my autonomy."

"When we invited him over, we just thought it might be nice for you to know someone young. We thought you all might be friends. The three of you." Beatriz nodded her head toward the bedroom, where Katy was likely now dreaming of sustainable microloans.

"I'm sorry."

"And you need to remember to lock the door when you come back in the house. Other people live here, too."

"Okay. I'm really sorry."

"Don't be sorry. Just stop it. Okay?"

Lily was surprised that Beatriz was going to make her lie. "Okay," she said.

In the bedroom, Katy was still up reading. She looked up when Lily walked in. "Hey," she said.

"Hey," said Lily, sitting heavily on the floor.

"Are you in trouble?"

Lily maneuvered her right sneaker off with her heel. "A little, I guess."

Katy sat up and stretched. "Hope he's worth it." She ran her fingers through her hair—her sun-dappled hair, Lily couldn't help thinking, though on anyone else it would have just been dirty blond. What was it about Katy that made you search for lyric descriptions?

"Well," said Lily, wiggling her toes. They were spectacularly, bafflingly dirty and she had no idea why. "He's interesting, anyway."

"You think so? I think he's hideously boring."

"Really?" Lily had told Sebastien he was boring on their first date, though, of course, she didn't actually mean it. He was, quite tragically, possibly the most interesting person Lily had ever met; he was so interesting that she'd figured that accusations of tedium could only goad him into being more interesting still. Lily didn't necessarily want to sleep with Sebastien; she did not think her fascination with him was sexual as much as anthropological, maybe, or zoological—but there was certainly no question that it was a fascination of some kind. And yet here was Katy, dullest of all possible humans, living at the precise center of all of the world's modest expectations for her, moving in confident strides toward the exact mean of her upper-middle-class life, saying that the most interesting boy in the world was boring.

"Of course he's boring," Katy was saying. She got out of bed and adopted a yoga pose on the linoleum—it was the archer, the bow, something or other. Lily didn't want to ask. "You didn't know boys like that in school?"

"No," said Lily. "An orphaned trillionaire in a haunted mansion? No. Did you?"

"I mean, you know he's just a hipster, right? You know he didn't invent sneering? If he lived in the U.S. he'd probably be a music blogger."

"Katy, his parents were *spies*."

"I'm sure he likes to tell you they were."

Lily was agog; she had never heard Katy talk like this. "Isn't your head starting to feel weird like that?" she said.

"Yeah, actually, it is." Katy dropped the pose, then erupted into a startling backward arch. Her T-shirt rode up, revealing the demure mollusk of a perfect in-betweenie belly button. Lily averted her eyes. "So what are you going to do about Beatriz and Carlos?" said Katy.

"I'm just surprised they care so much," said Lily.

"Well, I mean, they are getting paid to make sure we don't get killed."

"Who's going to kill me? Sebastien? I'd like to see him try."

"Or pregnant."

"Again, I'd like to see him try."

Katy laughed, and Lily felt a warmth with a sourness underneath. She didn't know when she'd started to worry about whether Katy thought she was funny. But it was true that she'd always been willing to be a mercenary in conversation; she had never been enough in love to refuse to trade on a man's quirks for good-natured laughs, and she was not, in this case, at all in love.

"He tried to give me a bracelet," said Lily. She remembered how Sebastien had handled it—with a light disregard, like it was something somebody had asked him to hold for a moment. "A diamond bracelet."

"He didn't," said Katy.

"He did."

"A real one?"

"I didn't let him do it." Lily had been a little surprised, actually, at how quickly he'd taken it back. She'd expected more of a fight; she'd already been formulating the opening chords of a generous and reasonable speech in which she would gently, with exquisite care and responsibility, turn him down.

"Very noble of you."

"I mean, I couldn't. It was his dead mother's or something." Lily remembered the blank expression on Sebastien's face when she'd asked about what had happened when his parents had died. She'd said "died" as a courtesy to him—nobody in her family could stand people who said "passed away"—but as soon as the word was out of her mouth it had hung heavily in the air, like a slur.

"Yeah," said Katy, "but he probably had a bunch. Of bracelets, I mean."

"Even so."

"Man," said Katy. "I wouldn't have turned down a present like that. That boy picked the wrong girl."

The remark echoed for a moment, and even though she knew Katy didn't really mean it, Lily found herself wanting to rotate the conversation somehow. "What did you love so much about Anton?" she said.

Katy maintained her pose a moment longer, then toppled. Even her toppling was graceful. "The thing that I loved the most about Anton," said Katy, and Lily could tell that she'd already thought a lot about it. "Was the way he made everything bigger."

"That sounds exhausting," said Lily. She felt firmly that things were already big enough; she certainly didn't need things to be any bigger.

"It was, sometimes," said Katy.

"So are you ever glad to have him gone?"

Lily expected Katy to pause and then say yes, sometimes, but instead she shook her head and shot Lily a terrible look—of generosity born of cosmic and enduring pity—from her spot on the floor. "No," she said.

"Do you think you should get over it, though? I mean, life is short."

"It's not short," said Katy. "It's terrifyingly long." Katy got up and cracked her back. Lily could hear the delicate pincer sounds of each of her vertebrae aligning themselves. "And for me at least, it just got a lot longer."

One night late in January, Sebastien awoke to a knock at the door.

He had been sound asleep, and he was surprised at how quickly he was flooded with joy—joy at the thought that Lily had been so eager to see him, that she'd been so bold on his behalf. Perhaps they had moved past the horrid bracelet debacle after all, he thought, as he staggered down the stairs in his boxers. It was this, exactly this, that was wonderful about having a person in one's life: As sociologists could attest, there was simply no knowing what people might do. Before Lily, Sebastien's days had been mired in reticulated sameness—he could just as easily find himself eating expired canned spaghetti at four a.m. as four p.m.; he might be asleep at three in the afternoon or drunk at nine in the morning; he might go out for walks in the middle of the night or he might not leave the house for a week. But now there was Lily, and she might (who knows!) show up at his house at any hour of the day or night, gloriously unannounced.

But when Sebastien opened the door, he could see—even in shadow, even in silhouette—that it wasn't Lily. It was Katy.

He was so surprised that he forgot to be ironic. "What are you doing here?" he said.

"I need to talk to you." In the dark, Katy's face was luminous. Sebastien could never quite shake the feeling that her eyes were somehow medically too big for the rest of her body.

"Does Lily know you're here?"

"Why should Lily know I'm here?"

"Okay, then. Fine." It was only when his heart began to slow down that Sebastien realized it had been racing. "What do you want?"

"I have a question for you."

"There are telephones, you know. There's the Internet. There's the daytime." Sebastien's mouth felt swampy, his mind still solidly lodged in some uneasy dreamscape, but he was beginning to wonder if it was perhaps earlier than he'd first thought. He ran his tongue along his teeth. It was, he realized shamefully, perhaps as early as midnight.

Katy cocked her head. "I need to know what's going on with Carlos."

"What are you talking about?" Sebastien leaned against the doorframe, suddenly aware of the cool night air and his boxer shorts. Well, and what should he be ashamed of? If Katy Kellers didn't want to see a sybaritic young gentleman with pale and blue-veined bare legs in his nightclothes, then she should have called ahead.

"He's in some kind of financial trouble, isn't he?" said Katy. "Isn't that what you said?"

"Is this a matter of some urgency? Are you being struck mad or insomniac by curiosity? Some of us have work in the mornings, you know. Not me, of course, but some people."

"I didn't want anyone to know I was over here."

"Well, I don't see how it's any of your concern what's going on with the Carrizos." Sebastien sounded cross, and he was further cross with himself for caring—privacy was such a bourgeois value, after all. "And I also don't know why you think I'd know."

"Of course you know. What else do you do besides sit there and watch everybody all day long? And there's that thing you said at the dinner."

"What thing?"

"About whether they were feeding us well. About the lawsuit."

"That was just a joke."

"I know Lily thinks that everything you say is a joke, but I don't think anything you say is really a joke. So—what, the Carrizos are being sued? Why?"

Sebastien rubbed his hair fretfully. "Something untoward with money," he said. "I think. Why does anybody get sued?"

"How do you know that?"

"I just told you I don't know that."

Katy looked at him sharply. "How do you *think* you know it?"

"It's gossip and hearsay," said Sebastien. "Truly mediocre intelligence. Do with it what you will. Which will hopefully be nothing."

"What could I possibly do with it?"

"I'm sure I don't know. I haven't had even a glimmer of imagination since approximately 1996."

"You're a strange boy."

Sebastien only hoped that the blankness on his face communicated the resounding unoriginality of this observation.

"I should be getting back," said Katy.

"So soon? A pity."

Katy retreated down the steps. Her beauty was so austere, so forbidding; there was something hard about it, as though she'd been chiseled from some rare mineral—whereas Lily seemed somehow organic, naturally arising.

"Might I ask," he said, as Katy was walking away, "whether you're going to tell Lily you came over here?"

"Why? Afraid it'll give her the wrong impression?" Katy turned her head away from him and kept walking. "Don't worry. There's a lot I don't tell Lily."

One day while Lily was out walking in San Telmo, a woman with a collapsing face shrieked at her.

The woman came from nowhere. Lily had been listening to her iPod, and all of a sudden the woman was right in front of her, yelling in Spanish too fast and distorted for comprehension. Lily tried to listen and pick out words even as she walked away—faster and faster, though she was careful not to break into a run—but it was useless: Listening to the woman was like listening to somebody talk in a dream, or through aphasia. Lily retreated into a doorway. The woman followed her there, still shouting. Her skin was leathery, and something about her eyes seemed wrong—the ratio of whites to iris was off somehow, maybe. She reached out and Lily fumbled in her pockets for coins. But when she looked down she saw that the woman wasn't holding her hands out to receive something; instead she was pointing at Lily, her hands like twin claws, and Lily was reduced to saying she did not understand, she was sorry, she was sorry, she did not understand. At this, the woman—seeming somehow satisfied, though Lily could not guess why—turned and dematerialized into an alleyway.

A moment passed, and Lily stepped gingerly into the street. With the woman gone the square was quiet, the sunbeams gathering into little pools on the concrete. A diagonal slash of light in front of Lily was bristling with dust motes, moving in a silent frenzy. Across the square, two young guys were drinking beers at a cervecería; they looked at Lily and laughed, and one of them raised his glass in a toast. Lily suddenly noticed an eggy wetness on her cheek, which, she knew immediately, was spit. That woman's spit was on her cheek. Lily wiped her face with the sleeve of her sweater—once, twice, many times—and she was half-way back to the Carrizos', still wiping, before she understood that that part of her face was just going to feel weird for a while.

For the rest of the afternoon, Lily felt the edgy weariness of ambient guilt. This had been coming in waves, between the Borges and the wine—the worrisome knowledge that she was basically on vacation in a country that was basically poor, at least by U.S. standards. She could not figure out how to regard her presence here. Was it good that she was in Buenos Aires, pumping her modest summer savings into the ridiculous exchange rate and coming out wealthy and dropping money into the economy? And trying—you could not deny that she was try-ing, and certainly she was trying harder than Katy—to learn the lan-guage, and make international connections, and foster cross-cultural understanding, and all that? She should be volunteering somewhere, perhaps. She should be suffering somehow. But then that seemed like it might be shallow, too, and maybe even worse, in a way that she had trouble unraveling. The whole study-abroad program had gone to an orphanage for an afternoon of work, and it had been so painfully clear how useless they all were—that small surmountable problems were being made for them to overcome, that tiny doable tasks were being left undone so that they might all line up and do them. And that every-thing was going more slowly because of all the translating and the extra explaining. That they'd basically made these people's jobs harder by their presence. That the real favor would have been to stay home. There was a particular kind of uneasiness that came from recognizing the profundity of your own uselessness. It was all so morally exhaust-ing. Lily worried about it, and then forgot to worry about it, and then worried about the fact that she'd forgotten. She recognized this as per-haps the second stage of culture shock, after elation.

Back at the house, Katy wasn't home, so Lily dug out her interna-tional calling card. She wanted to talk to someone about these things, and if that meant talking to a member of her own family, then so be it. Lily tried Maureen first, but she wasn't home. She could call Anna, she supposed, but she never called Anna. She honestly forgot about Anna sometimes—not the fact of her, of course, nor her role in almost all of Lily's childhood memories. But sometimes, it was true, the idea that Anna was living her own life at Colby felt less than totally real to Lily. This feeling was compounded by the legendarily ascetic hours Anna kept—going to bed and arising incomprehensibly early, which had always seemed to Lily like a conscious rejection of the world and its inhabitants. Sometimes at Middlebury Lily had woken up at one p.m. in time for her first class and thought of the terrifying fact that Anna had been awake for six and a half hours already, and the even more terrifying fact that this was nearly all Lily knew about her life. The things that Lily did *not* know about Anna's life were legion. Most important, perhaps, Lily did not know whether Anna was still a virgin. Worse, she did not expect to be apprised of any developments on that score, when and if they occurred. Lily had told Anna about her own first time, of course, and Anna had seemed both grossed out, which Lily understood, and also uninterested, which Lily did not understand—not only because sex was an objectively interesting subject, but also because Lily found it unfathomable to be repulsed by something and not also fundamentally curious about it. To Lily, those were essentially the same feelings. With Anna, it was not so. When it came to conversations about the really compelling, vulgar, transfixing realities of life, Anna was maddeningly equanimous; neither overtly interested, nor so prudishly avoidant as to acknowledge those subjects' power. She would talk about such matters when it was necessary, and what she would say about them then was inevitably practical. When Lily had told her about losing her virginity, for example, Anna had immediately asked if Lily was going to get on birth control.

"Really, Anna," Lily had said. She'd been trying to sound knowing and world-weary, but the truth was she hadn't given the matter much thought. She hadn't necessarily considered that sex was something she was going to keep doing; she'd been focused entirely on the hurdle of virginity loss, and being questioned about birth control now felt like being immediately grilled about postgraduation plans when you'd just come running into the room with a college acceptance letter. "If you are going to have any fun in college, Anna-Banana," said Lily, "you are going to have to learn to relax."

She and Anna had been closer when they were small—back then, at least, they had shared a serious interest. Like all children, Lily and Anna were generally bored by things that had happened before they were born—but the subject of Janie was, of course, the great exception, and it consumed them with a curiosity that was terrible and electric and shameful and insatiable. It was also, Lily realized now, probably normal, though they hadn't known that then. All they'd known at the time was that their inquisitiveness came out as cruelty. Lily had learned this the hard way when, at the age of four or five, she'd asked Maureen something horrifically blunt about Janie—something about the fate of her dead body, she thought, though she was not totally sure now and shrank from trying very hard to remember. The visceral, involuntary pain on Maureen's face in that moment had shocked Lily, as had the awful curdled quality of her voice as she answered, and Lily had suddenly realized that Maureen was very, very sad and was trying not to blame her for it. Lily could still remember the desolation of wondering—for the first of many, many times—if everything was more complicated than it seemed.

And so, because they loved their parents and did not want to hurt them, Lily and Anna had stopped asking questions. But their natural-born preadolescent morbidity—squashed and suppressed as it was—could not disappear entirely, and sometimes it came out in strange ways.

"We could die," Lily had whispered to Anna late one night. She was seven and Anna was five. It was the summer Lily slept in her Mulan sleeping bag every single night and pretended to camp. "Either of us. Don't you know that?"

"No, we couldn't."

"Janie died. We could die any time."

"Janie was very sick," said Anna sternly. This was the family's compulsively repeated mantra—to this day, Lily could hear it recited in an eerie, almost singsong chorus: *Janie was very sick, Janie was very sick*—and Anna was prone to slavishly parroting whatever Maureen and Andrew said, which Lily found annoying even when they were very small.

"Either of us could *get* sick, though," said Lily.

"Shut up," said Anna, her voice quavery. Even when they were little, Lily hadn't really known what would upset Anna. She had actually envied other girls who seemed to know exactly what would make their sisters sad, and what would make them angry, and what would make them tattle, and what would overwhelmingly gross them out. Lily didn't know those things; Anna was like an egg on a spoon that she was always dropping, even when she didn't mean to.

"We won't get sick," Anna had repeated fiercely, over and over, that night and many nights after. "We won't. We won't."

And she was right. They had not.

Lily squinted at the phone. The basement's artificial light was somehow shriller than usual, and she found herself dialing Andrew's number. Her father was either in on a Saturday evening or he was out, and either possibility had vaguely gruesome implications. Lily waited. An interminable row of numbers would be popping up on her father's caller ID. Lily could still feel dregs of the woman's spit on her cheek, though, of course, that was impossible. Andrew picked up the phone.

"Lily!"

"Hello, Father."

"To what do I owe the honor?"

"Just thought I'd check in on you." Lily had called him, but now she had to pretend that the calling was for reasons of business, not pleasure. "Make sure you weren't having too much fun without me."

"Clearly you needn't worry. What about you? Shouldn't you be out with that guy?"

Sebastien. Lily had mentioned him in a postcard ten days ago, feeling the thrill of the unconventional spelling and capitalization, giddy with the sophisticated joy of sending little stamps of excitement into the dull slog of the lives of the people she'd left behind. Now she wished she hadn't said anything.

"Do you think it's morally problematic to be on study abroad in Argentina?" said Lily.

"Ah, talk to your mom about this," said Andrew. "You know she's the only real Marxist in the family."

The fondness in Andrew's voice as he said this made Lily wonder, for the trillionth time, why her parents had split up—though she had to marvel over their inability to do anything, even divorce, with any real verve. It was very hard to tell how bad their marriage had been, exactly, as it was staggering around its terminal lap. It was certainly true that, for all their espoused progressivism, the family seemed to adhere basically to the national statistics about labor divisions in housework: Andrew seemed to make everything marginally dingier and dirtier without really trying as he moved about the house; Maureen swept quietly along behind him with a similarly effortless-seeming tidiness and order. But Lily knew it couldn't be that simple. There was a story that Maureen and Andrew told—sometimes separately, sometimes jointly, but always in a tone suggesting profound symbolic content—that Lily thought might contain some clues: Toward the end of Janie's life, apparently, the next-door hippie neighbors had brought over some crystals, and had stood on the porch (in Maureen's telling), smug, serene, beaming with the beautiful obviousness of the solution. Over the years, the crystals had become some strange and dark and utterly unfunny inside joke between Maureen and Andrew; whenever one of them turned to the other and said, emphatically, those *crystals*, it was clear that something tedious and adult was going to go sailing right over the heads of Lily and Anna, who knew better than to try to really probe the matter.

"I tried," said Lily. "She wasn't home. I'm stuck with you."

"Go dig latrines in Mongolia after you graduate," said Andrew. "What the hell else are you going to do anyway? You're a philosophy major."

"And women's studies."

"They're still regarding that as an area of academic inquiry?"

"I feel so useless."

"Well, you are useless, Lil. But the Peace Corps will still be there later. You might as well have fun now. Are you having fun?"

Lily felt deflated at the use of this word, "fun." She hadn't thought of Buenos Aires in terms of "fun"; she'd thought of it in terms of "transformative purity." But she realized now with a minor shock that it had been fun—the exploring, the psychic revelation of language acquisition, the drinking, the literary preening, the growing sense of herself as a fashionable waif in a foreign film. It had all been very fun until, somehow, it wasn't.

"Fun has been had," she said sadly.

"Well. Don't let mistakes get made. Listen, I've got to run. Garry Kasparov is on CNN in a minute."

"You love that guy."

"I *love* that guy. But listen—you're doing all right? Everything's fine?"

"Everything's all right, everything's fine. Blow Garry a kiss for me."

Andrew was gone, but Lily kept holding the phone to her ear, listening to the particular silence of a concluded phone call, staring right into the light above her until she saw black striations in her vision. She thought about the shrieking woman in the doorway. She tried to play back in her head what the woman had said, tried to retroactively unravel and translate it, but it was no use. The woman had been indecipherable, and would be incomprehensible now, always. Lily hung up the phone.

That night, Lily was on her best behavior with the Carrizos. She showed up to dinner early, asking Beatriz if she needed help with anything—though she was sure Beatriz could see her visibly hoping that help would not be needed—and decided to make a particular point to be more gracious to Katy. With Carlos, she knew, it would be easy: All she had to do to make him like her even better was to talk even more—

about the plotting of multinational corporations, the undeniably im-
perialistic ambitions of the United States, the dastardly scheming of
the IMF. Lily was dimly aware that she did not strictly believe all of this
stuff—a lot of it was the kind of talk you engage in to socialize, to an-
nounce your well-honed moral identity—but she was certainly not
going to quibble with an actual citizen of a developing economy about
the intentions of the IMF. And at any rate, Lily was not wholly sure that
Carlos really believed in all of it entirely, either. He regarded conversation as sport, and Lily loved anyone who regarded anything in life as
sport (except for actual sports).

"Nobody even believed there were weapons of mass destruction in
Iraq," she said to Carlos, to start things off. She poured herself a glass
of wine.

"Nobody," he said forcefully. "That's the big deception. Now everyone knows they were wrong, but what nobody understands is that
even *they* never thought they were right."

Lily nodded cheerfully. Maybe you could see Carlos's depression
underneath it all, though it was so different from the resigned white-
knuckled terminal WASP depression of her own family. Carlo's sadness wasn't the grim death march of Maureen's—who had basically
made a studied and understated decision to simply never enjoy anything again, ever. Instead, it seemed to push Carlos toward a fatal indifference that almost seemed like a kind of freedom. He probably
laughed as much as he did anything.

"George W. Bush's unresolved daddy issues are the only reason you
guys were even there," Carlos was saying.

Katy and Beatriz stayed mostly quiet when politics was discussed,
which it always was. This made Lily vacillate between the dark suspicion that Katy was politically ignorant and the even darker suspicion
that she might be politically moderate. Beatriz, she figured, was just
bored of Carlos, which Lily could understand.

"The felling of the Twin Towers was a symbolic castration of America," said Lily. "That's why the U.S. took it so hard." Somehow the mood
at the table was darkening. Beatriz was grimacing into her steak with

slightly more than her usual amount of exasperated chagrin. Lily looked at Katy for backup, but Katy stared at her levelly with what Lily thought might be some degree of tired amusement. Lily was alone.

The conversation bobbled onward, and Lily found herself issuing ever less provocative assertions and ever more lukewarm assents until she noticed that Beatriz had cleared the table and Katy had left the room and all that was left in the wine bottle was a few grainy ruby-red drips.

Afterward Lily found Katy on the bunk bed, reading. Lily stared at her for a moment, wondering what kind of perfect thoughtlessness could buy you such serenity. "What's that about?" she said.

"Governmental secrecy about inflation rates," said Katy, not looking up.

Lily didn't mean to say anything, and then she did. "Why don't you ever talk?"

"What?"

"Why don't you ever say anything at dinner? Don't you have any opinions on anything?"

Katy put down the article. "You're not serious."

"How would I know if you did? How would I know if you had a single opinion in your head?"

"There is no possible way you want me in that conversation."

"Of course I do."

"No. You don't."

"You're never going to change anyone's mind by sitting there and rolling your eyes."

"I wasn't rolling my eyes."

"You were. You were rolling your eyes as far back in your head as they would go." Lily could feel the wine sluicing somewhere back in her skull. She hiccupped. "I think you never want to say anything because you just can't stand to have someone mad at you. You just want to make sure everyone likes you. That's all you care about."

"Better than just wanting to feel right all the time, even if you're not actually doing anything to fix anything."

"I was the vice president of Amnesty International!" said Lily, throwing her shoe at Katy. It missed her by a wide margin. "I organized three petitions for a Free Palestine!"

Katy looked at the flip-flop appraisingly, then picked it up and handed it to Lily. "Calm down," said Katy. "We don't need to fight about it."

There was a pause. Lily hoped she looked less angry than she actually was.

"Maybe you're right," said Katy soothingly. "It's just—I don't know. I don't think they're good conversations. I don't think they're good for Carlos. He gets so drunk. He's so depressed."

"I am so sick of everyone being so depressed," said Lily. She was. Good Lord, how she was. Sometimes she felt like her own family was essentially the world's most passive suicide cult. Couldn't her host family at least have a different set of problems? "Doesn't anyone understand that you have to *try* not to be depressed?" said Lily. "You have to make it a marginal priority? You can't just get a free pass on your whole reality because you're so depressed? We're all going to be dead one day. We're all in the same boat."

Katy let this pass, and Lily could hear what she'd said swirl around the room in widening loops. She felt suddenly wretched and childish. She felt, suddenly and for the first time, like she wanted to go home.

"Why is he so depressed, though?" Lily said after a while.

Katy gave her a marveling look. "They're being sued," she said. "He's losing the business. Don't you pay attention to anything?"

CHAPTER SIX

February

The night after visiting the jail, Andrew dreamed of Lily. In his dream she was swaddled in an incubator, with tubes running in and out of her ears and eyes and nose. She was soft featured and infantile, yet the size of his adult daughter, and when she spoke—although Andrew could not understand what she said—she spoke with his adult Lily's low voice, clear and pleading, until he woke up.

Andrew was disappointed with himself. His whole life, his dreams had been dispiritingly common, crudely metaphorical, and always right on schedule: He'd dreamed of falling, he'd dreamed of unnoticed nakedness, he'd dreamed of forgetting about a class he was signed up to take, and later, to teach. He would have liked to at least be a little more original in a crisis.

Andrew got up and went to the bathroom. He turned on the light and watched himself appear, paunchy and red-eyed, in the mirror. Andrew had spent the last few years tracking his own aging through Maureen—both in how she looked and in how she looked at him—

each time he saw her. The last time, at Christmas, Andrew had realized that Maureen had dimmed into typicality: There were feathery wrinkles around her eyes and a persistent plummy color underneath; her hair was never quite as red as he remembered. It had finally happened: The best things about Maureen no longer showed. A stranger passing her on the street would never guess that she'd once jumped onto a train in Austria, or that she'd smoked dope in her closet and fallen down laughing into a pile of skirts, long before things happened that had made her fearful, that would make anybody in the world fearful. Joyous openness was, after all, a luxury. And sometimes Andrew was glad that Lily had somehow emerged from their lives carefree enough to do all the things she wanted to do. Other young girls felt this way, after all, and they went off on study abroad, and then after a semester they came home, behaving exactly as Lily would have: pretending to slip into Spanish or French by accident, ostentatiously mourning some newly beloved street food, telling stories they hoped would make other people admire their intrepidness as much as they themselves did. That's what Lily should have been doing in three months' time—she should have been out with her friends, all of them recently returned from different places, all of them exclaiming over how strange and light and leathery American dollars now seemed. But she would not be. Lily might be home in three months—but even if she was, she would no longer be a child, and she would not be saying the things that children say. And sometimes—especially now, when he thought of her sleeping in that cell, curled into herself for warmth—Andrew was not glad that she had had a chance to feel free and lucky in the world. Not even for a moment, not even if she deserved it. Because, really, who were they kidding? Their family had never been lucky. And Andrew and Maureen had failed Lily—failed her utterly—if they'd ever let her forget it.

Andrew tiptoed back to bed. Across the room, Anna seemed to be radiating resentful wakefulness, though she was very still; he feared that Anna was growing into the kind of daughter who would never tell him that he snored. Andrew lay back down. A line ran through his head: *There is no other life but the one we have.* This had been something of a mantra of his after Janie died: There was never anything more to her life in the world, he told himself, than the two and a half years she spent here. There are no other drafts, and no alternate endings. There is not a single day that rightfully belongs to our lives except for those that actually compose it.

Lying in bed, Andrew listened to the faint crepitation of a leaf against the window. He admired the recalcitrant light of the already diminishing moon. It was, after all, a very beautiful world.

Every morning at dawn, Anna donned her workout clothes and went off to run. She'd return silently, an hour or more later, and then sit in front of the mirror and pull the Band-Aids off her scabby heels while Andrew watched. At some point during her first year of college, she had turned into one long flank of muscle. In the afternoons, Andrew would make her go out with him somewhere—usually to the corner store, where he'd try to make desperate sport of all the exotic artificial flavors. Anna trailed behind him, suddenly lazy, her expression like a chunk of basalt.

"Chestnut-flavored yogurt?" Andrew would say, pointing. "Would you ever have thought?"

"There are a lot of things lately that I never would have thought."

Andrew did not blame her; she was doing her best. Learning to be an adult was learning that your best was rarely quite enough.

"Fig-flavored soda?" he'd say. "Bet you haven't had that before."

"I've never done a lot of this before."

On the third day after visiting Lily, while Anna was at the gym, Andrew went walking. He walked to bone-white cathedrals; he walked past houses with shrubbery growing onto them like stubble. There was dog shit everywhere, absolutely everywhere, and Andrew was impressed by the blithe acceptance of such—as though everyone had tacitly agreed that this was what the city was actually for. The sky was a pious robin's-egg blue. Andrew thought of what it would be like to be dropped live out of an airplane, and then fall streaking through this gorgeous sky, the color of a bluebird or a crayon. He thought of what it might be like to be too terrified to scream.

Andrew would have liked to be able to tell himself that they had all survived before, but the truth was, they hadn't. Lily's problem, he tried to remind himself, was entirely different from Janie's—Lily's situation was merely a function of a failure of rationality, a failure of communication. If Andrew could explain everything very slowly and carefully then all would be clear, and everyone would see that a mistake had been made. He didn't have to stop an oncoming tsunami or apocalypse or terminal illness; he didn't have to attract the attention or favor of a deity. All he had to do was describe, very clearly and persuasively, a true fact about the world: that his daughter had not killed anybody. Andrew was a professional explainer. To save Lily, he needed only to do better what he already did well. What could be simpler? What, in the end, could be easier? He should be glad to have such problems! There was no tumor in this daughter's body, no knife against this daughter's throat—only a handful of incorrect impressions deep in the minds of a few reactionary people. As threats go, these were not the worst.

Andrew walked past another church. Etched into its exterior were saints, forever without perspective, their halos gleaming like pennies. The church was closed. Andrew stood outside the elaborate wrought-iron gates and held on.

Anna came back at eleven and took a shower. In the afternoon, Andrew left her eating a room service sandwich and watching *Sex and the City 2* on HBO, which he'd ordered for her even though she told him she'd already seen it and that it had made her a worse and more stupid person. Andrew had the hotel call him a taxi and gave the driver the address of Lily's host family in Palermo. Sebastien LeCompte's house, Lily's emails had suggested, was right next door and enormous, and Andrew was hoping he wouldn't be able to miss it.

Some of the streets on the way to Palermo were questionable—

Andrew saw jigsaw structures made of plywood; shifty-looking men wearing only their undershirts; shredded hunks of pork, roasting on spits in the sun and attracting bevies of jewel-winged flies—but after they crossed Figueroa Alcorta, he relaxed. Out one window loomed some sort of museum, ornate as a cupcake, and the houses grew bigger and better until they were garish and tacky and tricked out in the taste of the full-blown nouveau riche. Things got calmer and cleaner once the taxi crossed into Barrio Parque; Andrew began to feel that he was in a neighborhood inhabited by men who'd made modest fortunes honestly. Finally the taxi rounded a dusty corner and onto Lily's street—Lily's former street—and Andrew was once again relieved. The house that must be Sebastien LeCompte's was unmistakable: It was right next door to the Carrizos', and was, as promised, huge and shambling and unkempt, visibly driving down the prices of all the other real estate.

Andrew couldn't help craning his neck to look at Lily's former house. It was nice, he was glad to see—he'd imagined open sewage, chickens in the yard, God knew what. Even so, what the lawyers had told him about the Carrizos did not sound reassuring. The Carrizos had certain attitudes about Lily, apparently—certain prejudices and suspicions—and Andrew certainly knew how grating she could be to people who didn't already love her. He glanced again at the house, trying to see into the courtyard, then shivered and admonished himself for being ghoulish enough to look. He averted his gaze and pointed to Sebastien LeCompte's mansion. The taxi driver eyed it skeptically.

The house was indeed immense: For once in her life, Lily had not been hyperbolic in a postcard. Three stories of mullioned windows squatted beneath a roof that seemed to sag on one side, giving the whole house the look of a shrugging person in a buttoned waistcoat. A winding path led to an enormous door that, Andrew saw when he reached it, was carved and expensive but missing a doorknob. The knocker was a snarling stone creature; Andrew found himself involuntarily snarling right back at it. He could have put his fist through the door and into the house's creepy interior. He did not do this. Instead, he knocked and took a few steps back. He was sweating. A warm and paltry wind kicked up and made him even warmer. He waited.

The door opened, at long last, and a thin, extremely young man appeared. He had brown hair and startling eyes and was dressed in a garment Andrew couldn't quite make sense of—was it a robe of some kind? A smoking jacket? Maybe, Andrew thought darkly, this boy was behind Lily's smoking. "Buenos dias," said Andrew, because he figured that this was the best way to start.

Sebastien LeCompte did not appear surprised. He only smiled a distant smile, revealing a set of teeth that must have been very expensive. "Why, *good day* to you, too, sir," he said. His accent was not what Andrew was expecting—it was nasally and harsh; the accent of British actors playing American. It did not match the outfit. "And what might you be selling?"

"You speak English?"

"I flatter myself that I do."

"Are you Sebastien LeCompte?"

"I flatter myself that I am."

In her emails, Lily had referred to Sebastien LeCompte as a "man" she was "seeing," phrasing that had seemed comical to Andrew at the time but that he'd clung to after her arrest—perhaps she *was* dating an adult, for once, someone who was reasonable and mature, someone who might actually be of some assistance to them now. This hope had diminished when he'd seen the security footage, and now, staring at Sebastien LeCompte in the flesh, Andrew could feel it almost disappear. What he was dealing with here was a boy: rail-thin, floppy-haired, tepid in his every gesture and glance, reflexively sardonic in his every utterance, the physical instantiation of his generation's taste in music. *Grow pulses, children!* Andrew wanted to yell, but he did not. The world was lucky Andrew didn't do half the things he thought of doing. Instead, Andrew extended his hand. He had to try—it was imperative that he try—to find out if there was any chance this boy could help them, in spite of himself.

"I'm Andrew Hayes," he said.

At this, something happened to the kid's face—he tilted it upward, and his eyebrows lifted almost imperceptibly. His nostrils flared. "Lily's father."

"Yes. Lily's father." Andrew paused. He tried to take the edge off his voice, just in case. "You've heard about Lily, I'm sure?"

Here, the kid seemed to recover himself. "Indeed," he said, snapping upright. "Most improbable. Though our children do have a way of surprising us, don't they?"

Andrew did not know quite what to make of this, but he knew he did not like it. He took a step backward. "Who's 'us'?" he said.

"No, no. I jest. I don't think your lovely Lily had a hand in the slaying."

Andrew dragged his fingers through his hair, feeling the resolute stubbornness of his own skull. "I am hoping," he said carefully, "that you can help me."

Sebastien looked at Andrew with placid eyes. "I am truly very sorry to hear that," he said. Andrew couldn't quite parse this one, either, but before he could ask for clarification Sebastien cleared his throat. "May I ask," he said. The jaunty spin had dropped out of his voice. "How Lily is faring?"

Andrew squinted. It seemed that the boy actually wanted to know. "Could I come in, maybe, and we could talk a bit?"

"Where are my manners?" Sebastien stepped backward into the shadows of the house and gestured, with elaborate gallantry, for Andrew to join him.

"Lily is horrible," said Andrew, stepping inside. "Thanks for asking. She's absolutely horrible."

Sebastien's reaction to this was obscured by the house's strange endemic darkness. Andrew blinked and a labyrinthine, anachronistic living room appeared—there was an arabesque clock on the mantel; an ancient piano teetering nearby; several sheet-covered mounds that Andrew fervently hoped were furniture. In the corner, a multicolored, very outdated map covered a window; a ray of sunlight illuminated a bright green nonaligned India. Andrew pointed to it.

"I thought the Soviet Union was done now," he said.

"Oh?" said Sebastien. "I hadn't heard."

He sounded truly bereft. This interview, it was becoming clear, was going to demand a different kind of patience than Andrew had thought to bring. "It was in all the papers," he said.

Sebastien nodded gravely. "My decorating scheme is very passé, I'm afraid. If you don't move things, it turns out, they don't tend to move themselves. I suspect that's why we still have all those Roman fora lying around willy-nilly."

Andrew half-nodded. He was faintly aware that it was probably unwise to keep obviously marveling at the house, but he couldn't quite bring himself to stop. This was where his daughter's boyfriend lived, and there was a cluster of chandelier pendants hanging from the ceiling, and Andrew was somehow positive that the entire room was cobwebby. On the mantel, Andrew could make out a collection of ancient liqueurs, a giant book that could only be the Bible, a vase with some flowers that looked like they had probably always been dead. On one wall was a tapestry—an actual tapestry, like something out of the national museum of a minor eastern European country. It was threadbare, of course, and depicting a hunt, of course: blue dogs harassing a red deer with anthropomorphic viciousness, the deer's eyes white with terror. Good God, the morbid pageantry of it all! How had the world ever produced a person like this? Had he been left alone for his entire childhood in this collapsing house with nothing but Evelyn Waugh books to read? And why, oh why, had Lily slept with him? Now Andrew had to worry about her self-esteem, on top of everything else.

"Where are your parents?" Andrew found himself saying.

"Well, that's truly the question at the heart of all human endeavor, isn't it?" said Sebastien gaily. "Where, indeed. You're a great thinker of our time—you tell me."

Andrew spent a moment in incomprehension, then felt a dull club of remorse. "Oh," he said. "I'm sorry."

"*Pas du tout*. Can I get you a drink?"

"No, thank you."

"I trust you don't object if I indulge?"

Andrew waved his hand in a vague gesture of permission giving and Sebastien LeCompte bowed his way into the kitchen. Andrew went to examine the mantel more closely. Next to the clock, in an odd thematic parallel to the tapestry, was a photograph of Sebastien with a murdered beast of some kind. Whatever it was had been shot near the heart, its wound wreathed by a ring of poppy-red blood. In the photo, Sebastien was even younger than he was now; his father—identical to Sebastien, theatrically swathed in various beige garments with compartments and buttons and bolts—had his arm around his son.

"You're sure?" said Sebastien, returning with a greenish glass of something that could only be absinthe. "I could even pop over to the corner store and get—what? Beer?"

Andrew shook his head.

"So," said Sebastien, sitting on one of the mounds and motioning to Andrew to do the same. "What was it that you wanted to discuss?"

Andrew selected a mound of his own. "Well," he said, tentatively descending. "I understand that you and Lily were—friends."

Andrew watched Sebastien fleetingly consider, and then reject, a sarcastic response. Instead, he looked at the ceiling and seemed to actually ponder the question for several long moments. "Yes," he said finally. "I think that we probably were."

"And you also knew the, ah. The deceased roommate. Katy."

"Briefly."

Andrew felt a contraction in his throat. "I am hoping you might help me understand what all of this is about. Why this is happening. Why they imagine Lily did this thing. Because it is outrageous, objectively. As I'm sure you agree. Objectively outrageous and unbelievable."

Sebastien stood and went to the mantel. He traced his finger along the photograph, making a curlicue in the dust, then regarded his finger distastefully and wiped it on his trousers. "Well, Lily didn't very much care for Katy, as I'm sure you've been made aware," he said flatly.

"I wouldn't say that," said Andrew. He swallowed, trying to unclench his throat. "They weren't close, maybe, but I don't think there was any particular hostility there."

"I trust you've read the emails? Or hasn't cable news reached America yet? Anyway, they were quite a spectacle down here."

Suddenly, Andrew wanted to snap this kid's skinny neck; suddenly, Andrew thought he understood homicidal rage. "I think 'spectacle' is probably overstating it," he said. "And, anyway, that's just how she talked. It's how many people talk. Many, many people say uncivil things about their friends in emails, and they are not arrested for it, because it's not actually illegal—not even here, in fact: I've checked. Whatever she wrote about Katy, she didn't mean anything by it. If you really spent any time with her, you'd know that."

Sebastien tilted his head to one side. "She did have a very particular idiolect, of course."

"Okay, look," said Andrew, standing up. He had had enough of this. His family needed him—again? or finally? either way—and he was not going to let this cartoonish Cheshire cat of a child stop him from helping them. "Listen. You are going to tell me some things."

Sebastien stared, and Andrew wondered how long it had been since he had received direct instructions of any sort.

"Tell me about the night Katy died," Andrew ordered. "Lily was with you."

"Yes."

"And you've talked to the police about this?"

"Briefly."

"Do they think you might be involved?"

"Probably."

"Why haven't they arrested you?"

"I was not actually involved." Sebastien looked down, and Andrew charitably allowed himself to consider the possibility that he might actually feel sorry for what he'd just said. Perhaps as penance, Sebastien continued—his voice a bit lower, a bit less theatrical, than it had been before. "There's nothing to tell you about that night. Truly. Lily was here. We talked and had some cocktails. We went to sleep around two. She went back to the Carrizos' in the morning. She came back over here after finding Katy. Then she called the police."

It was strange to listen to the boy speak so frankly—recalling events comprehensibly, constructing a linear narrative. The sun shifted, and two strips of cadmium midafternoon light fell onto the floor and across Sebastien's face, catching his freckles and making him look innocent and heartbreakingly young.

"The police came pretty quickly and cordoned off the house," said Sebastien. "They arrested her the next morning. I don't have anything else I can tell you. I'm sorry." He looked at his hands for a moment and then said, very quickly, "Do you think I could see her?"

For a moment, Andrew had wanted very much to suspect this boy. It was as though the universe was shoving Sebastien at him—here was a man, involved with two women, living right next door to both of them—and what a gift it would have been to have such an obvious answer. But now Andrew was confronted with the reality that believing in Sebastien's guilt would mean the beginning of believing in Lily's. And that was unthinkable.

"I can't imagine they'll allow that," Andrew said gently.

"Could I write her a letter?"

"Maybe."

There was a silence. "I'm sorry," Sebastien said finally, in that harsh, too-flat voice, and then he said it again. And then Andrew's feeling flipped over again, and he wondered, with a judder of suspicion that made all other suspicions seem shallow, just what it was that Sebastien was so sorry for.

"For what?" said Andrew. He looked around the place—its garish loneliness, its ghoulish ornateness—and he looked again at Sebastien: that goofy hair, that unreasonable outfit, that too-young face that shifted from guile to guilelessness with the movement of the sun. Andrew did not know why Lily liked Sebastien LeCompte, but he had to accept that she did—perhaps she even loved him. And one explanation for all of this trouble was that Lily was protecting this boy, against all reason, out of some strange sense of martyrdom or infallibility or perhaps something else altogether that Andrew might never begin to guess.

"What are you so sorry for?" said Andrew again meanly.

"I am sorry," said Sebastien, "for your absolutely abominable luck."

When Andrew returned to the hotel, Anna was staring listlessly out the window. The movie had ended and the screen had become a vivid aquarium blue, but she hadn't turned it off.

"Whatcha up to, Old Sport?" said Andrew.

Anna stared at him dully, unsurprised, though she'd made no move when he entered the room. Andrew suddenly wanted to go to her and take her bony shoulders in his arms. He wanted to curl up around her body and whisper "Hush," even though it was unlikely that Anna would ever require anyone to tell her to hush.

"Dad," she said. Even the way she said "Dad" sounded to Andrew like a kind of grudging concession. "Is Lily going to be okay?"

Andrew sat down on the edge of the bed and patted Anna's shoulder. "We are going to do everything we can for her."

"Jesus." Anna's voice was astringent. She stood up. " 'We're going to do everything we can for her'? You're such an irredeemable pessimist."

From the mouth of someone so young, the phrase "irredeemable pessimist" sounded rehearsed, obsessed over. Possibly, Andrew thought nervously, inherited. Or even worse, therapeutically processed. Andrew gave Anna what he hoped was an encouraging smile.

"I think she's got as good a shot as we could hope for," he said. Andrew had watched his child die. He was well beyond considerations of pessimism or optimism. But he did not want Anna to be, and he did not want her to have to understand. "I think the lawyers are terrific," he said. "And, of course, she's innocent. So we've got that going for us."

A shiver went across Anna's jaw. "Of course," she said. Her eyes were like bolts. She hated that he'd said it, maybe because it was so obvious. But then, Andrew wasn't above stating the obvious. He was the parent. More than anything, perhaps, that was his job.

"Once," said Anna, "just once, could you tell me that everything is going to be okay?"

Andrew nodded. "I could. I could tell you that. And it might be. That's certainly what we all are hoping and working for. But you're an adult now. And this might be a very long haul. And I want you to be prepared for anything."

"Do we? Do we eternally have to be prepared for anything?"

"It seems that we do, often enough."

Anna turned and faced the window. The light caught her flyaway hair, and she looked frenzied and, Andrew thought, angelic. His daughter. His one daughter, living and free. "I'm sorry, Old Sport," he said.

"I hate that you call me that, you know."

"I—you what? I didn't know that."

"You wouldn't have."

"You really hate it? It makes me feel ironical and literary."

"That is *exactly* why."

Andrew felt stung in a nearly physical way. He thought inexplicably of those furry little creatures in Australia, the ones with the vestigial, frighteningly nonmammalian stingers. "You could have told me," he said.

"Well, I just did." Anna stomped over to her suitcase and produced a plastic bag. Platypuses, that was what those animals were. "I bought these things for Lily," she said, pulling out soap, toilet paper, tampons. Shampoo with cursive writing on it. A razor.

"Where did you get all that stuff?" said Andrew. "Did you go out?"

"For Christ's sake, Dad. No. I went to the little store in the lobby."

"They're not going to let her have the razor."

"Okay," said Anna, putting the razor back in the bag. "Fine. But we need to get her these other things. She needs them."

"We can't get back there until Thursday, sweetie." Was he going to have to call her "sweetie" from now on? Surely that was worse.

"She needs them," Anna said again.

"I know," said Andrew. "But she'll manage. She's been managing already." He heard his own voice and realized he was angry. He wished he had gotten the things for Lily himself—even though it did not matter, not really. They could not see her until Thursday, anyway, and so it could not make a difference whether the things were purchased today or three days from now. And yet there was something galling about Anna having done it; Andrew imagined her walking into that lobby, flushed with exercise, meting out her foreign currency (saved from her various jobs, and then exchanged at a loss in the airport), and then selecting the best versions of whatever it was she thought Lily might need. All of this, all of this, was the job of a parent. In its unsentimental practicality it was, perhaps, the job of a father. It did not matter—of course it did not matter. And yet there was so little that could be done for Lily. Andrew couldn't help but feel it was ungenerous of Anna to do it all herself.

"You don't understand," said Anna, and Andrew heard the strange timbre in her voice that used to mean tears. She coughed herself into a more serious register. "You don't understand anything about it."

About what? he wanted to ask. About not being able to get what you wanted? Even the narrow-minded narcissism of children should be able to accommodate enough generosity toward their parents for Anna to understand that this was not true—probably not in anyone's case, and certainly not in his.

"We'll get her the things she needs, Anna," he said. The things you need and do not get and nevertheless manage to survive without—were those things ever really *needs*? If somebody's need was vast, and eternally unmet, and nonfatal, had what seemed necessary really only been desirous? After Janie died, everyone was always asking Andrew if he was okay, and he never knew what to say. Because what, really, was on the other side of okay? When you stopped being okay, you were just okay in a worse and different way.

"We'll get them to her just as soon as we can," he said.

Anna nodded seriously.

"You were very good to think of them," said Andrew. He hoped he sounded as tired as he felt.

"Well," said Anna, and her voice was stronger, the voice of an adult or a pragmatist. "It was the least I could do."

The next morning Maureen arrived.

Andrew had tracked her flight online in the hotel's business center, calculating how long it would take her to find her luggage and hail a taxi and traverse the city's allegedly Parisian boulevards. He waited until he thought she'd probably checked in to the hotel, then forced himself to wait ninety minutes more. Finally, he got in the elevator and rode down a floor—to room 408, which was, he figured, nearly directly below his own—and knocked on her door.

She appeared after a moment. "Hello, Maureen," said Andrew. He wanted to tell her she looked great, though the tone seemed off, and, anyway, she didn't. Her hair was messy—probably from sleeping thrashily on the plane—and under her eyes were two bluish pits of exhaustion. He tried to detect if she was thinner than usual; he couldn't tell.

"Hello, dear," said Maureen. She always called him something sweet and absolving and fond, and he always called her "Maureen." Andrew wasn't sure what this meant about who wanted or expected more from their postdivorce relationship, or who'd summoned greater depths of humanity or charity in their dealings, but he suspected that they'd both staked some kind of bet on their own way of doing things and he now felt fully committed to his own. They hugged with elaborate formality, which they always did, although Andrew never quite knew why. After everything they had been through together, they should slump against each other now like brothers, or puppies, or soldiers, or mental patients; the proximity of their bodies should be utterly meaningless. And yet a crisp distance had grown up between them, vinelike and intricate, and when Andrew touched Maureen, feeling the forbidding landscape of her clavicle through her T-shirt, he sensed the assertion of a new strangeness. She smelled like the airplane, vaguely clinical and foreign, nothing like her smell from their marriage—he remem-

bered the faint chivelike scent of her body underneath some rose perfume she had that always made him sneeze.

Maureen pulled away and patted him neutrally on the shoulder.
"How are you holding up?"

"Okay," said Andrew. "You know."

Maureen nodded and gave him that rueful look of hers he sometimes found so annoying—there was something about it that reminded
him faintly of an expression of reproach, as though Andrew had failed
her terribly but she was going to be a tremendous good sport about it.
Maybe that was the problem with this family—they were all in direct
competition with one another to see who could bend over backward
the farthest, who could suffer the most. But then, Andrew reminded
himself, he and Maureen had unlinked themselves in order to disrupt
these precise dynamics. They were not a family anymore; they were
only old friends, and pretty decent ones at that.

"How is she?" said Maureen.

"She seems okay," said Andrew. "She's holding up."

Maureen raised an eyebrow, but Andrew already knew that this answer was insufficient. Over the brief years of Janie's life and death, he
and Maureen had developed an involved shorthand, rife with pseu-
donyms and talismans and symbols, complete with its own vocabulary
and syntax and etiquette. Certain euphemisms were encouraged; others were scorned. Referencing the possibility of Janie's death was unacceptable, but it was also unacceptable to use the phrase "passed away"
to refer to the deaths of the other children on the ward—and the other
children died, too; they died horribly and they died quietly and their
deaths were the deaths that prophesied Janie's death, that made it
thinkable though, of course, not endurable, and certainly never men-
tionable. When Andrew and Maureen were forced to mark the fact of
the other children's deaths, they did not say that those children had
passed away. They said that they had died. They understood—they had
tacitly agreed—that anything evasive was disrespectful. *She's holding
up* was, Andrew knew, just about the worst thing he could say to Maureen.

Maureen pursed her lips. "How does she look?"

"The same. Mostly."

"Did she seem upset?"

"I mean, not visibly."

"What do you mean, 'not visibly'?"

Andrew squirmed. "I mean—she wasn't crying or anything."

"She stopped crying already?"

"Had she been?" In every conversation Andrew had had with her, Lily had seemed tired but brave, determined to show him that she was as tough as they'd always told her she was. Andrew thought of her now—crying and concealing this in order to protect him—and he knew that this was a bigger and worse kind of trouble.

Maureen's face was crumpling into an expression of terrible kindness. "Do you want to come in and sit for a bit?"

In the room, Maureen's clothes were spread across the bed, delicate cardigans and wool pants, things that looked all wrong for the weather. Maureen always dressed cartoonishly warmly, because she was always cold.

"It occurs to me that I don't have anything to offer you that you don't already have in your own room," she said, peering into the mini-fridge. "You want a soda? Granola bar? Shot and a half of vodka?"

"I'm okay," said Andrew, sitting heavily on the bed.

"Did you get her those things she wanted?" said Maureen. She was still bent over the mini-fridge. "The tampons and the shampoo and whatnot?"

"Anna got them."

"Oh."

There was nothing fraught about this "oh"—no hint of surprise or guilt-tripping, just the monosyllabic acknowledgment of information received—but it made Andrew defensive nonetheless. "You probably know better how she's doing than I do, you know," he said. "I mean, obviously."

"I'm sure that's not true," said Maureen, standing up. "It's just that she talks to me. She's a girl."

"They were all girls," said Andrew darkly. He wondered if Maureen had known about Lily's smoking, but he was afraid to ask; he felt that it would be understood to be his fault somehow—perhaps because he'd discovered it, perhaps because of some kind of labor division he'd never been briefed on (Maureen handles the sex, Andrew handles the carcinogens?)—and that he'd be revealed as a fool for not knowing why.

"They were all girls," said Maureen. "But you really can't blame me for that."

Andrew nodded, though part of him vaguely suspected that he could, a little. It wasn't that he didn't love his daughters—and yes, in a way, he still loved Maureen, with a strange and calcified love. But the fact of their united femininity could sometimes seem a bit prosecutorial.

Suddenly, a whip-crack sound issued from outside. "Jesus." Andrew hurried to the window. "Is that a gun?"

Maureen joined him. Across the street, in a small park, two young men were indeed holding guns, though nobody around seemed particularly nervous, besides a flock of scattering birds.

"I think they're just trying to spook the pigeons," said Maureen. She had not jumped when the gun went off. It was admirable and also suspicious, this tendency of hers not to jump.

"I wonder why," said Andrew, though he wasn't really wondering. He went back to sit on the bed.

Maureen lingered a moment, staring into the gathering darkness. "What did you think of the lawyers?" she said, turning around.

"They seem competent," said Andrew. This was a keyword from assessing Janie's doctors in the days before the Internet—when, after poring over medical texts at the library, after seeking third and fourth opinions, Andrew and Maureen had had to basically guess at who was right and what was true. The sheen of competence had always impressed them. It seemed possible to smell bullshit, and fear, even if you didn't know all the details.

"Good," said Maureen, coming to join Andrew on the bed. She

squeezed his hand dryly, asexually. Andrew looked down at hers—it was sturdy and unadorned, slightly shaky from the effects of the terrifying boatloads of caffeine she must have consumed. He knew she was letting him off the hook—that it was understood that there was more to say, but that, for now, she was going to pretend that he had said enough. "Well," she said. "I think you know what we could really use about now."

"Some crystals," said Andrew automatically. "Maybe in a pendant or something." It was generous of her to give him the punch line to this most ancient and exclusive of in-jokes—dating back to the day during the darkest season of Janie's illness when the hippie neighbors had called and invited Andrew and Maureen meaningfully over for tea and then had clutched their hands and given them a pile of greasy crystals instead. Maureen had laughed-choked-cried afterward: *Crystals? They schedule a fucking appointment like that and then they give us fucking crystals? Crystals? Crystals?* She'd said "crystals" over and over, with slightly varied intonations and ever more absurd facial expressions, until they were both laughing, laughing a complicated and manic and dangerous laugh on the floor, letting their aging bones hit hard against each other's, commenting on the amount of grime that had been allowed to grow on the linoleum. It was the grime of people on the edge, said Maureen, and then they'd laughed some more, but not because it wasn't true. In those days, Andrew had been closer to Maureen than he could have imagined being to anybody else—they'd had a closeness that was stranger and more frightening and more desperately necessary than anything he'd felt during the early days of their love. Maureen was the only one who could possibly understand the central fact and premise of his life; speaking to anyone else began to feel like a theatrical performance in which Andrew was increasingly badly cast. But this kind of closeness could go on only so long. After everything was over, they'd had absolutely nothing left to say to each other.

"A crystal pendant would be nice," said Maureen. "Though I'm thinking this situation might require more serious crystal intervention." She lay back in a chaste and exhausted heap, and Andrew followed her.

"Can you mainline crystals, I wonder?"

"Oh, that's an idea," said Maureen. "Maybe you can ask your students?" She was quiet for a moment, and Andrew imagined what the two of them would look like from above. They were two terrified teenagers in a foxhole, two infant children terminally conjoined at the cranium.

"I can't believe she did a cartwheel," said Maureen, not opening her eyes. "I mean, who knew she could even still do one?"

"Well, we spent enough on gymnastics."

"Christ, did we," said Maureen. "So many lessons."

So many lessons, it was true: art and music and ice-skating; Lily's every fleeting interest enthusiastically, abundantly indulged. Not to mention the many more practical investments—chemistry tutoring when she struggled, English enrichment when she excelled, SAT courses to propel her to the school and then, presumably, the career of her dreams. What costs had been sunk, what objections had been suppressed, to deliver their daughter into the open and waiting arms of her beautiful life.

"Whatever happened to her oboe?" said Andrew.

"That poor oboe. It suffered so much."

"Remember *Oklahoma!*"

During Lily's rendition of "People Will Say We're in Love," Maureen had leaned over to Andrew and remarked on how very much their daughter sounded like a Canada goose, which had made them both laugh hard enough to be shushed by other parents.

"God," said Maureen, laughing. "What a terrible mother I was."

"Speaking of terrible parents," said Andrew. "I went to see Sebastien LeCompte."

"Did you really?" Maureen's voice was hoarse, and Andrew thought of how tired she must be. "What's he like?"

"He's absurd. Affected. He looks like a homosexual pirate."

Maureen moved her head in the way she did when she was acknowledging that what you'd said was funny, and that she would laugh if she had the energy. "Well," she said, "she inherited her mother's taste in men, didn't she?"

"He looks like a postapocalyptic butler."

"A butler *and* a pirate? Astonishing."

"But he believes her."

"Of course he believes her. Why wouldn't he?"

"A reasonable question."

"I'm always reasonable."

"I know," said Andrew, a little testily. It was true: Maureen always had been reasonable. He was starting to wonder if all this reasonableness was maybe part of the problem.

"I want to say we should have never let her come here, but that's stupid," Maureen was saying. "This could have happened anywhere."

Maybe all the reasonableness—the latitude, the lessons, the open avenues of communication, the *floods* of communication!—was exactly their mistake. Lily had learned the oboe, sort of—but she had somehow never learned that the universe needed no excuse to fuck with you, no excuse at all, so you sure as hell better not give it one.

"It could have happened anywhere," said Andrew. "But it happened here." Lily. Dear Lily Pad. For the first two years of her life, she'd been their "only living daughter," their "sole surviving child"; she had been their gem—hard-won, hard-edged. They had harnessed their sadness in order to raise her, like rivers diverted to run beneath a city. After all of that, how could they not have told her everything she needed to know?

"Did we do this wrong?" he said.

Maureen was silent for a long while, and Andrew wondered if perhaps she had fallen asleep. But finally, just as he was about to tiptoe out of the room, she spoke.

"We may have to consider," she said, "that we have done a few things wrong."

CHAPTER SEVEN

February

On Monday morning, Eduardo went to the office an hour early. He had a meeting with Katy Kellers's family.

Above him, the sky was perfect, smugly blue, with a few blushes of clouds off in the west. On Mondays, Avenida Cabildo was covered with the weekend remnants of Universidad de Belgrano students' cavorting, and Eduardo kicked aside beer cans as he walked to the car. At nights he could always hear the young people laughing and roaring. They were, it seemed, a sentimental generation; they loved Cristina Fernández now that she was a widow and a populist. These students were so different from the students of a decade ago, when Eduardo had first moved to Belgrano—those kids had been broadly antipolitical, eternally unsatisfied, forever shouting Que se vayan todos! in the streets—but one thing the students seemed to share was a need for everyone to hear them, no matter what they were saying. Lying in bed at night, Eduardo would catch snatches of their conversations, the sonar rise and fall of their voices. The politics changed, but the talk stayed the same—always performative, always self-impressed, whether they were debating a debt default or complaining about a recession or adopting that tone of awful jokey charisma they thought might (finally!) get them laid. Eduardo could only figure that they talked so loudly because they thought they were brilliant and hilarious and that they were doing everybody in the neighborhood a favor by making them listen. Eduardo could not ever remember feeling that way; as a student, he had been cowed and chagrined. Though he did think he could remember—even now, as he dodged a patch of pink vomit, state funded, student produced—how the city had seemed grand to him once, how it had once had a certain clarity. When you're young you think it's the clarity that's intoxicating; later you realize you were only ever drunk on your own vision. Perhaps Lily Hayes, when she'd first come to Buenos Aires, had felt something similar.

On Eduardo's desk was a note from the secretary saying that the Kellerses were going to be late. Eduardo sat and called down for the newspaper. When it arrived, he was not surprised to find a grainy Lily Hayes staring back at him from the front page. The picture was a still from the Changomas security videotape; in it, Lily's face was tense, her expression suggestive, Eduardo thought, of some kind of barely subdued rage. Inside the paper, the story of Katy Kellers's murder was described in lurid fonts and blaring tones. Eduardo read with mild interest. The media was usually, though not always, a help to the prosecution. This made sense, in a way: After all, the media wasn't some abstract monolith; it was composed of people, people who—like everyone else—wanted a story they could believe. And by the time a defendant made it into the news, there was a high likelihood that that defendant was, in fact, guilty; the state had already applied its considerable resources toward establishing that truth. This presumption of guilt bled into the reporting, of course, and the handling of Lily Hayes's case was no exception: The media had managed to unearth everything she had ever written online (the coarse and callow emails, the narcissistic and weirdly long-winded diary entries on publicly viewable journals, the Facebook status updates that had endured out in the ether,

long after she'd forgotten them) as well as everything anyone had ever
written about her (her childhood friends had some interesting stories).
Eduardo was aware that all of this gave him an unfair advantage. Nevertheless, he could not bring himself to regret it. He was glad to live in
a nation that spent some amount of attention on the victims of crimes.
How could a country like Argentina be otherwise? You brutalize a
people for long enough, and they start paying pretty close attention to
brutality.

The Kellerses were announced, and moments later they appeared—
mother, father, and remaining daughter, all huddled in a little unit.

"I am so sorry for your loss," said Eduardo, extending his hand to
Mr. Kellers. This was the truest thing, and the most important thing to
say, and so it came first.

"Thank you," said Mr. Kellers. He took Eduardo's hand slowly, as
though he were moving through water, though his handshake, when it
finally came, was firm. His wife and daughter hung behind him. They
were small and fair and wore expensive-looking yoga clothes—soft gray
workout pullovers that looked like they were made of cashmere, form-
fitting black breathable fabrics that clung to their shapely hindquarters.
The whole family gave off some kind of sleek Los Angeles glamour even
though, as Eduardo kept having to remind people, none of them were
in the movie business. Glamour must have been in the air out in California; at a certain point, one absorbed and internalized and metabo-
lized it. And Eduardo could see how telegenic this family would be,
how tearful and wholesome; he could see how, in their press confer-
ences, they would almost certainly say the right things. It was not cynical to notice this. It was Eduardo's job to notice this. And the only way
he could help the Kellerses now was by doing his job very, very well.

Eduardo ushered the family into chairs and offered them glasses of
water. They responded with syncopated thank-yous, vacant and reflexive. When you looked at them more closely, the wages of their grief
became more apparent. The sister's lips were so dry they looked nearly
shattered. The mother's hair, pulled back tight into a ponytail, had
clearly gone without its touch-up dye job for longer than was typical; a

few stray hairs, white and brittle, fanned out from the part in her hair, where Eduardo could see a few blushes of skull, pink as the interior of a seashell.

His heart broke for all of them.

As quickly as possible, Eduardo explained to them the contours of the case—his belief in Lily Hayes's involvement, the certainty of another person's, his confidence that he was on the verge of putting the entire puzzle together. The Kellerses nodded in staggered nods, baffled and bereft.

After he had explained everything he could, Eduardo attempted a few forays at small talk (how had their flight been, and what arrangements had been made, and could they tell him a little bit about Katy—this last elicited such a soul-rending whimper from the mother that Eduardo found himself leaning away from her, as though he could somehow physically retract the question). At a certain point, Katy's sister began crying quietly, and the way her mother comforted her—giving half-conscious strokes that disowned with every gesture the idea that any of this could actually be made survivable, while quietly beginning to cry herself—made it clear to Eduardo that this was a scene that had been repeated many times already, and would continue long after they were back in Los Angeles and their part here had been concluded.

On their way out the door, Mr. Kellers paused. "How long have you been doing this work?" It did not sound challenging. He was just trying to keep track of all the new realities. That was his job.

"Seven years," said Eduardo.

"Do you get a lot of convictions?"

"Yes."

Mr. Kellers nodded crisply, as though pleased with a purchase, though both he and Eduardo knew that he had no choice about Eduardo.

"We'll meet in a few days," said Eduardo. "Once you've all settled in and have had a chance to process things a bit."

They nodded. Eduardo walked them out to their rental car. Mrs. Kellers produced sunglasses from her bag; they were huge and ornate, a throwback to less utilitarian times than these. The sister did not have any, and she looked painfully away—Eduardo had to think on purpose—into the sun's wretched brightness.

By the time Eduardo got home that night, a storm was starting. It was only seven o'clock, and he peered warily into the yawning maw of the evening; he could feel the black edge of depression clamping down on his shoulders already. Sometimes he thought of it as weather, and sometimes as a wild beast. Most often he thought of it as the lid of an enormous pot in which he was being set to boil; sometimes—like tonight—he could almost hear it clattering above him.

The wind was making heaving sounds, shuddery and mechanical, and the air smelled vaguely brackish. Eduardo gazed out the window into the rapidly descending darkness. He suddenly felt that he was staring into, or out of, a great shroud. He shivered and went upstairs to turn on the television. There was a thumping sound from somewhere downstairs, and he congratulated himself for not jumping. He went to close the windows in the bedroom. There was another thumping sound, this one undeniable. Perhaps the house was being robbed; perhaps a disgruntled former defendant had come back, finally, to kill him. Eduardo considered this possibility with abstract interest, then went downstairs.

Standing just outside the open door, her hair streaming wet, was Maria.

"Can I come in?" she said. Her face was electric, aflame within the wild dendrites of her hair. Eduardo felt as though he'd been slammed into a wall. He stepped away from the door to let her inside.

"I'm sorry. I still had a key," she said irrelevantly, holding it up and then falling into Eduardo's arms. He held her numbly. Because of the rain on her face, it was very hard to tell if she'd been crying.

"What's happened?" he said. "Are you okay?"

She looked up at him and laughed a little. "I'm sorry," she said. Her mouth was full and dark. "Do you mind if I take off my shoes? They're wet."

"Everything you're wearing is wet."

"You're so literal."

Maria kicked off her shoes and padded barefoot to the window. Her dress was plastered to her body. She was dripping on the carpet but did not seem to notice.

"What's wrong?" said Eduardo. She needed money, probably. If she did, he would not need or want to ask why. If she said she needed it, he would believe her. Everybody should have someone whose belief in them is unwavering, unconditional, always. "Do you need money?" he said. "Is that it?"

Maria shimmied her head in a gesture that was neither affirmative nor negative—it was more like she was shaking water out of her ear, or a thought out of her head. She turned and stared out the window for a moment, and by the time she turned back her mood seemed to have already shifted. Eduardo knew better than to be surprised.

"Doesn't it look like magic outside?" she said.

"It looks like a storm outside."

Eduardo had never believed in Maria's sign reading and portents and impulses; toward the end, he had stopped pretending to try, and most of the time statements of this kind provoked something terribly decretory and disappointed from her. But this time she just looked at him and clapped her hands and said, "Oh, but storms *are* magic!"

Eduardo shook his head. Either everything was magical or nothing was. "Do you want to take a shower or something?" he said. "You must be freezing."

Maria ignored this and turned back to the window. "I hear you've got a big case," she said. "That murderer of yours is gorgeous. Don't you think so?"

Eduardo shrugged. He had never found Lily Hayes beautiful, particularly, though he respected her alleged beauty's effect on the case: If she was thought to be beautiful, then indeed she was. "Is that why you're back?" he said.

It had crossed his mind once or twice, it was true—the acclaim that might come with a conviction, the way it might hoist him up in Maria's esteem. The way it might make her see, finally—but then, he did not know, really, what it was he thought she'd see.

Her face froze for a moment, and then she pouted and smiled. "Aren't you glad I'm back?"

"I don't know. Are you going to stay?"

She shrugged. "Did that girl do it?"

"Yes."

"I think so, too," she said with sudden fervor. "Girls are strange." Her eyes were like black little embers now, bright and fierce. She laughed once, manically, girlishly. "But then again," she said, "maybe not. Maybe she really didn't do it. Do you ever think about that, Eduardo? About what if she didn't do it?"

She shimmered over to him and began nibbling his ear. Eduardo felt a sickening sense of suspension. "Maybe she didn't, Eduardo. Wouldn't that be tragic?"

He should not, and yet it did not matter if he did. He'd only be left with his own solitary ruined heart either way. "It would certainly be tragic if she didn't do it," said Eduardo formally. He covered his ear protectively so that she would stop nibbling it. "But I assure you that it's also very, very unlikely."

"She fulfills a certain role, though, don't you think?" Maria moved away from him and crossed her arms. "She's got a symbolic function. She animates certain feelings. She's like the sacrificial virgin. Or the sacrificial whore."

"You're not talking seriously," said Eduardo. "I understand what you're saying, but you're not being serious. You're not really talking about this particular girl. You're speaking very abstractly right now."

Maria sighed, delicately and emphatically. "I'm just musing, of course. You're probably right. I'm sure you're right, Eduardo. I have never known a man of as much generosity as you."

Eduardo knew in his heart that this could not be true. And yet, here she was. She was here. Her face was sweet and even. How could he not almost believe it was true? It took so much strength not to believe it.

"I've missed you," she said, and he gathered her into his arms. Her smell was heart piercing; it did violence to all other memories. She kissed him on the neck. Perhaps this was manipulation, but Eduardo did not want to be cynical enough to be sure. He was open to being wounded. He was willing to be wrong. This was, he thought, the cost of being alive.

"You're so good to me," said Maria, as he carried her up the stairs to the bedroom. She sighed. "I don't know what I would do without you," she said, as he turned out the light.

He could have left it there—he could have backed out of the room and tiptoed down the stairs to pour a tumbler of whiskey and marvel at the stunning luck of his own life—but he did not. He waited for a moment in the darkness. He wavered.

"Maria," he said finally. "How much is it that you need?"

She sighed again. "Oh, Eduardo," she said. He could hear her burrowing further into the sheets. "It's kind of a lot."

The next day, Eduardo awoke to even breathing. Beside him, Maria was a hummock of sheet crowned by a spray of dark hair. Strips of light from the window, fat and white as candles, were flattening themselves on the floor. And Eduardo felt a quiet elation that quickly turned to energy. He wanted to go to work.

He would not have expected this from himself. He would not have imagined that, having somehow conjured Maria's return, he would be willing to even momentarily leave her again—let alone that he would actually *want* to go back to the jail to listen to the tearful exegesis of a murderous postadolescent's life. Eduardo's work was performed from love, but it was a very abstract love; he would have predicted that, blessed once more with a love that was concrete—that was sleeping right beside him—he would retreat, immediately and gratefully, into happy selfishness. He would have expected himself to want only to lie here now, lazy with his own luck, and let himself forget about the dead.

But he didn't. Eduardo looked at Maria, and now, more than ever, he wanted to help them. Ever since he'd met her, of course, Maria had been the compass he followed when charting paths to unimaginable sorrow. He'd known that it was important to have some emotional access point when dealing with victims' families, and so when he talked with them, he'd often spent a moment or two (a moment or two was all he could stand) contemplating what it would be like to lose Maria to violence. He had imagined the phone call, the terrible certainty he was somehow terribly certain he would somehow feel. But then she had left him, and now she was back, and the miracle of her return made more vivid to Eduardo, somehow, the unfathomability of her permanent disappearance. He thought of his grief over the past months, and he saw how shallow it had really been; now when he thought of the Kellerses—the father's slumped shoulders, the mother's shattered face—he could suddenly imagine, more acutely than ever before, a sadness that would truly be unending. He could imagine their unendurable rage, and the way they'd have to live in that rage in order to live at all. And he could imagine—finally, fully, with a terrible clarity—their need to have all of this witnessed. Eduardo had always known that victims' families were not motivated by revenge—some kind of biblical, primordial desire for hurt to accompany hurt—and he had always believed that society was built on a question of witness. But never before now—as he sat gazing at his sleeping Maria—had he felt so fully the power of a love that kept looking. All these years later, the Mothers still congregated daily at the Plaza del Mayo, wearing their white shawls. This is what Maria would teach him.

Eduardo rose and went to the kitchen. He left out some fruit and instant coffee alongside a note saying that he would be back that evening. He was halfway out the door before he turned around and went back upstairs, pulled out his wedding ring from the box where he'd kept it, and put it on.

. . .

At the jail, Lily Hayes looked worse already, somehow. Her hair was duller, her eyes more glassine; there were pockets of gray underneath them, as though she'd been stroked lightly by ash. Grimy yellow light from the window cut strange angles on her face. Whether or not Lily Hayes had ever been beautiful, there was no denying the swiftness of her unraveling: She was simply no longer the girl who'd stood in front of the Basílica Nuestra Señora de Luján, wearing nothing, inebriated with her own youth. Eduardo was always amazed at how contingent good health and looks and spirits were; most people tended to look terrible and act even worse after just a few days in a jail, and Eduardo routinely left his interviews deeply unsure of the durability of character. The truth was, he did not know how he'd fare in Lily's shoes. The other truth was, he did not want to know. The final truth was, he would never do anything that would force him to find out, and this ignorance was the reward—and maybe the only sure reward—of virtue.

Nevertheless, it was impossible not to feel some pity for Lily Hayes now, so Eduardo let himself feel it. This was the worst she'd ever had it, and things were likely to get a whole lot worse. And it was possible, of course, that she didn't even believe she'd done it; it was possible, after all, that she had galloping undiagnosed autism or some kind of horrific chemical imbalance or that she had been sexually abused as a child. Most defendants Eduardo saw had had lives that were hard from the start, lives that would have required enormous effort and luck and preternatural goodness just to properly begin. Eduardo did not think that Lily's life had been like that, but still, he had to acknowledge that it might have been. And even if it had not, she still might not know, not really, what she had done. Eduardo had encountered cases like that— when the perpetrator took a while to fully believe it—and he could imagine few things worse than enduring such a realization. A person who had murdered had ventured onto unmapped territories; he could not put his trouble into any kind of redeeming context, or situate it within any kind of myth; there was no consolation in the universality or inevitability of the thing. It was irreducible, and the suffering a per-son must feel in such times went so far beyond the pale of normal human suffering—so far beyond the natural landscapes of grief and loss and heartbreak—that only generosity could be extended to him. He was utterly alone in what he'd done. All that was left was for the details of his interminable aloneness to be codified and solidified, made formal in court. For a man like Eduardo, who feared loneliness so mightily, this fate seemed worse than any.

"Can I have a glass of water?" said Lily. Her voice was froggish and lower than the last time he'd heard it.

"Later," said Eduardo, spreading his papers out on the table. He al-ways made an elaborate show of doing this, as though the papers be-longed in a very particular order. "I have a couple of questions for you first."

"You're wearing a wedding ring today."

Eduardo felt an instinctive pull to put his hand under the table, but he resisted it. "That's so," he said.

Lily tilted her head back to straight. "Perhaps congratulations are in order."

Eduardo leaned back. "We're not here to talk about me."

"What's that, some kind of therapy talk?"

Eduardo smiled benignly. "It's just a reality."

The bottom line was that whatever might be wrong with Lily Hayes was not what really mattered: Justice was on behalf of the dead, and on behalf of those who remembered the dead. It was on behalf of the no-tion that lives, even mortal lives, mattered.

"Tell me about your life here," said Eduardo.

Lily looked at him evenly and licked her lips. "It's pretty dull, actu-ally." Her voice cracked slightly, and Eduardo realized that, of course, she had not spoken all day. "You're probably the highlight."

Eduardo was glad she could still make a joke, though he did not smile at it. "Here in Buenos Aires," he said. "Before all of this."

"I've told you everything already."

"Tell me again."

"Tell you what?"

"You lived with the Carrizos?"

"You know I lived with the Carrizos."

"And you liked them?"

"I like them."

"Tell me again about the night Katy was killed."

"I've told you already."

"Tell me again."

"I went over to Sebastien's. We had a few drinks."

"How many drinks?"

"I don't know. A few."

"Three?"

"Maybe more."

"Maybe four?"

"Maybe five."

"Maybe five. Okay. And you smoked some marijuana."

"We smoked some marijuana, yes."

"And where did you get this marijuana?"

Lily hesitated.

"I can absolutely assure you," said Eduardo, "that this is the very least of your problems."

"Katy gave it to me," she said.

Eduardo raised his eyebrows. "Did she?"

"Yes. I don't know where she got it."

"I see," said Eduardo. She was obviously lying about the marijuana—most likely trying to protect some idiotic study-abroad friend of hers from getting thrown in prison; even Eduardo occasionally found his nation's drug policy somewhat overwrought—but it probably wouldn't matter. And if it did, Eduardo would remember. "And what time did you and Sebastien go to sleep?"

"I don't know. Four in the morning, maybe."

"Four in the morning, you say. Okay." If Eduardo had worn glasses, he would have taken them off now. Instead, he squeezed the bridge of his nose. "But you're a relatively petite woman, and you'd had five drinks, as well as some unknown quantity of marijuana. Can you really be sure of what time you went to bed?"

"I don't know. It was late."

"Can you really be sure of anything that happened that night, for that matter? After so much alcohol and marijuana?"

"I mean, it wasn't LSD."

"I'll make a note of that." Eduardo made the note sardonically. He wouldn't have had to make the note even if she'd said something real, of course. But he had found that the churning muscle of his memory was most formidable when he kept it a secret.

"I know I didn't kill anyone," said Lily. "And I know we went to bed late, anyway. It was late."

"And you didn't hear or see anything suspicious that night?"

"No."

"But again, you wouldn't necessarily remember."

"I'm pretty sure I would remember hearing someone get killed, actually." Lily was becoming agitated, though this wasn't overt in her mannerisms yet; her distress was only faintly roiling her expression, like an animal ascending to the water's surface from its depths. "I think it would probably make a real impression on me, in fact."

"Lily," said Eduardo, leaning forward. "I'm going to ask you to imagine something. If you had done this thing, why would you have done it?"

"I didn't."

"Let's leave that aside for now. I'm just trying to get a sense of how this could have happened. I know you want to help Katy. I know you would have wanted to help Katy. Do you have any idea why someone might have done this to her?"

"No," said Lily. "I didn't do it and I would never have done it and I can never, never imagine why anybody would. And you can't make me say that I can."

Eduardo leaned back. "Okay, Lily. You didn't do it, okay. But you have to admit that you might have."

"I did *not*. I might *not* have."

"What does that mean?"

"You're trying to trick me. You must think I'm really unbelievably stupid."

"Nobody's trying to trick you, Lily," said Eduardo. Saying "nobody" rendered specific accusations vague while making the accuser sound slightly schizophrenic. "It really is a very simple question."

"For Christ's sake," Lily snapped. "If I'd done it, I would have had the sense to flush the fucking toilet."

Eduardo raised his eyebrows and opened his notebook. *If I'd done it,* she'd said. And even though Eduardo would have no trouble remembering it, this was one thing that he actually did write down.

"Okay, Lily," he said. "You're right. Enough speculation. I'm going to ask you a very frank question now. Forget *why* someone might have done this. Can you imagine *who* might have?"

She shook her head, her dirty ponytail swaying thickly. What insouciance that might have communicated in better times! "No," she said.

"No, really? No, you can't imagine a single other person who might have possibly done it? In the whole city? In the entire time you've been here?"

"No."

"What about Carlos? I understand he has a drinking problem."

"No."

"No, he doesn't have a drinking problem?"

"No, he couldn't have done it."

"What about Beatriz?"

Lily laughed joylessly. "No."

"Sebastien?"

She glared at him. "*No.*"

"Why are you so sure?"

Lily Hayes was not alone in her sureness: The police had not arrested Sebastien LeCompte after his initial interrogation, and in his gut, Eduardo did not believe that Sebastien had been present at the murder. Nevertheless, it seemed to Eduardo that Sebastien LeCompte was somehow the crime's original mover, standing off in the shadows, beyond the particulars of the evening; the ultimate cause behind all of the proximate ones. Since Lily's arrest, Eduardo had gone three times to Sebastien LeCompte's mansion to try to speak with him. Each time, Sebastien LeCompte had seemed not to be at home—though this was unlikely, since every report about the kid suggested that he had neither friends nor gainful employment nor romantic involvements beyond Lily and possibly Katy, who were now respectively imprisoned and dead. It was much likelier that Sebastien LeCompte was hiding. But he could not hide forever.

"I know Sebastien," said Lily.

"Do you? How well?"

"Well enough."

"Not well enough to love him, though. So maybe well enough to know not to?"

Lily glowered.

"How do you think your friend Sebastien felt about Katy Kellers?" said Eduardo.

"I don't know."

"But if you had to guess."

"I guess he probably liked her."

"You said they were sleeping together."

Lily looked at him witheringly. "*You* said that."

"You mentioned in your initial conversation with the police that Katy had learned about the lawsuit against Carlos Carrizo from Sebastien."

"She said she had."

"Do you know why the two of them might have had occasion to see each other?"

"He did live next door."

"Do you think they saw much of each other?"

"I have no idea."

"But if you had to guess."

Lily sat back in her chair. "This conversation is getting a little boring, you know?" She cocked her head to one side. This was not, in fact, an original pose for a young person in custody. Defendants might not always be so direct, but Eduardo had seen the rest of it often enough—the attitude, the facial expression, the body language, all of it designed to say: *I've got bigger problems than you.* But they didn't. Lily Hayes certainly didn't. Lily Hayes had never had a bigger problem than this one. It was quite possible that, before this, she'd never had any real problems at all.

"Boring?" said Eduardo. "This conversation that is trying to establish your guilt or innocence in the question of the murder of your roommate? These questions that are designed to get us closer to knowing who killed her? They bore you?"

Lily drooped her head and said nothing. Her ponytail looked deflated. "Can I have some water?" she said.

"No."

"I have a right to water."

"I have some emails I'd like to read you first."

Lily paled. "No," she said.

Eduardo did not like doing this. Lily Hayes was young and she was lost and she'd done the most horrific thing imaginable, for reasons that were probably inscrutable even to her. She was in a strange country and she was probably never going home. Eduardo had not planned on reading her the emails today. But if she was already going to be combative, then he would have to be, too. He would have had to do it sooner or later, anyway, and one could even argue that it was better to get it over with. Fulfilling the inevitable early was often—although, of course, not always—a kind of mercy.

Eduardo cleared his throat and flipped to the most important email: a missive Lily had written to her father her first week in Buenos Aires. It was something of an introduction to Lily's world; as such, it would serve as a natural introduction to the state's case, and Eduardo would likely quote it during his opening remarks.

"'The roommate,'" Eduardo read aloud in English, "'is Katy. She spends a lot of time reading her economics textbooks. She's brokenhearted from the recent departure of her boyfriend—right in time for junior-year study abroad, and she's surprised!'" Eduardo delivered all of this deadpan. In another context, he thought, this might be hilarious—his ponderous voice with its notable accent reading the words of a simpering, self-righteous young girl. "'You'd think she never watched a CW teen soap growing up,'" he continued. "'Then again, neither did I—you wouldn't let me!—but I turned out reasonably savvy, I like to think.'"

Eduardo glanced up at Lily. Her face was stony. If anything was breaking anywhere within her, he could not see it. He hadn't been sure he was going to continue, but now he decided he would, because he could see that Lily did not remember what was coming next.

"'She's probably the most typical person I've ever met,'" he went on. "'Her life has been really easy. You can just tell. She is from California, after all.'" Eduardo put down the paper. Lily's face was implacable and still. Perhaps there was the faintest suggestion of something unearthing itself, but whether this was fear or anger or self-pity or true and genuine remorse, it was very hard to say. "You thought Katy's life was easy?" he said.

Lily nodded shakily.

"Do you still think Katy's life was easy?"

At this, Lily began to cry. Eduardo did not like to do it, but he pressed on.

"Should I read to you from the autopsy report? And then we can talk about whether Katy's life was easy?"

"No. Stop. Please stop." Lily's face was flushed and patchy. In spite of everything, Eduardo did not like to make her cry. This wrenching and diabolical thing that she had done would be with her forever; it would cast itself backward into her past; she would have to understand—and everyone else would have to understand—that it had actually been with her all along. Her parents would remember her as the addled, orthodontiaed teenager she had once been, and it would be there. They'd remember her as a quick-witted preadolescent and a chubby-limbed toddler and a squalling, wrinkled infant, and it would be there; her mother would remember her pregnancy—the minor lightning of the child quickening, gathering itself into its life—and would find that it had been there, too. What Lily had done to Katy would blacken Lily's whole life—its singular irreducibility would stain every soccer game and family outing and first kiss—just as it would elevate Katy's whole life, transforming every moment, no matter how small-minded or mundane, into something fated and futile and grand. Everything for both of them had been straining toward this dreadful black horizon; it had been everywhere, it had been everything, even if neither of them had known it.

Eduardo put the email down. "Lily," he said gently. "You're in trouble. You're scared. You're confused. Of course you are. Who wouldn't be? That's natural. And I don't know exactly what happened that night. But the best thing you can do for yourself now—and the best thing you can do for Katy—is to be completely honest. That's the best way. I've seen lots of young people in trouble like you, and I can tell you—and I'm telling you this in all sincerity—that nobody ever improved their situation by lying."

This statement itself sounded like a lie, Eduardo knew, but actually it was, in his experience, generally true. The sooner a person admitted to what had happened, the sooner they could begin the long hard work of living with themselves. Something like what Lily had done could never be made right, of course; it could not necessarily ever be made much better. But it could be made varying degrees of worse, and Eduardo believed that honesty was the way to avoid that. And one thing was certainly clear: Lily Hayes had not done this alone. And the best way to learn who she had done it with, for now, was by letting Lily externalize the scene; allowing her to watch it from a distance, as though it had happened in a movie, or to somebody else entirely. Once she could see it that way, they could work on getting her to pull back the curtain and see herself there, too, standing in the corner.

Eduardo put his hands on the folder, palms up, in a gesture he knew to be subtly imploring. "Did Katy have a lot of friends in the city?"

"Just from the program," said Lily quietly. "And just girls."

Just girls. As though your gender could absolve you. Was this clev-erness, or was this denial? Eduardo turned his hands palms down. "Is there anybody else she knew?" he said. "Anybody you can think of? Anybody who had a problem with Katy, or anybody she had some odd dealings with?"

"No."

"It's a big city. It's a dangerous city, to be frank."

"No." Lily's voice was shakier.

"Any boyfriends, other than Sebastien LeCompte?"

Earlier in the week, Lily might have told him derisively that Sebas-tien LeCompte was *not* Katy's boyfriend. But now she just shook her head weakly.

"You must have known somebody," said Eduardo. "You've been in town six weeks. You had the job at Fuego. You knew so much about the city."

"No."

"The only way you can help yourself now is to think of someone. That's the only way you can help Katy."

Lily shook her head, but Eduardo could see that she'd thought of who she would say, if she had to say someone.

"Just one name," he said. "Just one name, and we'll check it out."

She closed her eyes. The hollows under her eyes had turned the color of eggplant. "Maybe Javier," her eyes still closed.

"What?"

"Javier." She opened one eye.

"Javier Aguirre? Your boss at Fuego?"

She nodded.

"You think he could have done this?"

"No."

"But it's possible."

"Anything is possible."

It was true. Anything was possible. Maria had left once, and then she had come back again. Anything was possible, unthinkable beauty and unthinkable horror, both. The sooner Lily saw that the impossible was possible, the better it would be for everyone.

"Thank you, Lily. That's very good. Now. Can I get you a glass of water?"

CHAPTER EIGHT

January

Because she could not bear to ask Katy about the lawsuit, Lily began looking around the house for clues. She tiptoed past the Carrizos' bedroom and paused there, listening for revealing snatches of conversation, but somehow only ever heard the TV. She gazed at Carlos's face searchingly during dinner; she tried to use words like "corruption" and "fraud" and "disaster" to see if any of them stuck. She realized that she was half-hoping to be able to bring some kind of treasured bit of information back to Katy—to drop some spectacular revelation casually into conversation as though it were common knowledge and then widen her eyes in shock when Katy expressed surprise. *"What?"* she'd squeal gleefully. "You didn't *know*?" But in spite of her best efforts, often enough Lily forgot to spy and missed the best opportunities—when the mail came in, when the phone rang, when Beatriz and Carlos spoke in hushed murmurs in the kitchen.

Around Lily, the city flashed from spectacular to hideous to ordinary, like a sky in a fast-motion video. In a strange inversion of what she'd experienced when she first arrived in Buenos Aires, Lily found herself lost in extended reveries about New England. She remembered the brutal wheels of white light coming off the rivers; the snarl of lemon-colored leaves in the fall, making crisp fragile sounds like dead insects underfoot. She remembered the celestial whiteness of winter mornings, the clean searing smell of apocalypse. She remembered the languor and contingency and drama of the summer: the heavy sulfur smell before thunderstorms; the understated nodding of the leaves, like they were acquiescing or drifting off to sleep. She remembered the way the light tongued the bark of the trees on summer late afternoons, the heartbreaking sense of time passing, time passing, time passed.

She had been away, she realized, only a month.

And when she turned her thoughts back to Buenos Aires, Lily found that the city no longer seemed so exotic. She caught herself effortlessly riding the Subte, confident in all transactions and maneuvers, without secretly feeling very independent and proud. She knew which restaurants were overpriced and which buses had pickpockets and how to avoid them both. She knew to expect sloppy cheek kisses from perfect strangers, and she had learned, finally, not to look so surprised when they came. On the weekends, she watched the tourists carrying around their cameras, timid and admiring, and felt a certain scorn. Lily was different from them now, and better; she had more in common with the porteños than the tourists. And when she saw a HELP WANTED sign at a Belgrano café/club called Fuego, she felt breezy enough to go in and apply even though she didn't have a work visa. She walked out fifteen minutes later with a job.

Lily's boss at the café was Javier Aguirre, a Brazilian with incredibly black skin. Lily was not sure she'd ever seen a person with skin so black—there was almost a purity to it, she thought: This was how people were supposed to look, before they began migrating north to snowy climes and growing pale and dumpy. Lily broke a wineglass her first night on the job and her drawer came up short the second—but Javier seemed to believe that this was a failure of competence, not of honesty, and he kept her on. Both times, Ignacio the weeknight bartender gave Lily cigarettes and told her dirty jokes to cheer her up afterward.

"What do you want a job for?" Beatriz said one night, rinsing cucumbers at the sink. "Don't we feed you enough?"

Lily frowned. She didn't know how to explain it. "Of course you do," she said. "This is just for spending money."

But it wasn't, really. Lily actually liked working at Fuego. She liked the banter with the waiters and the customers, and she liked the happy noises a table made when she brought them a tray of drinks, and she liked watching the strange people she would never otherwise meet—Javier, with his impish, impossibly white grin; Ignacio the bartender, with his sleepy eyes and his face like a tortoiseshell; one very fat regular who came in with a rotating array of very thin girlfriends. It was hard work, and Lily always felt harried—but she found she sort of *liked* feeling harried: Sometimes she caught glimpses of herself in the bathroom mirror, looking young and tired and put-upon, and was surprised at how satisfied she was with the sight. She didn't look her most attractive in these moments, certainly. But she did look the least like herself she ever had in her life.

"For the weekends," Lily added.

Beatriz shook her head. "God knows what kind of characters you'll meet."

She was imagining alcohol consumption, no doubt, illicit drug use, various unnamable and unknowable extravagances at the home of Sebastien LeCompte. And so Lily added, "This is just for extra money. For books. For travel," even though it hadn't occurred to her until that very moment to travel anywhere farther than she'd already gone.

After starting at Fuego, Lily began to see less of Sebastien. He often texted her in the evenings—oblique and faux-literary missives that seemed to always begin mid-conversation—and she'd glance at them while working and somehow feel that she'd already responded even when she hadn't. After coming home late she'd scroll through all the communiqués she'd missed, shielding the light from Katy's sleeping face, and resolve firmly to answer them the next day. But in the morning she'd be racing to her classes, guzzling the dregs of the instant coffee that Katy had made, and she would forget again. Finally, one Friday night—after some negotiating and bidding and counterbidding—Lily agreed to go over to Sebastien's for a drink. It had been nearly a week since she'd last seen him.

They had planned for ten, but Lily did not begin walking across the lawn until ten-thirty. Underneath her flip-flops, the grass smelled vernal and sweet. She knew Sebastien would never mention her lateness, and she took a terrible delight in knowing this fact and exploiting it. It was the kind of thing a boy would do.

At the house, Lily knocked on the door with her knuckle—using that gargoyle thing seemed to be a concession to affectation that she did not wish to make—and Sebastien opened the door quickly. Behind him, the house smelled musty, and Lily wondered when he had last left it. The must, the dark, the unnerving declivity to the floors—why had all of this seemed so tragically romantic once?

"Well, *hello*," said Sebastien. "You're a vision for sore eyes."

"You look nice," said Lily. He did. He was wearing a jacket. And sometimes Lily liked to irk Sebastien by saying dull things. It was a habit she found herself falling into—the more he wanted to talk in the abstract, the more she found herself commenting on the softness of his hair, the radiant greenness of the trees. Was she trying to get him to like her less? She had to wonder.

But to her surprise, Sebastien actually blushed lightly and tugged at the ends of his coat. "Well. I do try. And how have you been filling the many hours since I saw you last?"

"Oh, you know," Lily said, wrinkling her nose and stepping into the house. "This and that."

"The rigorous demands of the intellectual life, I suppose."

"Yes." Lily leaned in and kissed him, feeling the warmth of his cheek, the sturdiness of his clavicle. He would be so lovely if only he would stop talking. "It's all very draining. As you yourself know, of course."

"Of course," said Sebastien. He retreated to the kitchen, returning a moment later with two glasses of something amber.

"And as it happens," Lily said brightly, taking her glass, "I got a job."

"A job!" Sebastien set down his drink. "How adorably plebeian of you!"

For some reason, Lily had not wanted to tell Sebastien about Fuego. She'd thought he might see through it somehow; after all, a person as fake as Sebastien had to have some otherworldly insight into other people's vagaries. But as soon as Lily walked in the house she'd realized, with a gnawing anxiety, that she had not thought to generate any backup topics of conversation, and could not quite think what else they would manage to discuss.

"A job!" said Sebastien again, clinking his glass against Lily's. "Workers of the world, unite!"

Lily had known he would react this way; provoking this exact mockery was the conversational favor she was doing for both of them, and the fact that it had worked made her both pleased and sad.

"It seemed like a good way to get to know the city better," she said, taking a sip of her drink. Whatever it was made her feel like a very old man.

"A plucky young lass, just trying to make her way in the world?"

"Something like that."

"I certainly hope you haven't resorted to selling your rare charms on the street."

"I'm a hostess at Fuego."

"How very prerevolutionary France of you!"

"I think they'll make me a waitress after a bit."

"Well, shoot for the moon and you'll land amongst the stars, you know. People were always telling me that in high school, and just look at me now. Am I not a truly serious and substantive adult?"

Lily kissed him again, just to make him stop talking. His mouth tasted clean. "No," she said. "Even if we are drinking brandy. Are you trying to be?"

"Not often," he said, and kissed her back, more earnestly. Sometimes Lily could almost feel his heart beating through a kiss, though that was probably impossible. She pulled away and stuck out her tongue at him.

"Do you even know what you mean half the time?" she said.

"I do not," he said regally. "And that, I like to think, is part of my own rare charm." This made Lily kiss him one more time and take his hand—which was rough and boyish and vaguely callused, though she couldn't think what he might possibly do to make it feel that way—and lead him toward the bed. She suddenly knew that now they would sleep together. She had never decided to, exactly, but she had also never decided not to, which was, under the circumstances, a kind of decision. And he was, after all, a very dear boy, if only he wouldn't say so much nonsense.

On the bed, they wrestled for a bit until the moment came when Lily usually put the brakes on things; this time, she did not, and Sebastien pulled her hand to him. She gave a tentative stroke. She always forgot how hard these things were, and how quickly they got that way—she felt a little startled, every single time. She was still holding her brandy with the other hand. She put that down. Her heart was hammering out its fear now—forget the bravado, okay, she admitted it, she still got nervous about this stuff. This was going to happen, she realized. She was young and single and living in Latin America, and she had an outstanding collection of condoms. This is what she was here for. Her teeth were nearly chattering. Sebastien was kissing her. He took off his pants and his shirt and he started in on hers, all the while looking deeply grave. Lily wished he knew that he didn't have to look that way. He was on top of her, then inside her. His entry was unremarkable. Afterward he looked at her with that wondering, faltering gaze of his and said, "I love you."

Lily had been weaving her fingers through his chest hair—she secretly liked it, though she knew she had to pretend to other girls that she didn't—but now she stopped. This theater—this feigned vulnerability of his—made something within Lily go stony and sour. She did not want or expect him to love her, of course, but she did not understand the use of this phrase as performance art, either; it made her feel uneasy and a little insulted, though she could not think quite why.

"Uh-huh," she said. "I'm sure." She laughed wryly to give herself a moment to figure out what to say next. She would have to settle for something idiotic. "So." She sat up and began twisting her hair into a ponytail. "I've been meaning to ask you. Why is your house like this?"

"Like what?" said Sebastien. Lily was not looking at him—she was busying herself with her hair—but she could hear in his voice an emptiness, an echoing distance, like he was speaking from the bottom of a canyon.

"You know." Lily shrugged, trying to think of the right word. She couldn't. "Huge."

"It was the ambassador's quarters."

"Your father was the ambassador?"

"You and your internalized misogyny."

"Okay. Your mother was the ambassador?"

"No, I don't think either of them were, as a matter of fact."

"You don't *think* either of them were?"

"But they were building a new ambassador's house, I believe, and the ambassador at the time didn't have a family."

"Wow," said Lily. It was strange to think of Sebastien in the context of a family—a little solemn, towheaded boy, world-weary at the age of three. "That must have made your parents pretty happy."

"Happy! What a bourgeois concept. I can see why old Andrew and Maureen are so badly off, if that's the standard they're holding themselves to."

Sebastien knew Lily's parents' first names because that's what Lily called them, but she realized now—too late—that she didn't much care for his using them. "And they let you keep the house?" she said.

"As it happens, yes, they did. In their enduring gratitude to my parents' ultimate sacrifice. *Dulce et decorum est,* and all. There are rumors, it's true, that they were building a new house and this one was going to be condemned anyway. But I'm not sure I believe it, since I try never to believe in metaphors."

"What were they like?"

"The metaphors?"

"Your parents."

"It's very hard to say for sure," said Sebastien after a moment. "I don't think we actually got the chance to know each other all that well."

"That's—wow," said Lily again, and cringed. She could not believe she had said "wow" twice in the space of a minute, but there was nothing she could do about that now. "That's hard to imagine. I know my parents too well. There's nothing they do or say or think that wasn't prophesied by Freud a hundred years ago."

Sebastien was silent, and something about what Lily had just said started to sound wrong to her.

"I'm really sorry about your parents, you know," she said gently. She really was. Maybe she should have said that earlier, but there was never a normal time to say something like that. "That whole thing must have been so shocking for you."

"Shocking?" said Sebastien. "Well, it wasn't philosophically shocking, of course." His tone was didactic. "When you're this rich you're smart to expect some catastrophe. Have I mentioned to you how absurdly rich I am?"

Lily blinked. "What do you mean?"

"Oh, surely you know. If the universe grants you some favor, it's going to remember it and eventually make you pay it back. With interest. With criminally predatory interest, quite often. You don't believe that?"

"Of course not," said Lily, trying to sound soothing. She had the feeling Sebastien was angry with her, though perhaps it was only grief that she was hearing in his voice. Grief, she knew all too well, could make people savage. "I just think there's good luck and bad luck and that's it."

"I suppose you're better off not believing it," said Sebastien dryly. "You'd probably have a lot to worry about if you did."

"Well, I don't know," said Lily. She was trying not to sound offended. "My family had a baby die before I was born, and then they were basically grumpy paranoiacs for my entire childhood, and then they got divorced, so I guess if I subscribed to your totally unsupportable worldview, which I don't, I'd feel like now nothing really awful is in the offing."

"Oh, I wouldn't be so sure," said Sebastien. "I mean, that's pretty small potatoes, don't you think? No offense, as the kids say. But you didn't actually know the baby in question, correct? No offense, again, *il va sans dire.*"

Lily thought of Janie's scowling face, the grim determination of her rocking-horse rocking in the photo above the mantel. "Correct," she said hesitantly.

"And your parents getting divorced, I mean, that's just statistics. Nobody's going to even buy you a sandwich over that one."

"I suppose not."

"And that's it? No other calamities, no other disasters?"

"Well, my grandfather—"

"Please."

"Okay. No. No other calamities."

"And none of the things that have happened to your family were in the context of an elaborate system of morally redeeming societal oppression?"

"Well—no. No oppression."

Sebastien frowned like a doctor about to deliver terrible news. "Then I'd say you've got at least one relatively dreadful thing ahead of you."

"Do I?"

"Some sort of medium catastrophe in your future, if my powers of prognostication do not deceive me."

"Like what?"

"Well, maybe your husband will have an affair, but not just any affair. He'll be a very public official and have a very public affair and you'll have to stand with him in the rain at a press conference."

"Okay, I can handle that," said Lily, then shook herself. "I mean, what? No. I'm never attending some douchewad's press conference."

"Or you'll contract some kind of cancer that's eventually curable but permanently disfiguring."

"That would be sad."

"But you'd feel lucky to be alive."

"Of course."

"Of course. Your type of person is always so embarrassingly glad to be alive."

"What type of person is that?"

"I mean, really, what's in it for you? That's my question."

Lily stood up and grabbed her tank top and her skirt. She faced the wall as she put them on, then sat back on the bed.

"Or maybe you'll have a child who will be limited in some emotionally and financially exhausting way," said Sebastien. "Profoundly disturbed, you know."

Lily was suddenly seething with a palsied rage. She was sick of her parents' pain, but she was also defensive of it, and she hated that it was regarded as so morally neutral, so meaningless. They had been lucky in a lot of ways, of course. But it was one thing to know that your privilege was unearned; it was another thing entirely to feel that your sadness was, too—to have to be so pitifully glad, so pitifully sorry, for the modest perks of a dull and diligent middle-class life (TV, and Target candles, and a trip to Six Flags every year). Maybe that's why the whole family was so repressed. Maybe deep down they believed—as Sebastien apparently did—that, on some level, at the end of the day, they'd had it coming.

"This is depressing," she said to Sebastien, putting on her shoes.

"Get used to it, is all I'm saying."

"I am used to it. I am used to nothing else."

"I can't imagine," he said. "My life's been a laugh a minute."

. . .

Back at the Carrizos', light was still coming from underneath the basement bedroom door. Lily glanced at her phone—it wasn't even midnight. She opened the door.

"Hey," she said cheerfully. She felt sure her face was still flushed, and she did not really want to talk about it. "What are you reading?"

"A chapter about resurgent protectionism," said Katy. "Did you know that every year there are four million tons of maize that farmers can't sell either here or abroad?"

"I did not," said Lily. For some reason, this came out in an overly jaunty, Sebastien LeCompte type of voice.

Katy looked up. "You slept with him!"

For some reason, Lily felt a momentary gaiety—she wanted to shriek, *I did not!*, like Anna might have done as a child in the face of a true accusation—but she forced herself to remain calm. "I guess I did," she said. "It was fast enough that it's a little hard to say for sure."

"You harlot."

Lily laughed mirthlessly. "I suppose." The flash of gaiety was gone, and she felt a strange numbness in her chest, a mournful aching under her left flank. Perhaps she was developing pancreatitis from all the wine. Perhaps service industry work was disagreeing with her. Perhaps she was finally getting old, as everyone had always assured her she one day would.

"So," said Katy, closing her book with a decisive thump. "How was it?"

"Okay, I guess. We got into a weird fight afterward." Lily patted her hip bones through her thin skirt; they seemed to fit awkwardly into their sockets now, like jigsaw pieces put in wrong. "And he told me he loved me."

Katy's perfect mouth fell open. "No," she said. "He did *not.*"

"He did."

"Holy shit."

Lily sighed. "I just wish he knew he didn't have to try so hard."

"Is that what your fight was about?"

"No."

"What was it about?"

"Luck," said Lily. "I think."

"So, I mean, what did you say?"

Lily exhaled heavily. She was sobering up, which made her realize she'd been a little drunk. She wanted to hang on to the plucky sense of savvy she'd had when she'd responded to Sebastien's declaration. She'd had things figured out then—only an hour ago—and Katy was mucking things up with her naïveté.

"I mean, what was I supposed to say?" said Lily. "I said, like, 'Oh yeah, uh-huh, I'm sure.' Or something like that."

"Lily!"

"What?"

"You didn't."

"I mean, *really*," said Lily. "He doesn't mean it. You've met the guy: He never means anything." Lily already wished she hadn't told Katy. It was so tiresome having to explain everything to her all the time. "Anyway, I'm not an idiot. I'm just kind of disappointed that he thinks I am."

"I don't know, Lily." Katy blew on her bangs; they puffed out like an animal projecting aggression. "What if he really does?"

"Ugh, you're such a romantic."

"Maybe. But we're twenty-one! We're supposed to be romantics. Who wants to be so cynical at our age? There's something wrong with you if you're so cynical at twenty-one."

"I'm twenty. I'm twenty-one at the end of the month."

"So there you go. That's even worse."

Lily turned her back to Katy and began to undress. Normally she was pretty immodest—not because she thought so much of her body, but because she thought so little of it (what kind of vanity was required to think your body was so special it had to be protected from sight, when billions, literally *billions* of people, were built exactly like you?)— but it seemed strange to undress in front of Katy now, when she'd been with Sebastien only a few moments ago. She thought it might invite a new kind of evaluative scrutiny she didn't care to consider too fully.

"So what are you going to do for your birthday, do you think?" said Katy.

"What?"

"You just said you're turning twenty-one soon."

"Oh. Yeah. On the seventeenth. I don't know. Nothing. Go out somewhere, I guess."

"You should see if your boss will let you have a room at Fuego."

"He won't," said Lily. In the low light, she could see the fans of blue veins skirting her upper thighs. She had a hard time believing she was actually warm-blooded sometimes—her blood was just so visibly *blue*; it looked Arctic in origin. She could feel the vaguely unpleasant dampness and stinging from where Sebastien had been. Her face was slightly raw from his; Lily always felt that she was being vigorously *sanded down* when she kissed a man.

"You never know," Katy was saying.

"Sometimes you do. My boss doesn't like me that much. I drop things and my drawer comes up short."

"You drop things?"

"Well, I dropped one thing. A glass. Not like a whole platter of things. But trust me, is the point, about the party idea. It's not going to happen."

"Fine." Katy took out her textbook again. "You're awfully dour."

"I'm not dour," said Lily, wincing at how much she sounded like her parents. "I'm just a realist."

CHAPTER NINE

February

One night, amid all the rolling around, it finally happened. That beat of lulled momentum—the point at which Lily usually turned over, or lightly took Sebastien's hand, or asked him some jejune question, or got up to get a glass of water—came and went, and she continued to kiss him, with more urgency than she ever had before. In Sebastien's head, constellations, luminous and slow moving, were created and destroyed. His hand crept slowly, and then faster, to the side table to produce an atavistic condom. Afterward he said, "I love you," matter-of-factly. He meant it. He did not mean anything, but he meant this.

"Uh-huh," said Lily. She was trying to sound savvy and cold, or maybe she really was. Years of reflexive mordancy had left Sebastien with few tools to assess other people's emotional states. All communication was maneuver. And he felt oddly alone in the bed afterward, with the sheets now twisted into knots and the room growing dark in the evening chill, and Lily only a foot away from him.

Then she'd asked him something about his parents. (What kind of criminally banal pillow talk this was! He blamed the American movies.) She'd said that she was sorry about them—and she did look sorry, though frankly she also looked a little annoyed at having to be sorry—and remarked that the loss must have been "shocking." And this—not earlier, let the record show, not out of any sense that he was entitled to love (hers or anyone's), and not from any wounded pride (he had no pride to wound)—was when Sebastien had become angry. Shocking? His parents' deaths were *shocking*? Yes, shocking, of course, though expectations being wildly subverted was not, in the end, the most challenging aspect of that whole ordeal. He'd thought of the picture of his father on the mantel; his father had been young in that photo, Sebastien realized, only a little over forty. Surely one still wanted things at forty. Shocking? Sure. But primarily devastating, shattering. Life ending, as Lily surely had noticed. The wrongness of the word made Sebastien bellicose, and he'd led them into a stupid fight—transparent, pitiful, composed of serious nonsense—in which he condescended and dismissed, offering dark prophecies about Lily's future and his own. He monologued about all the bad luck she would one day have, all the medium-sized difficulties that would one day befall her. He didn't really believe any of it, of course—he didn't really believe anything—and he could feel the mood in the room darken: first with Lily's anger, then with her pedestrian defensiveness, her need to let him know that she had suffered enough already. That's all anybody wanted anyone to know about them—how hard it all had been, how valiantly they had tried, how much unseen credit they were due. Sebastien was tired of it. Sebastien was tired of everything. With every twist, Sebastien could feel the conversation taking him further away from Lily, but still he could not stop. He could have reached out then and touched her, he knew, except somehow it wouldn't have mattered. It would have been the same as not touching her. It would have been the same as getting up and closing the door and never touching her again.

. . .

Somehow, Lily's days were beginning to trace the same emotional arc, over and over again. She'd wake up in the mornings feeling jaunty and electrified, thrilled by her own life. She was young and nothing was really nailed down yet: It was true she was no longer a virgin; it was true she was no longer undeclared—but really, in the broadest sense, anything was still possible, and what a wonder that was. She walked around the city in the afternoons, watching herself in the third person—alone at cafés, at museums—and she mostly saw the person she had always wanted to watch herself be; a person for whom all the best things were still ahead. This feeling came back to her at nights, as she walked back to the Carrizos' from Fuego or from Sebastien's, the lights of the city shimmery and seductive all around her. There was absolutely nothing like a city at night. It was so easy to believe that everything that could possibly happen was happening somewhere right around her—just behind a closed door, just beyond her field of vision. And for all she knew, it was.

But between the mornings and the evenings, something was going wrong. A feeling came pricking at Lily in the late afternoons, when the sun turned a certain sickening rubescent color, casting light that made all the buildings look like glowing cinders. In those hours, Lily felt that she was kidding herself—that some central fiction of her life was growing worn with overuse, and that one day it would tear through completely. She would fall into a shaky melancholy then, as though coming down with a strange late-in-the-day hangover, and would have to go somewhere bright and capitalist and unreal to try to cheer herself up. Sometimes she'd find herself at a Changomas, staring at the children's cereal, or at the movies, watching dubbed American films that seemed to always use the same voice-over actors. She generally tried to stay away from email—it made her life in Argentina feel contingent and small and less urgent somehow; she was on the other end of the world, and she wanted to feel like it—but sometimes in these afternoon moods she'd succumb to a kiosko, where she'd spend a couple of hours reading blogs devoted to badly written expressions of widely held opinions. She'd watch the irradiated lobes of the computers grow brighter and brighter against the falling darkness.

Then evening would come, and she would walk out into the streets and gulp the still-warm air. She'd remember that she was so far away from home that she could actually wear a tank top in February. She'd take off the sweater she'd worn against the air-conditioning in the kiosko or the theater or the store. There would be a mild breeze against her shoulders, and she would feel it creakily cantilever her into the evening. Her old innate optimism would return. She would sense, with the tender and turbulent joy of a granted reprieve, that her life was not yet over. And she would begin to feel much better.

Sebastien did not see Lily again for a time. She began to bob maddeningly in and out of availability: Texts went unanswered for days; plans were made and canceled and made yet again. When she did materialize, she was abstracted, distant, always smelling slightly of burned chorizo. All of this, she fervently attested, was due to that infernal newly acquired job of hers. She would have Sebastien believe, apparently, that she had truly become absorbed to distraction in the minutiae of utensils and tips and the wrangling of emotionally abusive customers. She would have Sebastien think, apparently, that his palpably diminishing relative claim on her attention meant nothing.

One Sunday night, after watching an Antonioni film they'd both pretended to like, Sebastien and Lily lay together in silence. Lily's head was on his torso and he was stroking a strand of her hair with his thumb, admiring its multidimensional shininess. He was acutely aware of the rising and falling of his chest.

"So," said Lily abruptly. "What are you going to do?"

Sebastien kept trying to slow his heartbeat down and found it galloping ever faster nonetheless. "When, my peach?" he said.

"Now."

Through the window, Sebastien could see the gathering blueness of late twilight. He hadn't yet thought to get up and light candles. "Likely kiss you some more," he said. "If you're amenable."

"In general, I mean." Lily rolled over onto her back. Sebastien could see a cuneate piece of flattish pale stomach right above her jeans; he could see the knobby handle of her hip bone. "In your life."

"I can't imagine what you're talking about," said Sebastien, even though he could.

"I mean, are you just going to stay here forever?" Lily stretched elaborately. Sebastien could not get over the outrageous, unfussy healthfulness of her body. You could just see her frolicking in some creek somewhere; catching little frogs and crayfish and things with her bare hands because she hadn't yet been socialized to think those things were disgusting.

"You've got all this money," she was saying. "I mean, what do you want to do with it?"

Sebastien had known this would come eventually, but he was sorry it was coming already. "Support a revolving cast of lovely women, I suppose," he said. "Until I age into impotence, at least."

"No, really," said Lily. "You're a smart guy." Sebastien winced at this. Nobody felt the need to remark upon intelligence that they actually believed in. "You've got to go back to school at some point, right?"

"Not really."

"You could get a job, you know. Have you ever thought of that? I mean, I know you don't need to. I know you don't need the money. But it might be good for you. It might be good for you to get out once in a while."

"I've been out plenty. I'm retired now."

"It might make you less depressed."

Sebastien turned his back to her and stared at the cracks in the wall. Maybe, in a way, this bossiness was a good sign—maybe instead of reflecting grievous disappointment, it suggested a certain proprietary concern. "Who's depressed?" he said. "Depression is for the middle class. I'm having the time of my life."

"So you're just going to sit here and rot then?"

"Well, I've got to sit somewhere and rot. It might as well be here."

"That's awful."

"I'm sorry," he said, and stood up. He could hear his knees crack, and it made him feel old. You had to live so terribly long to actually *be* old, but Sebastien was starting to wonder if people began to feel that way quite a bit earlier, and spent their lives waiting for their bodies to match their souls. "Could you tell me more specifically what you're imagining? Some kind of a start-up? Socially conscious investments? Venture capitalism? Get involved in the what—dot-com boom? I assume that's still happening? Or maybe it's not too late to cash in on the tail end of the Gold Rush." Lily was visibly waiting for Sebastien to stop talking, but he could not. "Or should I set my sights lower, perhaps? Start taking in washing from the neighborhood? What are we thinking here? You tell me."

"You mean to say your plan is seriously to just sit here and order takeout until the day you die."

"This is everyone's plan, broadly."

"You're just like my family."

"I have to suspect that's meant unkindly."

There was a long pause in which Sebastien could sense Lily circling around what she wanted to say, thinking better of it and then veering back toward it again, each time getting a little closer. "You just want to wallow—" she finally began.

"Wallow! Who *doesn't* want a good wallow?"

"You want to wallow in the passive acceptance of death."

"As opposed to what? The active rejection of death? Or the active acceptance of death?" Sebastien grinned to show her that it was not too late for them to stop it. "The passive rejection of death, perhaps?"

Lily laughed a little. "You're impossible."

"I just want to know what my options are here."

"You are. Impossible." She kissed him again then, hard, but it was a complicated kind of kiss, a little bit vicious and fierce, and when he peeked halfway through he saw that her eyes were still open.

Her second weekend at Fuego, Lily picked up an extra shift and forgot to call Carlos and Beatriz to tell them. Halfway through the second shift she remembered, but the club was slammed, and she didn't even have time to pee until her break. At ten-thirty, as she maneuvered a tray of cocktails over to a tableful of Belgians, Lily spotted Katy standing at the bar near the door. It was strange to see Katy here. From a distance, she looked shy and beautiful and wide-eyed—like some sort of nocturnal jungle creature, a baby ocelot or something—and Lily could see that she'd already attracted the vulture-like attentions of several tables' worth of inebriated young men, as well as Ignacio, the tortoise-faced bartender. Katy did not seem to notice any of this. Lily looked down at her hands, bald and raw from the scalding hot water, smelling like the stewed detritus of the sink where she had, moments ago, despaired of ever dislodging an especially despicable layer of grime from a pan. Looking at Katy, Lily realized that she felt strangely self-conscious, as though Katy had caught her wearing a costume for a performance she'd hoped would stay a secret. Once Lily had been cleaning up puke in the men's room and a man had come in and smirked at her and said, in English, "I bet you wish you'd gone to college." And along with her indignation, Lily had experienced a sliver of pleasure at being mistaken in this way. This *was* a costume, of course. She didn't really need this job.

Now Katy was talking to Ignacio the bartender, who was pointing to the alcove where Lily was standing. She looked down and busied herself with some silverware until she felt a tap on her shoulder.

"Oh, hey," she shouted at Katy, trying to look surprised. *"What are you doing here?"*

Katy shouted something back.

"What?" said Lily. She really couldn't hear over the music. *Me gusta marihuana, me gustas tú,* sang somebody or other. The song was pretty old. Lily thought she'd heard it first in college, freshman year, at a frat party. Middlebury didn't admit to having frats, but they did, and it was a frat where she first heard this song. Lily glanced around the club and noticed Ignacio staring at Katy with a frankly hungry look. When Lily caught his gaze he raised his eyebrows at her inquisitively and nodded his head in Katy's direction. Lily made a face at him and pulled Katy farther into the alcove, where they were partially obscured. Katy said something else that Lily couldn't hear.

"What?" Lily hollered again.

"I said, what?"

"The bartender is checking you out."

Katy looked quizzical. Lily cocked her head in Ignacio's direction and gave a cartoon leer. Katy peered around the corner and waggled her hand in a semi-thumbs-up.

"Ew," said Lily, wrinkling her nose. "Really?"

"What?"

"What?"

"You are late," shouted Katy. *"Come home."*

"I can't," shouted Lily. *"I am working till two."*

Javier came over then, suave in a blue tie, and pointed at Katy. *"Your friend can't be back here,"* he shouted to Lily. *"Unless she wants to put on an apron."*

"Two," said Lily again, holding up two greasy index fingers. Katy turned to go, and Lily noticed Ignacio's noticing her leaving. There was something strange about a look of such appetite on a face so reptilian— though, of course, poor Ignacio couldn't help his face. Still, Lily felt a cold paranoia cauliflower along her spine for a moment before Javier clapped her on the back and suggested that now would be a good time for her to think about trying to at least pretend to do her job.

That night, Sebastien sent a text at four a.m. and Lily woke up to read it but forgot to answer. She forgot the next day, too, and the next day, and by the third day responding seemed fake and forced, but she made herself do it, and she tried to sound as unself-conscious and breezy as possible—"Hey SLC, sorry I've been MIA, wanna hang out tonight?"— as though she was a very popular girl and he was one of her many, many, many friends, no less precious to her because he was one of so many. His response came a day later, flinty and stiff—"I'd hardly noticed. You know where to find me"—and Lily knew that she'd done the wrong thing again, that she always did the wrong thing. Sometimes Lily wished she could float along in the kind of lighthearted solipsism that prevented grudges and bad feelings and lingering entanglements, that made it impossible to take anything too hard. But things in Lily's life never worked out this way. Sebastien's attempted gift of the bracelet weighed on her heavily, as did the sex, though she hated to admit it. She felt somehow obligated to him now; she felt that she'd treated him carelessly, and though she knew she'd treated him no differently from the way that many boys had treated her—no differently from the way that Sebastien himself would likely have treated her, if she'd let him— she still couldn't shake the acrid feeling behind her heart, the queasy sense of revolving guilt.

She called Sebastien the next morning and proposed dinner. She would bring it, she said. Her treat. He assented.

At least, Lily told herself, Sebastien was unlikely to bring up her recent absence. That was something she liked about him. Stoicism was not valued at Middlebury, where everyone wanted to endlessly talk and process and expurgate every little thing. If you hooked up with a boy he seemed to feel he owed you a real-time narration of his entire life, a live-blogging of his every emotional memory. If Sebastien LeCompte had been a Middlebury boy, he and Lily would already have agonized ceaselessly over the nature of their relationship, the question of monogamy, the issue of forward momentum, the prospect of looming distance and separation, the meaning of things, the meaningless of things. What a relief it was to be excused from all of that, anyway.

"I think old Sebastien's mad at me," Lily said to Katy that afternoon.

She and Katy talked about Sebastien a lot, partly because they couldn't find much else to talk about. Katy's family, apparently, was too loving and functional to merit discussion. On the question of politics, Lily sensed a level of conflict aversion in Katy that suggested that there might be conflict to be had if Lily pushed it, which, of course, she tried very hard to do—making flamboyant assertions, quoting outrageous statistics. But Katy proved impossible to rouse; she never agreed nor disagreed, only asked questions aimed at making Lily clarify whatever she'd just said. So Katy and Lily spoke most often of men, and they spoke of Sebastien most often of all.

"Oh?" said Katy. She was sitting on her bed and rubbing silver-dollar-sized globs of sunscreen around her eyes and chin and onto her breastbone. The smell of coconut filled the room. "And why's that?"

Lily shrugged. "I think he's on his period."

Katy nodded. "How's the sex these days?"

Lily was surprised that Katy would ask, but did not want to seem surprised. She wobbled her hand. "So-so," she said. "Are you going to the beach or something?"

Katy looked embarrassed. "It prevents wrinkles."

"Aren't you twenty-one?"

Katy hung her head. "I'm paranoid."

"Oh," said Lily. "Can I have some?"

"Sure." She tossed the bottle to Lily. "You want to do your hands, too."

Obediently, Lily rubbed the lotion into her hands.

"Do you think you guys will keep up after you leave?" said Katy, and Lily felt the flicker of nervousness that always came when Katy was inquisitive about Sebastien. It was possible that Katy still felt bad about calling Sebastien a bore, now that it was clear that Lily was going to keep seeing him. But somehow Lily suspected that there was more to it than that—that these conversations were Katy's way of being elaborately careful with her, as though Katy had decided that Lily was a person who required special handling, or special patience—and Lily did not like the thought of this one bit.

"Oh, who knows," said Lily. "Probably not, I guess."

Above them, Lily could hear the satisfying whir of Beatriz running the vacuum cleaner. This was one of Lily's favorite sounds of domestic life, alongside the sound of coffee brewing: It made her think of mornings, of getting the house ready for company. She closed her eyes for a moment to listen.

"No?" said Katy.

Lily opened her eyes. "I mean, let's be realistic."

Upstairs, the phone rang.

"He could visit you," said Katy. "It's not like he can't afford it."

Lily shrugged and scrunched her nose. The phone rang again. "I think I'll grab that," she said. She ran up the stairs, Katy following behind her.

Upstairs, the living room was flooded with light; the red curtains were waving slightly in the breeze, revealing and then obscuring a faint weal of cloud in the sky. The vacuum cleaner stopped, and Lily heard the distant, plangent sound of cathedral bells. The life these people had! She could stay here forever. She took a breath. The phone rang a third time.

"Sí?" said Lily, nearly breathless.

There was a pause.

"Ah, is Carlos Carrizo available?"

"I'm sorry, he's not here right now," said Lily. "May I take a message?"

There was another pause, and Lily reached down to the side table drawer to find a pen. When she opened it, she saw an ominous pile of paper: heavy documents and folders covered in what looked like some tedious bureaucratese. She didn't recognize the words, but something about them seemed heavy, resonant. Spanish, she decided, was too lovely a language for such matters. She shrugged the phone into the crook of her neck and motioned for Katy to come look.

"What?" Katy mouthed, but she didn't come over.

The man on the phone was giving his name and number, and Lily scrambled to grab a pen. She was writing the number on her hand as

Beatriz appeared at the top of the stairs, a basket of laundry on her hip. The man hung up.

"What are you doing?" said Beatriz. Her face was frozen, her eyes lightless, her hair pulled back very tight. Lily was still holding the phone, and she placed it back in its receiver overly carefully, as though she might now earn some belated credit for conscientiousness.

"I was just taking a message for you," she said.

Beatriz began to descend the stairs slowly, and Lily knew that the coming conversation was not going to be a good one. She wanted to turn around and catch Katy's eye, but she was somehow afraid; there was something so uniquely awful about the anger of an adult you did not know well. When did adult strangers ever get mad at you? Never in real life—only on the road or on the Internet. Lily flashed to an image of herself as a small child, being yelled at by a friend's mother for some infraction that was too abstract to be comprehended at the time. She remembered her terror; her strange distorting sense that the universe was actually aligned against her, and that maybe it always had been and she just hadn't noticed until then. Beatriz reached the bottom of the stairs and put down the laundry basket.

"Why did you answer our phone?" she said. She was not yelling.

"You weren't answering it."

"I was vacuuming."

"I was just taking a message for you."

"Do not answer our phone in the future. Do you understand? I assure you, the calls coming in are not for you."

Lily felt the strange cresting behind her nose that sometimes meant she was about to cry. "I didn't think they were," she whispered. She didn't understand why she felt so terrible. She hadn't done anything wrong. "I was only trying to help."

"And those?" Beatriz pointed to the disordered documents, still poking out of the open drawer. "What did you think you were doing with those? Helping?"

"Nothing!" Lily slammed the drawer shut. "I was just looking for some paper. I didn't see anything, I promise."

Beatriz moved back a step and took a deep breath. Lily could tell from her expression that she must look terrified, and she watched Beatriz decide to take things down a notch.

"In the future, please be respectful of our privacy and our home." Beatriz's voice was softer now, but Lily could hear how hard she was trying to make it that way, which was almost worse than if she'd sounded as angry as she actually was. Lily finally turned and looked at Katy for backup, but Katy's face remained open and neutral, ready to believe and be believed. If Beatriz had come down thirty seconds later, she would have found both of them looking at those papers. Katy would have come over to look. She would have. Lily was sure of it.

"You have a very lovely room downstairs," said Beatriz, picking up the laundry basket. "You should have everything there that you need. If you require something else, please ask me first."

With that, Beatriz took the basket down to the basement, and in a moment Lily could hear the washing machine.

Katy made a whistling sound. "Yikes," she said. "That was bad luck."

Lily dragged her thumb along the table near the phone. She wished there was some dust to pretend to brush off, some minor disorganization to feign absorption in, but the Carrizo house was always so spotless.

"What did those papers *say*?" said Katy after a moment.

"That's the thing," Lily said. "I don't even know."

By the time Lily hurried up the path to Sebastien's that night, pizza wedged on her forearm, she was already in a terrible mood. She had disappointed Beatriz, and now she was bound to disappoint Sebastien. It was a simple inevitability. She rang the doorbell and waited.

But really, she told herself, it was okay to try a little less hard for a boy. Sometimes when she thought about all the work she'd done in her life to make sure the men she knew were having a comfortable enough time—the vast amounts of effort she'd spent on this!—she had to cringe. With boys who were particularly recalcitrant on the phone, she'd sometimes actually written out questions to ask them before calling them up. Had anyone ever gone to such lengths for her? Would she have even wanted them to? Lily had earned a certain amount of disregard, she figured, and now was the time to extend it.

Sebastien appeared at the door after a moment. He was wearing a chestnut-colored waistcoat, the kind of thing you saw on academics in movies though never, in Lily's experience, in real life. His hair was appealingly mussed—it was growing out a little, which she loved, though she didn't dare tell him that for fear he would cut it out of spite. She smiled her friendliest smile. "Hello," she said. "Aren't you warm in that coat?"

"It's the mythical Lily Hayes! Goodness gracious!" he said, throwing his arms up and pretending to fan himself. "To what do I owe this rare honor?"

"I brought pizza," said Lily, still smiling. "Do you like pizza? You were an American teenager once."

"I was never an American. Nor, in the strictest sense, a teenager."

Lily gritted her teeth. "Can you forgive me nonetheless? And could you let me in, maybe? I want to set this down."

"Forgiveness is tedious," said Sebastien, ushering her through the door. Inside, the house was sweltering, lit by a bunch of candles that seemed now to have mostly burned down, making the room look wavering and medieval. Lily set the pizza on the dining table.

"You and your proto-Christianity, your Neoplatonism," Sebastien was saying. He opened the box and eyed the pepperoni skeptically. "Ah, and your pork products. Well, I guess living in a constant state of smug forgiveness is fair compensation for the freedom to consume unclean animals on your pizza. That's the great and central trade-off of the Abrahamic faiths, I've always thought."

"We can pick them off if you don't like them. And I already know you're angry with me, so you don't have to make quite so many allusions. And, I mean, you're not even making sense, even in terms of just your own internal logic, right now."

"Angry with you, my jonquil! Perish the thought."

"I'm sorry I was so out of touch this week," said Lily carefully. "I was busy."

"I understand. I've been swamped with a million and ten things myself. The kids and their interminable soccer practices, don't you know."

"Sebastien. I said I was sorry."

"And I said I was indifferent."

For some reason, Lily didn't want Sebastien to know how tiresome she was beginning to find him. She didn't want to admit it entirely to herself, either; she felt premature nostalgia (already!) for the way she'd felt about him in those first few weeks, and she still held out some slim hope that the feeling might return. There were moments, after all—there was a certain way Sebastien had of looking at her when she first arrived at his house, his face open and unguarded and so beautiful in its architecture and its youth—that still made her stomach flip. But then he'd begin to talk; invariably at length, invariably ironically, and Lily would feel herself drifting off somewhere. One time Katy had compared Sebastien to a dead fly frozen in the amber of his house, and this image, worryingly, had stuck with Lily.

She found two dusty plates in the cabinet, rinsed them, and put them down on the table. She put slices of pizza on each of their plates, then took a bite of hers. Sebastien did not.

"Are you on a hunger strike?" she said. He looked shiny and a little unwell, and Lily felt—acutely, momentarily, and for the very first time—the paucity of her attraction to him. "Would you care to state your demands?"

For once, Sebastien LeCompte said nothing.

Later, after a fitful and underwhelming round of intercourse, Lily was restless. She sat on the edge of the bed, facing away from Sebastien, and put on her bra. It was still early; the stars were dim topazes in the sky, only beginning to leak their modest light. The fight with Beatriz crouched on Lily's sternum like the pressure of an oncoming heart attack. She sighed heavily. Sebastien said nothing. Lily wanted to go somewhere. They never went anywhere. She sighed again.

"Something troubling you, my sweet?"

"I'm bored," said Lily, ferreting into her tank top. "Can we go out?"

"Where would you like to go?" Sebastien was lying on the bed, still naked. He was exotically non-shy about nudity. Before sex, Lily always liked this quite a lot about him; afterward, she liked it a little less.

"I don't know." Lily rotated her shoulders in their sockets. They cracked audibly, and she was glad when Sebastien flinched. "Just somewhere. Out. You pick."

Sebastien sat up and looked at her with an expression of intense mock-seriousness. "Lily Hayes, are you perhaps not your very best self tonight?"

She spun her shoulders again, though this time they didn't crack. "Maybe not," she said.

Sebastien sat up. "What's wrong?"

The straightforwardness of this took Lily by surprise—she'd expected him to maintain his usual tone—and made it seem possible, all of a sudden, to tell him what had happened. Not that it could help— you might as well talk to a Magic 8 Ball about your problems. But she supposed it couldn't hurt much, either.

"I got in trouble with Beatriz," she said.

"Again?"

"Yes, again." The situation seemed monstrously unfair somehow— bigger and more serious than a mere misunderstanding—though Lily still couldn't quite pinpoint why. Sebastien stood up, put on his boxers—finally!—and came to sit next to her, resting his head on her shoulder. Lily knew he meant it ironically—it was a commentary on, a parody of, such gestures—but his hair was soft, and his skin was warm, and she hoped that he would stay there for a minute, anyway.

"I certainly hope *I* wasn't responsible," he said.

"Not this time, you'll be relieved to know." Lily's fingers wound their way into Sebastien's hair and stroked his skull lightly—he was so well made, really. "She freaked out because I answered their telephone."

"The gall!"

"I know! I mean, in general, I understand why Katy never gets in trouble. Katy never sneaks out at night, for one thing."

Sebastien's eyes flickered lightly. "Doesn't she?" he said, and Lily felt again the fleeting, uncomfortable suspicion that everyone around her knew more than she did.

"Well," she said. "I guess I don't know. I mean, I do sleep in the same room as her, though. She'd have to be a pretty good sneaker to sneak out all the time. And she doesn't really seem like the sneaking type."

"Hmm," said Sebastien. Lily stopped stroking his hair and patted his shoulder so that he'd sit up.

"But I mean, getting in trouble for stuff I actually do wrong is one thing. Getting in trouble for something like that while Katy is standing *right there* is just dumb."

"It's the principle of the thing, you're saying? Abstract notions of justice and right?"

"It's that Beatriz just hates me no matter what I do. It's like, if Katy and I are both doing the *exact* same thing, Beatriz attributes benign intentions to Katy and malign ones to me. But maybe I have benign intentions, too. Sometimes, at least."

Sebastien pulled her to him then. He smelled slightly oniony, which Lily sort of liked; she found herself pleasantly surprised by his moments of undeniable masculinity, and the way they offset his light eyes and freckles and cerebralism. Sometimes she wished she could tell him this; so many times when he went on and on and on she'd wanted to take his hand or grab his thigh and tell him, *Stop it. Just stop it. I was impressed already.* But she felt that this would disappoint him somehow; that it would be vulgar; that it would be conventional. And sometimes Lily wondered if maybe she wasn't the person he was actually trying to impress, anyhow.

"Benign intentions?" said Sebastien, kissing her temple. "I thought you were a wicked woman."

"I guess maybe I am," Lily said glumly. "I mean, that seems to be the prevailing assessment."

"All right, my sulking salmon," said Sebastien, clapping her fraternally on the shoulders. "Let's go out. I'll grab my walking stick."

Outside, the moon was huge and cantaloupe colored, looking too heavy for the sky. Lily had thought the walking stick thing was a joke, but Sebastien had indeed produced one from one of the cavernous back rooms and now carried it majestically, tapping on the ground from time to time. His parents had bought it in Fiji, he said. It had chips of abalone shell that glowed like the eyes of something nocturnal, and Lily gave it a wide distance as they ventured through a thin woods and over a small hill toward where Sebastien had said there was a river.

Lily wanted to frolic. The creepiness of the walking stick made her nervous in a giddy, childish, not entirely unpleasant way. And outside, in this soft summery evening, the trouble with Beatriz did not seem so important. You could not get everyone to like you; you could waste your whole life trying, and still it would not work. Lily did a cartwheel. Sebastien held the walking stick in the crook of his elbow and golf clapped. She did another—passably, she thought. They were pretty hard to do now; she had no idea when they'd become so difficult. But this was like a lot of things, she supposed—you wandered away from something for what felt like a minute and by the time you thought to come back to it, it had already been gone for a very long time.

Lily had only three months left in Argentina.

They walked until they reached the river. Above it, the sky was clear, and the moon was so big that Lily could see its whorls; it looked like a chalky thumbprint in the sky. The moment might have been romantic—Lily could feel Sebastien gearing up to take her hand, to kiss her—but she wanted to shake off the feeling. She felt mischievous, scheming; she wanted to make Sebastien do something frivolous, something that he simply could not look cool while doing. She didn't know why she hadn't thought to take him out earlier. It had always seemed too egregiously typical, she supposed. But now she saw that being in the world had wrong-footed Sebastien in a way she rather liked; she felt that she was now on a sort of home field advantage.

"Do you want to play Pooh sticks?" she said.

"What?"

"Like in *Winnie-the-Pooh*?"

"I'm afraid I'm unfamiliar."

"You never read *Winnie-the-Pooh*?"

"My parents' tastes skewed more continental, I'm afraid."

"You drop a stick in the water and see whose stick gets to the other side of the bridge first."

"It sounds like a thrill."

"Well, it was a game for fictional stuffed animals, so yeah. It's dumb. Let's play. Find a stick." Lily had never thought to do this before, either—to just go ahead and tell Sebastien to do something. She was forever being deferential, forever letting him set the terms of their conversations, forever allowing him to lure her farther and farther into swampy and sardonic terrain on which she'd never have a hope of standing upright. But now they were outside, and the sound of the river was making it hard to banter, and Lily knew that Sebastien would do whatever she told him to do.

"What?" he said.

"Go find a stick," she said severely. "Make sure it's a good one."

Sebastien gave her a baleful look and walked off into the woods. Lily ran off into some scrubby weeds and found a twig. She ran back, breathless. Her hands were dirty. This was friendship; this was the stuff of memory and future nostalgia. They reconvened on the bridge.

"Okay," she said, peering into the water. Below them, the river was roiling obsidian; the reflection cast by the moon was shaky and insubstantial. "Let go."

They let go. Lily grabbed Sebastien and pulled him to the other side. A stick emerged a moment later, and then another. "I can't tell which is which," said Lily. She was laughing a bit more buoyantly than she ordinarily might. This was her little impulsive adventure, after all, and she knew she had to make it feel as though they were having joyful and terrifically arbitrary fun. In the modern world, this was usually the girl's job. She'd seen enough movies to know.

"It's mine," said Sebastien. "I'd recognize it anywhere. Mine won."

"You cheated!" said Lily. She hit him. She'd been planning on accusing him of cheating all along, no matter what happened.

"You let me win!" he said.

Lily spanked him playfully and then grabbed his hands and pulled him to the ground. She was trying to be a spritely elf of high spirits and curiosity. She was trying to be a person who might cause trouble sometimes—but only because she was so lively and nonconformist, only because she was so special, and not because she ever meant any harm.

Lily strung her fingers through Sebastien's. They lay in the grass for a long time and Sebastien told her many things about the constellations. And although Lily knew for a fact that at least some of the things he was saying were wrong, she decided to pretend that she did not.

That night, lying in bed—after taking off her shoes in the entrance, carefully picking her way across the linoleum, and closing the door to the basement with the most exquisitely gentle of clicks—Lily could not sleep. Within her, a tremendous sea of unease was twisting into a cyclone; the dreamy magic of the evening was over, and she was left with a stark and uncomfortable fact: Beatriz hated her. Beatriz *hated* her. And not just for things she did, but for things she had not done. Katy managed to fly below the radar, and why was that? Was it only because her face was so pretty, and so pretty in such a sweet way? Was it because she never ventured an opinion at dinner? Or was there something she was actually doing right, something that Lily could actually learn from? Was it true that Katy was somehow paying more attention?

Lily sat bolt upright. "How did you know they were being sued?" she said.

It was possible that Katy was asleep—it was late, the lights were out, and Katy had not spoken when Lily had entered and climbed the ladder to the top bunk, her toes painfully monkeying around one rung and then the next—but somehow, Lily did not think so: The room vibrated with some other awareness, and Lily suddenly felt sure that Katy had been waiting for her.

There was silence. Lily felt the minor heave of Katy rolling over. "Sebastien told me," she said at last.

At this, Lily nearly bonked her head on the ceiling. "Sebastien told you? How?"

"I went over there to ask him."

Lily lay back down. Her heart was pounding. She tried to keep her voice steady and light. "I didn't know you guys were friends."

Lily could feel Katy shrug. "We're not, really."

Not really friends, as Lily well knew, could mean any number of things. It could mean enemies, or frenemies, or fuck buddies, or fuck frenemies, or any countless variations thereof. It would be far too horrid to ask for clarification, of course, so Lily did not. "I thought you couldn't stand him," she said instead.

"Well, I said we *weren't* really friends. And anyway, no, I can totally stand him."

A realization was opening up in Lily, a knowledge of galactic vastness and obviousness. Of course. She thought of the way Katy always steered the conversation toward Sebastien—who really cared that much about some other girl's sex life? She remembered the night after that first dinner, when Sebastien and Katy had stood on the porch together—Sebastien looking flustered, Katy smoking a cigarette (who would have thought?). Lily had seen them from the basement bathroom window, though she hadn't cared enough to really think about it at the time. But she saw now that Sebastien had probably preferred Katy from the start and had settled for Lily only as a consolation prize. And perhaps the two of them had had some ongoing whatever—

attraction or flirtation or fling—its exact nature did not really matter; it did not really change anything. Sebastien might even really love Lily, for all she knew, with a sort of diffuse, redirected, anonymous love. That's how most boys were, in her experience; they could love with real tenderness, but their love was almost always aimed at a woman's most generic qualities—her sweetness or softness or relative beauty, her archetypal feminine characteristics, whatever Freudian maternal shadows she cast—and so it was fungible, nonspecific. Empty, finally, even if it was technically real. Just look at Harold and the accounting major! Lily had been wise to practice a strategy of passive resistance, of conscientious objection, throughout that entire relationship. Boys were all the same, even Sebastien, who had seemed so promisingly weird. All he really wanted was a woman (any woman!) who was sweet and reasonable and attractive. And Katy was all of these things—she was, in fact, more of these things—than Lily would ever be.

"Anyway, he may not be my favorite person in the world," Katy was saying. "But it's very obvious he's totally nuts about you."

To this, Lily said nothing. She rolled over. She stared at the ceiling for a long while. She did not sleep. And this time, she was positively sure that Katy was not sleeping, either.

CHAPTER TEN

March

On Wednesday, the DNA results came in.

As Eduardo had expected, there was nothing of Sebastien LeCompte anywhere in the house. As Eduardo had also expected, there was nothing of Javier Aguirre, the nightclub owner whom Lily had named. What was more, Aguirre had supplied an ironclad alibi—a night at a strip club, complete with security footage you did not want to see and bookended by ATM withdrawals. The DNA that was all over the crime scene—in the semen in Katy's body, in the spots of blood on the carpet, in the contents of the astonishingly unflushed toilet bowl—derived from a man named Ignacio Toledo, who'd been a sometime bartender at Fuego and had apparently not shown up to work since Katy was killed.

Toledo had been arrested twice before—once for possessing paco cocaine and once for vandalizing a car, though what he'd really been trying to do, no doubt, was steal it. He'd testified against his friends both times and had spent eighteen months in Villa Concepción for the second conviction. He didn't have a history of violence, at least not that the state had noted, but that did not matter. We all create our histories as we live them; every killer had once lived many years as an innocent. And if there were two great democratizers of violence, in Eduardo's experience, they were prison time and paco cocaine.

As Eduardo had further expected, there were also several substantial signs of Lily Hayes at the scene of the crime—on Katy's mouth (the defense would try to explain this via the improbable CPR), on one of Katy's bras (Eduardo couldn't quite imagine what they would come up with for that one), and, most incriminatingly, on the knife. Eduardo knew what the defense would say about that: It was a kitchen knife, after all, to which the whole household had had access. In the interviews Eduardo had conducted, neither Beatriz nor Carlos Carrizo could summon a single memory of Lily cooking anything, ever; furthermore, Lily herself had never once mentioned cooking in Eduardo's previous conversations with her, during which he'd established an extensive accounting of all the usual aspects of her daily life. Still, the panel would likely find it perfectly plausible that Lily *might* have handled the kitchen knife at some point during her stay with the Carrizos— and really, who could be perfectly sure that she had not? In the end, in fact, it was the bra clasp that was murkier—and in some ways, more important. Here was an object that Lily should have had no occasion to handle, and here was proof that she had.

"Why did you tell us that Javier Aguirre did this?" Eduardo asked Lily. She was flanked by her two lawyers, who had been hired days ago by the Hayes family but only recently become cognizant, it seemed, of their client's ongoing propensity for unsupervised chats with the prosecution. Eduardo knew both of them slightly: Velazquez, whose bald head gleamed so forcefully it looked spackled, and Ojeda, who was so fat that you had the sense that, if you were very, very quiet, you might actually be able to hear him getting fatter. Ojeda was good at his job— he was brilliant and ruthless and clinically efficient—and he deployed his fat, Eduardo was sure, as a method of getting people to underestimate his capabilities. Eduardo couldn't help but feel a grim admiration for this tactic, as well as a certain affinity with it. Velazquez and Ojeda would forbid Lily, of course, from speaking with Eduardo in any more conversations pertaining to her role as a defendant. But her mention of Javier Aguirre as a possible suspect meant that any hypothetical prosecution of him would mean Eduardo's calling Lily as one of his own witnesses, and even Lily's lawyers could not stop him from speaking with her about that.

"I didn't," said Lily.

"You could be charged with slander, you know. There could be a civil case."

"I didn't tell you that he did it."

"Do you want me to read you the transcript?"

"You forced me to say someone!"

Eduardo pretzeled his face into an expression of bewilderment. "How did I force you? Were you threatened? Were you in any manner physically coerced?"

Lily looked down. Her unwashed hair made heavy curtains around her face; behind it, her eyes were quartzitic and glittering. She did not answer.

Eduardo leaned forward. "Why, Lily? Why did you name Javier? Did you have problems with Javier? Problems at work?"

Lily shook her head. "I never had a problem with Javier."

"He did fire you, though."

"For the party, yes."

"I've heard you were having problems before that."

Lily bolted upright. "Who said that?" she said. It would have been touching were it not so perverse: She actually still cared about how her job performance had been perceived.

"You dropped things, I understand. Your drawer came up short."

"I was new!"

"You gave us this name, Javier Aguirre, and that has led us down the wrong track."

"I didn't mean to."

"But we've been on the right track all along, haven't we, Lily?"

"All right," said Velazquez, standing up. "That's enough of this."

At night, Eduardo listened to the recordings of his interviews with Lily, hoping to hear something new. It seemed to him that time had forked lately, that his life was running on parallel tracks. In every moment there was Maria: her smooth back, the aquiline sweep of her nose, the perfect and enduring certainty of her sleep. And in every moment, simultaneously, there was Lily; fragments of Eduardo's conversations with her coursed through his consciousness likes tides.

You slept all day, you're saying? And you didn't think it was odd that Katy didn't appear? Not even once? You didn't think to look for her?

I did look for her. Jesus Christ. I found her!

Again and again, Eduardo listened. Again he pressed play, and again he was walking into the jail, his dress shoes squeaking against the floors, the sense of obdurate underlying filth everywhere made more potent by the astringent smell of cleanser all around him. In every moment, it seemed, he was staring at those same taupe walls, the light through the high windows above them alternately gray and dull or yolky and rapturous, depending on the time of day. In every moment, it seemed, he was standing underneath the enormous PROHI-BIDO FUMAR sign, wishing he could have a cigarette, his head growing marginally lighter with either fury or discouragement or settled, piercing clarity.

But you didn't think to look for her earlier.

I thought she was asleep.

On the tapes, Lily's voice had a slight elusive lisp that Eduardo had never noticed in real life. And the tapes had other, less trivial secrets to reveal. Slowly, Lily's connection to Ignacio Toledo was taking shape in Eduardo's mind. At first, Ignacio Toledo did not seem to fit into Lily's life. But once you looked closer—once you knew Lily Hayes like Eduardo did—you saw that, in fact, he did.

Most important, perhaps, he was the opposite of Sebastien LeCompte. Sebastien LeCompte was handsome, for a particular taste, as well as wealthy beyond imagining. But he was also, by all accounts, impossible: sphinxlike, maddeningly detached, forever circling around life and speech, both, in half-ironic, riddle-filled whirlpools. What better rebellion for someone like Lily than a night with a man who was none of these things—a man who was uncomplicatedly masculine, straightforwardly working class? This was the girl, after all, who'd taken photos of a pantsless boy, a deformed woman: a girl on a quest for authentic Argentinean grotesqueries, things she could do and see so that later she could tell about having seen and done them. Next to Sebastien LeCompte, Ignacio Toledo would seem completely real and more than a little dangerous.

Lily would not have known how dangerous, of course, when their night began. But then, she would begin the night not knowing how dangerous she herself could be. And so the evening would begin with a minor cruelty: her rage at the breakup with Sebastien and his involvement with Katy would lacquer over her smaller rage at being fired from Fuego, and she would go there to find Ignacio Toledo, the one person with whom she could exact revenge on everyone—Sebastien and Katy, Javier, even Beatriz Carrizo (who would surely have blanched at the thought of such a man in her house for tea, let alone for homicide)—all at once. It was masterfully efficient, really, even if Lily had not been entirely aware of what was impelling her moves that night, as Eduardo presumed she had not been—her motives were massed within the mammoth blue iceberg of her subconscious, looming undetected below the blind, white fragment of her thoughts. And so Lily would go to the club as it was closing, perhaps not quite knowing why, but feeling reckless and competent and bold. You look upset, Ignacio Toledo might say to her, and offer her a drink on the house. I'm not supposed to be here, she might say. He would raise his eyebrow and press a finger to his lips and say, I won't tell.

From then on they would be coconspirators—first in a second drink, maybe, and then a third. Afterward they would leave the club, and at some point Toledo would produce the paco—and although Lily did not take it (her drug tests revealed only marijuana), its nearness would give her a proxy shot of adrenaline, a mutinous thrill at witnessing something so much closer to real subversion than whatever was voguish among the high-achieving white children of Vermont. Eventually Ignacio Toledo would propose some plan for the evening, and Lily would agree to it. She probably hadn't known him well—that much was probably true. But she'd wanted to have an adventure; she'd wanted to go out and explore the dark corners of the city. And, at this point in the evening, Ignacio Toledo probably still felt like something of a chaperone.

Eduardo did not doubt that they had not planned to kill Katy. The unflushed toilet alone made this clear. But they'd gone back to the house—drunk and high and wanting something from Katy that she would not give, or perhaps trying to give something to her that she would not take: drugs or sex or money (hers or, perhaps, the Carrizos') or some combination thereof. And perhaps Katy had threatened to call the Carrizos, or perhaps the cops, and suddenly Lily—her aggression deformed by drugs, her inhibitions shattered by alcohol—felt all of her resentments surge forth into a rage. This violence was not inevitable for her; she was not a person who would have killed somebody eventually anyway, no matter what course her life took. But she had always been a person who *could* have killed somebody—as, in Eduardo's experience, a terrifying number of people were. It was this potential, ultimately, that she'd brought to the crime. Ignacio Toledo brought the drugs, the criminal history—maybe even the idea, the initial spark of brutality that set that whole room ablaze. But Lily had brought the template: the latent sociopathy, the entitlement. And, in the end, she'd brought the opportunity. After all, she had provided the house—there was no sign of a break-in—and, in doing so, she had provided Katy.

Again and again, the tapes ended; again and again, Eduardo climbed into bed next to Maria. It was her return, he knew, that had enabled him to see the truth in Lily—that had given him the courage to keep looking until he saw it—without being blinded by the wrong stories or paralyzed by their repetition. The television people were obsessed with Lily Hayes, as well as entirely convinced of her guilt. But it had become clear to Eduardo over the weeks that they were convinced for all the wrong reasons; their certainty might be correct, but it was essentially reactionary, unearned. The world did not know Lily like he did. Stills from the security footage were paraded alongside pictures from Lily's own camera, and the TV was forever running images that were widely thought the worst: There was Lily at the church, her bosom spilling wildly; and there she was mid-kiss with Sebastien on the day of Katy's death; and there she was in front of a condom display, her eyebrow raised into a bemused isosceles triangle, only a few hours later. Those photos were bad, of course. But, Eduardo thought, they were not as bad as the others, the ones that didn't feature Lily herself—the woman with the blood blister, the small naked boy. That's where the real Lily Hayes was—not as a subject of the photographs, but as their merciless off-stage director. It was too bad, Eduardo often thought, that the TV didn't run *those* photos. But expecting the media to realize their significance would be like expecting a dog to look where you were pointing, instead of at your finger.

Whatever the quality of the world's certainty, Eduardo still liked to imagine delivering the justice that it wanted—this was, of course, only human. And he knew that if Maria hadn't returned to him, he could have drowned in the potential consequences of success, as well as the potential costs of failure. It was true that Eduardo had failed before. Not often, but occasionally—once quite notably, when an accused murderer and rapist, fully prosecuted in the media, had been let off because a junior policeman had behaved cavalierly with the crime scene semen. This had not been enough to disqualify the case in and of itself, but the fervor—the "zealotry," a stern TV commentator had said—with which the DNA had been collected had meant that the most important piece of evidence had been disallowed in court. Eduardo's arguments were worth nothing then. After the verdict, he had walked out of the courtroom and into a cluster of journalists punching away on their obnoxious little BlackBerrys, which they'd all managed to buy before the shortage. Eduardo had been all over town looking for one—to Movistar in Palermo, to Claro in Recoleta—but to no avail, and so he had to walk all the way back to the office to begin sending the necessary apologetic emails.

And if Maria had not returned to him, Eduardo could imagine losing himself now under the weight of his fears, the shadow corollaries of his each and every hope. If she had never left him, in fact—if Eduardo had never known the pain of that loss—things could be even worse than that: He might have become consumed with worldly ambition, the wish to have this success propel him solidly into the professional realm he deserved to inhabit—the realm she deserved to have him inhabit—so that their lives might thrum, at last, to some sort of hazy, satisfying conclusion. But losing Maria and then getting her back again had given Eduardo a deeper vision of loss, just as Dostoyevsky's mock executioners must have given him—as he rose, shaking, to find himself still alive—a keener understanding of the resurrection. Eduardo was wiser now, and he was able to look, and listen, and be ready for whatever he might learn.

All day? You thought she was asleep all day?

I was asleep.

Eduardo's certainty was no longer growing. But it was moving. It was shifting from his cerebellum to his gut: His hair pricked now when he heard Lily's voice on the tapes. He did not yet know how the killing had transpired, exactly, or what strange combination of drugs and lust had fueled it. But now—when he looked at pictures of Lily's oddly faraway expression, that strange flatness around her eyes—he was beginning to understand, more viscerally than he ever had before, that she really had done the thing he was saying she had.

You were asleep, or you thought she was asleep?

I don't know. Both.

You were simultaneously asleep and under the impression that Katy was asleep?

Their conversations threaded around so much that Eduardo would sometimes grow confused by their redundancies, their repetitions, their minor adjustments in syntax; he'd feel himself getting lost in the sifting of relevant and irrelevant changes.

And then you attempted CPR.

Yes.

Had you ever performed CPR before?

No.

Had you ever taken a class on how to perform CPR?

No.

So tell me again exactly what you were trying to do?

And yet Eduardo persisted, letting Lily's voice echo within him as he got ready in the mornings—staring into the chrome mirror with one eye closed, shaving incipient whiskers off his chin. Every day Eduardo looked the same, and yet there was a part of him that believed he was watching himself grow better, and that one day all of this virtue would suddenly reveal itself somehow.

Tell me about Sebastien LeCompte.

I have told you everything I know.

Remind me.

Literally everything. I have told you things I don't even know.

You've told me things you don't know?

Because you made me guess.

You've lied to me, you're saying.

No!

Eduardo knew he should never be grateful for his work, since having work to do meant that evil had been done, and that suffering had occurred. And so he tried not to think of this new momentum as a kind of happiness, though of course that's what it was.

You didn't like Katy. There's no crime in that.

I did like Katy.

You didn't.

And even if I hadn't—

Even if you hadn't, what?

The truth would emerge, like secrets rising out of the sea, like fossils stepping out of their clay, like everything that makes us understand our world and, at long last, ourselves.

But you were nice to Katy, nonetheless.

Yes.

Nonetheless what?

What?

You just said you were nice to Katy nonetheless.

You *said that.*

In every moment, Eduardo was tiptoeing into the bedroom; in every moment, Maria was putting down her book in a hurry. She was fiercely private about what she read for reasons she would never discuss. Eduardo had learned long ago that Maria's secrecy could hurt him if he let it, and that ignoring this secrecy was his only armor, inadequate though it was.

"What does she say?" Maria would ask, putting down her delicate gold-chained bifocals, hiding her book underneath the sheets. Her toenails were buffed to opaline; her skin was nearly translucent. In the light of the reading lamp, she seemed to glow from within.

"I can't tell you that," Eduardo would say.

"She isn't saying anything. I can tell."

"She's not saying anything she hasn't said already. I'm listening to tapes."

But this wasn't entirely true. Lily may not have said anything new, but Maria had taught Eduardo to listen to her anew—and upon reflection, he had realized that the most damning thing that Lily had said in the interviews was not something that either of them had even realized was damning at the time. Argentina had always felt like a dream, she'd said. Nothing that had happened to her there had ever seemed totally real. And the night she killed Katy, Eduardo now saw, must have seemed the least real thing of all—merely the part of the dream that curdles into nightmare in the final dark moments of the night. It must have seemed as bad as that, and nothing worse. It was Maria who had taught Eduardo to see this; it was Maria who had taught him to look beyond the signifier to the signified. He would tell her some of these things one day. He would thank her for them.

"Patience, mi amor," Maria would whisper, patting him fondly on the thigh. "She will say something soon."

On Wednesday, Andrew took Anna out to Tigre, north of the city, to see the ocean.

"It's not really the ocean," Anna said, looking up from the pamphlet she was reading. She was sprawled over a handrail because there was only standing room on the train. Andrew was trying to ignore the public service signs above her head, obviously warning against malarial mosquitoes. They were both wearing splashily patterned shorts and flip-flops, packed in some fit of optimism or delusion he could not now fathom.

"It's just a delta," said Anna.

Andrew shrugged. "It will still be fun."

When they were little, Lily and Anna had loved the sea. Andrew and Maureen had usually taken them in the summers—going early to beat the heat, piling into the car with Cokes wilting in the back, sometimes getting there before the sun had even burned off the dew, while the fog still rolled in like tulle. Andrew would read *The Economist* while the girls buried and unburied him. Sometimes they'd go in the winter, when the weeds were scraggly and the snow stretched out like sand and the water was a dimpled sterling. Andrew and Maureen would fill a thermos with hot cocoa and get the girls comically bundled in brand-new pastel snowsuits. When she was pregnant with Lily, Maureen had wanted to keep some of Janie's things for the next baby. But Andrew could not abide the thought of seeing another toddler in Janie's clothes—it felt too nightmarish to contemplate—and so Maureen had conceded the point, because in those days there'd actually been a very simple rule about who conceded what: Whenever there was a way for one of them to ease the other's pain in any way, they did. And so the new snowsuits had been bought, along with the new diaper bags and the new toddler shoes and a new arsenal of stuffed dogs and bears. Andrew had repainted the nursery. The Beatrix Potter décor was changed to Winnie-the-Pooh.

"What about it is going to be fun, exactly?" said Anna.

"We'll rent a canoe," said Andrew. In the pamphlet, Tigre was brimming with nuclear families paddling happily in red kayaks. It was strange to Andrew that other people came to this country for vacation. "We'll ride on a boat. Don't you still like boats?"

The train stopped and the doors opened. Anna was backlit by sun and Andrew had to squint to see her. "Tomorrow," she said. "I want to go with you to meet with the lawyers."

Tomorrow, Andrew and Maureen would be meeting the lawyers to discuss the DNA findings. Lily's DNA, it seemed, had appeared on Katy's mouth—which was not surprising, considering her CPR attempt—as well as on the murder weapon—which was actually not surprising, either, considering the murder weapon was a kitchen knife belonging to the Carrizos. Lily's DNA had also appeared, a bit oddly, on one of Katy's bras. Reassuringly, most of the DNA collected near Katy's body was from someone else. All Andrew knew about this person was that he was a man, and already in the system, both of which facts were suspicious, and thus encouraging. After hanging up the phone, Maureen had stared at Andrew emptily and said, "Well, you might as well take Anna somewhere, since there's nothing else we can do today." He'd been glad for the chance. In the days since Maureen had arrived, Anna had moved mostly into Maureen's hotel room, and the two of them had spent their evenings together, whispering and watching telenovelas and, Andrew realized once when he picked them up for breakfast, drinking their way through the minibar. This made Andrew feel strangely frustrated; it wasn't that Andrew was the bad cop and Maureen was the good one, it was just that Maureen was both. Andrew could no more let Anna drink something out of the minibar than he could stop her from doing so, right in front of him, if she decided she wanted to. The fact that she didn't was, he understood, a courtesy that she extended to him—like still calling him "Dad" and

Maureen "Mom," when Lily had long ago begun addressing them by their first names.

"It's going to be boring, sweetie," said Andrew, ushering Anna out of the train and into the depot, which smelled oppressively of pastries. All around were kiosks selling gum and soda and tabloids. Andrew tried hard not to look at the headlines.

"Boring?" said Anna. "Are you kidding me?"

"Excuse me, do you speak English?" A worried-looking couple with a map was standing in front of them.

"No," said Andrew, hurrying Anna out of the depot. Outside, the sky was blazingly blue, the palm trees obnoxious.

"Dad, what the hell are you doing? They were just trying to ask directions."

"Well, we can't exactly give them directions, can we? Now, will you look at this?" Andrew gestured grandly. Before them, beer-colored delta water lapped desultorily against the hulls of rental boats. Nearby, a man was giving a bikinied woman a piggyback ride. Andrew could not understand what would impel an adult woman to allow herself to be carried like that. The entire town seemed to smell of coconut sunblock and Quilmes. Andrew could hear the woman's thighs slapping against the man's back.

"Dad," said Anna. "I'm trying to talk to you."

"Listen, sweetie—oh, shit." A mosquito was buzzing menacingly close to Anna; Andrew bent to swat it away from her leg—which was denuded and well moisturized, he noticed: How did she possibly have the energy to keep shaving her legs?—and then stood back up. "It's going to be a big conversation."

"I know it's a big conversation," said Anna. "That's exactly why I want to be there." Another mosquito veered brazenly toward her other leg, and Andrew waved that one away, too—though this, he saw, was perhaps a lóst cause. He couldn't really protect Anna from malaria, or a lingering death, or an interminable unjust detention. But it had to be better to keep pretending that he could.

"Dad," said Anna, "you have to stop that."

Andrew stood. Across the street, he could see, was a little stand selling ice creams and Cokes. "Do you want an ice cream?"

"Jesus Christ, Dad. You're trying to ply me with ice cream? I'm not nine."

"Anna, I'm sorry. You can't go to the meeting. They only want to talk to me and your mom, anyway." This was not technically true. Andrew marched Anna across the street to the ice cream stand. "Uno helado, por favor," he said to the vendor, smiling brightly.

"What flavor?"

"Um. Chocolate, please."

"Why don't you want me there, Dad?" said Anna. "Seriously. Tell me. Do you think you're going to hear something you don't want to in that conversation?"

"Well, of course we will." Andrew lowered his voice. He wished he didn't have to know that the ice cream vendor spoke English. "It's a gruesome thing that's happened, and we're going to hear all about it. And it's happened to a girl only a few years older than you. Which is part of why it's not a good idea for you to come along. This trip is upsetting enough for you already." Andrew rifled in his pocket for change.

"I know all that, Dad," said Anna. "That's not what I'm wondering."

"What then?" Andrew handed her the ice cream and was relieved when she took it.

"I'm wondering if there's something else we might hear that we don't want to." Anna sounded careful, and Andrew wondered fleetingly, uncomprehendingly, if she was talking about Lily's sex life.

"I don't know, sweetie," he said. He saw now that it was a mistake to have brought Anna here. It was too much; she was too young; her just-begun life with all of its own rich dramas and disappointments was being put completely on hold, and for what? "But please don't worry." He pulled Anna to him, and she allowed this, barely, holding her ice cream away from her body with exaggerated awkwardness. Andrew could never get over how tall Anna was, how substantial and lanky; her body had grown into its own authoritative spin on his genetics, like she was the product of some kind of unholy tinkering with recombinant DNA. The possibility that a child of his could grow to nearly his height, could one day live to outlive him, was nearly as unthinkable as the fact that such a creature could ever die. It was possible, Andrew realized with terror, that he needed Anna here. She had, after all, already done more for Lily than he, or anyone else, had been able to. But none of that was any excuse to let her stay.

"Anna," said Andrew, "do you think you'd like to go home?"

"What?" She wriggled out of his embrace. Andrew had meant it as an offer, but he realized it had come out as a kind of threat.

"We could get Uncle Phil to pick you up at the airport and drive you back up to Colby."

"I don't want to go back."

"You'll need to go back eventually."

"When Lily's free. She needs me here now."

"Anna, look." Maybe Andrew would just be honest. Maybe, for the first time in a long time, he'd just be direct. "I need you here. Lily needs you here. Your mom needs you here. But just because we all need you here does not mean you have to be here. And while we figure all of this out, Maureen and I need to be your parents. We are still your parents."

Anna was letting the ice cream melt onto her hand now, in a show of indifference either authentic or feigned. Andrew tugged off his backpack and started rummaging through it for the antibacterial hand wipes that he knew Maureen would have packed.

"Do you understand, Anna?" Andrew found the wipes and marveled—for the millionth time—at Maureen's somber resourcefulness, her capacity to predict and prepare for all manner of future disasters, large and small. "I want you here. I need you here. But there have to be limits. We have to protect Lily. We have to protect you. And what we need from you tomorrow is to stay in the hotel."

There was a sort of solar wavering in Anna's expression, but then it seemed to downshift and she smiled. Andrew handed her the wipes and she licked the melted ice cream off her wrist. "Okay, Dad," she said.

"Okay?"

"Yes. Okay. Now, do you want to see about renting a kayak?"

. . .

The next day, Maureen and Andrew rode in silence to Lomas de Zamora. Andrew clutched a paper bag with an egg sandwich for Lily; he'd just bought it and already it was leaking, turning the paper oily and translucent. At the jail, Maureen paid the driver with a twenty-peso bill and Andrew was sure she'd get her change back in counterfeits, but he didn't have the heart to comment on either of these things.

In the waiting room, they sat. Maureen hadn't been to the jail before, and Andrew was glad that he was able to direct her through the metal detector, to point her toward the bathroom, to show her that things were not as awful as she might have imagined they would be. They waited. Maureen pawed through her bag and produced her wallet. Poking out of the billfold, alongside receipts and her United Airlines boarding pass, Andrew saw the blue tip of her passport. He nudged her.

"You shouldn't carry that around," he whispered.

"I know," she said apologetically.

This was where Lily got it, no doubt—Andrew had never realized it before, but now it seemed obvious. Maureen had lost one child to death and another to incarceration, and yet here she was, breezing around town with her passport in her bag and accepting back fistfuls of cash as change without even holding them up to the light.

"Do you want to read something that will break your heart?" said Maureen.

"No," said Andrew, because he was a little angry with her. "Not really."

Maureen ignored this—she understood that Andrew did want to see the thing that would break his heart, that he couldn't bear not to see it now that it was on offer. She produced a journal from her overstuffed bag.

"Flip to the page that's paper-clipped," she said, handing it to him.

The paper inside the journal was creamy and expensive and lined with Lily's handwriting, and Andrew realized with an anguished stab that Maureen (or Anna) had thought to buy Lily a notebook and a pen and had figured out how to get it to her. He read.

Things I Will Do At Home:
—eat a steak
—volunteer at a nursing home
—practice the oboe
—get up early enough to watch the sunrise 4 x per year (one per season)
—be nice to everyone
—set up a fundraiser for Katy
—apologize to Harold
—apologize to Sebastien
—apologize to Mom and Dad

Andrew stared at the sheet—the clean white paper, the handwriting shaky (from what? he wondered. From malnutrition or terror? Or merely from years of Internet use?)—and his eyes filled with tears. He knew from much practice that the best thing to do now was to keep his eyes down and to open them very wide so as to prevent spillover. It was the line about being nice to everyone that really got to him. To Lily, this whole disaster must indeed seem the result of not being nice enough. She hadn't killed anyone, but she'd written a few mean-spirited emails. And now she was in jail, those emails paraded around everywhere as evidence of her depravity. Of course she was promising to be good, promising to be a lamb, promising never to think a mean thought, or any thought, ever again, if only they would let her out.

"'Mom and Dad'?" said Andrew.

"I know. Who knew?"

"Where did you get it?"

"She had the lawyers mail it."

Andrew stared again at Lily's handwriting. Something about it made him afraid of what she might look like this week; he didn't like to admit it to himself, but he had some doubts about her internal resiliency. She wasn't the fussiest of all possible middle-class children, of course. She'd always worked in college; in the summers, she worked more than full-time, refusing offers of financial help—this stemmed from some kind of confused and contradictory sense of self-sufficiency that accepted sizable government loans and even more sizable parental tuition payments and rejected all other forms of charity—and it was clear that she actually enjoyed reveling in temporary, self-imposed poverty. Toward the end of her paycheck, Andrew knew, she ate mostly popcorn and hot dogs from her movie theater job. But all of this, of course, was because she'd had a childhood characterized by neither deprivation nor ostentatious wealth: a childhood in which modest de-sires were firmly affixed to what was actually possible. She did not know to regard the absence of comfort with fear—partly because she wasn't particularly materialistic or entitled, but partly because she did not believe, not really, that such a state could ever truly be permanent. And that *was* entitled, Andrew saw now—that expectation of the uni-verse's benignity. Lily felt she did no wrong, and that this demanded that no wrong be done unto her. The simplicity of this thinking beg-gared belief. It was almost too perilously sad for Andrew to contem-plate.

A security guard finally appeared and led them down the hall, Maureen clutching Andrew's hand. In the visiting room, Lily was sit-ting with her head down just where Andrew had left her the last time. He fought the image of her sitting there all week long, waiting for their return.

Maureen went to Lily and gathered her up into her arms. "Mom," Lily hiccupped, bending her head into Maureen's lap. Andrew leaned over both of them and pecked Lily on the cheek. Her hair was in clumps, and she smelled of oil and dirty laundry. Andrew did not know whether this was defiance or despair, or which would be worse.

"Sweetheart," said Maureen. She gently cupped Lily's head, as though she were a newborn—fragile, tender-fontanelled. "I love you, I love you, I love you."

This should have been the first thing Andrew had said when he'd visited. This should have been the first thing, not the last. Andrew patted Lily's shoulder, then reached into his bag for the sandwich. "We brought you this," he said. It was chorizo with egg—she'd loved this sandwich so much that she'd actually written home about it—and it had been Andrew's idea to bring it to her. Lily lifted her head now and stared at the sandwich plaintively, as though she could not remember what one was supposed to do with such a thing.

"Aren't you hungry?" said Maureen.

"I don't know," said Lily.

"Why don't you take a bite, and maybe you'll find out that you are?" said Maureen. This was a trick of hers that Andrew remembered from when the girls were little and prone to low blood sugar—they'd run around and forget to eat and then they'd cry, and Maureen would have to coax them into taking bites of grilled cheese until they calmed down. Now Maureen handed Lily the sandwich, which she held limply for a moment before taking a tentative bite. She chewed for a very long time, as though she wasn't producing enough saliva to get the job done. She held her hand over her mouth daintily—a strange affectation she'd picked up from someone at college, made odder now by her grubby hair and oily skin, as though she were some *Grey Gardens*-style fallen aristocrat. She'd never been a vain child, their Lily—she always had a grass stain on her overalls or an eyelash on her cheek or a bit of cookie in the corner of her mouth; she was forever picking up cats and dogs against their will and getting animal hair all over her clothes. But she'd always been basically clean, basically presentable. The way she looked now was not entirely like herself.

Maureen must have been thinking the same thing, because she said, "Sweetie, here," and began rummaging once more through her enormous bag. "I brought you a brush."

Lily stopped chewing but didn't swallow. "Are you serious?"

"I think it'd be a good idea to try to clean up a bit for the lawyers," said Maureen.

"Are you fucking serious?" There was a flaky bit of egg on Lily's lip, or maybe it was a piece of dry skin. "You want me to brush my fucking hair? *That's* what you're worried about? That's what your priorities are?"

Andrew looked at Maureen. In the old days, Maureen had been very, very strict about language—one time Lily had sworn at her when she was on the phone with one of her friends, and Maureen had calmly unplugged it—but now her expression was pleading and subordinate. "Sweetheart," she said.

"Stop calling me that, okay? Just stop it. I'm an adult. If you're old enough to have everyone think you killed someone, you're old enough to have your fucking parents stop calling you fucking sweetheart."

"Everyone doesn't think you killed someone," said Maureen. "We all know you didn't kill anyone. I just think it would be a very good idea for you to look like you haven't. And like you haven't given up on yourself entirely, either."

"Well, what if I have?" Lily snarled.

"This is part of the problem," Andrew ventured, and both Lily and Maureen turned to look at him like they were surprised he was still in the room.

"What are you talking about?" said Lily. She didn't even sound angry. He wasn't the parent worth her anger.

"Impressions matter, is all I'm saying, sweetheart."

Andrew was only reiterating what Maureen had literally just said, and so he could not understand why Lily and Maureen were both looking at him like he'd just now revealed himself to be the cruel man they'd always suspected he might be.

"Are you joking?" Lily said, turning back to Maureen. "Are you two joking? Because you never used to have senses of humor."

"Okay, Lily," said Maureen. "Okay." She was making gentle curlicues on Lily's back now, and somehow Lily was allowing this. Andrew flashed to an image of Lily at age three or four—it was summer, and she was sprawled out on the couch in tiny shorts, licking a bright blue Popsicle and singing along to the theme song of some wretchedly long-running soap opera while Maureen traced letters through her

T-shirt. The light of that long-ago late afternoon was silvery through the picture windows; in the corner, the monitor crackled with the sounds of baby Anna, sighing in her red inscrutable dreams, and maybe all of them had thought for a moment then that their lives would turn out to be tolerable after all. *I love you,* Maureen wrote, over and over, long before Lily could know what the shapes she was making meant. *I love you, I love you.*

"Okay, okay," said Maureen, and Andrew saw that she was leaning over with the brush and taking it gently to Lily's hair, and that Lily was not resisting. Andrew expected Maureen to say something—to coo a little, or offer something comforting, or in some way acknowledge that Lily was submitting where before she had defied—but she did not. She just kept brushing with one hand and stroking Lily's back with the other, and slowly Lily's hair returned to normalcy, and she began to look like a regular girl on a particularly bad day, but not necessarily in a particularly bad lifetime.

Velazquez and Ojeda entered the room, and Maureen and Andrew stood up to greet them. Lily remained seated. Andrew did not like this new passivity of hers, this tolerance of manhandling and ordering and planning by others. The lawyers sat and spread manila folders out on the table. They did not coddle Lily, or tsk over her, or offer expressions of sympathy to anyone. Maybe this was because her situation was not as bad as some they'd seen, or maybe it was because it was much worse and they'd already entirely given up. Or maybe—and, Andrew had to think, most probably—it was just because the lawyers were absorbed in the particular details of their own lives, and were already looking forward to the dinners that waited for them at home.

"Well," said Ojeda. He was already sweating; his tie was tied too tightly and had the look of a purple silken snake throttling him about the neck. "The bottom line is that the DNA results are fairly good for us. First and most importantly, there's DNA everywhere from a man— a man with a criminal record—who will now become the prosecution's central suspect. He's been arrested twice—once for drugs, once for try- ing to steal a car—and served nearly two years in prison. This is the man who committed this crime, and we can't stress how significant it is to have him already identified."

Maureen and Andrew nodded. Lily's head listed to the side, her expression grave and still.

"Lily's DNA was present in three places, however," said Velazquez. "On the victim's mouth, on a bra which may have belonged to the victim, and on the knife. Our first concern is with the knife."

"When you say 'the knife,' " said Maureen, "you mean the one that was—used—in the crime?"

"The murder weapon, yes."

"My DNA is on that?" said Lily in a small voice.

"Well, it was a knife from the kitchen," said Velazquez. He was looking at Maureen. "It was a *communal* knife. Beatriz Carrizo's DNA is on it, too. And Lily surely had occasion to use it for cooking. Didn't you, Lily?"

"Sure." Lily nodded and clasped her hands in her lap—a little prissily, Andrew thought. "I'm sure I did."

"Can you think of a specific time you might have used that knife for cooking?" said Ojeda.

"In particular, can you think of a time when somebody might have *seen* you use that knife for cooking?" said Velazquez.

Lily's face paled, suddenly looking as fragile and ovoid as an egg. Andrew struggled to produce a memory, any memory, of Lily cooking anything, but he could not. Lily was notoriously and stridently indifferent to cooking. On Thanksgiving she'd stand around holding forth and drinking wine while Maureen basted the turkey, Maureen mashed the potatoes, Maureen chopped the squash. Maybe Lily would be given the occasional minor task—ferrying something from the counter to the table, polishing a glass, finding a ladle—but Andrew had never seen her voluntarily reach for a cooking gadget of any sort, and he seriously doubted she had recently taken an interest.

"Well," said Ojeda, "you don't have to remember right this second."

"As for the victim's body," said Velazquez, "the fact that your DNA was on her mouth fits with your account of attempting CPR."

Andrew cleared his throat, and the whole table turned to peer at him. "Excuse me," he said. "But shouldn't that be pretty fatal to the prosecution's case? That there's DNA evidence that Lily tried to save Katy, just like she said she did?"

Ojeda looked at Andrew evenly. "It fits with our narrative, yes," he said. "But the prosecution will find a narrative that also fits."

Andrew opened his mouth and then closed it again.

"Finally," said Velazquez, opening another folder. "The bra clasp. This, too, could be easy to explain. Lily did live there. The bra might have even belonged to her, for all we know." He produced a picture from the envelope and pushed it across the table to her. Andrew leaned over. The photograph was of a white bra with a tiny blue flower at the clasp. "Lily, did this bra belong to you?"

Lily frowned. "I don't know," she said. "It might have."

Velazquez glanced at Ojeda. "You don't know?"

"Sweetie," said Maureen.

"No," said Lily, looking quickly away from the picture. "It wasn't mine."

"Did you and Katy ever share clothes?" said Ojeda.

"No," said Lily faintly. "I mean not that I know of. She wasn't really my size."

"No matter, no matter," said Ojeda, making a note on his pad. "You might have picked it up sometime. Your laundry might have gotten mixed up. You lived together—anything is possible. It's not surprising that your DNA is on some of her things. And there were irregularities with the evidence collection, anyway. None of the DNA results have been obtained or handled with the rigor they should—that's not unusual, sadly. Establishing that lack of rigor will be our approach for any results we can't otherwise work with. But you don't need to worry about any of that now, Lily."

Velazquez leaned forward. "The real question here, Lily, is the other suspect. This is the person who committed this murder—that much we know, and the prosecution knows it, too. So what they're going to try to do is place you there with him. And in order to do that, they're going to have to say you knew him. In fact, they're going to want to say you had some kind of a relationship with him."

In an earlier lifetime—in an earlier week—Lily might have said, "But I didn't," as though this counted for something. But now she stayed quiet and nodded somberly, accepting this latest outrage without comment.

"So it's very important that you tell us now if you knew him, and if you did, what exactly your acquaintance with him was." Velazquez pushed forward another picture—this one of a leathery-skinned man with a sleepy gaze—and Lily leaned forward to look. Her expression was open and a bit curious, as though she thought it was possible that perhaps she'd known him after all, that perhaps they'd slept together, that perhaps she'd actually done all the things they said she had, and had somehow forgotten.

"Oh. Yeah. That's Ignacio. He works at Fuego." Lily looked up, her eyes wide. "They think he did this?"

Ojeda and Velazquez exchanged another glance. "What were your experiences with him?" said Velazquez.

"None," said Lily. "I mean, hardly any."

"It's important that you try to remember this very carefully," said Ojeda. "If you say you never spent any time with him, never spoke with him, and the prosecution finds evidence that you did—even once—that will be very, very bad for us. I'm sorry, Lily, but that's the reality."

Lily looked more closely, and a new faltering look came over her face—whether it was recognition or invention, Andrew couldn't be sure. "I don't know," she said. "He worked there on weeknights, I think. We talked sometimes, I guess. Not very much."

Ojeda nodded. "I see," he said. "And was there anything else? Any other particular exchanges with this man? Any other dealings with him?"

Lily shook her head.

"And I'm sorry, Lily, but we have to ask: Did you have any romantic or sexual involvement with him? Anything whatsoever?"

"We can ask your parents to step out for a moment here, Lily, if you'd prefer."

Lily shook her head again. "No," she said. "They can stay. There wasn't anything like that. Like I said, I knew him from work. Just a little." She put her head in her hands. "Jesus. I remember him staring at her that night."

"Which night?" said Velazquez sharply.

"The night Katy came to see me at work."

"When was that?"

"I don't know." Lily bit her lip. "A week before my birthday, maybe?"

"A date would be more helpful."

"Maybe the tenth?" she said hesitantly. "The tenth of February? Around then. And I saw them kissing. Well, I think I did. At my birthday party. On the seventeenth. I think."

This time, Ojeda and Velazquez did not exchange a glance; perhaps, this time, they did not need to. Velazquez leaned forward. "Lily," he said. "We will talk about all of that at length, and very soon. But first, I need to ask you another question, and it is very important that you tell us the truth. Do you understand?"

Lily's eyes grew even larger. "Yes," she said.

"Did Ignacio Toledo ever sell you drugs?"

"Think carefully, Lily," said Ojeda quickly. "It would not be a good idea for you to get this answer wrong."

Lily exhaled heavily, and Andrew could tell that she had been holding her breath. "Yes," she said.

Maureen drew back, as though recoiling from a gunshot.

"Just weed," said Lily. "And just once."

"I see," said Velazquez. "And when was this?"

"This was the day I was fired."

"Again, a date please."

"Maybe the eighteenth."

"Katy Kellers, you'll recall, was killed on the twentieth. So this was two days before that?"

"I guess so," said Lily. "Yes."

"And Lily, I'm sorry, but I have to clarify: The marijuana that Toledo sold you—was that in addition to the marijuana that you told the prosecution you got from Katy?"

"What?" said Maureen. She turned to Lily. "What are they talking about?"

"Lily," said Ojeda urgently. "We are not going to scold you. We are here to help you. But in order to let us do that, you need to tell us the truth."

Lily stared at the table, her eyes wide. "No," she said. "I mean, no, I never got any from Katy. Just Ignacio. I lied about that before."

The lawyers looked at each other and nodded. She had gotten this answer right. And Andrew saw how Lily could be persuaded to change her mind. He saw how she could be persuaded to say anything at all.

CHAPTER ELEVEN

February

When Lily awoke it was late, the sun streaming in dusty and luxuriant chords through the window. Below her, Katy's bed was empty and neatly made, and Lily's suspicions of the night before seemed unwarranted, possibly paranoid. After all, anything that happened with Katy and Sebastien was really none of Lily's business. She was young, she was open-minded, she was philosophically opposed to reflexive monogamy, and if Katy and Sebastien had had a flirtation—or more—it had nothing to do with her. She was free to go find flirtations—and more!—herself, and maybe she would. Maybe she just would.

And over the next few days, Lily was generally friendlier to both Katy and Sebastien than she'd ever been before. Being warm toward them was actually a relief from the elaborate invisibility campaign she was conducting at home—the only way to avoid inadvertently provoking Beatriz's wrath again, Lily figured, was to stay far, far out of sight. She stopped watching television with the Carrizos in the evenings, she excused herself from dinners early, she tried to stay out of the house as much as possible. Housework was a difficult negotiation; Lily was afraid of seeming entitled and equally afraid of seeming presumptuous, and so she found herself striking odd balances—like washing her own plates to sparkling by hand and then leaving them near the dishwasher for Beatriz to load with the rest of the family's. She even began eating less, as though to say that she could not be sure anymore that food was not also begrudged her. She knew that it was all a little much—she remembered adopting similar poses in moments of aggrieved chagrin in childhood, performing ornate shows of brave despondency in the face of such grave injustices as bedtime, and she knew that she should not be acting this way as an adult. But she could not help herself. And at any rate, if Beatriz noticed—or if she felt at all sorry for the way she had spoken to Lily—she did not show it.

At school, Lily skipped more and more of her classes. All the rumors about study abroad were true, it turned out—you really only had to show up for the tests. At Fuego, she was learning how to be more authoritative in her movements and more efficient with the dishware. Her Spanish vocabulary relating to food and beverages was expanding exponentially. She started jutting out her hip while taking orders, and she began taking smoke breaks with the kitchen staff, for which occasions (and these occasions only) she purchased her first pack of cigarettes. On these breaks, everyone stood around sounding very, very bored with Fuego, and Lily tried to sound bored, too. Feigning this boredom was one of the many minor thrills that, in aggregate, made the job one of the top thrills of Lily's life.

In bed, on nights when she bailed on Sebastien, Lily found herself making mental lists of all the things that she would do when she got home. She would eat all the American brands that she barely ever actually ate but suddenly acutely missed: banana-flavored Laffy Taffy, Skippy peanut butter, Coffee-mate creamer in decadent seasonal flavors. She would follow the news more carefully so that she could talk about it with Andrew. Most important, she would go outside more. The hills around Middlebury were so lovely—purple in the fall, apple green in the summers—and they seemed so close that you could walk up one. And maybe you could—she had never tried! Why had she never tried? She would do that when she got back. She would walk in the woods with the faintly heaving shadows. She would call her friends—especially the ones from high school, the ones who'd disappeared into a seemingly endless array of second-tier liberal arts colleges in upstate New York—and ask them about their lives. She would be a better sister to Anna. Instead of text messages, she'd send her care packages, full of items responsive to the needs of a long-distance runner. She'd think later about what those might be. And, maybe most important, Lily would reconnect with her parents. She imagined going to long languorous brunches with her mother, long sunset walks with her dad—why was there somehow never any time or appeal for these things when they were actually available? She blamed the Internet, somehow. But no matter. Buenos Aires was making her a better and wiser person. She would be twenty-one in a few days. And when she got back, things would be different. She would go camping. She would walk through slow-moving autumns. She would get up early and watch frosty New England sunrises.

The night of her birthday, Lily pre-gamed with Katy in the bedroom. They traded sips from a bottle of vodka that—along with a plastic water gun shaped like a shark, a pretty rainbow-colored Buenos Aires shot glass, and an enormous and yolky chorizo egg sandwich that was still warm when unwrapped—had been Katy's birthday present to Lily. For a moment, staring at the sandwich, Lily had felt a flicker of suspicion—Was Katy trying to suck up? Was she trying to beg forgiveness? Was she trying to be funny?—before she told herself to quit it.

"Thanks so much!" she said, waving the sandwich. "You know I love these."

"Yay!" said Katy, giving Lily a hug. "This is going to be such a fun night!"

Lily boisterously agreed that it *was* going to be a fun night. At Katy's urging, Lily had asked Javier about celebrating her birthday at the club and, to Lily's surprise, he had agreed. Now Lily watched as Katy dressed—in tight jeans that Lily had never seen before and a shiny black shirt that looked wet and metallic in the light—while listening to Beyoncé. Katy bopped and bounced and shook her finger, acting out the dance from the video.

"I think this song has really changed gender relations in our generation," said Katy, still bouncing. She was already a little drunk. Lily cocked her head. Normally she was the one to make grand pronouncements, espouse sweeping theories. But tonight she didn't really feel like speculating on anything bigger than her own life. "Don't you think so?" said Katy.

"I guess," said Lily. Katy's high spirits were making her edgy; she would have liked Katy to be in a somewhat less good mood. "Did you bring those from home?"

"What?"

"The jeans."

"Oh. No. I bought them here." Katy switched to "Alejandro" by Lady Gaga, then spun around and tried to check out her own derriere, which was so much smaller and shapelier than Lily's as to be unrecognizable as the same body part. "They're so tight I think they're going to give me a urinary tract infection."

Lily nodded but didn't laugh.

Katy put on her best Gaga face. *"I know that we are young and I know that you may love me . . ."* She giggled. "Ugh. I shouldn't have eaten so much cake."

Lily nodded again and took a swig from the bottle. Beatriz had indeed made a homemade cake—pink frosting, a swirling and calligraphic Feliz cumpleaños!, the works—but Lily hadn't been able to enjoy it. She still felt bad about the incident with the phone call, as well as preemptively guilty for however she would be getting in trouble tonight. Somehow, Lily knew, Katy and Lily would both come home late and drunk, but Lily would be the one to get a lecture from Beatriz tomorrow—Lily would cough, or trip, or break something coming in the door, or leave a telltale receipt behind somewhere. And Beatriz would wind up yelling at Lily while Katy slept, or highlighted her economics textbook, or watched the whole scene, innocent and mute. Lily was fairly resigned to this sequence of events, but she was not exactly looking forward to them.

"This song is just that Ace of Base song," said Katy. "'Don't Turn Around'? It's the same tune. Don't you think?"

"I did in 2009," said Lily. She walked to the mirror and leaned toward it, mouth wide open, to apply some eyeliner.

"Is Sebastien coming tonight?" said Katy.

Lily turned to do the other eye. This time her jaw cracked when she opened it. "No," she said. She could feel the shot she had taken; she was enjoying the sense of life opening up. In the mirror, she dusted her freckles into oblivion; she made her expression hawkish and sharp. What did Sebastien know? He didn't know anything about her. He didn't even know it was her birthday. This thought gave Lily such a delicious stab of privacy that she started chanting it in her head as a kind of incantation while she did the rest of her face: *He doesn't know it's my birthday, he doesn't know it's my birthday.* In the mirror, Lily painted her cheeks mauve, her eyes purple, her lips a severe and sexual red. She was becostumed, she was bewitching. She hiccupped. She was buzzed.

"Why not?" Katy said, and Lily could tell she'd already said it once.

"I didn't invite him."

"You didn't *invite* him?"

Lily shrugged. She liked the disturbing concavity of her clavicle when she shrugged; it was the only time she really looked skinny. "I just don't think he'd have a very good time," she said, in a voice that was higher than her own.

This was true—Lily did not think that Sebastien would have a very good time, but that was because she planned to have the kind of night he would not have a good time witnessing. If Sebastien liked Katy more than Lily—still or originally—then fine. That was only reasonable. That was, in fact, only right! But Lily was a modern woman, and men at the club hit on her sometimes, and tonight it was her birthday. Once she made out with someone else, everything would be even again between Katy and Sebastien and her: They'd all be equally progressive people with an equal number of fantastic possibilities before them. There were no hard feelings. All was fair in love and war, and this was neither.

"I don't know," said Katy. "I bet he'd want to be invited."

"Eh," said Lily, and shrugged again. "Maybe it's time to meet someone new."

Katy frowned a moment, and Lily saw her sober self—endlessly concerned with feelings and appropriateness, Lily had always thought, though now she had to wonder—shine through for a moment. But then Katy smiled and said, "Well, maybe. You do look hot."

Lily made herself laugh and wiggle along to the song. "You think so?" She twirled around and then slapped Katy lightly on the arm. "And how about you, missy? Ready to put down your widow's weeds and have some fun?"

Katy blushed—blushing always made Lily look like she'd just had some kind of fit, but it made Katy look tawny and healthy and shining. "Maybe," she said.

"Maybe!" squealed Lily. She was not naturally a squealer, and she didn't much care for the voices she found herself employing when she was trying to be friendly to other women. But this was, like many things in life, a necessary evil. "Listen to you. What, do you like someone?"

Katy blushed even deeper. "Maybe," she said. "Not yet."

At Fuego, Lily quickly saw how much she was going to enjoy knowing people that Katy did not know. She found herself waving manically at coworkers she didn't usually talk to, using first names more than was usual or required, making reference to fairly mundane incidents as though they were in-jokes ("Hopefully no more guys ordering Patrón tonight, right, Roderigo?" she said; Roderigo looked confused). "Oi, Hector!" she shouted at Hector. "Can we get a couple of vodka tonics?" She handed Katy her drink with theatrical magnanimousness, as though Fuego were her home and Katy her guest. Katy accepted her drink happily, then handed it back to Lily almost immediately and went off to find a bathroom.

Lily made her way to an unobtrusive corner and gulped her own drink, nodding her head along to the music. She could feel the beat in her chest, more insistent than her own heart. She nodded at some coworkers, but they were all working. She made small talk with a couple of kids from the program who had wandered into the club in the hopes of free drinks. She began sipping Katy's drink. She experienced a flush of awkwardness at standing alone, then a surge of liberated spunky indifference, then a second wave of chilling and recalcitrant discomfort. She finished Katy's drink and headed back to the bar. As she was paying—because it was understood that you didn't take more than one round for free—she saw Ignacio the Tortoise out of the corner of her eye. He was in the back alcove, near the kitchen, and he was with a woman. Lily squinted. The woman was Katy. The woman was Katy, and Ignacio was grabbing her ass with two hands. Lily did a double take. When she turned back, they were just talking. Did Katy look upset? Did she look traumatized? It was hard to say. Around her, the club was a wavery, hilarious smear, and Lily felt very far away from everything. She grabbed her drink and marched over.

"I need you to come with me," she said, pulling Katy's arm. She tried to look distressed so that Ignacio would assume some dull girl problem was at hand, but then she felt actual distress breaking through on her face, and she realized there was no need to pretend.

"What?" said Ignacio. "What are you doing?"

"Come with me," said Lily. She pointed to the bathroom and spilled her drink a little on the floor. Katy shrugged apologetically at Ignacio the Tortoise and followed Lily to the women's room. In the tawdry bathroom light, she looked at Lily hard, one hand on her hip.

"Are you okay?" she said.

"Are *you* okay?" said Lily. "That's the question."

"What are you talking about?"

Somehow Lily couldn't remember exactly why she'd brought Katy into the bathroom, but she knew there was something important they needed to discuss. "We need to talk," she said.

Katy looked solemn. "Okay," she said.

"We really need to talk," Lily said, and then stopped. She careened around her own brain for a moment before tripping on the sharpest object. Suddenly she was filled with the piercing confidence that comes from unraveling a conspiracy. "Why didn't you defend me?" she said.

"What?"

The toilet flushed and a girl came out, staggering and fawnlike on her high heels, and washed her hands without using soap. Out of a strange retroactive sense of propriety, Lily waited until she left to continue.

"From Beatriz."

"What? When?"

"When she found me looking at that paper." Yes, that was what it all came down to. Katy had betrayed her, and now it was time they finally discussed it.

"Defend you? I don't know what you're talking about."

"Beatriz just doesn't like me," said Lily. "That's all. It's just not fair."

"Well, Carlos likes you," said Katy. Lily knew then that Katy was a little drunk too.

"Carlos likes everybody," said Lily.

"No. He doesn't like me. He thinks I'm boring because I'm quiet."

"He doesn't."

"Isn't that what you think, too?"

Lily mulled this. It was so obviously true that she did not know what to say. She'd thought this was the kind of truth that had been so thoroughly tacitly acknowledged as to be well beyond mention—like when a thin girl complains ceaselessly about her body to a fat friend, and the flagrant cruelty of this is both mutually understood and mutually unspeakable.

"Did you ever think about how it might make Beatriz feel that Carlos likes you so much?" said Katy.

Lily felt a blank cotton taste in her mouth. "It's not like that," she said.

"I know it's not. But don't you think it might feel like that to Beatriz? All the drinking and laughing and debating? And you're so young and gorgeous?"

Lily shook her head. Katy should really not have said "gorgeous." She really should have opted for a smaller word. Lily's mouth was twitching with real heft and persistence now; she kept waiting to lose it entirely and begin crying, and she kept not quite doing this—but neither could she get the twitching under control, and she knew she must look like a waiter trying so comically hard not to drop a platter of dishware that you just wish he'd go ahead and throw the whole thing on the floor.

"I'm not saying she thinks anything's happening," said Katy, who was watching Lily's face with some alarm. "Of course not. I just think that if you want Beatriz to like you better you might think about toning it down some with Carlos."

"Toning *what* down?" Lily nearly wailed. She could not figure out what Katy was referring to. It wasn't how she dressed. It wasn't what she and Carlos talked about. It certainly wasn't the way she acted—she did not touch Carlos's arm, she did not bat her eyelashes coquettishly, she did not tilt her head back and laugh, she did not twirl her hair. She knew she didn't; she wouldn't like herself if she did.

"Just," said Katy. She bit her lip. "Your personality."

"My personality?"

"Just, you know. The things you do."

"*What* things?"

"Well, like, answering the phone is a perfect example."

"That was only polite! What are you talking about! You wouldn't have answered the phone?"

"Well, think about it. They have an answering machine, right? So it's not like they're going to miss this once-in-a-lifetime phone call telling them they've won the lottery and never find out."

Lily gaped. Another gaggle of girls—shiny-shirted, shiny-haired—

entered the bathroom and spilled together into one stall, where there was shuffling and shushing and sniffing and then, finally, giggling.

Katy lowered her voice. "Then also, Carlos is running a business, right?" she said. "And you know they're having legal troubles—"

"As if I even care about whatever is going on with that stuff! As if I could even *fathom* anything more boring!"

"So a message anyone might give would probably be pretty technical. And you know, your Spanish isn't that good—"

"It is good! I understand everything they say!"

"They talk slower to us. They talk way slower to us. Do you understand everything strangers say? And on the phone you can't see the person, which makes it a ton harder."

The shiny girls exited the stall, wiped their noses, straightened their hair in the mirror, and left.

"And then," Katy went on, "what do you think it seems like for some random young girl to be answering the phone at their house in the middle of the day? Do you think it might seem strange to someone? Do you think it might be the kind of thing that could make Beatriz a little bit embarrassed or uncomfortable?"

Lily's lip was quivering again.

"And then, finally, you're so upset that Beatriz is mad at you, you're creeping around the house all the time seeming *so* sorry, but did you ever actually tell her you were sorry? I mean, you explained, but did you ever actually apologize?"

Lily was silent. She had not.

"See, it's not that you're actually *doing* anything," concluded Katy, with the air of finally finishing a speech she'd long been anxious to deliver. "It's just that you don't think about these things."

Katy was right. Lily didn't think about these things. She didn't want to have to. She didn't want to tiptoe through her life—she wanted to act impulsively; she wanted to be understood and, if need be, forgiven. She wanted everyone to know that she meant well. She wanted everyone to fucking *relax*. Her ears were ringing, her nostrils filled with a lethal silver smell, and for a moment she thought she might pass out.

But then she recovered, and refocused, and straightened her shoulders. She was going to be herself, and she was going to say what she meant, and she did not care what anyone else thought about it.

"I don't mind about you and Sebastien," said Lily. "Whatever it is."

Katy took a step back, her eyes wide. "There's nothing with Sebastien."

"Ignacio, though, is *seriously* gross. Really, you could do better than either of them."

"What are you talking about? There's nothing with Sebastien. You're being nuts."

"No, I really don't care."

"There's nothing to care about. You want to call him and ask?"

"Exactly." Lily felt a strange twisting despair, an aloneness shocking in its completeness and profundity. She wondered if this was because she was drunk or if she sort of always felt this way but was so repressed that being drunk was the only thing that could bring it forth. "I'm sorry," she said, lunging at Katy with a sloppy, ill-advised hug, and not at all sure what she was sorry for. She caught a glimpse of herself in the mirror and saw that her eye makeup had smeared. She licked her lips and tasted the sodium of her sweat alongside the blunt chalky taste of her makeup.

"That's okay," said Katy, patting Lily's shoulder, obviously surprised at the shape the evening had taken. In the mirror, Lily looked garish, cartoonish. What the hell was she trying to prove? Who the hell was this for? Sebastien wasn't even here. She had the kind of headache that came from crying, even though she hadn't been. And Sebastien wasn't even here. Sebastien didn't even know it was her birthday.

CHAPTER TWELVE

March

When Eduardo went to Sebastien LeCompte's house again, it seemed as abandoned as it had on his earlier visits. For the fourth time, Eduardo walked up the dusty unkempt path, for the fourth time he knocked the heavy knocker, for the fourth time he brushed away cobwebs from one of the first-story windows and squinted into the house's interior. It was mostly dark, as usual, but this time Eduardo could see what he thought were candelabras in the corner, partially obscuring an uncurtained western window, casting hand-shaped shadows on the floor. The furniture was draped in white sheets, looking like sand dunes.

It was strange to Eduardo that a house like this could exist in Buenos Aires—or, really, anywhere. It was so glaringly a relic of another time—a time when dapper intelligence men in other parts of the world spent their time warring with their counterparts over cocktails and tennis, though down here they were mostly focused on making inadvisable military hardware sales—and if it had been cared for, it would have been lovely. It had fallen apart through neglect, though, and Eduardo could not fathom why a boy with so many other options would want to stay in it—or, for that matter, why a house like this had been relinquished to the ownership of a spoiled teenager in the first place. Eduardo could only assume it was a murky form of payoff for whatever unpleasantness had befallen Sebastien LeCompte's parents; and perhaps, after all, this was a fair trade.

Eduardo walked to the side of the house and tried to peer in the windows there, but those, arbitrarily, were hung with heavy green velvet curtains. He walked around to the back of the house and stared into the copse of woods behind it; he had not gone there on his previous visits. He was about to turn around and investigate the undefended back window when his eye landed on a small patch of feverish green. A garden. Eduardo moved closer. He saw sprigs of plant life, newly watered, alongside the hanging bulbs of some kind of vegetable Eduardo did not recognize. Could this be the work of Sebastien LeCompte, playboy and layabout? Perhaps the house had squatters.

Eduardo made another lap, banging on every window, saying loudly and methodically, "I know you're in there. I know that you are in there." When he rounded the corner to try the front door a final time, there, standing barefoot on the footpath, was a disheveled postadolescent in striped pajamas.

"Hello," said Eduardo. "You must be Sebastien LeCompte. I'm Eduardo Campos." He produced and flashed his ID, but the boy was not looking. "I work for the state."

"You're finally here," said Sebastien. "I've had the table set for days." There was a frisson of domestic haranguing in his voice, which Eduardo took to be some kind of grim joke. But then the boy gestured into the house, and through the open door Eduardo could see that the table was indeed dustily arranged—arrayed with plates and knives and dull pewter goblets, place settings for a family of depressed ghosts.

"I want to talk with you about Katy Kellers," said Eduardo, pocketing his ID. "Might I come in?"

"What kind of a host would I be if I said no?"

Inside, the room was populated with perhaps a half dozen large objects—more than Eduardo had been able to see from outside—all obscured by muslin sheets, making the house feel like a winter residence of a rich family away at the shore. On the mantel crouched a wizened, arabesqued clock that had stopped working some late afternoon—or early morning—a very long time ago. Eduardo was somehow quite sure that it had been a very long time ago. Next to the clock was a photo of a young Sebastien, standing next to a man who was obviously his father, presiding over a dead tapir. In the center of the room was a teetering, moldering Steinway. Here, indisputably, was true status wastefulness; it was too bad the eternally shouting students weren't around anymore to shout about this.

"Care to sit down?" said Sebastien. He pulled a sheet off of one of the objects, and looked surprised when it turned out to be a sofa. He patted it invitingly for Eduardo, then unveiled a different couch for himself. Eduardo sat.

Eduardo pointed to the piano. "That looks like it used to be expensive."

Sebastien turned to it with an expression of mild interest, as though being directed to remark on a minor museum piece. "Oh, appallingly so, I should think," he said.

"Do you play?"

"Yes. I'm fabulously talented but, alas, intensely private and protective of my gift. Do you? You really ought to favor us with a number."

"Another time, perhaps."

"I'd offer it to you as a present if I didn't fear it might feel a *tad* too snug in your car."

Eduardo ignored this. He pointed to the picture of Sebastien and the tapir on the mantel. "He's a beauty," he said. "You shoot that fellow yourself?"

Sebastien turned around to look at the picture. "That? Oh, that's not me."

Eduardo looked again. The older man was exactly identical to the person Eduardo was currently sitting across from; the child had his every feature in miniature. "Your brother, then?" he said.

"No relation. I picked the thing up from a flea market. Why, you think you see a resemblance? How strange—I never noticed."

At this, Eduardo made a pretend note on his pad. It was curious that Sebastien would lie so early, and for so little. Often people who knew they were planning to lie tried to establish as much credibility as possible ahead of time: They volunteered extensive and accurate information about themselves, they made disclosures, they answered the vast bulk of verifiable questions with showy and elaborate detail, they readily admitted ambiguity wherever they could spare it—as though any of this mattered in the slightest. As though the law had come to investigate their general characterological deceitfulness, not the very specific issue at hand—what they saw, where they were, what they did, on a very particular day or night. Given this widespread tendency, Eduardo normally commenced interviews with a series of straightforward questions to which he already knew the answers and to which most people were more than willing to truthfully respond—name, age, occupation, various other publicly available contours of their lives—in order to establish a pattern and a rapport and, sometimes, to allow the person to relax. An interviewee's relaxation tended to work in Eduardo's favor, though few people understood this. A person who was terrified throughout an entire lie detector test—for the true statements as well as the lies—would be impossible to read; it was the relative relaxation that provided the gauge, which was why Eduardo usually tried to create it in his interviews.

But the usual approach, Eduardo saw, would not work with Sebastien LeCompte, and would only bore them both. He feigned another note on his pad. "You knew Lily Hayes how long?" he said, not looking up.

Eduardo could hear Sebastien drumming his fingers softly on the muslin. "I already gave a statement to the police."

"Jog my memory," said Eduardo, looking up. "We're starting over. You knew Lily Hayes how long?"

"About a month."

"And how did you meet?"

"The Carrizos invited me over for dinner. We struck up an acquaintance."

"And how would you characterize your relationship with her?"

"Mind-bogglingly sexual."

On the whole, Eduardo would have preferred talking to almost any of his usual characters—a small-time drug dealer with oily facial hair, a clinical sociopath, a burbling schizophrenic—to talking to Sebastien LeCompte. It was important that Sebastien not see this. "You were close, then?" said Eduardo.

Sebastien leaned back and crossed his arms and appeared to cogitate. "Might we define our terms here?"

Eduardo folded his hands neatly in his lap. Indulging some stalling only underscored its futility.

"When we say 'close,' what do we mean?" said Sebastien. "I mean, in a sense, we were as close as two people can possibly be, and in another sense, we knew each other not at all."

"Could you be more specific?"

"Probably not."

"You were sleeping together?"

Sebastien's jaw dropped open theatrically. "Truly, you push my chivalry to its limits. How is one to answer such questions and remain a gentleman?"

"You were having a romantic relationship with Lily?"

"I was trying to, certainly."

"Tell me about the night Katy died."

"I think if you'll refer to your file, you'll see you have the whole sordid tale right there."

Eduardo could feel the dull blade of a headache beginning to saw against his temple; he fervently wished he could tell this child to quit wasting both of their intelligence on such small battles. "You know," he said, wedging his voice into its most avuncular tone. "You're really not helping Lily this way. Maybe you're not trying to. I wouldn't want to presume. I understand you're a legendarily unknowable fellow. But if you want to be helping Lily, you should probably understand that you aren't."

Sebastien's face was blank. A breeze blew through the window, making a faint rustling sound in the curtains.

Eduardo leaned forward. "Tell me about the night Katy Kellers died."

"Lily and I spent the night here. As I have frequently said."

"And what did you do?"

"We watched a movie."

"What movie?"

"Are there no limits to your sadism? You people are really going to make me admit to this again?"

"What movie?"

"*Lost in Translation.* We watched *Lost in Translation.* If I'd known you were going to be locking her up the next day, if I'd known I would have to tell so many strangers about it, I would have been sure it was something more obscure."

"And you fell asleep when?"

"Probably around four."

"And you woke up when?"

"Around eleven."

"And Lily was with you the whole time?"

"Yes."

"You're sure of that?"

"Yes."

"Might she not have stepped out while you were asleep?"

"Not possible."

"How do you know?"

"We sleep tangled in each other's arms. Shared lucid dreams, sex every hour on the hour. Truly a cosmic connection we have."

"I see." Eduardo made another note, his pen scratching dryly. "And, given that connection, how do you imagine Lily felt about your liaison with Katy Kellers?"

Sebastien made a guttural sound, the dregs of what was probably supposed to be a disbelieving laugh. "Liaison?" he said. "Is that what they're calling such things these days?"

Eduardo gritted his teeth but was careful to keep his lips slack. "Something shorter? A onetime incident, perhaps?"

"I suppose you'd call it a zero-time incident, if you're really interested in crunching the numbers." Sebastien's voice now was something well beyond flat—it was polished, it was Simonized.

"You are saying you did not sleep with Katy Kellers?" said Eduardo.

"Goodness, you're tedious."

"Not once? That's your statement?"

"Not once. Never. I am fairly sure I'd remember."

"That's not what Lily Hayes reported."

"On this, and on this alone, I fear Lily Hayes is mistaken."

Eduardo's headache was moving from the flanks of his head into its center; it was burrowing down, settling into itself, getting ready for the long haul. Eduardo would not let it bleed onto his face. "You don't have to lie to me," he said, because of the headache. It was his first misstep.

Sebastien scoffed. "If I had anything to lie about, I would absolutely have to lie to you," he said. "But as it happens, I don't. And I did not have any kind of conjugal relations with the deceased. And I'm frankly appalled you'd even ask such a vulgar question."

Eduardo pressed on. "Lily and Katy," he said, "were seen having a fight at Fuego on the night of Lily's birthday."

At this, there was some little sub-physical twitch in Sebastien's face, some kind of barely suppressed psychomotor agitation. Eduardo stared at Sebastien long enough to let him know he had seen it. He never commented on changes in facial expression during interviews— if he did, it would become clear to the interviewee how ephemeral such things were, how easy it was to dispute another person's perception, how quickly two people's interpretations of an event became equal and opposing forces and canceled each other out. Leaving facial clues obviously registered and pointedly unremarked upon made people feel that they had revealed something significant but as yet unutilized. This threw them off and edged them closer to actually saying something valuable, which, of course, was all that could ever actually matter.

"You're telling me that it wasn't you they were fighting about?" said Eduardo.

"I assure you it was not," said Sebastien, recovering mastery over his face.

"What, then?"

"I don't know. What do women fight about? Bra size? Sexual dominance? Competing predictions about the likely consequences of Mercosur's limits on trade restrictions? I don't know."

"Tell me what you heard of it. Maybe the two of us can piece it together."

"I don't know. I wasn't there."

"You weren't at Fuego that night?"

"No."

"You are telling me that you did not attend your own girlfriend's birthday party?"

"As it happens, no."

"We can check that, you know."

"Modern police work is becoming so terrifyingly good."

"Why did you stay away? Because it didn't seem like a good idea to have to deal with Lily and Katy in the same room?"

Sebastien LeCompte raised his head. "I stayed away because I was not invited." His voice had to be some new category of deadpan; it was his singular invention in this life, his sole contribution to this world.

"It doesn't do you any good to lie to me about these sorts of things," said Eduardo. This was actually true. The little lies could not possibly help.

"I marvel at your continued insistence on this point."

"Why wouldn't Lily Hayes—your girlfriend, the girl you were sleeping with—have invited you to her birthday party?"

"I think that's probably a better question for Lily. Do let me know what you hear." There was a fibrousness in Sebastien's voice now, and Eduardo suddenly understood that he was not lying about this—and, though it might not be the only true thing he had said so far, it was the only true thing that actually meant anything to him. As such, it was a detail that would now need to be energetically pursued.

"That's a pretty aggressive thing to do, wouldn't you say?" said Eduardo. "To not invite your own boyfriend to your birthday?"

"Well, I might not say aggressive. It was certainly very *emancipated* of her. These twenty-first-century women, right?"

Eduardo knew by now that there was no tonal variation between sincerity and irony when Sebastien LeCompte talked, and he could tell that this strange speech characteristic—this sort of semantic monotone—was deep and ubiquitous and actually authentic to him, though, of course, perhaps somewhat amplified by the context of the interview. The implication of this was that even if Sebastien LeCompte was rarely serious, he was not absolutely always joking. Eduardo decided to try something new.

He leaned forward, then pulled back and shook his head a little and leaned forward again. "You know," said Eduardo, making his voice sound confiding, conspiratorial, as though he were an actor who was tired of being in the same bad play as Sebastien and it wouldn't hurt if they took a cigarette break backstage for a moment. "My wife is rather erratic, too."

Sebastien's eyebrows rose in studied amusement, but he said nothing.

"She gets angry at me every other day, and to be honest? I have no fucking clue what it's about half the time. I truly do not. It's a giant guessing game. Did you find that with Lily sometimes? No, it's okay, you don't have to answer that. Of course you did." Eduardo almost added something like *We've all seen her Facebook posts, after all,* but he decided against it. Alluding to some widely known fact about Lily here might not be a bad idea—it might actually induce Sebastien to chuckle ruefully, naughtily—but referencing material that had been acquired in the course of the investigation could only snap Sebastien back away from Eduardo. If he'd bent to him at all already. Which, it was quite possible, he had not.

"But you know, Sebastien, the thing is, when my wife is angry with me and I have no fucking clue why and I have to guess—the thing is, sometimes I do actually guess right. If I really, really think about it. Maybe only a quarter of the time, but still, that's not statistically insignificant, you know? So tell me. If you had to hazard a *guess*, why do you think Lily might have been angry with you that night?"

Still, Sebastien said nothing; his face was so blank that it did not even look like a blankness that was orchestrated to conceal. Eduardo would not have thought it was, if he hadn't known better.

"And, of course, Lily was angry with you and Katy both," said Eduardo. "We know that much. So that's probably a clue. What might have made Lily angry with you and Katy at the same time?"

Still, on Sebastien's face, an expression of total noninvolvement. It was not blatantly evasive—he did not look down, he did not look away, he did not fidget or blink too much or touch his hair. He sat with his hands curled lightly at his lap; his pose was one of total calm and attention and patience, as though he were the one awaiting the answers, not the other way around. He was pretty good at this, Eduardo thought. Maybe he should have gone into the family business.

"Well," said Eduardo, standing up and handing Sebastien his card. "Think about it. Don't worry. Sometimes it takes me a while to get it, too. But do get back to me with whatever you come up with."

And at this, Sebastien—finally rousing from his fugue state and showing Eduardo to the door—responded that he assuredly, enthusiastically would.

Andrew and Maureen stood drinking on the hotel balcony and did not speak. A floor above them, in Andrew's room, Anna was sleeping. Three miles away from them, in jail, Lily was waiting. Andrew and Maureen were sipping mini-bottles of vodka straight, letting the alcohol macerate their mouths. Across the street was an office building, dark except for a single room that glowed like an illuminated postage stamp. Above it, the stars were opalescent pinpricks, looking so cold and distant that Andrew couldn't quite believe they were fire. It was not right that he could stand here and see these things when Lily could not. Once, years ago, while flying over the North Atlantic, Andrew had spotted an eerie pale dot in the black ocean below him. It had reminded him of that famous picture of the earth from space—tiny and luminous, like a glowing pearl in the void—which everyone had thought, for about thirty seconds, might bring world peace. Squinting at the dot, Andrew had thought it was an iceberg, or the reflection of the moon on a whale, or some heretofore undiscovered Arctic bioluminescence. Or maybe, he'd thought, just maybe, it was something else. Andrew was surprised at how ready he was to believe it might be something else—how ready he was, also, to keep quiet about it, to make it a secret between him and the universe. He'd been almost all the way to England before he realized it was only the reflection of the airplane.

The rest of the interview with the lawyers that afternoon had been repetitive and interminable. Andrew had tried to take notes but had eventually fallen into a fretful underlining of the notes he'd already taken. After the revelation of Lily's drug purchase from Ignacio Toledo, nothing new was revealed; she'd stuck faithfully and reassuringly to her story about the day of the crime, and in its repeated tellings the narrative seemed to move from the specific to the archetypal—like a Bible verse or a Beatles song, it became too familiar to actually hear. Lily told the story so many times that Andrew nearly felt he was watching it unfold before him: He could almost see the ghostly shadow of stoned Sebastien LeCompte, he could almost hear the coppery yelping of the game shows that Lily had watched while Katy's undiscovered body—good God—lay a floor below her in the basement.

By the time the lawyers finally left, Andrew and Maureen's visit was over. Maureen had tried to persuade Lily to eat the rest of her sandwich, but she did not; they'd left it on a crusty pile on the table, even though Lily said that the guards would probably make her throw it away. Then they'd both kissed her on the cheek, and she'd clung to Maureen for longer than the security guards had liked, and then it was time—again—for them to leave her.

"Come on," said Maureen, tugging on Andrew's wrist. "Let's go in-side."

Andrew followed her into the room, vodka between his forefinger and thumb, and shoved aside a pile of newspaper clippings so that he could sit on the bed. In the corner of one of the articles, he could see the edge of that awful picture of Lily from her own camera, standing in front of the church with the immodest décolletage and the too-bright smile. Andrew turned the newspaper over, and Maureen joined him on the bed. She smelled like moss and cedar and some new late-in-life perfume. She smelled mostly like a stranger.

Maureen sighed. "I can't believe she lied about the drugs."

"Well, she didn't lie, I don't think," said Andrew. "Not really. She just didn't volunteer that information."

"She should have known better."

"She's scared. She's with lawyers. She doesn't know what to say." Andrew ran his hand through his hair. "Anyway, it was just a little dope."

"Just a little dope? Down here? Jesus Christ. Just a little dope would have been a big enough problem, even if she hadn't happened to man-age to buy it from a murderer." Maureen sighed again and shook her head. "God. You know, I can't even really let myself think about it, but it could have been her. It so, so easily could have been her, instead of Katy."

"I know," said Andrew. It was true. It could have been her. It *had* been her once. It had been Janie.

Maureen traced her pinkie along the rim of her vodka, then put it in her mouth. "Do you think I was unreasonable about her hair?"

"You weren't wrong."

"But do you think I was unreasonable?"

Andrew flashed again to that photo—the forbidding sobriety of the church, Lily's bosom spilling out of that ridiculous tank top, which had probably cost her less than the equivalent of three U.S. dollars some-where. Could she not afford a shirt containing enough fabric to actu-ally cover herself? They would have bought her one! Didn't she know that? Is that all it would have taken? Andrew shook his head. "It just might have been a little late, you know?"

"What do you mean?" Maureen's voice was vinegary.

"I just mean," Andrew said slowly. "It seems like there are things we should have talked to her about. In terms of how she presents herself. Probably a while ago."

"Me, you mean." Maureen was chewing audibly on her nail. The physiology of her anxiety was like a childhood language Andrew hadn't known he still remembered until now.

"Us, I mean."

Andrew did not know if this was really what they had done wrong—but clearly, they had done something wrong. And really, how could they not have? They had just been trying to keep it together, and Andrew was still proud of them—he would never stop being proud of them—for having managed as long as they had; in situations like theirs, it was usual to divorce much earlier. Right after Janie had died, of course, there'd been a moment when they'd teetered. Maureen's mother had come to stay; she was rigid and humorless even under the best of circumstances, her face flat and white as a Japanese empress's. The three of them moved through those days with the insensate numbness of creatures of the very deep sea: They were little translucent crabs scrabbling along near the volcanic vents, they were blind and mute and looming dumbo octopi. Maureen walked around with an expression of enduring, ferocious blankness, and Andrew had known she would not have noticed then if he'd let her drift away, or if he'd drifted away himself: into the geriatric Peace Corps, perhaps (they had a branch, he knew, for sufferers of late-onset idealism), or the arms of a younger, undestroyed woman. It was nearly unbelievable to Andrew now that they'd even bothered to bathe and dress, let alone hang on to their marriage for a time. He could see how an outsider might think they'd been saints, though, of course, that wasn't true at all—they had, in fact, been utterly devoid of compassion for anyone besides Janie and each other (and, for a brief time right before the death, only Janie; and, for a brief time afterward, only themselves). Janie's death was the monstrous planet around which everything else orbited. Even the other children at the hospital lived and died merely in relation to Janie; viewed in one light, the death of another child could seem like a harbinger of Janie's departure, the hideous reality that made the more hideous potentiality more real; viewed in another, it could feel like dodging a bullet (and, as Churchill had said, there's nothing so exhilarating as being shot at without result). And if only a certain percentage of children with X were doomed, and if child Y died, would that mean it was statistically more or less likely for Janie to die, too? Andrew and Maureen would actually talk about this. Maureen would point out that they were conflating probability with odds. Neither of them would point out that in the narcissism of their grief they had forgotten the other child, forgotten the other family—who were somewhere weeping, picking out a tiny gold-limned coffin. There was no other family, there were no other children. There was only Janie and Maureen and Andrew, at sea on a little boat, and all the continents of the world submerged.

How did they love each other again after that? How did they even look at each other? But they did, somehow they did, and there were the years of Lily and Anna: chubby hands, dandelion-down hair, adorable little pets—a tuxedo kitten who eventually grew to a murderous twenty pounds, a precious lop-eared dwarf bunny who transformed into a sexual predator overnight—and life had been livable, at least until the girls went to school. But once they did, the show was over: The stage lights dimmed, the orchestra was dismantled; the audience, drunk on their own lives, disappeared into the night. And Maureen and Andrew found themselves staring at each other, alone together at last.

Andrew nearly wanted to say some of these things to Maureen, but he looked down and found her in a shallow and hard-earned sleep. He rose, careful not to crinkle the newspapers, and turned out the light.

Andrew rode the elevator up one floor, then stood for a moment in the harsh yellow light of the soda dispenser, listening to the snorkeling of the ice machine, before walking back to his room. He dipped his key and watched the console flash green and opened the door.

Anna was not in the room.

She was not in the closet, not in either bedroom, not in the bathroom. Not, when Andrew went downstairs to check, at the gym. She had not been seen by the hotel concierge. Andrew headed back toward his room to put on his sneakers. He was not about to rouse Maureen from sleep to confess that he'd lost another daughter.

This time when he opened the door, Anna was sitting in the corner on the floor, long legs folded up around her as though she were a piece of obsolete video equipment. Andrew wavered in the doorway. "Where were you?" he said.

"Have you been drinking?" said Anna. In the moonlight, her hair looked nearly gray, and Andrew thought he could almost see her as she would someday look—in some future unimaginably far, that Andrew would never live to witness.

"Excuse me, have *you* been drinking?" he said. "Just where the hell have you been?"

"I'm nineteen years old," said Anna, standing up. She was shorter than Andrew by a good three inches, but her litheness and youth conspired to make him feel towered over. "You can't keep me locked up here. I'm not the one in jail." She hiccupped.

"You can't just take off like that. This is a dangerous city." Andrew's voice was shaking. "Do you know how worried I was?"

"Afraid someone will kill me?"

"Christ, Anna. Yes. Obviously. Among other things." Andrew wanted to go to her and take her in his arms, but he could not bear the thought of her shrugging him off.

"Other things? What other things?" said Anna. "Like that I'll kill someone, maybe?"

"Stop it," said Andrew, with volume. Anna looked surprised. Because Andrew normally spoke so gently, nobody ever remembered that he had a voice that carried when he wanted it to.

"Dad." Anna wobbled again. "Would you still love her if she did it?"

"Stop it," said Andrew again. "Sit down."

She did.

"Take off your shoes," said Andrew, even though he didn't know why he was telling her to do this. She wouldn't run off again without her shoes, maybe. Or maybe she would. Maybe he had no idea what his daughters would or wouldn't do. Maybe Andrew just wanted to tell Anna to do something and watch her actually do it. "Hand them to me," he ordered.

She did. Andrew was feeling marginally more under control. "Okay then," he said. "I'm going to get us some water."

Andrew went to the bathroom and ran the water until it was cold. In the mirror, the skin around his eyes and mouth were furrowed; his teeth, he could see, were yellowing by the day. It was very clear to Andrew that he was older now than he had ever, ever been before; worse, he strongly suspected that, from now on, he was only going to get older still.

Back in the room, Anna was sitting on the bed. Andrew handed her a glass of water, then drank his own in one gulp. He wiped his mouth. "She didn't do it," he said.

"I know." Anna looked into her water balefully. "But what if she had?"

"That's not a useful thing to think about."

"Everything's useful to think about. That's a direct quote from you. You have actually literally said that."

"Well, not this."

"Hypotheticals. You always say you truck in hypotheticals."

"Anna—"

"Counterfactuals, right? That's your word. So what if she did it? What if she had done it?"

"Stop it."

"Or what if I did? What if I did something terrible?"

Andrew squinted into his glass. He remembered when Anna and Lily were small and terrified of their nightmares and would come crawling into bed with Andrew and Maureen to make them promise not to die. Andrew had never been inclined to promise this, since, in fact, he and Maureen *would* someday die, and the best of all possible outcomes was that Anna and Lily would have to watch them do it. And Andrew had imagined some future reckoning, some kind of confrontation (though when this would occur exactly, he was unclear) when

Anna and Lily would point at him with accusing fingers and go back to the videotape and say *Look, you promised not to die, and look, you did die. You promised not to and you did.* Lying to them about this most irreducible fact seemed to Andrew an unforgivable deceit—he was giving them the wrong idea about absolutely everything if he gave them the wrong idea about this.

But Maureen had not agreed. She felt that the children were children, and that they needed a promise in order to sleep at night—on this one particular night, the wind shivering through the white pine trees outside their windows, their sheets vaguely redolent of lavender— and that by the time Maureen and Andrew died the children would be grown and with children of their own and they would understand the lie, and would look back and forgive them.

And so Andrew and Maureen had promised: They had looked their two living children in the eyes and promised not to die. And Andrew remembered how this had assuaged Anna—how, sleepy with relief, she had tugged at her ear and grabbed her stuffed rabbit, Honey Bunny, by one felt foot and dragged him up the stairs—but how Lily had remained awake, staring at them with her fierce agate eyes, saying, "That's not true. I know that you can't promise that. I know that that isn't true."

Andrew made a decision. "You wouldn't do something terrible," he said to Anna. "You couldn't do something terrible. But if you did, I'd always love you. That's our job." Probably, this wasn't a lie. Probably, he would still love her. This was the elasticity and permanence of parental love; everything vile about your children was to some degree something vile about yourself, and disowning your child for their failings could only compound your own.

Anna looked at him hard, and for a moment Andrew saw her as a child, yawning and pacified, swinging her rabbit from her hand, turning around to pad up the stairs. And then the look changed, hardening into something brittle and unyielding and wise, something that could know things that Andrew didn't know, that Andrew might never know.

"No," she said finally. "You wouldn't."

CHAPTER THIRTEEN

February

The day after her birthday, Lily awoke to a bright dawn. Preposterously pink light streamed in through the windows; it was like waking up in the middle of a conch shell, and Lily felt a sense of emergency—apocalypse, war, alien invasion—before realizing that this was only a sunrise. This happened every morning; every morning she was bathed briefly in this otherworldly light, and she was never even awake for it. She propped herself up on her elbows. It was strange, maybe a little violating, that the room could turn this color without her noticing. She popped her head over the side of the bed to look at Katy, feeling, as she did so, the first ominous heave of what she knew would be a daylong hangover. Below her, Katy was composed, even in sleep. At the sight of her, the whole of the previous evening came back to Lily, and she remembered that she was going to have to break up with Sebastien. She lay back down.

Lily was sorry she had to end things with Sebastien, but she saw no alternative; she was outmaneuvered, and to do nothing now would only make her a chump. Lily didn't know how she'd gotten herself into a situation where being a chump was even possible—being, as she was, about as committed to transparency and low-stress, drama-free entanglements as a person could be—but there it was. Lily hadn't asked anything from Sebastien—she hadn't even wanted anything, really: She hadn't required him to make any promises, she hadn't put him in a position where he'd need to tell her any lies. The fact that he'd treated her poorly anyway could only mean that he'd wanted to.

Lily rolled over and stifled a groan. She'd been childish, she saw now; she'd wanted everyone to be liberated and generous with one another, and somewhere along the way, she'd started believing that that meant people actually would be. Why had she believed this? Was it because she'd watched too many reruns of *Friends* growing up? In which everyone jumped in and out of bed with one another but no one got hurt and the truly sacred, eponymous relationship—friendship—remained intact? Or maybe Lily's problem was her parents' fault; perhaps it was some kind of inherited naïveté. Maybe it stemmed from Maureen and Andrew's allegedly hippie-ish youth (though the only supporting evidence for this characterization was Maureen's claim that she'd gone barefoot for the entire summer of 1971), or maybe it somehow came from Andrew's outmoded, overly sanguine scholarly worldview—all the end-of-history-Francis-Fukuyama shit he'd committed to twenty years ago and now had to wearily, disingenuously maintain in article after article. Lily did not know. All she knew was that she was going to admit it when she was wrong. It was true that in her generation people didn't have to be cruel and deceitful in order to get what they wanted—unless being cruel and deceitful *was* what they wanted, in which case they had a whole new vista of opportunity to be that way. Whenever Lily herself had juggled dates, she had done it because she really *liked* a few men at once—she wanted to talk about politics with one of them and she wanted to talk about music with another and with a third she wanted to go on playful midnight adventures to search for free furniture on the street when the first of the month came and everybody moved out of their apartments. And in this spirit, Lily had done new things: She went to a rally for a union, even though she'd always found labor issues terribly dull; she found a child's abandoned skunk piñata on the street and kept it in her dorm for half a year; she attended a concert of an intolerable band whose music was like the forceful overthrowing of the concept of music, and after a while she found herself dancing, actually dancing, even though she still didn't like the songs. The reason Lily didn't want a boyfriend was because she actually cared for all of these men. They were all her friends, and Lily's friends mattered to her; she was not in love with any of them, but she would have given any one of them a kidney. She understood now that this was not how Sebastien felt about her. A situation like theirs arose not because a man liked too many women, but because he hated too many.

Lily was, she realized, monstrously thirsty. She padded down the ladder and went to the bathroom to guzzle water directly from the faucet. When she stood up, she caught sight of herself in the mirror and startled. What was wrong with her face? Her eyes were raccooned with makeup, of course, but that wasn't it. Last night Lily had thought she looked a bit fierce—masquerading semi-convincingly as the kind of girl that she was secretly intimidated by—and normally in the mornings after a night out she just looked goofy, like a person whose Halloween costume had fallen apart because they were having too much fun at the party. What was it that looked different now? Lily leaned closer and studied her face. Recently, faint sickle-shaped lines had appeared around her mouth; Lily had known, on some level, that these were wrinkles—fetal wrinkles, proto-wrinkles, whatever—but still she'd regarded them up until now as temporary blemishes, something she might yet grow out of, like acne. She pulled away from the mirror. The lines were barely visible, but they were there, and they were, she realized, part of the reason she looked different: She looked older. Not old, of course—but old enough to seem a little less victorious in sloppiness, like a person whose immaculate beauty has faded enough that their stern glasses finally really do look dowdy. In the morning light—makeup smeared, hair disastrous—Lily didn't seem like a person whose costume was unimportant. She seemed like a person whose costume was very important indeed. Lily bent and scrubbed her face, leaving black streaks on the hand towel, then furiously scrubbed at that until the motion stopped her. She threw the towel helplessly in the hamper, trying not to think about who might find it, and retreated back down the hallway.

The sun was still coiling around the bedroom, gathering itself up into corners, as Lily climbed back into bed. There was a ray of light on her pillow. Maybe it wasn't violating at all, the way the light snuck in like this—maybe it was lovely. It meant that there could be beauty, benevolent and unasked for and all around you, even if you didn't know it. There was something bittersweet about this, but perhaps there was also something hopeful. Soon enough, Lily would be on the other side of breaking up with Sebastien. And soon enough, Lily would be awake early enough for this light; she vowed to remember it, to set an alarm to gratefully greet it. But not today. Today, she was tired. And so Lily lay back down—deliciously, guiltily, with the decadent weariness of the newly old—and sank back into sleep.

When Lily woke again, it was ludicrously late, the light outside her window already aging. Sleeping into the afternoon always gave Lily a dreadful feeling—as though she'd wasted an entire life, not only part of a day—and she bolted upright. She looked at the clock and scoffed. It was almost three-thirty. There was a real possibility she was going to be late for work.

Ten minutes later Lily was racing along Avenida Cabildo; above her, the skies were opening up into an uncharacteristic late afternoon rain, contributing to her general sense of persecution. She arrived at Fuego soaking wet but only five minutes late. Javier was sitting at the end of the bar poring over some papers. He shot Lily a subtle smirk. She ducked her head and hurried to grab her apron, trying to look diligent and humble. But when she glanced back in Javier's direction, she saw that he was motioning her over to him. This felt ominous, though Lily reminded herself that absolutely everything today felt ominous. She walked to the end of the bar.

"Hey, Javier," she said. "What's up?"

"Feeling okay today, Lily?"

She laughed ruefully and bobbled her hand back and forth. "Not too bad. A little tired."

"Well, don't worry about that. You can go home now."

"What?" Lily gestured toward the break room, where the schedule was posted on the wall. "I'm on the schedule for tonight."

"I know, Lily," said Javier. "But it's not working out."

"What?" Lily felt like she'd bitten on a blade. "Why?"

"I expect my customers to make scenes, not my waitresses."

"What?" Had Lily made a scene? Maybe, by very, very puritan standards, she had. "But it was my birthday," she said, inanely.

"Well, your birthday present is you got to make a scene," said Javier. "Happy birthday. Now you're fired."

"But I mean, I wasn't even working. I mean, I was off the clock."

"Yes. It was a favor for you."

"Doesn't that mean I was just a customer? So I get to make a scene, too?" Lily laughed lightly, but Javier did not.

"Really, Lily, did you actually like this job? Did you think you were any good at it?"

Actually, yes: Lily had thought she was good at it. She'd thought she was okay at it, at any rate, and getting better. She'd thought that the customers and the other staff liked her. They laughed and jovially caroused whenever she came around, anyway, and she'd always thought that this was good-natured, maybe even fond. But just like things with Beatriz, and Sebastien, and all men, and possibly all things and all people, Lily saw now that perhaps there had been a different, more menacing undercurrent to all of this teasing—something she hadn't detected, or had willfully mistranslated, in order to be happy. "I did like this job," said Lily. "I do like it."

Javier's face softened a bit, and he said, "Well, I'm sorry, Lily. But I know you don't actually need this job."

"I've never been fired before."

"Have you ever worked before?"

At this, shamefully, Lily's eyes filled with tears. Why did everybody always want to think the worst of her? "Of course," she said emphatically, and waited a moment to see if this might earn her a reprieve. When she saw it wasn't going to, she told Javier she'd go clean out her locker.

A few minutes later, armed with her water bottle, book, and street shoes, Lily walked out into the already diminishing day. The rain had stopped. She really never had been fired before; it had been years and years, in fact, since she'd been in any kind of trouble at all, if you didn't count Beatriz's scoldings. She was still shaky from the conversation's blunt smash of adrenaline—so much like the brief narcotizing energy that comes, when you're hurt, just fractionally earlier than pain.

"Hey."

Lily turned. It was Ignacio the Tortoise, leaning up against the side of a dumpster. Lily flashed to the image she'd seen—or thought she'd seen—of Ignacio and Katy, his hands on her ass, flashing in the strobe lights. Lily had wanted to ask Katy about it last night, but she'd been so drunk that she couldn't be certain, and now that she and Katy had finally fought and reached a delicate, tentative peace, she wasn't sure she'd want to reopen the issue.

"Hey," said Lily. "I just got fired."

Ignacio shook his head. "Bad luck," he said. Lily could smell the pungent stink of weed. He must have just been smoking.

"I guess. Hey." Lily felt suddenly bold. She was already a derelict employee—she might as well be a minor criminal, too. "Can I buy any of that from you?"

Ignacio raised his eyebrows in an expression of amusement. "Of course," he said. "You want a baggie?"

"Um, I guess so."

Ignacio began reaching into his backpack.

"Oh, now?" said Lily.

Ignacio looked around the empty alleyway. "You want to do it later?"

"No, no," said Lily. "Now is great."

Ignacio nodded and produced a small plastic bag with a few black rosettes in it. "For you, forty pesos," he said. Lily was hoping he would hurry. "A discount. Since you've had a rough day."

Lily found a damp fifty-peso bill in her purse, then handed it to Ignacio and grabbed the baggie. Sweat was breaking out on her back, and she scurried away from him without taking any of the change. "Thanks," she called behind her, as she walked out of the alleyway and into the street.

"Hey," said Ignacio. "Anytime."

Lily turned onto the street and immediately nearly ran into a woman with an army of tiny dogs trotting alongside her. The dogs were so small that their heads bobbed savagely at the pace they were going; the smallest dog's eyes were white with cataracts that shone like mother-of-pearl.

"Permiso," Lily muttered. The woman gave her a look and walked away.

Lily would not tell Sebastien about the firing, she decided, as she headed toward the Subte. She would not tell Sebastien, or Katy, or Beatriz, or anyone. She could not bear to. And anyway, she could probably find a use for the freedom of nights with nowhere to go and no one to answer to. Lily's awareness of the baggie in her purse was contracting and relenting like a pulse. She had nothing in mind, particularly; no plans or schemes or mischief or, beyond Katy and Sebastien, really any friends. But whatever you did was simply more your own when no one else knew you were doing it. In front of Lily, a scarp of periwinkle dusk was falling over the streets. Around her, the bars were just beginning to rouse to life. And out in the city she might find anything, anything at all, except someone who was waiting for her.

. . .

Lily was careful to stay out of the house until her usual hour. When she returned, she found Katy in the living room, watching cartoons. Lily halted at the door and considered turning around—but then she'd be out later than Beatriz expected her to be, and she didn't want to risk that. Instead, she paused in front of the living room.

"Hey," she said. "What are you watching?"

"I don't know," said Katy. Next to her sat an economics textbook with an uncapped pen as a bookmark. "It's totally surreal. I turned it on like an hour ago and I can't turn away. How was work?"

Lily had been anxious about seeing Katy and had expected to feel something moving gingerly between them now, but Katy sounded nonchalant.

"Fine," said Lily. "You know." On the screen, a talking rodent with crazed eyes was doing somersaults. "This is a weird show."

"Yeah. It kind of makes me wonder why I ever stopped watching cartoons. I guess because I went to middle school."

"Age is really no object." Lily walked over to the sofa, still holding her purse. She didn't want to leave it unattended in the house—Beatriz probably had drug-sniffing dogs in her employ. "A lot of my friends watch them all the time."

"Like, currently?"

"Yeah."

"Why?"

"I don't know," said Lily, sitting down. "They think it's hilarious."

"Our generation has such a weird thing with little-kid stuff," said Katy after a moment.

"What do you mean?"

"Like coloring books and ironic T-shirts with dinosaurs and stuff."

"I guess. It's premature nostalgia."

"Do you ever feel that way, though?"

"What way?"

"Like you could go back to some time that's passed? Like you catch yourself thinking, why don't I go there anymore, and why don't I see those people and attend those parties, and then you remember it's because that life is gone? And that you can't?"

Lily nodded, even though she wasn't sure she ever did feel that way, exactly. Under the regime of Maureen and Andrew, there had been no confusion about which way life was headed, or what its ultimate destination would be. Still, Lily had never heard Katy say anything like this before, and she wanted to offer something in return.

"Maybe it's because when we're kids we don't really believe time only moves forward," she said. "And then you learn it does, but you never really get your head around it."

"You think that's it?" said Katy.

"Yeah." The red muskrat bopped manically on the screen. "Maybe." It sounded like it could be true, and so maybe it was. After all, you hadn't told a child a story until you had retold a child that story; children awoke to sentience in their lives with fables and fairy tales already familiar, and maybe this meant that the first stories they heard never felt like linear narratives at all—maybe they were more like rituals, passion plays, establishing a sense of life as recurrent and recursive, a sense that everything that happens is somehow always happening. "Like you know how when you're a little kid you really think you live in a story?" said Lily.

"I don't know," said Katy doubtfully. "I don't think so."

"Oh, man," said Lily. "I really, really felt that way. I totally thought I lived in a story. I was really pretty confused about it, actually. I was always thinking, here's the part where *this* happens."

"Where what happens?"

"Well, like." Lily thought for a moment. "Like this time that my parents got a man to dress up as Winnie-the-Pooh and show up on the porch for my fifth birthday, for example."

"That sounds terrifying."

"It wasn't, though! That's the thing—I wasn't terrified at all. I think I'd seen so many movies about ordinary children's lives turning magical that I saw it as basically my birthright." It was true: Lily remembered it vividly. When she'd seen Pooh coming up the walkway, she'd clasped her hands together in a gesture of such hushed, old lady-ish happiness that Andrew and Maureen had laughed and taken her picture. "Who's that?" Maureen had said, her voice suspiciously girlish, the way it always was when she was telling children lies—it was a tone that Lily had half-noticed even then, though she'd merely registered it as the voice that Maureen used when something incredibly special was happening. But what Maureen and Andrew hadn't known—what they never had known—was that Lily was not actually surprised. She wasn't surprised at all. In that picture, what she was thinking was: This is it. It's finally happening. This is the part where the magic starts.

"It sounds like you've got really good parents," said Katy.

"I do," said Lily, surprising herself with the force of her sincerity. "I really, really do."

The next day, Lily left the house at the usual time. She had promised herself she would end things with Sebastien that day, but she found she was stalling—watching the shifting trapezoids of birds against the sky, feeling a pleasantly lonesome wanderlust. The rain had left the chestnut smell of waterlogged leaves in the air. Lily was enjoying this brief purgatorial reprieve; she could afford, she figured, one more day of it. And so she rode the Subte to the end of the line and back; she stalked the parameters of the zoo, which was closed since it was a Sunday. No matter, thought Lily; after all, half the fun of a zoo was smelling it! She laughed out loud, rounded a corner, and saw a booth with a fat red pay phone at its center.

She flitted her fingers through her pockets and smiled when she found coins. Who would she call? Maybe Anna. As soon as she thought of her sister, Lily felt a violent longing, which was weird, and she actually dialed most of Anna's number before hanging up. Anna was busy, after all; Anna wasn't good on the telephone; Anna, it went without saying, would never have lost a job of any sort, even one as dumb as Lily's. Most of all, maybe, Anna was a grown-up, and sometimes Lily wished she weren't. But there was nothing to be done about it: Anna simply wasn't the same little girl who'd helped Lily try to contact Janie's ghost on a Ouija board—a plan endlessly discussed and then, finally, one summer night, thick with humidity and black magic, attempted— and who had, when the indicator began to move, wet her pants.

Before she'd decided whether she wanted to talk to him, Lily found she'd called Andrew. The phone rang three, four, five times, and Lily was surprised by how relieved she felt when he finally answered. "Hello?" he said.

"Hey, Andrew. It's me."

"Thank God. You see that many digits, you have to assume it's Interpol."

Lily paused to let him know that, if they were in the same room, she'd be rolling her eyes.

"How's it going down there, kid?" he said.

"Pretty good," said Lily. "But listen, I have a serious question for you." Now she would have to think of one.

"Oh, Jesus."

"Not that serious. Don't worry." Lily tapped her thumb against the bottom of the phone. "Do you like your job?" she said finally.

"What a question," said Andrew. "What's with these getting-to-know-your-parents probes lately? Is my dean hiring you to spy on me? Have you joined a twelve-step program of some kind?"

"Not yet!" said Lily. "Well, do you?"

Andrew exhaled heavily. "I suppose," he said. "It's interesting, anyway."

"Is it, though?" said Lily, finding an angle. "Is it still interesting? I mean, do you still feel like you learn things from it?"

On the other end of the line, Lily could hear Andrew consider; one thing that was nice about old Andrew was that he actually thought about it when you asked him a question.

"Well," he said finally. "I learn what your generation thinks about things, anyway. And I do like watching them learn, which I guess is a kind of learning."

Lily sighed. She felt bad for her parents sometimes; everything good that would ever happen to them pretty much already had. The arithmetic of their lives was complete. It was wonderful, of course, to have things to lose—but from now on, that was all they would ever do.

"You're always telling me how great your generation is," Andrew was saying. "Tell me one great thing."

"We're better with technology."

"Well, hallelujah."

"We're less racist."

"Okay, I'll give you that one." Andrew paused. "Lily Pad? Are you all right?"

Andrew hadn't called her Lily Pad in forever; it was a name dating back to her cradle years, when he'd made up nonsense songs for her: *Lily Pad, Lily Pad, stop your crying, don't be sad! Lily Pad, Lily Pad, go to sleep, don't make Mom mad! Lily Pad, Lily Pad, cease to fuss, be kind to Dad!* Lily had liked the nickname when she was very small. But it had turned mortifying in her preadolescent years, when the word "pad"—along with most other words, people, and events—could send her into paroxysms of humiliation, and she had begged Andrew to abandon it.

"I'm all right," she said, hoping she sounded stoic.

"You sound down. You sound like your mother."

"Do I? Nah. Just a little tired."

"Well, get some sleep, why don't you?" There was a momentary lilt in Andrew's voice, and Lily thought for a fraction of a moment that he might actually be about to sing to her. It seemed possible, at least, that he was considering it. If he was, however, he must also have been considering how viciously Lily was likely to mock him for it, and so he restrained himself. Lily had trained him well. There was something a little sad about that, maybe.

"I love you, Dad," said Lily, with feeling.

"I love you, Lily!" said Andrew, sounding startled. "I love you very, very much."

Lily returned to the Carrizos' house at her usual hour and caught herself half-hoping to find Katy watching television when she got there. Lily could almost imagine this becoming a nightly ritual—something sweet and arbitrary and inexplicable, something she'd remember fondly in the years to come. But tonight, Katy was nowhere to be found. Instead, there was Beatriz, sitting at the kitchen counter with a glass of water and a newspaper, and when Lily walked through the door she looked up, her mouth already forming that most beloved phrase of hers. "Where were you?" she said.

"At my job," said Lily wonderingly. She set down her bag slowly and stretched, hoping she looked appropriately tired.

"I thought you lost your job."

"What?" Lily found herself picking her bag back up, perhaps out of a sense that she might need to be prepared to flee at any moment.

"I thought you were fired," said Beatriz.

"Where did you hear that?" Lily was mystified. Had Javier Aguirre called up the Carrizos to tattle on her? What would possibly provoke him to do that?

"I'm not trying to make you feel bad about the job, Lily." Beatriz began folding up the newspaper. Lily could not believe that there were still people who knew how to do this. "But I do need to know where you are, especially at night, and I can't have you lying to me about it. I am responsible for you."

No, it could not have been Javier. He didn't have the Carrizos' number; Lily didn't think she'd ever even mentioned their names to him; and anyway, it would make no sense for him to do something like that—it was too overly vindictive, too overly engaged. Too overly concerned, in a way. So how did they know? Did they have eyes and ears all over town? Who were these people, anyway?

Beatriz put her hand on Lily's shoulder. "Lily," she said. "Look. I understand that you're embarrassed."

This was something that Lily herself might have admitted if Beatriz had waited a moment longer. But it was unendurable to be told you'd embarrassed yourself; there was something too presumptuous about having your shame taken for granted. And so Lily found herself ducking Beatriz's hand and running to her room, where she lay on the bed and, horrifyingly, began to sob. She told herself to stop it immediately. She told herself that in acting this way she was losing her grip on all the finely threaded claims on adulthood she'd only just begun to establish. But this thought only made her sob harder, and eventually Lily gave in to the sobbing, and—out of the same impulse that made you want to wreck something completely once it was wrecked only a little—she let it get louder and messier than even she felt was really necessary.

The next day, the Carrizos left for their nephew's baptism, and Katy went off somewhere with her even-tempered lady friends. To celebrate, Lily cut her classes and spent the day skulking around the house. Beyond opening one of Katy's drawers to check her bra size (32B—Lily was not sure what she was going to do with this information), Lily behaved herself. She flopped carelessly on the sofa just because she could. She picked up the phone's receiver and then set it back down. She rifled through the kitchen cabinets and inspected Beatriz's incomprehensible cooking gadgets. But she opened no private drawers belonging to the Carrizos—Beatriz probably had everything booby-trapped, anyhow—nor did she brook the grim border of their bedroom door. She enjoyed only the meager proprietary feeling that came from washing her own dish, from changing the television to a new channel. Left to her own devices, Lily actually was fairly trustworthy—but, she thought bitterly, nobody would ever know it.

When evening fell, Lily began the walk across the driveway toward Sebastien's, dragging her feet on the grass. She had told him she'd be over at seven-thirty and was already late; she could not possibly put it off any longer, she knew. And anyway, the anticipation was always worse than the thing itself—the anticipation and the memory, of course. And the anticipation of the memory was maybe the worst part of all, at least for Lily. In her life so far, Lily had managed to remember with stunning clarity every truly painful conversation she had ever had; they ran through her head like incantations, like important speeches memorized during childhood (Lily wished she could still remember speeches—why was it that nothing could be tattooed onto your brain like something written there against your will when you were young?). The coming conversation with Sebastien would be no different, Lily knew, and she did not relish the thought of it replaying in her head for a lifetime—the scene made somehow grimmer and more ludicrous, both, by its setting in that ridiculous room, before that awful tapestry, which, she now thought meanly, Sebastien had probably commissioned to be made to look threadbare.

Across the yard, Sebastien's house grew larger and larger, and then it was upon her. Lily stood for a moment on the porch, feeling, over her sadness, that strange flutter of excitement that often came to her in darker moments. It was a sense of detached curiosity and potential energy; a feeling that here before her was an important event she might witness, an important mystery she might solve, an important challenge she might rise to meet. This sensation had been with Lily from the first missteps of her childhood—she remembered it from the time she'd killed the banana slug, and the time she'd accidentally made Maureen cry over Janie—but it had had more sinister incarnations, too. It had been with Lily the time Anna had broken her ankle doing gymnastics in the living room; it had been there when she sat in her sixth-grade classroom and listened to the teacher try to explain what had just happened to the buildings in New York City.

Lily raised her hand to the knocker. Standing here now, undeniably, it was with her again—the same feeling as when she'd sat among her subdued classmates (sixth graders being too young to know what to be scared of or sad for and too old to fall into reflexive hysterics regardless); the same feeling as when she'd raced up the stairs and into the hallway and dialed 911 while Anna screamed in the background. Alongside the terror and the rabid sort of mania there was also something like elation. It was the elation of jumping off a bridge, perhaps— the momentary delirium you'd feel in the free fall—but whatever it was, it was with her now, as she knocked on Sebastien LeCompte's door for the last time and heard him moving toward the door. *Here we go. This is it.* Lily closed her eyes. *Someday we'll all be dead, but we are not dead yet.* She held her breath. *And something is finally happening.*

CHAPTER FOURTEEN

February

By the last night, the night Katy died, Sebastien already knew it was over.

Lily appeared at his door at nearly eight o'clock—late—and he took her coolly into his arms. He could smell the baseness of bleach, the dried beer spilled on her shoes, something skunk-cabbagey in her hair—now that she worked, Lily always smelled like the world. She submitted to his embrace with the resignation of a person who has already planned to take away something enormous, and so has no trouble giving something trifling.

"Sorry I'm late," she said, even though she must have known that he would never have remarked on it. She sounded too careful, too kind; he could hear in her voice the magnanimousness of the already decided. Sebastien had so little of her, he knew; he always had. Still, what could he do? He had to proceed as usual. He had to act as though what was clearly happening was not.

"Are you?" Sebastien was exhausting even himself now. "I never notice Newtonian time, myself."

Lily nodded vacantly—he had to think: tolerantly—and wiggled away from him, kicking off her shoes. Sebastien would not fritter their last moments with indignity and anxiety, he decided. He would not paw at her and beg for her love and stroke her hair and say, What's wrong, my love, what's wrong, what's wrong? He was his parents' son, after all. If there was anything he could endure, it was solitude. If there was anything he could endure, it was abandonment. If there was anything he could endure, it was everything.

"Do you mind if I pour myself a drink?" said Lily.

She had never asked this before. "I'll pour one for you," said Sebastien. "Did you eat at home?"

"They're out of town," she said, padding off to the bathroom. "Beatriz left us some leftovers."

She closed the door and turned on the water, and in a moment Sebastien could hear the beeping of her phone. He was not surprised. This was the way of things. She was young, and she was alive, and she belonged in the land of the living. Sebastien would not try to strong-arm her into this sarcophagus of a house, to lie with him in his post-mortal life for all eternity.

Lily came back from the bathroom and mustered a smile.

"Do you want to watch a movie?" said Sebastien. He'd meant to say, "Would the lady care to indulge in some of the more mediocre of our cinematic arts?"—but, for some reason, everything sardonic was curdling somewhere in the back of his throat. He felt himself regressing, turning into someone young and uncomplicated, someone who had never had to be brave.

"I guess," Lily said dully. She was tugging at her split ends with the fretfulness of a trauma victim. Maybe, after all, she was not so special—just a pretty girl, a little less than conventionally gorgeous, a little more than conventionally bright, affixed with all the conventional scraps of luck that came with a conventionally privileged life. Maybe, Sebastien told himself, she would be easier to forget than he was imagining.

Sebastien put *Lost in Translation* into the DVD player and turned off the lights. Lily produced a joint, lit it, then passed it to him wordlessly. Sebastien was surprised but was not going to ask; instead he took a long drag, hoping for some kind of emotional blunting. On the screen, a mute Scarlett Johansson moved through a frenetic Tokyo. Sebastien began to feel the waves of weed, its surges of calm and twists of paranoia. Time passed. He did not touch Lily, and she did not touch him. The movie ended. Sebastien looked at Lily, who was still staring at the darkened screen. He was not ready for it, but he also knew he never would be.

"Let's skip the histrionics, shall we?" he said.

"What histrionics?" said Lily. Her pupils were enormous from the weed and the dark.

"Please don't insult my intelligence," said Sebastien. He realized immediately that the "please" made it sound like a request, not a demand.

"I have no idea what you're talking about."

"We're done here, aren't we?" Sebastien hated, absolutely hated, what this new energy of hers was doing to him: rendering him silent, monosyllabic, ordinary. If he could have been angry with her for anything—which he couldn't yet—it would have been for this.

"Sebastien." Lily turned her head away from him—whether in bafflement or sadness or anger, he was not sure. "I don't mind about you and Katy, you know."

A new sense of doom was dawning in the back of Sebastien's head, but he felt too stupid now to comprehend it. His tongue was thick and ungainly. "Me and Katy what?"

"I don't mind. Really. I know it has nothing to do with us. I'm not possessive."

Sebastien was trying very, very hard to understand, but the weed made it impossible to follow a sentence from its beginning to its end. Lily looked sad.

"But I do think that maybe we should probably spend less time together," she said.

To this, Sebastien said nothing. He could think of absolutely nothing to say.

"I'm going to take a walk," said Lily, standing up. "I need some air."

"I'll come with you." Sebastien scrabbled upright. He was not at all sure, in that moment, how he might go about executing the physical act of walking, if Lily had assented. But he also knew that she would not.

"No," she said. "I want to be alone. We'll talk about it in the morning."

"As you wish," said Sebastien, and gave half a sloppy bow for aesthetics.

She was gone for a long while. Later Sebastien would try to remember exactly how long, but it was hard to say precisely; the weed had made his relationship to time somewhat suspect, and all the minutes she was gone felt longer and harder and more robust than they possibly could have been. He remembered that he stared out the window at the Carrizos' house for a time. Across the yard, all the lights were off. Later, Sebastien would spend endless nights wishing he'd been watching the garden, wishing he'd been attentive to the shifting of any shadows that might have been moving there. But he'd spent so much time watching the house for its light that all he would ever remember of that night was its darkness.

Sebastien was never really sure if Lily ever came back. He dreamed of her all night—he dreamed that they spoke, he dreamed that they kissed, he dreamed of her returning, again and again and again. And somewhere in the sea of his dreaming, he thought that she actually did return, at some point, and lay beside him, at least for a while. But he could not be totally certain, because he went back to sleep very quickly. He wanted to be with the Lily who loved him.

In the morning, when Sebastien woke, she was gone. Golden bars of light illuminated the map on the wall—all the places he had either already gone or would never go. There was nowhere on that map that he hadn't been yet but would one day see, he remembered thinking. In the bed next to him, the sheets were still slightly damp and sweet with that adolescent perfume that Lily wore. She was gone, and Sebastien thought—dramatically, implausibly—that he might never see her again.

But he did. She was back again that afternoon, running up the steps, her face sheet white except for a bright red spot on her cheek, and she was crying with a wild and ragged and frightening abandon, crying like she never cried afterward, crying like nobody else ever saw her cry, throughout the entire thing. Her hair was streaming all around her. And Sebastien stood on the stoop in terror thinking, *What's wrong, what's wrong, my love, what's wrong?*

PART II

CHAPTER FIFTEEN

February

The next morning, a pair of police officers showed up at Sebastien's door. After a surreal, hallucinatory trip to the store to buy a toothbrush, Lily and Sebastien had retreated back to his house. Lily had spent the night weeping and throwing up—sometimes simultaneously—while Sebastien brought offerings that grew increasingly outlandish over the hours: water, then toast, then some restorative fried eggs at four a.m., then some fortifying vodka at seven. She refused all of it. At some point Sebastien slept a bit, he thought—at any rate he collapsed on one of the sofas for a while—but one channel of his consciousness seemed to remain on all night, and when a knock on the door finally came the next morning, he did not really feel that it had woken him up.

Sebastien went to the kitchen sink and ran a wet comb through his hair. He was still wearing yesterday's clothes. Another knock came, more aggressive than the first. He went to the bathroom and opened the door, where Lily was sitting with her back against the porcelain flank of the bathtub. She looked up. Her face was clayey and blanched, like she was a victim of internal hemorrhage. "Is someone here?" she said.

Sebastien extended his hand to her. "Come on," he said.

They opened the door to a pair of police officers, young and vigorously well groomed, and Sebastien made an elaborate show of offering to make them some coffee. This was a bluff—he did not have any coffee—but the officers weren't interested, anyway. They told Sebastien and Lily that they'd like to take them down to the station. They wanted, they said, to have a conversation.

In the car, Sebastien was relieved that the police did not make Lily or him wear handcuffs—Sebastien was given to understand that agents of law enforcement were always on the hunt for opportunities to practice needless barbarism. Having his hands free meant that he could rest one of them lightly on Lily's—not quite holding it, just floating on it—in a gesture that he hoped seemed present, not proprietary. He had to assume that they were still broken up.

The word "conversation" had made Sebastien think that he and Lily would be speaking together with the police, but this, it seemed, was not the case. They were split up almost immediately: Sebastien led down one dark hallway and Lily down another, into conversations that were separate—and, as it turned out, very, very long.

Sebastien was interviewed first by one of the officers who had come to the door. The questions he posed were straightforward, and for once Sebastien didn't embellish his answers—even though, after years of conducting all conversations as though they were being recorded, he knew that this one actually was.

"How did you spend the evening?" asked the officer.

"Watching a movie," said Sebastien.

"All evening?"

"Mostly."

"What else?"

Sebastien did not know what Lily was saying to her interrogators, or if she was saying anything at all, though he almost felt that he'd be able to detect her answers—that he'd be able to sense them through some kind of magnetic shifting out in the universe—if only the cop would stop talking to him for a moment and just let him pay attention.

"We talked," said Sebastien. He felt a poisonous sense of decay alongside a vile clenching feeling. He realized that he'd been gearing up to lie long before he knew that he would have to.

"You were together all evening?"

I am going for a walk, Lily had said. It would be hard to make someone believe that he had not asked where, but truly, he had not. The only thing that had mattered then was her impending departure; the destination or even the duration of her leaving seemed, in that moment, beside the point. Through heavy marijuana-befogged lids, Sebastien had watched her walk out the door. And somewhere in that moment— or somewhere a bit before it, or a bit after—Sebastien had felt all causality in the universe collapse. The only thing that had seemed thinkable then was staring at the blue menu screen of the DVD player—it was transfixing, bewitching. He'd felt himself drifting ominously close to the ceiling; he had actually tugged at the bedspread to keep himself from hitting it. He'd thought he might be dying; he'd reminded himself he was not. He'd felt a coldness billowing up from somewhere deep inside him, like a vent blowing caustic air from a subway, or a spring bleeding water from some vast subterranean aquifer, or an oil rig spewing its cobalt bile from the earth. He had lingered on each image as it came to him, forgetting for long moments what feeling he was trying to figuratively capture. But then the vicious internal chill would remind him, and he'd fear that he was learning something about himself—something terrible, something that he could never unlearn.

He had been very, very stoned.

"Yes," said Sebastien.

"You were together *all* evening?"

But who was to say Lily hadn't been beside him the whole time? It had seemed as though she'd been gone a long while, but perhaps she had not been. It had seemed as though she was leaving the house, but maybe she never had. And once Sebastien had told the first lie, it was easy to tell the second.

"Yes," he said again.

When the first officer left, the second officer appeared and conducted the same interview over again; somehow Sebastien understood—though he didn't know why—that this switching off meant that all of these conversations were merely the preliminaries. The second officer had the kind of face one wanted very much to lie to, but Sebastien resisted the impulse to introduce any new deceits. Instead, he stuck to his first set of answers, and this time he felt—and, he was sure, sounded— much more certain of them than before.

Afterward, the police drove Sebastien home. It was dark outside, which meant it had to be very late. They dropped him at his house, and he went inside to wait for Lily to come meet him. A week later, he was still waiting.

Slowly, it became clear to Sebastien that they were not going to let him see Lily—though he went every day (rather gallantly, he thought) and asked. Only family was allowed to see her, they said, and only on Thursdays. They did let him leave her things: notes, phone cards, and, in a fit of inspiration and bribery, a journal and pen. But they never let him in, and Lily's father—who had appeared at Sebastien's door one day, bristling with the politest rage Sebastien had ever seen, and clearly half-expecting to find Sebastien in the midst of committing a homicide in the foyer—said that they were unlikely even to allow Sebastien to call her.

Sebastien had expected to encounter some opposition in going to the jail—enough, at least, so that he might feel that he was suffering along with Lily on some small level. Beyond submitting his DNA sample—a terrible indignity made endurable only by the thought that he was doing it for her—nothing much had been asked of Sebastien; he wished he could throw himself into the awful place where Lily was, beat his fist against its walls, demand that it hurt him, too. But everyone at the jail was maddeningly polite, even apologetic, when they told Sebastien, for the fifth or seventh or tenth time, that no, he could not see her. When he argued, they shrugged the divested shrugs of people who are enacting a script they did not write and did not necessarily even think was very good. One of the security officers—a woman, blinking down at Sebastien from behind bulletproof glass—even seemed to find his situation somewhat sweetly amusing, and eventually Sebastien began to understand that she would actually have *liked* to let him see Lily, if she could have. But she couldn't. When Sebastien realized that he wasn't up against anything he could actually see, he grew exhausted. He stopped going to the jail for a few days. And then—finally, lamentably—he bought a television.

The television, in general, proved to be a bad idea. When the Telecom man arrived to install it—surprised not to be replacing or supplementing another set—Sebastien explained that he was looking to get information about a particular story in the news. He could not have fathomed then how much information he would get. The daytime news channels, in particular, seemed to cater exclusively to people exactly like Sebastien—people without work or diversions, people who had nothing to do but sit around, underdressed and agape, and obsess over every single detail of the case of the murdered Katy Kellers and the accused Lily Hayes. The reporting was speculative and circular and redundant and endless, and Sebastien found himself disappearing into it for many strange, amnesiac hours. After a day with the television, Sebastien had seen the news cycles begin and end and begin anew; he had witnessed each anchor repeat him- or herself nearly verbatim several times over. The anchors' surprise never diminished with repetition—the fact that Lily had apparently done a cartwheel during her interrogation, for example, was marveled at with an astonishment that seemed to grow only more vigorous over the hours. By the end of the first day, Sebastien suspected all of the anchors of traumatic brain injury. By the end of the second day, he suspected them all of genius. He tried to track the variance in tone and emphasis, the subtle shifts in syntax, the inversions of word order, as they recounted the same news item again and again; it occurred to Sebastien that they might be speaking in a code too sophisticated and nuanced for the crude instruments of quotidian comprehension. After all, *wasn't* there something fundamentally different about the meaning of *Lily Hayes was widely known for her erratic behavior* and *Lily Hayes's erratic behavior was widely known*? After two days with the television, Sebastien began to feel that there was.

From what Sebastien could gather, the television's suspicion of Lily seemed to hinge partly on the order in which she had done certain things on the day after the murder. The most damning fact, it seemed, was that a delivery truck driver had seen Lily running across the lawn with blood on her face before she called the police at Sebastien's. On TV, this point wound up yielding two different insinuating questions, asked over and over by a rotating handful of commentators—though always in the same tone of energetic inquiry that invited viewers to believe that these important queries had only just occurred to them (the commentators), and that they (the viewers) were watching substantive thinking in real time on live television and that this was why it was worth paying for cable.

The questions were these: 1. Why, the pundits asked, had Lily not called the police first before running to Sebastien's? (Unless, of course, she was running away in guilt, trying desperately to leave the scene before the law arrived.) 2. And *why*, pondered the pundits, had she stayed at Sebastien's that night—mere steps from where Katy was slain—since she could not know that the killer would not return to the neighborhood? (Unless, of course, she knew precisely who the killer or killers were, and exactly how afraid of them she really needed to be.) The suppressed premises of these questions seemed contradictory to Sebastien but, apparently, to no one else; they were always paraded out together and were often mentioned in nearly the same breath, as though the one compounded the other instead of substantially subverting it.

Though the bulk of the information was repetitive, every day the TV unearthed some new bit of trivia: Here was Lily's report card (she'd only been making Bs in Spanish!); and here was a picture of Lily as a child in a school play (dressed as a green pepper and clearly overacting); and here was an unkind Facebook message exchange Lily had had with a friend about a third girl (whose name was redacted but who was, in Lily's estimation, "just unfuckingbelievable"). Sebastien would catch himself feeling fascinated by and a little grateful for the information the TV dug up for segments about Lily's online persona—at the end of the day, *is* this the social network profile of a killer?—before remembering to feel horrified and then ashamed. He'd vow to guard against this curiosity, though he did not turn off the TV. Somewhere along the line he had convinced himself that if information was power, then rapt information gathering was loyalty.

In odd moments Sebastien would startle to see an image of himself on the screen—though he shut his eyes whenever they showed that episode near the Changomas condom shelf or the shot of him and Lily kissing, mouths visibly open, the police tape flapping behind them. (One of the lesser tragedies from this great tragedy, Sebastien figured, was that he would never be able to kiss anybody ever again.) He began to imagine what his whole life might look like as told through security camera videotape: Here he is jubilantly pouring coffee at a Cambridge 7-Eleven during that Harvard admitted students' visiting weekend; here he is hunting for a suit to wear to his parents' funeral, his face oyster-gray and formless; here he is shopping for cereal at his corner bodega, again and again and again, alone. All of these images existed somewhere out in the universe, Sebastien now realized, and they would show a version of his biography if somebody ever decided to collect and arrange them. And Sebastien saw how convincing the security tape telling of his life would be—to the average viewer, or even to him—no matter how many other true things were missing.

The worst was when they ran images of Katy—which they did, at cruelly frequent intervals, nearly as much as they ran pictures of Lily; often, they showed their pictures side by side. Katy's image filled Sebastien with a sort of mental vertigo every time it appeared; he could not yet make his brain automatically register her as dead. Her deadness simply did not seem intuitive—maybe because the deadness of vague acquaintances felt uncomfortably similar to their aliveness. Sebastien had glimpsed Katy occasionally in real life, and now he glimpsed her occasionally on television; she was still beautiful, still remote, still a person he did not really know. No matter how hard he tried, Sebastien could not make her seem as dead as she actually was, and always would be. He badly wished he could do this; not managing it seemed disrespectful, somehow. And each time Katy's image appeared, before Sebastien fully remembered what had happened, he experienced a momentary anxious feeling—fractional, subconscious, pre-lingual—that she was a person he had been charged with protecting and had somehow forgotten.

And those moments forced Sebastien to consider a question he'd been trying hard to avoid: Why, he wondered, had he not been arrested along with Lily? Sebastien went back to that day again and again. Already his memory was shrinking from looking at it straight; the day was saturated in a blinding, otherworldly light, beginning with the moment he saw Lily come running across the lawn. Sebastien hadn't known yet what was happening, and for an instant he'd thought she was coming back to apologize—he'd imagined she was weeping with the fear that she'd created irrevocable damage between them; he'd hoped she was finally revealing that, like him, she'd had a frangible and hidden heart all along. Was there a moment, when she buried her head in his shoulder and sobbed, when Sebastien was glad she'd been returned to him this way—glad that she'd been returned to him any way at all? There was not. But Sebastien had also congratulated himself momentarily, retroactively, for this virtue—and that, he knew, was just as bad or worse.

If they were handing out prison terms for murky moral impulses, Sebastien figured, he might as well go ahead and turn himself in.

Every day, Sebastien watched for developments at the Carrizos'. They'd been summoned back suddenly from their trip (to witness the baptism of some northern nephew, according to the women at Pan y Vino and the news), and at first Sebastien thought they were staying sequestered in the house, though he did not see them. Teenagers drove by at night honking and yelling, but Carlos never emerged to shoo them away. The car was sometimes there and sometimes not; its comings and goings, along with the illuminations and cessations of the lights in the house, seemed to reject all logic. But this, in a way, made sense to Sebastien. Normalcy and sanity had been suspended, after all. Katy was dead. Lily was in jail. The Carrizos' car, unsurprisingly, was no longer adhering to a regular schedule.

It took Sebastien a week to understand that the Carrizos weren't living in the house anymore. He'd been staring dumbly out the window, wearing his overly warm smoking jacket, at two in the afternoon, and he actually slapped himself on the forehead when he realized it. The Carrizos weren't living there anymore. Of course they weren't. Who could stand to live there anymore? The house was haunted, it was horrifying. And, no less important, it was a crime scene. The Carrizos weren't living there anymore. They were just coming and going to pick up their things.

It took Sebastien nearly another day to fully register that this meant he'd been living all alone on the hill—all alone truly, for the first time in his life—ever since Katy had been killed.

And still—out of the force of habit, or the force of something else— Sebastien kept watching the Carrizos' house, feeling a strange revulsion every time he glanced across the yard. The sun was the wrong intensity these days, always too weak or too brutal. The grass was the wrong color, too—it had begun to turn a rusty red, the symbolism of which Sebastien noted with no small amount of superstitious horror before realizing it just meant the Carrizos had stopped watering the lawn. In the late afternoons the house cast long shadows that didn't just move toward the street—they seemed to *creep,* Sebastien couldn't help but feel, with sneakiness and intentionality. The days were beginning to last forever. In the hideous and unrelenting evening light, Sebastien drew sheets around the windows.

He forgot to be afraid of the killer, though he knew that he should be. Believing that Lily had not killed Katy—and this he believed utterly—had somehow made it difficult to fully believe that Katy had been killed at all. But indeed she had been, and Sebastien tried to imagine the person who had done it. He summoned an image of a man—lurking around, staking out both houses, perhaps, maybe entering the Carrizos' by accident; after all, there was far more to steal at Sebastien's. Maybe the murderer had killed Katy by mistake. Maybe it was Sebastien he should have killed, if he was going to absolutely insist on killing someone. Or maybe the killer had been looking for Lily— perhaps he'd known her from that awful club where she worked, where boys with popped collars and Euro-lascivious hair went to preen and overpay for cocktails. Perhaps he was one of those, or perhaps he was not one of those and wanted to be. Or maybe it really *had* been Katy the killer was after, for reasons that Sebastien did not expect ever to fathom. Each theory was disturbing in a different way, though they shared one disturbing element: that the killer, whatever his plan, had seemed to know that Sebastien presented no threat. The killer had somehow surmised, correctly, that Sebastien was not a person to worry about—that he'd probably be too cowardly to do anything should he hear the screams, and that he'd probably be too stoned and inert (and blasting Air, as it happened) to even hear them in the first place.

And so, out of respect, Sebastien tried to be afraid. He should be thinking about moving, he knew. He should, at the very least, be thinking about putting real locks on the doors. But he wasn't afraid, not really. When his parents died, he'd been afraid—and not merely afraid, but deeply paranoid in a way that felt final, and somehow true. This feeling had reached its apex two days after the crash, the day of Sebastien's own flight back to Argentina, when he'd been completely convinced that whoever had killed his parents had followed him right through the post-9/11 security performance art and into Logan International Airport to finish the job; every single person Sebastien saw that day seemed to him to have been cast in his own story—a story that had always been straining, it turned out, toward this single, terrible ending, all along. Sebastien tried to invoke some of that fear now, sitting alone on the hill. But he could not. He did not feel afraid, exactly.

Instead, what he felt was a surreal, disowned dread; he kept having dreams where he'd remember with a sickening feeling that he'd been entrusted with the care of something—once an infant, once a puppy, once a small furry invented creature that looked a bit like a guinea pig—and had forgotten it for far too long, and went hurrying back, frantic, knowing it was already too late. A fear so abstract and meta-physical could drive a person crazy, Sebastien saw. And after a while, he began to feel that it might be an odd sort of relief to have an actual murderer show up—so dissolute was his anxiety, so vast was his long-ing for a horror he could actually see.

The 911 call itself was finally produced, as Sebastien had known it eventually would be. He had not been there when Lily made it—he'd been sprinting across the lawn to be ready to direct the police to the basement—but this became hard for Sebastien to remember as he lis-tened to the recording, over and over and over again, along with the rest of the world. On television, the tape opened up new landscapes of syntactical and tonal speculation, previously unplumbed depths of slander, entire undiscovered universes of improvisation; the news channels reacted to its emergence with unrestrained—and, Sebastien felt, unseemly—glee. At one point, Sebastien happened across a show where a "vocal analyst" was offering his expert opinion on what Lily's speech patterns revealed about her psychological makeup—even though Sebastien felt that the vocal analyst, in addition to being a charlatan, was possessed of a very unrepresentative sample of Lily's voice: On the 911 tape, she simply did not sound like herself. (Sebas-tien was not entirely convinced that it was Lily's voice at all, in fact, and he had half an idea to call up the vocal analyst—maybe the next time he did a call-in show, maybe at home in the middle of the night—and tell him this.) Instead of sounding breathless, as she often did, the Lily on the tape sounded somehow the opposite; she sounded as though she had only breath and could not remember what she was supposed to do with it, or what it had ever been for.

Sebastien came to hear the tape so many times that it became impossible not to think of it as a loop or a cycle, or as a kind of mythic event that was somehow always occurring because it never had; like literature or drama or sacred texts, the tape seemed to demand the present tense. On the tape, Lily's voice sounds like it's being removed from her body with pliers. She gives the Carrizos' address before she says anything else. Throughout the call, she speaks English to the dispatcher and never seems to notice. *Qué es su emergencia? She's dead, she's dead, oh my God, oh my God, please hurry, oh my God, she's dead. Quién? Katy. My roommate. God, please hurry.*

All of this, of course, gave the anchors their new favorite question. If Lily was so sure that Katy was dead, they asked—breathlessly, delightedly—then why had she so valiantly attempted CPR? *I don't know,* Lily said miserably, according to the leaked police report that ran without ceasing. *I guess I thought maybe she wasn't dead at first. But then by the time I made the call I just knew that she was. I just knew.*

And this was another thing Sebastien wished he could tell the television, or at least tell someone: He had known it, too, somehow, as he stood holding Lily outside the Carrizos' house. He had known that Katy Kellers was dead. It was a certainty as distinct and undeniable as a physical sensation, though somehow deeper than that—not like the chill of the sun moving behind a cloud, but like the particular sense of forsakenness this brings. The police were fanning into the house, and Sebastien was standing behind Lily, holding her by the shoulders, then the elbows, feeling her heartbeat rattle in her body. She was clenching her hands so hard that her whole body shook. This ferocity scared Sebastien; it suggested a wretchedness that he would not have been able to bear in anybody, but especially, especially, could not bear in her. This was why he had kissed her—first lightly, and then a second time more forcefully. It certainly wasn't lust driving him to do it; it wasn't even tenderness, quite. His only thought, really, was to distract her, to make her hands unfreeze from the terrifying shape they were taking.

The cameras never caught any of this, though. Instead, they showed

Sebastien leaning into Lily. They showed Lily's face, strangely slack and empty and looking, the commentators said, nearly bored. And they showed Sebastien kissing her and kissing her again, while the men outside the house rolled the police tape, drawing a line between Katy and everyone else.

CHAPTER SIXTEEN

March

At ten a.m. on Thursday, a taxi arrived to take Andrew, Anna, and Maureen back to Lomas de Zamora.

Anna sat wedged between Andrew and Maureen, whose hair was still wet from the shower; Andrew could see several wiry, lunar-white strands near her temple. The violently familiar smell of her shampoo filled the cab, casting Andrew uneasily back into the unplaceable past—he felt as though he'd awoken in some unknown, long-ago year of his life and had no idea whether great joy or great sorrow awaited him. Andrew's sense of time was jostling; he simply could not believe how much of it had gone by—not the years since he'd last regularly ridden in cars with Maureen and Anna together, not the week since he'd seen Lily—and how little of it seemed to have properly passed. So much seemed entirely elided over somehow, like the hours lost to anesthesia.

At the jail, they were ushered in quickly. Andrew let Maureen and Anna walk ahead, not wanting to deny Lily one instant of her mother.

And so he was trailing behind, unable to see anything, when he heard Maureen breathe in sharply and say, "Oh my God."

"What? What's happened?" said Andrew, hurrying into the room. Over Maureen's shoulder, he could see that Lily was sitting in her usual spot, in her usual position, except that this time, she was bald.

"Oh my God," said Maureen again. "What did they do to you?"

Lily had her hands spread out on the table again. Andrew had so hoped to find her in a different position this time. "I got lice," she said.

Maureen cupped Lily's head in her hands. Her face was concave with horror, and Andrew knew that part of what she was imagining was how Lily would now look on TV. "How did you get lice?"

"Everyone has lice."

"They couldn't have given you a special shampoo?"

"Mom," said Anna.

"Mom, seriously?" said Lily, ducking away from Maureen. "There's no shampoo. There's definitely no *special* shampoo. We barely have soap." The weary condescension in her voice was strangely, momentarily, consoling; Lily had used this voice many, many times, after all, for many, many occasions. A line ran through Andrew's head, possibly remembered, possibly imagined: *Mom, it's college, of course they have coed bathrooms!* But as soon as Andrew summoned that line he realized there was something different—something troublingly different—about Lily's tone now; he recognized it after a moment as the complete absence of triumphalism. For years, Lily had thought that she knew more about the world than Andrew and Maureen did, and for years, she had been wrong. Now she was finally right, and she did not want to be.

Andrew looked again at Lily's baldness. Her hair wasn't actually entirely gone, he saw now; it was chopped off in pieces on one side, messy and askew, and shaved to a smooth bulb only near the top. It was the kind of thing she might have done to herself, actually, under different circumstances. Andrew flashed to an image of a different kind of Lily—rebelling and experimenting and trying out new identities; adopting lesbianism, briefly or permanently, at one of the Seven

Sisters schools; coming home with a shaved head the Thanksgiving of her freshman year and saying *you don't understand, you don't understand, you just don't understand,* no matter how strenuously Maureen and Andrew assured her that they did, they did, they absolutely did. This image flipped to a more frightening one: a different Lily, in a different sort of wayward twenties, as a cult member or religious supplicant; her hair, in a gesture to humility, arranged into the tonsure of some sort of Eastern monasticism; saying to Andrew and Maureen *you don't understand, you don't understand, you just don't understand,* and this time it being true. That picture dissolved, and finally Andrew was struck with the one that would stay with him, no matter how he tried to shake it: the stunning, horrifying image of a Lily condemned. He saw a bald Lily burned for witchcraft, a bald Lily enduring the Spanish Inquisition, a bald Lily loaded onto a cattle car headed east. Andrew knew these comparisons were inapt; he knew that in invoking them he was hysterically overstating his daughter's trouble while diminishing the suffering of history's real victims, and that this was as disrespectful as it was useless. But Andrew couldn't stop seeing those other Lilys, and his knees nearly buckled when he thought of them: all young and bald and innocent; all beyond the reach of his help, or anyone's; all eternally living out stories with endings that the world now knew.

"It's okay, Mom," said Lily. Maureen was standing beside her, trying not to cry. Lily reached out and patted her in an odd swiping motion; the gesture was unnatural, as though Lily had read a manual on touching someone you loved but had never seen it done. "Don't cry. It's just hair."

"I know," said Maureen. "I'm not crying." But it was clear that she was, or that she would be, though there were no tears. Maureen had the ability to visibly defer crying, if it was not a good time to cry. This was something Andrew had seen her do many, many times.

"It's okay, Mom," said Lily again. "It's okay. I'm okay."

Maureen's face continued its silent internal collapsing. Watching this was far more excruciating, always, than her actual crying would have been. It meant that something had happened that she could not endure, and that she would not endure—just as soon as she endured it a little longer.

In the taxi on the way back to the hotel, Maureen stroked Anna's head. "I know it's not what's important," said Maureen. "But her hair was just so pretty."

The rest of their time with Lily had been halting and quiet—with the urgency of the first visits over, a strange sharp-edged shyness had overtaken all of them. In an especially painful moment, Lily had actually resorted to giving them listless recommendations about what to see in the city. Perhaps this terrible new awkwardness was because of Lily's baldness.

"We always wanted red hair," Anna said to Maureen. "I mean, really red hair. Like yours."

Or perhaps it was merely the oddness of the four of them, alone together in a room—though they'd congregated with some regularity after the divorce, it had usually been at holidays or weddings or funerals or other special occasions, in the presence of relatives or mutual friends or one of Lily's beleaguered suitors.

"Blame your father and his dominant genes," said Maureen.

But probably, after all, the strangeness hadn't been because of Lily's hair or the posthumous assemblage of their nuclear family. Probably it was because Lily was in jail, and after an hour the three of them would be leaving without her. And even if Lily knew rationally that there was nothing Andrew and Maureen could do about it, how could this abandonment not feel to her like a betrayal? After all, when the time was up and the security guards arrived, did Andrew or Maureen physically fight them? Did they grab Lily and try to make a break for it? Did they throw themselves in front of her and tell the guards that they could take them but they could not, could absolutely not, take their daughter? They didn't. Instead, they rose and hugged Lily and whispered promises and encouragement and then, at the appointed time, they left, widening the new, terrifying chasm between Lily and everyone else. Andrew could almost hear it happening. He'd certainly heard it in Lily's voice—*We barely have soap,* she'd said, and in that "we," it seemed to Andrew, she had signified allegiance to a different realm. In some very fundamental respects, and through no fault of her own, Lily now had more in common with the worst people in the entire world than with her own family.

"Really, it was so beautiful," said Maureen. "Like yours."

"It wasn't beautiful," said Anna. "Mine's not, either. Like Lily said, it's just hair." But she did not shrink away from Maureen; in fact, Andrew thought, she settled in closer to her.

That night, Andrew dreamed of flying away. When he woke, he stared at the ceiling fan above him, waiting for the sedative effects of its cyclonic whir. In three days, he was supposed to be leaving Buenos Aires. His plane ticket was already booked.

Andrew had had the flying dream often when Janie was sick. In the dream, there was no question as to whether he was flying away for good—he knew that he was delirious with the wickedness of precisely this—though he was always unable to make his way through the elusive dream-memory and figure out how he had ever let it happen in the first place. All he could really remember was the exhilaration: In the dreams he flew low enough for a detailed aerial view of the world; for some reason he seemed always to be headed north (to Canada, perhaps—like an escaped slave? Or like a draft dodger?), and whatever had allowed him to leave in the first place was already far, far behind him, and he could not account for it. This wasn't so different from the way it must feel to do inconceivable things in real life, Andrew thought. There wasn't a single cell in our bodies that was the same as the day we were born, and yet we were still held responsible for everything all of our former selves had ever done.

Nevertheless, after the dreams Andrew had always felt a guilt that was nearly tactile—not unlike the guilt he used to feel after the occasional sex dream (about old lovers, or old almost lovers, or students) back when he and Maureen were first married. Andrew could scarcely believe now that such trivialities had ever mattered so much to him. There had been great stretches of sexlessness between him and Maureen during those dark barren months when Janie was dying, and touching each other seemed unthinkable (not forbidden and thus alluring, but beyond comprehension, outside the realm of possible occurrences, something belonging to paraphysics or myth), and Maureen had even told him once that she did not care if he slept with someone else. Andrew's actually acting on this was, as Maureen surely knew, implausible (who would he possibly have slept with?) and yet he did not take her offer as a dare, or as a taunt, or as a trap. When Maureen said she would not care, Andrew really believed her. During that time, and exactly as psychology predicted, Andrew was dreaming of losing his teeth.

Andrew got up and put on his bathrobe. He switched on the light. Outside, a cadaverous alley cat was mewling at a garbage can. He opened the door to the living room and jumped. Anna was sitting on the edge of the couch, watching the television with almost no sound.

"Hey," said Andrew. His voice was craggy. "Why are you up?"

"Why are you?"

Andrew shrugged and began rifling for coffee filters. He opened the mini-fridge and stared into it dumbly. "Do you want a yogurt?" he said. Anna pointed to the yogurt she was already holding. Andrew closed the refrigerator.

When he went home, the idea was that he would try to resume his life. He would meet with Peter Sulzicki, the lawyer; he would meet with the accountant; he would, perhaps, make an appearance at his classes. From now on, he and Maureen would alternate weeks in Buenos Aires—a jointly devised plan that Andrew knew he couldn't postpone forever. Trading weeks meant that Lily would always have a visitor, and that Andrew and Maureen would each be able to keep a foot—or at least a toenail, as Maureen had said—in their former lives. It was understood that they would have to do this because they'd need the money and small interim scraps of sanity their jobs afforded them.

It was also understood, though never mentioned—much like the possibility of Janie's death was never mentioned until it was already a reality, already in the past, already an event they were moving further away from with every second that passed—that they might never get out of this thing. They might, in fact, be in it for the long haul, and they had to try to keep now whatever they would need for the duration. Andrew had discussed this explicitly with his dean, who had listened with tented fingers and uncharacteristic generosity. He had a full beard and seemed to know how much everyone expected him to stroke it; Andrew suspected that he did not do this out of spite. Even so, he had been kind. An extra TA had been assigned to Andrew's class. A grading schedule had been worked out.

Andrew poured himself a coffee and padded over to the couch. On the TV, a reporter was interviewing an athlete. "Who is that?" said Andrew.

"A tennis player," said Anna.

"Oh." Why didn't Andrew ever think to turn on the TV? It was such a friendly presence. He cocked his head to one side and let the Spanish slip around him; it was a uniquely tantalizing feeling—that sensation of something eddying just beyond your comprehension. "I didn't know they did tennis here," he said.

"He won the U.S. Open."

"Oh."

"Is he saying anything interesting?"

"I don't know. I mean, I guess probably not."

Andrew rose and went to the window. He leaned his head against the glass. Outside, the light was sepulchral and thin, and Andrew remembered the light from his dreams: the sun tilting through the clouds, casting vast lattices of shadow on the ground; Andrew, above it all, skimming over stands of majestic northern firs, great meadows of allium flowers, rattling trains on trestle bridges. In the dream, Andrew was always struck by how easy it was to do all of this. He was always amazed that he had not done it earlier.

Andrew turned back around and found that Anna was frowning at him. "Am I supposed to ask you if you're okay?" she said.

This, Andrew knew, was not an expression of genuine concern. It was a tactic of confrontation, inherited from Maureen and based on the premise that the speaker had silently suffered more than you had—more than you could ever even imagine someone suffering—and that condescending to deal with your weakness now was merely the latest trial to be endured with superior resilience and grace.

"I am okay," said Andrew. "Of course I'm okay. Obviously, it's probably not great about your sister's hair."

"Well, I mean, it's the kind of thing she probably would have done to herself anyway." Anna grabbed the remote and turned up the volume on the TV. "She's always been weird."

Andrew considered this. Had Lily been weird? She was high-spirited, certainly, and maybe there were times when that had put her out of sync with her peers in various small ways. It was true she hadn't worn a bra until a bit later than she should have—this had been a point of principle, and she'd been earnest and humorless on the matter—and there had been something a little strange, and more than a little funny, about a child so young fighting a battle so old and so lost. But that only meant that she had ideas of her own. Andrew, through his squeamishness, had even been a little proud of her. "Weird?" he said. "You think so?"

Anna raised her eyebrows and said nothing.

"How do you mean, 'weird'?" said Andrew. Lily was a little socially awkward, maybe; it was possible that she wasn't quite as naturally intuitive about other people as girls were usually expected to be. He remembered a phone call from her sometime during her freshman year in which she'd complained about an entry-level political science class. She couldn't do it, she said, because she couldn't figure out what worked for people—why were certain slogans effective and others ineffective, why were some unguarded moments seen as winningly humanizing and others as gaffes, why did people trust certain politicians and mistrust other ones? Why, she wondered, had "It's the economy, stupid" resonated so widely as a phrase?

"Well," Andrew had said, "I suppose because it *was* the economy, stupid."

"That doesn't really matter with that stuff, though," said Lily. "It was just some magic formula or something."

"Is that the kind of thing they're teaching you there?" he'd said worriedly.

"I don't know how you do it," she'd said. "How do you ever guess what people are after?"

"I don't," he'd said. "I guess what states are after. Much easier. They behave like cue balls."

On the TV, the show had gone to a commercial, and Anna's eyebrows were floating farther and farther toward her hairline. "Never mind, Dad," she said. "If you guys never saw it, I'm not going to be the one to tell you."

"Anna," Andrew said sternly. "You are clearly trying to say something. I would like to know what it is." Lily was maybe a tad socially inept—but that wasn't "weird," per se, as Anna so uncharitably put it. And she was maybe a tad smarter than the bunch, which made the bunch a bit inaccessible to her—but that was certainly not an extraordinary state of things. And anyway, the gulf between Lily and most people was very, very slim: She was smart, but she was not as smart as she thought she was. A slight overestimation of one's intellect was a useful sort of self-deception, Andrew thought; it pushed a person toward confidence and risk taking and high standards. This was a quality that Andrew had seen countless times in his boy students and almost never in the girls, and so he couldn't help but find it somewhat endearing in a daughter.

Anna stared at the television. If she did not want to answer, Andrew had no idea how he was going to make her. But then she turned to him, her eyes full of a terrible adult patience that he had never seen before. "Do you remember," she said, "when Lily killed that animal?"

Andrew began to laugh, but he could hear that his laugh sounded frightened. "No," he said.

"It was a banana slug or something. You really don't remember?"

"A slug? Why would I remember something like that?"

"She and her friend killed it."

"I see."

"They found it in the backyard. She was seven, I think."

"And this slug," said Andrew. "Its significance was what, precisely? Was it a special pet of ours? A work colleague of your mother's?"

"It was Lily's idea. She kind of goaded her friend into it. It was pretty disturbing."

"Disturbing? Come on, Anna. If she was seven, you were what, five? I'm not sure your concept of disturbing was at its most sophisticated."

Anna shrugged. "She liked killing it. You could tell."

Andrew could hear how little Anna expected him to believe her, and how little she cared that he wouldn't, and he felt, suddenly, an overwhelming, choking sadness that turned to anger in his voice. "Oh, and what?" he said. "You're going to tell me next she was wetting the bed and setting fires while I wasn't looking, too? It was a slug, Anna. Put it in perspective. Killing a slug is not torturing a puppy."

"I don't think you would have noticed if she was doing that, either."

"Jesus Christ!"

"I'm not saying she was doing that," said Anna. "She wasn't. I know that because I know what she was doing and I know what she was like."

"Have you been feeling unattended to lately, Anna?" said Andrew. "Are you maybe a little jealous of your sister right now?" He knew this could not be a useful thing to say, but he was angry, and he had long ago decided never to yell or raise his voice when angry. Losing your temper never made your case for you; it only made you sound foolish and sputtering and inarticulate—whenever Andrew heard people bellowing sloppily into their cell phones he couldn't help but think how much more serious their anger would seem if they could keep it calm and well reasoned and under control. When Andrew was angry, he tried to be communicative and nondefensive, to explain intentions and interpretations, to make "I" statements. He tried never to let aggression bleed into unsullied areas; he tried to keep hostility quarantined, the better to effect its excision. But not even Andrew could be calm all of the time, and when he felt himself becoming too angry to stay that way, he had a signature tactic of his own: attempting to ascertain the true origins of his opponent's behavior. This move had the benefit of seeming completely high-minded (nearly academic, even), communicating how completely irrational he found the other person's behavior (so totally beyond the pale of comprehension that he could only assume—indeed, he *had* to assume—that there were other dark forces at work within them), and being, of course, impossibly maddening, all at the same time.

"I'm sure this trip has been hard on you," said Andrew. *At least you're not unjustly detained in a foreign country!* he wanted to scream. *At least you're not dead! Because it could be a whole lot worse than this, Anna, Old Sport.* "I know we've been very focused on Lily. And maybe you're not getting what you need from us right now. But, sweetheart, this is not the right way to act out. This is not the right thing to do with those feelings. This is not a good way to get attention."

Anna was seething. "You're being a fucking asshole, Dad."

"Okay. You got me. I'm an asshole. We're all down here trying to help your sister hang on to her life just to torment you. Because it's my idea of a good time. Because I'm an asshole."

"You know that isn't what I mean."

"Well, what do you mean, exactly? Please elaborate. We've got all the time in the world, Anna. We certainly don't have any bigger concerns right now."

Anna screamed at him then, swore and screamed like she never did during her adolescence, though Lily sometimes had, and then slammed out of the room. And Andrew sat on the bed for a time, patting himself on the chest, as though he could smooth over the divots that had lately been gouged into his heart.

. . .

Andrew went downstairs a few hours later, ready to broker some kind of stopgap peace. He knocked on Maureen's door and she appeared.

"Hi," she said.

Something about seeing Maureen when he'd expected Anna made Andrew consider her face anew: the fractal lines around her eyes, woven like bits of tapestry; the way they somehow made her eyes seem brighter by contrast. He was relieved to see that she had not been crying, at least not recently.

"I can't leave," said Andrew, surprising himself. It was not at all what he'd thought he was going to say.

"What?" Maureen held open the door. Andrew stepped over a pile of Anna's gym clothes and into the room.

"I just can't," he said.

"Because she cut her hair? We've got bigger problems than that." Maureen went to the window and opened the curtain. In the gray wash of light, Andrew wasn't sure whether he could actually see the red in Maureen's hair. Maybe he only sensed it, like a pentimento from an abandoned painting.

"Anyway, we've talked about this," said Maureen. "You have to go back. That's where your life is."

"Is it?" said Andrew fretfully. "I don't know. It keeps moving around."

"Maybe you're just misplacing it." Maureen sat on the unmade bed. "The wages of age, you know."

"It wouldn't be the only thing, these days." Andrew joined Maureen on the bed. He rocked his shoulders through their sockets. "Your daughter's mad at me," he said after a moment.

"I know."

"I see," said Andrew grumpily. "She said something?"

"What was it about?"

"Surely you already know that, too."

"I don't. Really."

Andrew stared into the silent television screen. There was something oddly comforting about this; he felt a sudden, unreasonable hope that it might materialize into an oracle and offer up a prophecy. "She said something about Lily," said Andrew. "She said something about her killing an animal."

"Oh," said Maureen mildly. "Did she mean the slug?"

"What?" said Andrew. "Yes. Why didn't I know this?"

"I don't know."

"I mean, why does absolutely everyone else know this? It is not an exaggeration to say that this has probably been *literally* on the evening news. I don't understand why I didn't know this."

"Me, neither. She cried about it for, like, a week."

"Why did she do it, then?"

"I have no idea."

"Well, anyway," said Andrew darkly after a moment. "A slug isn't really an animal."

"No."

"I actually think it's pretty misleading of Anna to characterize a slug as an animal." Andrew closed his eyes. "I have to wonder if she's actually pretty angry at Lily."

"I'm sure she is," said Maureen. "I mean, aren't you?"

"Mad at her? No. Why would I be?"

"Well, she's made some pretty dumb decisions."

"She's a kid."

"She's made some pretty dumb decisions even for a kid. She's done things we wouldn't have done at her age. She's done things Anna wouldn't have done."

"I suppose."

Maureen sighed. "It's just—you really do want them to turn out to be smarter than you."

"Of course," said Andrew mournfully. "I mean, what's the point otherwise? That's the whole thing. Just saying, okay. We've tried, we've done our best with ourselves and our lives, we've done all right. But the best hope is that something else might do better."

"You cede your competence to its next incarnation," said Maureen. "That's why it's so terrible and astonishing."

"And boring," said Andrew. "With Lily, at least."

"It was boring! She was *such* a boring baby, wasn't she?" Maureen laughed. "Why was that? Is that an awful thing to say?"

"Babies are boring when you're not terrified, I guess," said Andrew. It was true. Janie had probably been boring, too, but they'd been too scared to notice. "Being mortally terrified will make anything interesting. Bet you're not bored now, are you?"

"Nope! Riveted!" Maureen laughed again. "Oh, we don't have the best luck, do we?"

"Not the absolute best." Andrew was saying, "One could imagine better"—but then he stopped talking because he and Maureen were kissing. He had not noticed that they were going to kiss. Perhaps there had been a brief fillip of intention—perhaps his hand had been on her face momentarily—before it happened. But it would be impossible to say for sure whose fault it was; they both maintained plausible deniability, he felt, throughout. The rest was muscle memory; a routine so routine that it was elevated nearly to ritual. All the thousands of times they had done this. It was strange the things you still remembered, whether you wanted to or not. They were like aging dancers performing the first ballet of their youth, just to see if they still knew how.

Afterward, they slept. For the first time since arriving in Buenos Aires, Andrew did not dream.

On Thursday, Ignacio Toledo was apprehended in Ciudad Oculta.

He was not the kind of person Eduardo had been expecting. It was difficult, in fact, to tell what kind of person he was at all. Toledo appeared in Eduardo's office wearing a heavy brown coat that he declined to remove, even though the air was stifling. Unlike most paco fiends Eduardo had known, he was not jangling with the twitchiness of a nervous system with broken shocks, nor was he particularly derelict; it was hard to imagine him standing around a prison yard, cooking kerosene and sulfuric acid on a spoon. In one light, in fact, Ignacio Toledo actually seemed to possess an odd sort of charisma: He had lazy half-open eyes and the kind of carved, rugged features that seemed to speak of great masculine stoicism. When you first glanced at him, you saw a person who might have been a lover to Katy, or to Lily, or to both; a person who might even—maybe—have inspired lethal passions in one of them.

But then you blinked, and when you looked at Ignacio Toledo again, you saw something else. You noticed that he had bags under his eyes the shape and color of fire bellows, that his teeth looked like they were older than he was; you noticed that his gaze was somehow jumpy and leering simultaneously. Or was it? Eduardo was not sure. Uncharacteristically, when it came to Ignacio Toledo, Eduardo was not quite sure about anything. Even Toledo's appearance without a state-appointed lawyer was difficult to unpack. With Lily, that decision had been born of a naïveté that was arrogant to the point of suicide, and maybe something similar was at work here. Or maybe it was more calculated with Toledo—perhaps this decision arose from the idea that accepting a lawyer was a tacit admission of guilt. But this was only a different kind of naïveté, ultimately, and there were moments when Eduardo wondered if Ignacio Toledo was purposefully inviting Eduardo to believe in either kind. Eduardo did not know and was not moving toward knowing; every time he found himself approaching a sense of Ignacio Toledo, something about him shifted—so subtly, so apparently guilelessly, that Eduardo could never be totally sure that there'd been any change at all. It was like catching a fractional glimpse of a fish through the reeds, turning back only in time to be sure of the motion—which may have been, after all, only your own shadow on the water.

"Look," said Eduardo. He squinted, as if this could somehow correct for the strange psychic parallax that seemed to be at work here. Out the window behind Toledo, the sun was a garish pumpkiny orange. Eduardo was already frustrated and had had to pee for an hour.

He should have seated Toledo facing the window, but now it was too late to change places.

"You've got nothing to lose now," said Eduardo. "We know you were there. Your DNA is absolutely everywhere."

When Eduardo had said this to Lily, it had been a bluff—but this time it was true, and it was maddening that Toledo was acting as though they were playing some game of strategy at which Eduardo might yet be outsmarted. What did he hope to gain from this? Could he be dumb enough to believe that Lily was the one they were completely sure of, and that admitting to having had any dealings with her would be a fatal mistake? Eduardo was not sure he believed in a stupidity so vast. After all, Ignacio Toledo must *know* that his DNA was everywhere; he must *know* that his own involvement was so well established that he should be willing to implicate absolutely anyone—including Lily Hayes—for exactly as long as Eduardo would let him try. But instead, Toledo had remained mostly silent, while Eduardo thought with increasing longing of the urinal.

"I wasn't," said Toledo.

Eduardo held up his hand. He was trying to stop Toledo whenever he began obviously to lie. "Absolutely *everywhere*," said Eduardo severely. "We know you were there. This is not a question."

Now Toledo was wringing his hands in a way that seemed nearly animalistic one moment and just generically distressed the next. Perhaps he was thinking of faking an insanity defense; if so, it was a very, very subtle performance. Nevertheless, any such attempt would be problematic, since it would naturally cast suspicion on anything Ignacio Toledo might be persuaded to say about Lily Hayes, which Eduardo still hoped would be plenty.

"What *is* a question," said Eduardo, "is exactly what Lily Hayes's involvement was. Her DNA was also at the scene of the crime, and we're trying to figure out why. Do you understand?"

Eduardo was beginning to consider the possibility that Ignacio Toledo did not really believe in DNA; it was, after all, very hard to imagine someone so divorced from the modern world that they'd literally leave their shit in a toilet at a crime scene. Eduardo felt slightly deflated at this prospect. It was so cheap to catch a man like this—like winning at a game of football because the other team suddenly picked up the ball and ran.

"This is Lily Hayes," said Eduardo, pushing her picture across the table. "I'm sure you recognize her." Eduardo tapped on Lily's face but did not look at it. He did not like looking at the photo; he did not want to see again the gestures of mortality underneath Lily's relative youth and health—the gray below her eyes, like thumbprints of news script; the teeth already yellowing, like a sepia photo fading into age. The Lily in the picture thinks she's escaped the confines of childhood and eluded the claims of adulthood, but she is wrong. Consequence, like mortality, is after her already; it is just over her left shoulder—even though she doesn't know it, even though she doesn't feel it, even though it doesn't yet cast a shadow.

Eduardo leaned forward. He thought he caught a whiff of something vaguely briny, subaquatic, on Toledo, but then it disappeared. "I understand you spent ninety-seven days in jail last year for vandalism."

Toledo shrugged. "You seem like you'd know better than I would."

"You must have enjoyed your time there," said Eduardo. He leaned back and his chair skittered sideways on a broken caster. A faint look of disgust either did or did not flicker across Ignacio Toledo's face. He yawned, revealing teeth that were strangely small and sharp, like little broken buttons.

"Excuse me, hello?" said Eduardo, rapping on the table. He bit the inside of his lip, willing himself to attention. "Listen. The only thing you can do now is help us understand how Lily Hayes was involved. This isn't only the best thing you can do for your case at this point. It's also basically the *only* thing you can do for your case. This is it. Do you understand? This is the last choice you'll get to make in all of this. This, really, is the only one."

At this, something decisive seemed to flash in Toledo's face—the whites of his eyes grew momentarily larger, perhaps, or then again maybe they didn't—and Eduardo felt a queasiness that he recognized as the onset of unwanted certainty.

"Do you not believe me?" said Eduardo. "Go ahead and get yourself a lawyer. He's going to tell you exactly the same thing. I assure you."

There was another freighted silence. Eduardo tried to breathe shallowly so as not to jostle the mounting pressure in his bladder. And then—finally—Ignacio Toledo began to speak.

"Yeah, I knew her." Toledo sighed with unexpected theatricality. "We talked sometimes and I sold her some weed once. The night it happened she came by really upset just as my shift was ending. She'd been fired a few days before and I didn't want Javier to see her and get even angrier, and she seemed to really need to talk to someone, so I offered to buy her a beer. So we went out and, well, it turned into a pretty crazy night."

"Okay," said Eduardo. "That's helpful. Thank you. Did anyone besides you see Lily come by Fuego that night?"

"I don't think so." Now Toledo seemed to be working something around the corner of his mouth, though Eduardo couldn't quite catch sight of it properly—every time he looked at Toledo straight on, he stopped. "I mean, I saw her in the back alley, and I tried to sort of hustle her away. Because like I said, I didn't want Javier to find out she was there."

"I see. And then what happened?"

"Well, we went out—"

"Where?"

Toledo looked down and squinted into his lap. When people were lying, they usually rolled their eyes upward—but then again this was widely known by anyone who had regular occasion to lie or be lied to. "I don't remember," he said. "A place on Juramento. I can check."

"That would certainly be helpful. Did anyone see you there?"

Toledo shrugged. "I don't know. I mean, it was really crowded—like completely packed—so I'm sure people saw us, but I don't know if anyone would really remember us."

"I see. And you didn't happen to make any of your purchases with a credit card that night?"

Toledo shook his head.

"Of course not. Go on."

"Well, anyway, we got really drunk, and then. Well. I know this part isn't going to make me look so good, but I guess I should probably tell you the whole story."

"That would indeed be wise."

"Well, then we smoked some weed and took some paco. And anyway, all this time, Lily was telling me all these crazy stories about Katy, about the kinds of insane sex stuff Katy was into. I mean, I'd seen the girl around a few times myself and that was definitely the vibe I got from her. And somehow we got it into our heads that we should go back to the house and try to get something going with her. The two of us. It was Lily's idea, really, but I'd seen Katy around a few times and thought she was pretty hot, so I was game. We got there and she was up for it, and things got started. But at a certain point Katy just started freaking out—"

"Slow down. Freaking out how?"

"Threatening to call the people whose house it was, threatening to call the cops. Lily started screaming back at Katy, and then I slapped her, just sort of to calm her down, get her to snap out of it. Then Lily hit her and Katy sort of tried to hit her back, and I was thinking this was maybe still part of the sex stuff, like maybe they did this all the time. I mean, I guess they'd had a pretty crazy fight at Fuego just a couple of nights earlier. I didn't see all of it, but that's what I heard. So anyway then Katy came swinging at me and I got in there, too, and, anyway, it was really fast, and like I said—"

"And when did the knife come in?" Eduardo said this dispassionately. One could not let emotion corrode these things. He had to think of what it would be like to lose Maria. He had to believe that somebody—somebody rational and humane—would go about the careful business of doing all of this when he was unable to; he had to believe that somebody would stand back from the mosaic and try to make sense of the whole.

"I honestly don't even know," said Toledo. "I was really drunk and frankly pretty high. Maybe Lily grabbed it, or maybe I did. Or maybe even Katy did. I mean, I'm sure your tests will show what happened, but I honestly don't know. It was a mess. And in what seemed like a minute Katy was on the ground, and it seemed like she was hurt pretty bad. I asked Lily if maybe we needed to take her to the hospital but Lily said no, it was her problem, she would take care of it and would keep an eye on her and would call for help if she needed it. So anyway, naturally I left then. I definitely didn't think Katy was dead at the time. It never would have occurred to me that she could be. I thought she was like, passed out. Every night at Fuego some girl or five passes out. I didn't know that Katy had died until I saw it on TV the next day. And I had no idea what the hell had happened, or what had happened after I left, so I figured it was best to just lie low and see what happened next." He shook his head. "It's horrible. It's absolutely horrible. I really can't believe it at all."

"Thank you," said Eduardo. "I do appreciate your being so forthcoming."

Toledo shook his head. "I just wish I'd known what Lily was really like, you know?" he said. "Then maybe I could have stopped it."

That day, Eduardo left work early. Outside, the evening was balmy, the light still dripping off the buildings like icicles. He had decided he would walk home.

Eduardo was, overall, very satisfied with Toledo's confession. In a broad sense, of course, no murder confession could ever be truly satisfying, because you could not hope for a real answer to the fundamental question of *why* one person murdered another. That question was on the order of cosmic questions about meaning and love and mortality, and it was not the job of a newspaper or a court to unravel it. In most cases—and this case, it seemed, was no different—there was no answer that could ever make a normal person understand.

Across the street from Eduardo, a small protest was beginning. The students were yelling *Putos Peronistas!* this year, but they were yelling something every year. Eduardo stopped for a moment and marveled. All that vanity and self-congratulation, and all for not being dead or old yet. As though this, in and of itself, was some kind of accomplishment. Eduardo kept walking.

But even without a satisfying answer to that most elemental question—the question of why—Toledo's story made sense. The story did not need to force a jurist or a prosecutor or an average person to empathize his way into comprehension, after all. It did not need to make them see how an event like this could happen; it needed only to convince them that it had. And on that score, the confession worked. Significantly, it drew a narrative line between the triplicate data points of Lily's DNA: on the knife, on Katy's mouth, and on the bra. The defense could tell a heroic story about CPR to explain the mouth, but that story would not explain the bra, and Ignacio Toledo's story explained both. It further explained the hours between when Katy Kellers died, according to the pathologist, and when Lily Hayes was seen streaking across the yard with blood on her face: If she and Toledo had not realized that Katy was mortally wounded, then Lily probably *was* surprised to find her dead. And all of this fit with the fact that clearly neither Lily nor Ignacio Toledo had expected the night to turn out the way it had; even before it was tested, the visible presence of DNA at the crime scene had strongly suggested that Katy's murder had not been premeditated—had perhaps not even been entirely intentional.

Toledo's story made sense of all of this, too. And more important still, from the panelists' perspective, it was unlikely that Toledo could know that it did. Realizing that Toledo had an incentive to lie about Lily's involvement was one thing, after all—believing that he'd had the foresight to craft such a comprehensive, multivariable lie was quite another. And most crucially, perhaps, Toledo's story was really only a continuation of the stories the judge panelists would have already heard from Lily herself: her suspicions about Sebastien and Katy leading to the fight with Katy at Fuego leading to Lily's firing leading, finally, to this. The alcohol, the proximity to drugs, made more explicable the gulf between Lily's past behavior and her behavior on this night. And although it would have been better if Ignacio Toledo and Lily had been seen together, they had both independently supplied reasons why they might have tried hard not to be: Toledo wanted to keep Lily out of sight of Javier Aguirre; and Lily had, by her own belated admission, purchased illegal drugs from Toledo—which must have seemed like a pretty serious problem, before Lily learned just how serious problems could be.

It was true, of course, that Eduardo did not need Lily any longer to successfully prosecute the case. He had Ignacio Toledo—both his story and his DNA—and there were prosecutors, Eduardo knew, who would now begin to see Lily Hayes as a murky distraction, a person whose guilt was quickly becoming inconvenient. There were prosecutors who would want to edit her out of the narrative in order to tell the jurist panelists a cleaner, less subtle story—a story in which all the victims and villains looked the way they usually did, and all the motives were fairy-tale clear—and, depending on how much they thought it would strengthen the state's overall case, there were prosecutors who might even offer Ignacio Toledo a modest deal in exchange for excising Lily from his confession. A deal of that sort could be breathtakingly, vanishingly modest—since Ignacio Toledo had absolutely nothing to lose—and there were prosecutors who would see all of this as an overarching win: one small moral concession for a broader moral victory, an indisputably pragmatic trade-off. There were prosecutors who would shrug and send Lily off into her life, keeping her guilt a secret between them. They would console themselves with the thought that she was very unlikely to do anything violent ever again. And they would tell themselves that—either way—the prosecution of Lily Hayes, as that of all people everywhere, was ultimately in the hands of God.

But Eduardo could do none of this. He had heard a line once that had stayed with him, both for its elegance and its wrongness: *It is the final proof of God's omnipotence that He need not exist in order to save us.* Where had Eduardo heard that quote? He did not know, but he knew he did not believe it. The way to assure morality on Earth was not to behave as though there was a God, even if there wasn't—it was to behave as though there was no God, even if there was. We must act as though ours is all the judgment and forgiveness that is ever forthcoming, if we want any hope of getting anything right. Maria was a living reminder of that charter, if Eduardo could have ever forgotten it. Human love meant the witness of human lives, and Maria was witnessing Eduardo's, even if no one else was. And dropping Lily's prosecution would be a rejection of the single mission that was, whether divinely charged or not, the only mission men are tasked with. In the end, it would be an act of moral violence done not only to Katy Kellers, but to Lily Hayes, as well, and even, in a small way, to Eduardo himself: It would be a denial of all of their humanity. The difference, really, was only a matter of degree.

Eduardo stepped into the street, and a motorcycle whizzed by him. He leaped out of the way, swearing, and fell sideways onto his knee.

"Cabeza de pija!" he bellowed. The kid was already half a block away and did not turn around—only dug his knee into the bike, as though it were a sentient creature that could actually respond to him. Eduardo hated, hated, the motorcycles. Syncopated waves of new objects were always flooding the country, responsive to the lifting of this or that trade restriction—Eduardo woke up one day and everyone suddenly had a BlackBerry, or were standing in lines that snaked around corners in order to buy a flat-screen TV, or had a fucking motorcycle. Sometimes Eduardo could understand the appeal of living in a closed neighborhood—just pulling your arms over your head and trying to wave away history's vicissitudes. He straightened out his knee. It was decidedly—perhaps a bit disappointingly—undamaged. He stood up. He could feel his whole body shaking. The rest of the walk home, he favored his knee a bit more than he really had to, for the benefit of anyone who might have been watching.

When Eduardo reached the apartment, he stood in the doorway

for a moment. Since Maria's return, he had become accustomed to taking the temperature of a room before he entered it; today, he could feel
the low ebb of the apartment's energy. The kitchen was mostly dark. In
the few strands of vermiculated light coming through the window, he
could see that the small mess from breakfast was still sitting on the
table; the coffee was still stewing, now cold, in its pot.

The one remaining problem with the case, as Eduardo saw it, was
Sebastien LeCompte. The alibi he provided for Lily was deeply nebulous, and he was not a person any judge would be inclined to trust,
even with a far better story. Nevertheless, Toledo's account—with its
multiple acts and multiple locations—would be harder to square with
Sebastien LeCompte's testimony than a simpler narrative might have
been. It was easy enough to believe that Lily had left Sebastien for an
hour or two without his knowledge; four or five hours—which is what
Eduardo feared Toledo's story implied—would mean that the panelists
would be forced to decide that either Sebastien LeCompte was lying or
Ignacio Toledo was. And LeCompte and Toledo struck Eduardo as
about equally disingenuous seeming; really, you might as well flip a
coin between them. Eduardo switched on the light.

"Hello," said Maria. She'd been sitting on the couch, perfectly still,
and had not spoken when he entered the room. "Did I startle you?"

"No." She had, but Eduardo never physically startled.

"I went to church today," said Maria. "I wanted to visit your pal." She
meant Jesus. Eduardo was wary of this topic of discussion. Maria's firm-
est and lowest opinion of Eduardo centered on the myth of his blind
religiosity and—in part because she seemed to enjoy it so much—he had
long since given up trying to explain his actual feelings on the matter.

"I hope you communicated my regards," said Eduardo, pouring out
the coffee. He flexed his knee again and felt a vaguely satisfying pulse
of pain. Those fucking kids.

"Oh, I didn't have to," said Maria.

Eduardo turned on the faucet. He believed in God in the same way
he believed in his own consciousness; Eduardo would no more have
tried to prove that he actually felt God's presence in his life than he

would have tried to convince someone that he actually heard his own inner monologue running through his head. He would have liked to explain some of this to Maria, but she was not a very good listener when it came to such things.

"He knew all about your regards already," said Maria, in case Eduardo hadn't gotten it. "I mean, obviously."

Eduardo dislodged a plate from its swamp of waterlogged rice. He was glad that Maria had left the dishes; he could pretend not to hear her when the water was running.

"It's funny," said Maria, "that people talk to God so much, when He's the one person who you shouldn't have to explain anything to."

"Mmm," Eduardo said. He was trying very hard not to argue. It was atheists, he often thought, who were the true fundamentalists—forever trapped within their own limited circuit, utterly without humility, smug in the laughable confidence that the universe was somehow specifically set up for human understanding, like an algebra problem designed to be challenging but reasonable for a particular age group. How did that idea not undercut its own argument, while being hopelessly unimaginative and narcissistic at the same time? But there was no point in saying any of this. When Maria got in this mood, there was no point in saying much of anything.

"People think that's true of lovers," said Maria, "but it's not. Right, Eduardo?"

He turned off the water and grabbed a dish towel. There were a few options before him now, and he ran through them. He could remain silent, which would only provoke Maria to keep talking. He could say something conciliatory, which would have no effect, or something withering, which would either sate or excite her. Or he could gamble on something silly—make a joke, flick water at her, try to create a hallucinatory, wavering moment in which she might still decide she didn't feel like fighting.

"But people like to tell God everything," said Maria. "He must get bored listening to all of those thoughts."

Eduardo handed her a dish to dry.

"Even yours, Eduardo," she said, swiping at it feebly. "Do you think you're ever boring our Lord? Do you think He's ever just pretending to listen? Just trying to be polite?"

Eduardo had decided what to do. "Not everyone can be as patient as you are," he said. He kissed her on the forehead for good measure— once begun, it was important to really commit to appeasement—and was relieved when Maria laughed merrily. It had worked.

"Oh, Eduardo," she said, drawing her hand to her cheek. "I'm a nightmare. I don't know why you put up with me. Oh!" She clapped her hands and went to the couch. "Did you know you were in *Clarín* today?" She produced the paper from the sofa cushions and handed it to him. The article was a profile. It had been written and researched months ago, its publication endlessly deferred. But now here it was, resurrected at last, occupying a respectable square chunk of the page. Eduardo glanced at the photograph accompanying the article. Through some strange newspaper sorcery, it made Eduardo appear far more handsome than he was in real life.

"Did you read it?" said Maria.

"Not yet." Eduardo stared at the photograph. It was a weird trick of angling or light, he thought; it gave the completely wrong impression of his face. And in giving the wrong impression of his face, it seemed to give a wrong impression of his entire life—nobody with that face could ever be as lonely and as heartbroken as Eduardo had so often been.

"They make you sound so smart," said Maria. Like all of her compliments, this one was slightly askew and, like all of her compliments, Eduardo was happy to have it.

"Thanks," he said, giving the photograph one last look. It felt fraudulent, embarrassing, somehow, to see it. He almost wanted to ask the newspaper to issue a retraction.

"That really looks nothing like you," said Maria, hovering over his shoulder.

Eduardo kissed her on the cheek this time, hoping she'd take weariness for tenderness. "No," he said. "I guess it doesn't."

. . .

That night, Eduardo stayed up in his office. He folded the newspaper to his picture and set it on the desk, then took out the picture of Lily Hayes—the one he normally did not like to look at, the one taken before she was guilty but when she was already the person who eventually would be—and set them side by side. Pictures were so deceptive, he thought, pressing his thumb into Lily's face. What had she known about herself then? What had the people who loved her known? Perhaps they'd felt a difference in her somehow but had had no vocabulary to name it. Maybe this had been something like the color blindness of the ancient Greeks, before words had ushered in vision—we do not see that which we have no language to understand. Or maybe Eduardo had misunderstood that entire concept entirely. Maybe he'd been getting it wrong all along.

He went to the kitchen and turned on the coffeepot. It hissed and sputtered like a roused animal, and he hoped Maria could hear it. He padded back into the office and opened the window. Outside, it was raining an invisible nocturnal rain. He sat back down and put his cheek to the table. He stared at the photograph of Lily Hayes. Her prosecution was something that was owed to her—just as much as, if not more than, it was owed to Katy Kellers. In his head, Eduardo spoke to Lily: *We must act as though our understanding, as limited as it might be, is the most panoramic and complete understanding possible. We must act as though everything in this life counts; as though we have only one shot to get things right. We must act as though nobody would see the truth if we did not see the truth.*

He would tell Maria some of these things someday, he thought.

Eduardo opened his eyes. Outside, somehow, the sky was already, relentlessly, brightening to the color of tallow. The rain had stopped. It was possible that Eduardo had slept.

CHAPTER SEVENTEEN

March

It was ten days before Sebastien finally saw Beatriz Carrizo again.

He'd been staring at the computer for nearly an hour, trying to decide whether to buy lightbulbs online. Leaving the house was beginning to feel impossible. The women at Pan y Vino went silent now whenever Sebastien came in—though whether from hostility or sympathy or politeness (since, like everyone else, they were doubtlessly spending most of their waking hours talking about the trial), he did not know. But whatever the case, Sebastien's going anywhere or doing anything had come to seem like an elaborate imposition on everybody else, when before it had seemed like an imposition only on Sebastien himself. He certainly hadn't been in the market for yet another reason to stay indoors. And he found that there was something strangely anxiety producing about not being able to leave the house without ruining someone's day (and he reminded himself that he'd managed to ruin Andrew's without even doing that much); it seemed to consign him to the realm of the mythic and the monstrous and the deformed—and was, perhaps, the reason he was waffling so much over ordering the lightbulbs online. To do so would be a concession to a new, more disfiguring reclusiveness. After that, it would be only a matter of time before mothers started warning their children about him to get them to behave. Sebastien shook his head and closed the Amazon lightbulb page. He glanced out the window. And that's when he saw a bent figure moving hurriedly across the yard.

Sebastien jumped. The fact that he had not noticed Beatriz until she was already halfway between her car and the house made him uneasy, as did the strange tension in her gait. She had always been elegant, regal in a way that seemed beyond considerations of age. Now her walk was a sort of scurrying, and it made her look like an old person or a criminal or an animal—something that had long stopped caring, if it ever had, about what anyone watching might see.

Sebastien hurried to put on his slippers and opened the door. Outside it was gaspingly hot. A current of pre-storm wind was beginning to pick up; the trees were relinquishing their leaves as though they were shedding armor; the sky was gray and laden, threaded with rays of black rain clouds that reminded Sebastien of blood poisoning. He ran across the yard, his slippers whisking against the grass. No amount of wind could touch the heat—the heat was virtuosic, it was unimpeachable. Sebastien wanted to catch Beatriz before she went too much farther; he was not superstitious, but neither was he interested in going anywhere near that house. He got close enough to her to shout.

"Señora Carrizo," he said, waving.

She froze in place and looked at him, eyes wide. It was possible she did not recognize him from the distance. He should not have startled her. He ran closer. It was beginning to rain.

"Hello? Señora Carrizo?" Sebastien waved his arms. He was aware that he probably did not look his best, running across the yard in the rain, gesticulating like a person with some kind of neurological disorder. "It's me!" he yelled, stupidly. "Sebastien."

But Beatriz Carrizo was backing away from him, slowly at first, then a bit faster, in a mad and socially inept sort of scramble.

"I'm sorry," she said. "I don't want to talk to you." Sebastien could see that she would have liked very much to turn her back on him and run away, though she was unwilling to actually do this.

"Please," he said, coming closer.

"No," she shouted, putting up her hands as though feigning entombment in a box. "Stay back."

"It's me, Sebastien," he said. Maybe she really couldn't see him. Maybe her eyes were bad. "Your neighbor?" He pointed ineffectually back at his house, to remind her.

"Don't come any closer," she said, and Sebastien heard the flickering arpeggio of fear in her voice, and finally he understood, and stopped running.

The rain was coming harder now, flattening Sebastien's hair against his head. He raised his arms in a gesture of defeat, of meaning no harm. "I just want to talk to you," he said.

"I'm sorry," said Beatriz again, before hurrying up the steps to her house—her former house—and slamming the door.

After that, for the first time, Sebastien felt that the Carrizos' house was actually watching him back. The lights still went on and off, the car came and went at strange hours, and though he did not see the Carrizos—and though now he knew better than to try to go over there to speak with them, even if he had—he could somehow feel their wariness; he could sense them turning their attention to his house and finally considering, with elevated heart rates and shortened breaths, who might actually live there. Sebastien still could not quite bring himself to fear the murderer returning to the hill. But he could feel the Carrizos' fear and it worked on him like a contact high, making him edgy in moments when he was thinking of something else and not remembering that he was the person the Carrizos were afraid of. It was such a strange injustice, to watch a woman skitter away from you in terror. Though in a way, that moment had made Sebastien feel closer to Lily; he liked sharing the plague of suspicion with her—even if it was only in miniature, even if it did not count for anything, even if he could not have told her about it, anyway.

It was a few days before Carlos came to the door. Sebastien watched him approach but believed until the very last moment that Carlos must have other business somewhere—maybe he had something to say to the garden flowers, maybe there was something on the porch he wanted to vandalize—and, even after hearing steps on the front walk, Sebastien still jumped to hear the querulous sound of the knocker.

He went to the door, and Carlos was standing on the porch, gaze cast downward, looking as though, had he been a person who was inclined to wear hats, he'd be wringing one in his hands right now.

"Yes?" said Sebastien.

"Yes, hello," said Carlos. Sebastien felt a current of mutual embarrassment flash between them—embarrassment that such a thing as a murder had occurred, and that they both knew it had occurred, and that it had occurred somehow on their shared watch, as well as embarrassment at the abject, frenzied hysteria the situation now necessitated (anything less than that would, after all, be inhumane), as well as embarrassment at their joint failure to completely participate in it. Carlos laughed apologetically. "I was just admiring this knocker you've got here. What is that?"

"It's a bust of my grandfather," Sebastien said automatically.

"Ah." Carlos looked down quickly and cleared his throat. "Well. I'm sorry if Beatriz was rude to you the other day. She's sorry, too."

"Oh," said Sebastien, fixing his eyes on Carlos's shoulder. He could not guess what was expected of him here. *Please, Carlos, don't think of it for a moment! What's a suspicion of murder between neighbors? I certainly hope Beatriz hasn't been fretting over it.* "All right," he said.

"You know, it's a difficult time right now," said Carlos regretfully. "She's scared. You can imagine."

"It's an unspeakably dreadful thing, what's happened," said Sebastien. It came out with more intensity than he'd meant it to.

Carlos squinted, even though the light was behind him. "Yes," he said. "Katy was a very sweet girl."

"It must be an absolutely terrible time for you," said Sebastien. He meant it. He did not mean anything, ever, but he meant this.

Carlos inclined his head and looked at Sebastien directly for the first time. "For you, too, I'd imagine."

"Worse for you, I'm sure," said Sebastien. "It was your house. And, really, I didn't know Katy that well."

Sebastien had meant this as a kindness—an acknowledgment of the magnitude of the Carrizos' pain, a deferral to their closeness to the situation—but it seemed to hit Carlos wrong somehow, and his expression changed, and there was a creeping feeling along Sebastien's neck.

"You knew Lily well, though," said Carlos.

Sebastien recognized Carlos's new expression as one of suspicion. And—perhaps because this time he was, on some level, expecting it—Sebastien found himself looking at Carlos with frank suspicion right back. "You know she didn't do it, right?" he said.

Carlos retreated by a step. "Beatriz is just shaken up."

"But you do know that, right? You really know that?"

At this, Carlos shook his head slightly. "I've recently realized I'm too old to think I really know anything."

That night, Sebastien sat up donating anonymously to Lily's parents' travel fund.

He'd found the site immediately after its conception. It had clearly been erected by one of Andrew or Maureen's baby boomer friends—its pleas for money or frequent-flier miles were written in outlandish, early Internet fonts, floating above family pictures of the Hayes family at wholesome New England destinations. On top of Mount Washington, Maureen, Lily, and Anna bend against the wind, matching red hoodies pulled tight around their faces; Lily pretends to hold on to a railing for dear life. After each donation, Sebastien felt a brief sense of calm; he was glad to finally have found some way to spend money that didn't make him feel wretched. He would make a great philanthropist yet, he thought, after completing his fifth donation. He laughed and got up to fix himself a drink.

When he sat back down, he Googled the word "suicide." A toll-free hotline number popped up above the search results, and Sebastien felt the hairs on his arms stand up, just as they always did. Sebastien had discovered this search engine curiosity right after his return to Buenos Aires. NEED HELP? the message above the number said, a question that Sebastien found oddly, overwhelmingly touching, though he did not know what entity could be said to be asking it. The computer? The aggregated information of the Internet? The kind person in Mountain View, California, who had thought of this idea in the first place? The anti-suicide lobbying group that had demanded it? Sebastien did not know, but still the message had made him cry the first time he saw it—for the impersonality of the algorithm that was behind it, and for the pure indifferent public-spiritedness that was behind *that*. He took a sip of absinthe. It almost did not matter, he realized, what the intelligence generating the message was—whether it was conscious or unconscious, singular or plural, animate or inanimate. The message was simply concern cast out into the universe—toward him or anyone or no one. No matter what it was, it had helped him once, and no matter what it was, it could not know that it had.

Sebastien palmed his cheek, then clicked back over to Lily's travel fund website. He zoomed in on the picture of Lily on Mount Washington. He touched her hood, putting his finger directly on the computer screen. Lily's face was scrunched and red, her eyes wet with tears from wind or laughter. Sebastien clicked on the Donate button. He was about to click again when he heard a knock on the door.

He startled and looked at the clock. Somehow, it was already eleven a.m. The knock came again, and Sebastien scurried to the bathroom to swallow some toothpaste and run a comb through his hair. There was a third knock, and Sebastien ran to the door—tripping over the leg of a piano bench and swearing loudly—and opened it.

On his stoop was a girl—young and reddish haired and wiry, like a vehicle built for efficiency.

"Hi," she said. "I'm Anna."

Sebastien was stupefied. He tried to summon Lily's description of her sister but could produce nothing specific; Anna had floated around the edges of Lily's anecdotes, a pixelated smudge of sidekick, consigned to the modal past tense—*Anna and I always used to do this, Anna and I would always go there*—and listening to the stories it would have been easy to think, to the extent one thought about it at all, that Anna was still six years old somewhere, pigtailed, mischievous (though not quite as mischievous as Lily), eternally trailing after the shadow of her older sister. Sebastien had detected no animosity in these narratives, only the profoundly tangential nature of Anna's role in Lily's world today. What could you say about someone like Anna? You were children together, that's all. But now here was an adult Anna, standing on Sebastien's porch and, presumably, in the very center of her own life.

"Don't tell me I look like her," she said. "I already know."

She did not, in fact, look all that much like Lily, in Sebastien's estimation. Their features were similar, but Anna seemed mad about it, somehow—as though her face was just a mask of Lily's face that had been foisted upon her against her will and that the cruel townspeople were now forcing her to parade around the square in.

"That's an interesting knocker you have," she said.

"I got it at a rummage sale," said Sebastien, unfreezing. Why weren't her parents watching her? he caught himself thinking, then could not believe he was thinking it.

Anna frowned and leaned closer to it. "It's a griffin, right?"

"I'm sure I never asked it such a personal question," said Sebastien. It came out snappish. He didn't want to seem surprised that Anna had known, but he was, a little, and he saw that she could tell.

"Lily always did have weird taste in boys," Anna murmured, as if confiding in the griffin. She stood back up. "I'm a classics major."

"Oh," said Sebastien. "Lily didn't tell me that."

"Oh, yeah? What major did she say I was?"

Lily hadn't mentioned it, of course—though Sebastien would have imagined (had he been forced to imagine) that Anna might have been studying business, or finance, or some other soulless discipline of the sort pursued by compulsive exercisers. "Lily didn't talk about you very much, I'm afraid," he said.

"Well, yeah. I mean, I'm not Lily, am I?" Anna gazed sourly past Sebastien's shoulder and into the house. "Could I come in, do you think?"

Sebastien gestured an elaborate *by all means*. Anna walked inside, squinting against the room's patchy light and nodding faintly, as though confirming to her own silent satisfaction that everything was exactly as she'd thought it would be. Sebastien was irritated. *You try having lights under the circumstances,* he wanted to say. *You try having furniture.* At least there was a sheet over the television; Sebastien still could not bear the thought of anyone—even a stranger, and even now—knowing that he owned one.

"Forgive me for asking," said Sebastien, "but why are you here?" He'd been planning to offer Anna a drink but now he wanted her out of the house; the expression on her face was too much like the one he'd been afraid Lily would have the first time she came over, and on the whole, this encounter with Anna was starting to feel too much like an alternate, wholly unpleasant version of the inaugural one with Lily.

"Shouldn't you be asking how you can help me?" said Anna.

"I'm afraid I presumed you would not hesitate to tell me."

"I have to ask you a question."

Sebastien mimed loading and firing a gun.

Anna nodded again, as though Sebastien had just done something that she'd been assured many times that he would. "My sister dumped you, right?"

"I beg your pardon?"

"Would this be less weird if we were sitting down?"

Sebastien waved at one of the sheeted lumps. He wished Anna would remark on the lumps—it would be much better if she would—but she did not. Instead, she lifted the sheet to look under it—it turned out to be an oak bench—before sitting down.

"I wouldn't feel bad about it," she said. "My sister dumps a lot of guys. She even dumps guys she's not even really dating. It's sort of a hobby of hers."

"We all need to pass the hours somehow."

"But I guess what I'm wondering is, did she do something particularly awful to you? Or did you guys do something awful together?"

"Forgive me," said Sebastien. "But I am really struggling to imagine how you're seeing any of this as your concern."

"The night Katy died, I mean. I don't want to know about anything awful that happened any other night. That really wouldn't be any of my concern, you're right."

Sebastien could feel angry horror rising through him, and he was beginning to be unable to bear the sight of Anna's face. He closed his eyes. "Did I sell out your sister for revenge, is what you're here to inquire?"

Anna gave him a flat look. "I just think it's strange that she's in trouble and you're not, that's all."

"Is that a question?" said Sebastien. "Or is this morning's program only going to involve a lecture segment? What a thrill it is to be the recipient of personal disquisitions from *both* Miss Hayes the Younger *and* the estimable Andrew Hayes, PhD. Of course, it's true that a less easygoing fellow might start to find all this a tad pedantic."

Anna raised her eyebrows. They were high arched, like Lily's, which made her look even more surprised than she probably was. "My father came to see you?"

"He did indeed."

"I didn't know that."

"To live is to learn. Your father came here, and we had a truly unendurable conversation, and I am starting get an unhappy picture of the Hayes family's manners, particularly as they pertain to *barging in*. It's a miracle Lily is as affable as she is."

Anna's forehead was still slightly unsettled; Sebastien could see that this revelation had thrown her off, and that it was time to capitalize on this. "Speaking of your Andrew," he said, "does he know you're here? Or does Maureen?"

"Do Andrew and Maureen know I'm here?" Anna's face clenched— this was a sort of airless, noiseless laugh, Sebastien supposed, though it looked strikingly like some kind of medical problem. "No. They don't keep terrifically careful track of me."

"That seems odd, considering."

"Not really."

"Why's that?"

"They've never been overly interested in me. They really only had me because they thought I'd be important for Lily's psychological development. I was like a kiddie Mozart CD for her. Or didn't she tell you that either?"

Sebastien looked at his feet. "Lily's take on it, I think," he said carefully, "was that you both felt a bit extraneous to Janie. That was her name, right?" Even though he already knew.

Anna nodded, then shook her head. "They would have had Lily anyway, though. No one ever talks about that. Janie and Lily, that was supposed to be their family. Two kids. I was just the sub, and no one seems excessively happy that I got off the bench. To use an American sports metaphor that, I'm sure, seems pretty vulgar to you. But all of that can be a good thing sometimes. It means I can do stuff I might not be able to otherwise. Like come here and talk to you, for example."

Sebastien flashed, suddenly, to a memory of his father. Growing up, Sebastien had noticed—first vaguely, then with growing attentiveness— the way his parents lied about their work. Their strategy seemed mostly to involve making their jobs sound very, very boring, and the more Sebastien understood how interesting their jobs really were, the more he marveled over the fact that this approach was actually effective.

When Sebastien's parents were queried about their profession, they gave breezy, dismissive, self-deprecating answers, countered the question with a question, and—just like that—the subject was changed. Invariably, whomever they'd been speaking with was only too happy to do the talking; invariably, it was what they had really wanted to do all along. Sebastien had asked his father about this once, in one of their only direct conversations about such matters. Sebastien was always trying to find the right questions—questions based on tacit mutual understanding, questions that did not demand any concrete answers— and this question, it turned out, was one of them. His father had even looked a little bit pleased that he'd asked it.

"That's an applicable life lesson, my boy," he'd said. "Nobody is really paying attention to you. Most people don't really get this. They think they must count more to other people than other people count to them. They can't believe the disregard could truly be mutual. But it's a useful thing to learn, you know, if you can manage not to feel too sorry about it."

Sebastien had listened and nodded gravely. It was thrilling and terrifying, realizing how easy it was to hide how unlikely it was that anyone would come looking for you if you did.

"I understand," he said to Anna.

The light through the window shifted, and Anna turned to look. Sebastien followed her gaze. Outside, feathery clouds sculpted the sky. When she turned back to him, her face was sharp again. "I want to know why you weren't arrested," she said. "Especially considering you were sleeping with Katy."

At this, Sebastien could feel his heart seize, then begin to race. He spent a moment trying to calm it down before he spoke. "Why does everyone think this?" he said.

"Well, who *was* she sleeping with, then? She was involved with someone, apparently."

"I don't know. 'It isn't any of my business'—is that the charmingly late-capitalist phrase one hears? But I am certain it wasn't me. I do believe I'd remember." A wretched thought came to him. "Is that what Lily thinks?"

Anna said nothing.

"I wasn't. Tell her."

"Whatever." Anna waved her hand, as though trying to decline something Sebastien was physically offering her. "The point is, everyone thinks you were, so, given that, why weren't you arrested?"

"You want my own opinion on why I wasn't arrested?"

"Yes."

"It's an honor to be consulted."

"Please don't be a shit."

Sebastien ignored this. "In my opinion—hubristic and limited and self-serving as it is—I suppose I was not arrested because they can confidently rule me out."

"And why is that?"

Sebastien opened his eyes wide, hoping to give the impression of marveling over the fact that Anna was going to make him explain this. "Well," he said slowly. "They know a fellow was involved, and they know that that fellow was not me. I don't want to go into the gruesome reasons why they know these things, but I'm assured yours is an unprecedentedly indelicate generation. You've seen *Law and Order*, I trust?"

"You could have both been involved. That happens all the time."

"Well, yes," said Sebastien. "But they know that only one gentleman had a biological role in the events, which would make my role—what, exactly? Aesthetic? Spiritual? Light direction? Was I the key grip? It's all a little narratively awkward, even for that horrid prosecutor's crazed imagination."

At this, Anna's face seemed to close, and Sebastien knew he'd made a mistake. What was he doing? He was joking, perversely, horribly. How could he ever go testify on a stand in front of normal people? He couldn't even talk to Lily's sister without convincing her of his total unsoundness, if not his actual guilt.

"I'm sorry," he said. "But you understand what I'm saying. You're a reasonable person. I apologize for my flippant tone. One gets a little defensive in emergencies, as I'm sure you've noticed in your sister."

"This is true," said Anna coldly. "Though my sister doesn't exactly need an emergency to be defensive, does she?"

Sebastien hadn't meant to be digging for information here, particularly, but still he felt a shameful welling of hope at the thought that he might have found some. "What do you mean?" he said.

"Well," said Anna. "She's got something of a persecution complex, right? Thinks the whole world revolves around the gaping vacuum of her needs? Thinks she's the only one in the universe for whom pragmatism is a major crisis of the soul?"

Sebastien was stunned. He opened his mouth and closed it again. His teeth clacked together audibly.

"Haven't noticed any of this?" said Anna. "No, I suppose you wouldn't. Someone who thinks their need is the vortex of reality can make anyone attending to those needs feel pretty central, too."

Sebastien would put away these claims; he would save them for later review. At some point, he knew, he would greedily consume them; he would be willing to consider their every angle, as well as their possible truth. But for now, Anna had said an incredibly uncharitable thing about a person she was supposed to love—a person Sebastien himself loved—and who was, at this very moment, defenseless, in every possible sense of the word.

"My heavens," said Sebastien. Chivalry, regretfully, demanded bitchiness. "And Lily said you didn't have an original thought in your head."

"Ha," said Anna. "I don't, of course. But in my family, knowing that *is* the original thought."

Sebastien blinked. "Lily loves you," he said. "For whatever it's worth. And she has absolutely no idea that you hate her."

"I don't hate her." Anna shook her head vigorously. "I love her. How could I not? I mean, everyone wants to love Lily. That's the whole thing. Everyone wants to love her, everyone wants to think she means well. And it's not that she doesn't. It's just that she can't see how much it matters whether people *want* to give you a break. That's why she's in this mess. It's because for her whole life, she's been playing by different rules from everyone else."

"Rules!" Sebastien scoffed. "Pah! What rules? It's anarchy and law-lessness all the way down."

"That's not true," said Anna. "There are rules for people, and there are different rules for Lily. Or there were, anyway. And she never knew it, which is why she's in so much trouble now. Because she couldn't stop herself from doing that cartwheel, or from talking to that asshole prosecutor without a lawyer, or all these other dumb things. Because she never had to learn to live in a world that didn't necessarily *want* to go easy on her." Anna stood. You really could tell that she was an athlete—her posture was impeccable, nearly militaristic, reflecting more alertness than Sebastien could ever remember feeling in his life. "Anyway," she said. "Okay. This has been less than totally illuminating, but I guess I believe that you didn't consciously screw my sister over."

"How flattering."

"Well, that's definitely what I'm going for, so." Anna shook her head, and when she spoke again, her voice had softened. "No, I mean, I know you care about her. I can tell. You know there's a site where you can donate? For my parents' travel and stuff." She opened her bag and pro-duced a pen and paper—Sebastien was relieved he was not going to be summoned to locate these objects in his own house—and scribbled the address of the website. She was, he noticed with mildly senseless surprise, left-handed. "If you really do want to help. That's how you could help."

"I'll do that."

"Maybe you will."

Anna turned to leave. In profile, she looked more like Lily than she had from the front.

"Tell her that I didn't sleep with Katy," said Sebastien. "Please."

"I don't know that that's true."

"Tell her that I said it, anyway. Put it in scare quotes. Do an impres-

sion, if you have to. Adopt a funny voice. Say it's an unconfirmed report. But tell her I said it."

"Okay," said Anna. "I will."

She was out the door, and Sebastien spent a moment walking aim-
lessly around the room. He stared at the ingots of light coming in from
the windows; he stared at the bleached humps of his furniture and
tried to see what Anna would have seen. Then he padded back into the
kitchen and heard the strangely sickening crunch of wheels on gravel.
He opened the door just in time to see Anna get into a car with Eduardo
Campos and drive away.

Eduardo had driven out to Palermo on something like a whim. He'd
been short-tempered all morning at the office, and had no meetings
scheduled for the afternoon. When he walked outside at noon, he
found that the sky above him was pearlescent, like the interior of a
clamshell, and that he did not wish to head straight home. Maria might
call him at the office, of course, and be surprised to find him gone—
but it would not kill her, Eduardo decided, to have to wonder about his
impetuousness for once. It would not destroy her to have to sit for a
moment with the fact that she did not know where he was, and that
there was nothing she could do about it. And in light of Ignacio Toledo's confession, it was time—high time—that Eduardo paid Sebastien
LeCompte another visit.

When he turned up the hill toward the mansion, Eduardo found
himself involuntarily glancing over at the Carrizos' house, then scolded
himself for doing it. It was, after all, just a house. And this case was,
after all, just a case—even if it had consumed the city, then the country,
then decent chunks of the world; even if it had animated innumerable
listless attention spans; even if it had brought teenagers out at night to
honk and yell. Eduardo reached the top of the hill and killed the engine. At the Carrizos', all the lights were out. What was the lurid appeal
of this place, really? Murder was incomprehensible, yes—but when

you got right down to it, so was almost everything people did. Eduardo got out of the car. He endured a brief, ghostly longing for a cigarette, like a twinge from a phantom limb. And then Sebastien LeCompte's door opened and Lily Hayes walked out of the house.

Eduardo felt a surge of adrenaline. He looked again. But no, of course it was not Lily. Of course, it was the sister. He'd seen the girls' resemblance in family photos—their matching quadrilateral faces, bracketing the redheaded mother and the mild-eyed father (who appeared, at least in pictures, to be constitutionally incapable of any sort of combativeness). But the sisters were, apparently, much more alike in real life. They were not exactly identical—this one was more compact and her skin looked better, though Eduardo couldn't tell whether this was due to a bit less living or a lot more attention—but these differences seemed circumstantial, especially now. This girl—who had still not seen Eduardo—was just a Lily who exercised and wore sunscreen. And Eduardo was struck now by the unnerving sense that these girls were not different people at all, but just the same girl in different lives.

"Hello," he called jovially, in English. "You're Anna."

The girl froze. Eduardo would have expected her to jump. "I know who you are," she said, squinting at him. "And I'm not talking to you."

This was just like Lily—to tell him something in the act of declaring that she would tell him nothing at all. "How was your conversation with the young gentleman?" Eduardo nodded his head toward the house. He was grateful for the extra layer of formality that speaking English granted his diction. "I was about to go in there, myself, but I find I need a moment to prepare myself mentally. He is a maddening person to speak with. As perhaps you have already found."

Anna scoffed. "You're not going to make friends with me by doing that," she said. Her voice was exactly like Lily's; Eduardo could have closed his eyes and heard the voice from the tapes. "In fact, you're not going to make friends with me at all. I'm not an idiot."

She probably thought that by putting her refusal up front, she was making it clear that she was savvy and severe, a person Eduardo would really have to contend with. Nonetheless, it was another revealing disclosure. Anna would not talk to him because Anna was not an idiot, and the corollary of this, obviously, was that Lily *was* an idiot: Lily had talked to Eduardo—unwisely, idiotically—and now they were all here dealing with her mess. There was judgment in this, and resentment. And Anna, Eduardo was realizing, might not know that yet.

"Look, I'll be honest with you," said Eduardo, running his hands through his hair. There was no use in playing on Anna's resentment directly. No matter how she felt about Lily, surely her moral self-concept hinged on ignoring these feelings—surely, if she knew she might be letting those feelings reign now, when Lily was at her most vulnerable, she would never, ever forgive herself. "The truth," said Eduardo, "is that I'm not at all sure about this."

Anna cocked her head to one side and stared at Eduardo with an expression that she must have thought looked like disbelief.

"Your sister is a strange girl," Eduardo continued. "As I'm sure you know. She's said and done some pretty erratic, pretty incriminating, things. It's very hard to know what to make of it all." Eduardo looked at the ground and bit his lip. He wanted to seem as though he was struggling to decide whether to say what he really wanted to say. "But I'm not sure," he said again, finally. "And I certainly don't want to waste the state's resources if I'm wrong."

He looked back up at Anna, whose expression of feigned shock was already fading. The only way that she would speak to him would be if she felt she was helping—by being cool-headed and wise enough to explain her sister, who could no longer be trusted to safely explain herself. Even if somewhere deep down Anna knew that speaking to Eduardo must be a very, very dangerous prospect—even if somewhere even deeper down she knew that this was part of why she wanted to do it—she would need to believe, always and utterly, that she'd truly thought she was extending herself on Lily's behalf.

"The charges can always be dropped," said Eduardo. "But only if I can find another way to make sense of all of these things. I haven't been able to, so far. Your perspective might be helpful." Anna dipped her head. "I'd ask your parents," Eduardo added, "but I'm not sure they'd be willing to talk to me."

Anna snorted. She even snorted like her sister. "I doubt they'd be very helpful," she said. "They don't exactly know Lily very well."

Eduardo nodded evenly. "Well, I guess that's pretty common with parents."

Anna—torn, Eduardo suspected, between wanting to withhold the acceptance that would come with agreement and avoid the engagement that would come with dispute—said nothing.

"Look," said Eduardo. "How's this? We go get a cup of coffee. I won't ask you anything about that night." He would not say "Katy." He would not say "death." He would certainly not say "murder." "We'll pretend it never happened. If I bring it up, you can go ahead and leave. But maybe you can tell me a few things about your sister. Maybe you can translate a couple of things for me. Or whatever else you want to tell me. Whatever you think I should know. You talk, I listen. You're in charge. You want to leave, you leave. Does that sound fair?"

It was worth trying, but, of course, Eduardo did not expect it to work. This meant that he had to be careful not to show his surprise when, as he turned back toward his car, Anna Hayes actually followed him.

"I talk, you listen," she said, as she got into the passenger's side.

Eduardo nodded and, to show Anna how literally he was taking the rule, said nothing.

At the café, Anna sat with her arms crossed and pointedly refused to look at her menu. "I hate what you do for a living," she said.

Eduardo laughed. "Me, too, some days."

They had driven to the café in silence. If Eduardo had asked her anything in the car, she could still have demanded that he take her back, which, of course, he would have. But now that they were at a café and had ordered coffee there was a trip wire of courtesy encircling their conversation—even if Anna became angry and wanted to leave, she would understand that Eduardo would need to get the check and pay before he could drive her home (this was, after all, just reality), and this would give him some extra time to work with. He was betting that Anna was afflicted with the same learned courtesy as Lily, and that—as he had with Lily—Eduardo could use it to his advantage. So he was surprised when Anna leaned back and looked him right in the eye and told him, in a mature and well-considered voice, that she thought he was a monster.

"Really," she said again. "A monster." So here, Eduardo saw, Anna's similarities with her sister ended. Lily's commitment to politeness had rarely wavered in their interviews, not really, no matter how angry and exhausted and terrified she was. She had tried to revoke it a few times— tried to walk back to the position she'd held before she'd been so fault- lessly polite, as though he might forget—and occasionally she'd even attempted to insult him. But she was too awkward at this to ever seem truly venomous; she always reminded Eduardo of the infant pit viper he and Maria had come across once—it had been tiny, furious, hissing with such comic valiance that they'd stopped whatever fight they were having and laughed. But Anna, Eduardo was seeing, was different.

"A monster?" he said. "Really? How so?"

The waitress brought their coffees, and Anna waited for her to leave before she answered. "You're a person with no empathy," she said.

Eduardo took a sip of his coffee and leaned back. "For Lily, you mean."

"For anyone."

"Do you think you're a person with empathy?"

"Yes."

It was what anyone—anyone in the world—would say, but Anna's response did not sound reflexive. It sounded like she had actually, at some point, considered the question—which, of course, meant that, at some point, she had actually wondered. "Do you have empathy for Katy?" said Eduardo.

"What would that mean at this point?" said Anna. Her voice was harsh. If this was a painful question, it did not show on her face. "I didn't know her, and now she's dead. I'm sorry for her family, but she never existed for me, so I don't feel anything for her. You don't, either."

"I don't?" Eduardo had expected Anna to say—emphatically, emotionally—that she did have empathy for Katy. He was glad that he never sounded surprised, even when he was.

"No," said Anna. "You're not really interested in Katy. That's not what you're in it for."

"Well," said Eduardo. "I suppose if I was really interested in Katy, instead of the law, then I'd be a much bigger monster than even you think I am." He put his hands faceup on the table and stared at the radial symmetry of his palms. He was always struck by the recurrences of shapes in nature—by the clean economical indifference of recycling the same structure for a feather, and a leaf, and a heart. "If Lily had committed this crime," he said without looking up, "what do you think would be the most empathetic way to treat her?"

"She didn't do it."

"I understand you think that."

"She didn't."

Eduardo looked up. "We're speaking abstractly. I'm just shifting your premise to ask you if it changes your conclusion about my sense of empathy."

"I am not shifting my premise." Anna sounded disgusted. Perhaps she was starting to believe that this was all Lily would have had to do. "My sister is a good person. She is a wonderful person. She didn't do it, and you don't understand a thing about her."

Eduardo nodded quickly. "I think that's true. I think I don't understand her very well at all." He trilled his fingers lightly on the table. "I'm not saying she's, like, beyond comprehension. She's not even that unusual. It's just that you, personally, don't understand her."

"I certainly don't understand why she did what she did."

"She didn't do what she did. I mean, she didn't do it at all."

"Can I ask you a hypothetical question?"

"No."

"What do you think would have made Lily act like she wasn't her-self?"

"You're just going to ask me the question anyway? Doesn't that mean your first question was hypothetical?"

"I think it means it was rhetorical."

"You want me to tell you what imaginary circumstances could have made Lily commit a crime that she did not commit in real life. For our imaginations."

"We can speak more broadly than that."

"You're unreal. Are you actually any good at this job?"

"Maybe not." Eduardo traced his coffee's meniscus with his spoon. "But that's why we're here, isn't it? Because I'm doing my job badly and you are going to help me do it better by telling me where I'm going wrong? So, I'm listening. What would you like me to know?"

Anna was silent. She'd spread her fingers out on the table, stretch-ing them slightly beyond their natural extension, in a gesture Eduardo recognized from Lily. He wondered if this was a shared long-standing habit, or something new that Anna had unconsciously adopted only after seeing her sister in captivity.

"Because I certainly have plenty of questions I could ask you, if you don't feel like you have any," said Eduardo. "Really, it's your decision."

"She didn't do it."

"Yes. You've expressed that opinion." Eduardo put down his spoon and flipped open his notepad, landing on a grocery list written in Ma-ria's loopy script. He squinted, pretending to study it. "Okay. Here's one. Was Lily much of a gymnast?"

"What?"

Eduardo put down the list. "She did a cartwheel when she was first interviewed. Did you know that?" Of course Anna knew this. Every-one knew this. If a random consumer of news anywhere in the world knew two things about Lily Hayes, the first was that she had murdered Katy Kellers, and the second was that she had done a cartwheel the very next day.

Anna glared. "You'd probably want to move around, too, if you'd been cooped up for hours and hours."

"It was a pretty good one, actually," said Eduardo. "Was she a very talented gymnast, growing up?"

"A lot of girls can do cartwheels."

"You look like you're both pretty athletic." They weren't. Anna was the only athlete in the family. Eduardo tapped his spoon against his cup. "But still. You'd think she'd realize that it looked a little odd. A little heartless. Given the circumstances. I mean, she's a very smart girl, right? This is what I'm discerning from her academic history, at any rate—good grades, a 2300 on the SAT." It had been a 2280, and he took a sip of coffee to give Anna a chance to correct him. To her credit, she did not.

"She's just naïve," said Anna. "She just had no idea that anyone was going to hold any of this stuff against her."

"And why was that, do you think?" said Eduardo. "Was she not accustomed to people holding anything she did against her?"

Anna slammed her eyes to the ground. Eduardo took another sip of his coffee, letting the silence between them sit. "I understand Lily's nickname used to be 'Lil the Pill,' " he said at last.

"You've got to be kidding."

"Am I right that, in English, 'pill' is slang for a 'tiresomely disagreeable person'?" It had been her nickname as a child, a fact that the press had decided to willfully misinterpret—suggesting that the word "pill" might connote trouble of a particularly sexual variety, or be a reference to a drug habit of some kind. Eduardo had uncovered no evidence to support either of these conclusions.

"It was from when she was a kid," said Anna. "You cannot possibly be serious."

"Did she earn the nickname by being a tiresomely disagreeable person?"

"What are you talking about? She was a kid. This is ridiculous."

"You find this irrelevant?"

"I don't *find* it irrelevant. It *is* irrelevant."

"Okay," said Eduardo, closing his notepad with a thump. "Maybe you're right. Here's a question that you may find more relevant. I understand your sister had a history of killing animals?"

Anna blanched and looked down at the table, but seemed quickly to realize that she'd need to look Eduardo in the eye in order to answer. She raised her head and locked eyes with him. He could feel how uncomfortable this was for her, and not just because of who he was and what they were discussing. In her gaze was a bone-deep, lifelong discomfort with eye contact in general—Eduardo should know—and yet she did it anyway. "That's not true," she said.

"No?" said Eduardo. "She never killed an animal?"

"No," said Anna. There was a wavering in her face, but not her voice.

"Not one?"

"No." This time she sounded angry. "She hated people hurting animals. She hated aggression of all sorts. She was a vegetarian in high school. She hated that picture of Sebastien and that dead animal. She even talked about it after she dumped him."

After she dumped him. There was a millisecond-long flicker in Anna's eyes as she heard her sentence land. And Eduardo understood, all at once, that Anna had made a mistake, and that she knew it was a mistake, and that she could not tell whether Eduardo had noticed it, or whether it mattered if he had. Lily and Sebastien had broken up the night Katy died. And Lily had spoken with Anna, apparently, that same night. Eduardo took a sip of his coffee, finally letting Anna look away.

"I've seen that picture of his," said Eduardo. "Gruesome." He opened a sugar packet with his thumbnail and took some time shaking it sloppily into his cup. "What did you say to Lily about it?" He would not ask her to report what Lily had said, only to reflect on what she, Anna, had advised. He would not let her know what kind of a mistake it was—he would show her neither its nature nor its size.

"Well," said Anna carefully. "I didn't actually talk to her."

"Ah." Eduardo nodded. It was a voicemail, then. Lily's emails had been scoured, of course, along with the calls she'd made from her cell phone; all of that was chronicled and accounted for, and there was no communication to Anna and the United States on the night Katy Kellers was killed. But it would seem Lily had called Anna from somewhere else—Sebastien's landline, perhaps—and, unbelievably, it would seem she had left a message. Eduardo felt a flutter in his chest, a little scherzo of near laughter. He clenched it back. "So why did she call you, do you think?" he said lazily, stirring his coffee. His best maneuver, now as always, was projecting a sense that his grip on facts was vague.

"She was upset," said Anna.

Eduardo probed his spoon further into the cup, scraping it against the granular sludge of sugar on the bottom. It made sharp little bell-like sounds against the porcelain, which seemed somehow louder than they should have in the empty café. "She seems like she'd be a tough person to console," Eduardo said to his coffee. "Under any circumstances."

"I guess that's why I didn't answer," said Anna. She blinked when the spoon hit the cup.

"Well, that's understandable," said Eduardo, motioning to the waitress for the check. "To tell you the truth," he said, and this time he actually was, "I'm not sure I would have, either."

CHAPTER EIGHTEEN

March

Andrew awoke to Maureen's lunging toward a ringing phone.

"Hello?" she said. She'd been startled into the gulping shock that always accompanied her sudden awakenings, and hadn't yet managed to sand down the rough edges of panic in her voice. This, Andrew knew, had nothing to do with Lily's situation; this was long-standing, possibly endemic. Maureen would sound this way at home, at one p.m., on a Sunday, with a telemarketer.

"Lawyer," she mouthed. She'd become comically disheveled during their nap, another classic characteristic. *I want to know where you went and what you did and whether you took pictures,* Andrew used to say to her in the mornings. It was one of the many small things about her that Andrew had neither particularly treasured nor particularly disliked and so had not, until this moment, particularly remembered.

"I see," said Maureen. Her face, Andrew noticed, was blanking. "Oh, God." Andrew raised his eyebrows. "Okay. Yes. We'll be there. We're on our way." She hung up.

"What?" he said.

She shook her head. "Lily has done something incredibly stupid."

Oh, something else? Andrew wanted to say. His mood was still fossilized from the mirth of the morning; he sat up straighter in order to shake it off. He said, again, "What?"

Maureen ran her fingers through her hair. "She's said some really stupid, incriminating things."

"What things? To whom?"

"To Anna, I guess. On the phone. There was a voicemail."

"What? When?"

"That night. There was a voicemail. We need to get Anna."

"Okay," said Andrew. He stood up, pulled on his pants, and began walking to the closed door of the other bedroom.

"What are you doing?" said Maureen, as he knocked. "She's in your room," she said, as he said, "Isn't she in here?" Maureen's look was floundering, and Andrew could see that Maureen knew Anna was not there but was willing to check anyway, because she would not want to be too confident about what was or was not possible anymore.

"I mean, isn't she in your room?" said Maureen.

And instead of saying no, Andrew said, "We'll go look."

Outside, the sky was high domed, impossibly distant. Andrew had an image of it floating farther and farther away from them—perhaps in forgetfulness, perhaps in disgust, perhaps in total indifference. The sky seemed suddenly like a child's balloon, like something you could lose if you weren't careful or weren't paying attention.

Anna had not been in the room.

In the taxi, Andrew squeezed Maureen's hand lightly, and she squeezed back. Their refusal to console each other was their way of offering consolation; they were so far past reassurances. For this, and maybe for only this, Andrew was grateful.

When they reached Tribunales, Ojeda and Velazquez were already standing outside the office building, waiting. Andrew could see the flare of one of their cigarettes and he wondered pointlessly which one of them smoked. Behind them was another figure—Andrew saw a sheet of russet hair, the severe right angle of a substantial jaw, looking like cast silver in the early afternoon light.

"Oh my God," Maureen breathed, and he knew that she was seeing Lily. The possibility that this person actually was Lily was low—for one thing, Andrew realized, this person had hair—and yet it held them there for a moment, as they rose and got out of the car, seeming to move against some sort of aquatic resistance, like the density that fills the atmosphere when you're running from terror in a dream.

"It's Anna," said Andrew.

"Of course it is," said Maureen. And Andrew knew, with a seam of certainty that opened within him like an old scar, that they were doomed, once again.

Anna began running toward them. "Mom," she said. "Dad." Her running was smooth and intentional and competent, even though she was crying—truly, she was her mother's daughter. Even so, Andrew could feel the doom in the air around him. He could have reached out, he was sure, and fluttered his fingers through it. "I'm sorry," said Anna. "I'm sorry, I'm sorry, I'm sorry."

Sebastien is sleeping, said Lily's voice on the tape. Eduardo could hear in her voice a desperate treble—something he wasn't sure he'd ever heard in their conversations, or even in any of the other recordings.

I just came back, she said. *I just—what's wrong with me?*

Anna's iPhone was, of course, subpoenaed; the relevant message was, of course, retrieved. This only took half an afternoon, since the voicemail, though deleted, had been helpfully stored in the iPhone's deleted messages vault. Eduardo listened to it over and over, of course—first alone, many times, and then with the person who would need to try to explain it.

Jesus. I don't know what I did.

Lily sounded hazy on the tape; altered, no doubt. But this line meant she'd been in possession of her faculties, mental and moral, and that she'd known she'd committed a hideous wrong. She'd known it enough, after all, to call her sister and sob about it. And you could hear in her voice that she really was sorry for whatever it was she had done. Nothing, nothing, could be more damning than that.

Once more, Eduardo restarted the message; once more, Lily's voice filled the room. Once more, she said, *Sebastien is sleeping.*

Eduardo looked across the table at Sebastien LeCompte. His face was ashen. Eduardo glanced down at his notepad and began to form the obvious questions.

Sebastien sat across from Eduardo Campos, waiting to be made to listen again to Lily's voicemail. Its content, as Campos was once more explaining, had raised some new issues.

"Lily says quite clearly that you are sleeping in the other room," said Campos. "As you can hear."

All around Sebastien, everything was white and unreal. He swallowed.

"You told me that you were with Lily all night," said Campos. His hair was glistening with an indecipherable sheen—either sweat or gel, Sebastien couldn't tell. "But the tape tells me that, in fact, she left. You'd lied about that."

This was true, and yet Sebastien felt his brain cleave with a dizzying shock at the accusation. Why? It must be because he'd told the story so many times that he'd begun to remember it the way he told it. This had happened to him sometimes as a child—he'd embellish a story slightly and then eventually lose track of which narrative zigzags were real and which had been added later for flourish. Now—confronted with the evidence of Lily's departure, bludgeoned by the memory of that night—Sebastien felt almost as surprised as he would have if he'd been told something he actually hadn't known.

"I don't think so, no," he said shakily.

"That's all on tape, too, as, of course, you realize. This isn't a question of you convincing me my memory is fuzzy. It isn't, as it happens, but you don't have to take my word for it. You can take your own."

Campos hit a button, and now Sebastien's own awful voice filled the room, telling of how he had spent the entire night with Lily, how she had stayed beside him, how he was sure of it. Sebastien felt a surge of distaste for the person speaking—it was automatic and instantaneous, like a bias he knew better than to indulge but could not help feeling, for a brief panicked second, before his superego roused itself for policing. Who was that person? Did he think he sounded unconcerned? Did he think he sounded *relaxed*? Did he think he sounded like he had any control over the situation—any control, even, over himself? Sebastien was sad for that kid. He was disgusted with that kid. Most of all, he was very sorry that he was now going to have to clean up that kid's mistakes.

"But it was only a moment," said Sebastien. His guilt was unending, stereoscopic. His guilt was like a pain so great that you stop believing it's coming from you at all and start believing that it's coming from the universe; it was no longer within him, it was around him. You knew this, he told himself. Remember? You knew all of this already.

"I mean, I'm not a mathematician," said Sebastien. "I'm not Euclid." Even as he spoke, he could hear the weakness of what he was saying— he could hear the shrillness of his indignation, the overstatement of his scoffing. "But that voicemail is, what? Thirty seconds? Are you saying she was, like, stabbing Katy while she was listening to Anna's outgoing message? Or, like, in between sentences? Or what?"

Eduardo Campos leaned forward. He smelled medicinal, so it must be gel in his hair. Sebastien didn't really need to have it explained to him, but still Eduardo did—more patiently than Sebastien himself would have, if their places had been reversed. "The problem," he said— and he really made it sound like a problem, he made it sound like it was both of their problems, like it was everyone's problem—"is that there's nothing besides you accounting for Lily that night. Your word is all we have."

Sebastien's word, Campos did not seem to think he needed to mention again, was already dubious. And with the voicemail, it had been rendered null in its entirety.

"Okay, yes. As we've both learned, I was wrong." Sebastien bent his head slightly, giving Campos a moment to appreciate this concession. "But that's not really the question. The question you're really after has nothing to do with whether I was right or wrong about that one particular moment. The question is what she did when she was out of the house. What, realistically, she could have done. If she even left the house at all. And so you're going to tell people that she stepped out for a brief midnight murder, as one does, and then slipped back in to call her sister back in college before climbing into bed and *sleeping* the rest of the night next to me? Because I woke up at some point in the early morning and she was asleep next to me. And, okay, I get that you're thinking that I'm not trustworthy and so who cares. But without showering? She didn't use the shower. She came back from a little light impulsive murder spree and didn't even shower? Don't you have a way of checking that?"

"We do." Now Campos's expression was actually gentle. Sebastien could see that he had begun to understand that Sebastien's confusion wasn't genuine—that it was desperate, delusional, that he was constructing the kind of convoluted narrative people invented to make the real seem less real. "And we could have," said Campos, "if you'd been honest with us from the beginning. But, as you undoubtedly realized even as you were speaking, we cannot now go back in time and establish whether Lily Hayes took a shower in your house several weeks ago. Alas."

Sebastien's mouth flooded with a tannic taste. He was beginning to realize how minor the points of dispute here were; he was beginning to see that you did not build up good credit by getting most of the story right. And, frankly, he did not question the correctness of this. It didn't matter whether he was a liar in general, or whether the bulk of what he'd told everybody had been true. At the end of the day, he'd lied for Lily, which meant he was willing to lie for Lily, which was the only relevant fact about him in relation to this case, and possibly the only relevant fact about him in general.

"She broke up with me that night, you know. That could have been what she was talking to Anna about."

"When?"

"When she talks about the mistake."

"It could have been," said Eduardo agreeably. "But we certainly have no reason to think that. Did she seem to feel that breaking up with you had been a terrible mistake?"

Sebastien said nothing.

"Look," said Eduardo, putting his hands on the table in that oddly supplicating gesture of his. "I'm not going to tell you that being honest is your best way to help Lily. I know I've been saying that to you for a while, and whether you believed it or not, it was once actually true. But I'm not going to say it now, because I'm not convinced that it's true anymore. I don't think you can help Lily at this point. All I know for sure is that you can still hurt her. You have hurt her with this lie. You have hurt her as much as Lily has hurt herself. Because now we do not know anything with certainty."

And then Sebastien listened while Campos listed all the things that they could no longer know with certainty. Had Lily and Sebastien actually smoked weed together? (Because she had smoked weed with somebody.) Had they actually watched *Lost in Translation*? It was baffling to Sebastien, this extension of rigorous skepticism toward all the mundane things—was this the kind of movie Sebastien usually watched, and was this the amount of alcohol that Lily usually drank, and why would she have come over and spent so much time with him anyway if she was only planning on ending things afterward? Come to think of it, had Lily really even been there at all that night? As Sebastien listened, he could feel the entirety of the night unravel—he watched it erase, all the mistakes disappearing, beginning with Katy's death and ending with Lily's breaking up with him, or maybe the two things vanishing simultaneously, until none of it had ever happened, none of it had ever happened at all.

Or maybe, Sebastien thought, this was too ambitious. Maybe he needed a more modest request; maybe he needed only to erase Anna. He imagined Anna not coming to see him. In his mind, he unspoke their conversation, unknocked the door, undrove the taxi back to the hotel where Lily and Anna's parents were sleeping, then woke them up.

Eduardo Campos had stopped speaking. Sebastien felt a great cistern of grief inside him. It would swallow him whole one day; one day, he knew, he would drown in it. Sometimes he wished he could walk toward it with stones in his pockets and get the whole thing over with.

"Here," said Campos, handing Sebastien a telephone. "I assume your parents had a lawyer."

"Seriously, what the fuck?" Andrew said to Maureen on the drive back to the hotel. It was evening, and the taxi's headlights briefly spangled the wall of the jail. Anna had had to stay behind to talk to the lawyers. "Maybe we should all just go home."

Maureen did not answer.

Anna's iPhone had been subpoenaed that afternoon; the incriminating voicemail had been produced. Anna had deleted it but apparently not deleted it enough somehow, a fact that Andrew vacillated between attributing to Anna's technological ineptitude and to some subconscious desire of hers to do violence to her sister. He could not bear to think seriously about which was really likelier. On the message, Lily's voice had been strange—though not strange in the same way as on the 911 call, which she would make only twelve hours later. In her call to Anna, Lily's voice was faraway and hoarse, and too relaxed somehow. It was almost unrecognizable to Andrew, and he'd nearly said this—he'd nearly challenged the idea that it was Lily's voice at all—but then he'd stopped himself. He was learning.

In the message, Lily sobbed weakly. She lamented the fate of the dead animal in Sebastien's picture; she warbled about a mistake she had made. It was not a confession, of course—it meant nothing, less than nothing. The mistakes Lily had made in her life were so heartbreakingly minor that Andrew was not sure she would even remember them when she grew up. And yet the time of the call was within the span during which the pathologists posited that Katy had died, and Anna—curiously—had seen fit to withhold the message. It was not certain that the fact of the withholding, per se, would be allowed in court. But it was certain that Anna would now have to testify—about what she'd felt when she first heard the message, and about what she'd later feared it might have meant.

There was something else wrong with the message, though it took Andrew a while to figure it out. He'd heard the story of the night Katy died so many times that it was like an incantation, like a children's song predating language or memory. Hearing the story on the voicemail was disorienting, like walking into a room with the furniture moved; every time he listened to the message, the version he'd heard before momentarily superimposed itself over this new one. Until, after a few listens, he'd caught it.

I went to the river, Lily had said. Most people's voices seemed higher when recorded, but hers had sounded lower. *I went to the river.* In the stories Lily had told of that night, she had not mentioned a river. And *I* went to the river, she'd said. I, not we. What had happened at the river? Nothing had happened at the river. What did it mean that she'd gone to the river? It meant nothing that she'd gone to the river. And yet in the previous tellings of the story, there had never been a river.

Out the taxi window, the moon was a glowing auricle in the sky. The light it cast made Maureen's face look angular and not quite realistic, as though she'd stepped out of a painting from one of those movements that sought to portray people not as they appeared but as they actually were.

Andrew rolled down the window and let the air rush in at him. He thought of his Lily, alone at night, leaving Sebastien LeCompte's house and going outside—for her own reasons, innocent and unknowable, both. It was terrifying to think of Lily doing anything alone at night. It was more terrifying—much more—to think of her never doing anything alone ever again.

Andrew thought of the phantom river with his phantom daughter beside it. It would have looked icy, probably, in the moonlight. Lily had merely done what Andrew had dreamed of doing so many times when Janie was sick, so many times since then: Without telling anyone, without asking anyone, she had opened a door and walked away.

"Andrew," said Maureen. He could feel her looking at him in the darkness, and he turned his face to meet her gaze.

"Yes." Out of the vast thicket of preexisting worries and sorrows that Andrew knew intimately, a new unnameable fear was seizing him. It released him and then seized him again, a clonic coursing, gripping and then relenting.

"You watched that security footage of her at the store?" said Maureen. "With Sebastien?"

"A few times, yeah."

"Me, too." The taxi rounded the corner to their hotel. Maureen turned back to the window. And she was still looking away from Andrew when she said, "Did you ever know that she smoked?"

CHAPTER NINETEEN

July

Sebastien went to court every day for three weeks before Lily finally took the stand.

It was obvious as she testified that she'd been told to speak clearly and slowly; it was obvious that she'd been told to make eye contact. It was a mercy that nobody had told her to smile—that this was a performance that did not require cheer—because the smile she gave in pictures, Sebastien thought, really could make someone wonder about her. Her Spanish was much better now. Her hair was growing in, but its shortness made her face more severe, more frank, than it usually was. She wore an array of mock turtlenecks, often in pale pink—which struck Sebastien as so bizarre, so clearly not a choice she'd made; they reminded him of a picture he'd once seen of a skinny African child wearing a donated vanity T-shirt designed for some family's 1993 reunion barbecue. The incongruousness of Lily's shirt had to have been part of the strategy, Sebastien figured. It must have been chosen not only for its modesty, its subdued femininity, but also for the way it showed the world that Lily was a captive now—that she was a prisoner, that she would take whatever shirt you gave her and wear it gratefully, that she was sorry, that she had not killed Katy Kellers but she was still sorry for everything else, she was sorry for the way she was and what she had and who she'd been, and that she had learned her lesson, and that the world could afford to forgive her.

Sitting in the courtroom, Sebastien listened to Lily explain the cartwheel—slowly and carefully, while making forced eye contact with a different arbitrary stranger every few seconds. She had done the cartwheel, she said, not to mock or disdain Katy's death, and not to try to seem defiant or brave. She had done it, she said, simply because she'd felt helpless. She'd wanted to show herself that she could still do this one small thing. Maybe she couldn't do anything else, but she could still do this.

And then, sitting in the courtroom, Sebastien listened—again—to the voicemail. The sound of Lily's recorded crying filled the room. Sebastien still wanted to believe that that voice was crying over him. But he knew better now than to let himself believe something he so badly wanted to.

In the end, it was a relatively quick trial.

By the time Eduardo and Adelmo Benitez, the instructor judge, brought the case before the court, the story was neat and compelling. The DNA evidence had Lily handling the murder weapon; the delivery truck driver had her present and bloodied at the scene of the crime; her ruined alibi left Ignacio Toledo's confession essentially unchallenged and unchallengeable. All that was left to do was stand back and watch motives orbit Lily like planets around a star.

First, Katy weighed in from the beyond, with her cryptic message about the new romance in her life, the one she was afraid would upset Lily terribly. Next was Beatriz Carrizo, shaking more from holy anger than from nervousness, describing how Lily had spied and snooped and snuck out and been fired from her job, how not one week had gone by—literally not one week—when she hadn't been in some kind of trouble or another. But really, the bulk of the work was done by Lily herself—bit by bit and word by word, in the emails, the voicemail, the fight, the lies—making Eduardo's case more convincingly than even he could have done, long before she ever took the stand.

Next came Lily herself, speaking first for the defense. By now her Spanish was excellent, newly and finally fluid. She'd learned idioms and slang. She had, you could be sure, learned swears. Her Spanish now was the kind of thing you could dream in and rely on, and Eduardo was sure that she was sure that if she could have had the chance to do everything over—if she could have dubbed the last few months into *this* Spanish—that none of it would have happened. But, of course, it would have, and anyone could have seen it; her perverse callousness toward Katy required no articulation, and thus no translation. If anything, Lily came across worse in this improved Spanish than she had before. The newly jovial emphasis in her speech—her unself-conscious willingness to really commit to the accent—clashed strangely with her dispassionate account of Katy Kellers's life and death. When her Spanish had been broken, limited, there was a sense that perhaps the nuance of her experience and perception was being lost; that perhaps a fuller, more sympathetic picture existed just on the other side of fluency. But now when Lily spoke you could be sure she knew what she was saying; and so when she issued some gigglingly inappropriate non sequitur about the quality of Katy Kellers's orthodontia, one of the judges frowned and removed his bifocals and made a note of it, sure that whatever he was hearing was exactly what was meant.

Accordingly, in his examination of Lily, Eduardo could afford to be low-key. He spoke to her quietly, gently, and delivered only one serious jab. He needed only one.

"You say that you performed CPR on the victim when you found her body?"

"That's right."

"Lily, could you tell the panelists here the steps of CPR?"

She could not.

The impact statement came next. This was delivered by Mr. Kellers, eloquently and poignantly, the remaining members of his beautiful family making a tragic tableau behind the prosecution desk.

Then there was Anna: poised and self-contained; speaking crisply, with the terse composure of a law enforcement official, about all of Lily's many fine qualities; and giving very good answers to all of Eduardo's questions but one.

"I just didn't think Lily would have wanted anyone to hear that message," she said.

Eduardo tilted his head and furrowed his brows. "But why would you have worried about anyone else ever hearing it?"

Next came Sebastien LeCompte. He spoke tenderly of Lily when questioned by Ojeda, but even the mitigating assertions that he made about her—even the ones that Eduardo knew for a fact were true— wound up sounding somehow sneering and false. Perhaps this was due to stage fright. Perhaps it was due to the difficulty of entering an arena with one's credibility already compromised, and the automatic inau- thenticity that came with overcompensation (Eduardo remembered this from his own early attempts to network at law school, when he'd been so unpracticed and reluctant that he wound up coming across as even more transparently craven than his colleagues). Or perhaps, Eduardo thought, Sebastien LeCompte had actually forgotten how to mean anything. Perhaps he had never known.

In any case, there was no denying that Sebastien LeCompte had, like Lily, contributed to the obstruction of justice. Eduardo could have highlighted this fact in his questioning—he could have leaned on it, made Sebastien feel its threat, made the panelist judges see its import. But in the end Eduardo decided on a different approach, for its efficacy as much as for its humanity. At heart, after all, Eduardo did not believe Sebastien LeCompte was really dangerous to anybody, or that the mis- takes he'd made were likely to be repeated outside of his own life. So the kid had lied to protect his girlfriend: This only showed that he had enough sense to see that she was guilty and enough loyalty to love her anyway. And, at any rate, it was abundantly clear that Sebastien LeCompte already had a prison.

And so instead of pursuing Sebastien's deceitfulness, Eduardo chased his ignorance. What had Lily's birthday party been like? he asked. Sebastien had not been there. Why had Sebastien not been there? Because he had not been invited. And how did Lily feel after having been fired? Sebastien did not know. And why didn't Sebastien know? Because Lily had never discussed it with him.

It was in these faltering moments of admitting his own agnosticism—and in these moments alone—that Sebastien LeCompte finally sounded like he was telling the truth.

Last came Ignacio Toledo. It was hard for Eduardo to confidently guess how he was coming across to the judges; in certain moments he struck Eduardo as evidently self-serving, and Eduardo was not at all convinced that the panelist judges were convinced that he was telling the whole story. But they were even less convinced that Lily was, after all that they had heard. And—since Ignacio Toledo's testimony involved a lot more self-recrimination than Lily's did—perhaps it seemed to them intuitive to split the difference. Ignacio Toledo was sentenced to fifty years in prison. Lily Hayes was sentenced to twenty-five.

Afterward, the camera crews mobbed Lily Hayes's family on the courthouse steps.

"Were you surprised at the outcome?" they asked.

And Andrew Hayes looked wearily at the camera and said that at this point in his life he was fairly sure that nothing could ever surprise him again.

Lily wrote to Sebastien only once during the trial. It was an odd letter, formal and paranoid and strangely anonymous, as though she'd written it without knowing who, if anyone, would ever read it. It was mostly about her parents: about how their visits were still at the center of her life, the thing that pinned her entire mind to the wall, but how every time they came she became obsessed with their leaving, consumed by thoughts of the minutes that had already passed, terrified of not feeling what she wanted to feel and not saying what she wanted to say during the time she had left with them. She wrote that she had to funnel her whole life, her whole secret heart, into these few moments, and that then they'd come and go and she'd spend the whole week worrying that she hadn't gotten the visit right and vowing to do better the next time. But she didn't, she said. She always found herself growing somehow abstracted, her attention half-deflected toward their departure. She wanted the visits to be something solid, she wrote, something she could fully get her arms around. But instead they were like everything else: They were diffuse, spurious things, like atoms, like seconds, like all the stuff you had to depend on but could never really trust.

The night of the sentencing, Eduardo took Maria out to dinner. At the restaurant, they were overly polite, like strangers who'd each been told that the other was freakishly given to offense. Eduardo knew he was being superstitious in not inviting anyone else out with them—he knew that he was trying to avoid an outburst of the sort that had happened after his promotion all those years ago. And though he was disappointed in his own childishness, he was far more disappointed that it did not seem to be working. Lately, their relationship had seemed to Eduardo like a coin spinning ever slower, far past the point at which you think it must surely, surely land.

That night, next to him in bed, Maria whispered a question into his ear when he was nearly asleep.

"Would you still love me if I killed someone?" she said.

The question crawled into Eduardo's ear and hooked him out of his sleep, and it echoed within him for a moment, like something from a dream, before he realized it was real. "Did you say something?" he said.

"Well, would you?" Maria was on her side, head propped up on elbow, ear cupped in her hand. Eduardo had the impression that she had been staring at him for a while.

"What are you talking about?" He sat up. "That's ridiculous. You'd never kill someone."

"But would you love me if I did?"

"But you wouldn't." He turned on the bedside lamp. Maria looked up at him, her face owlish and expectant. She did not sit up. "You wouldn't be yourself if you did."

"You get so philosophical sometimes."

"No, really. You wouldn't. There would be no 'you' to love."

"But what if you don't know that? What if I already have killed someone? Would I still be me? And if I'm not me, who am I?"

"You haven't killed anyone."

"You're right. But what if someday I will?"

"Don't be morbid. You won't. Do you need me to promise you you won't so we can go to sleep?"

She smiled. "You don't know I won't. You don't know me that well, really, after all." Her face was strangely serene, and she seemed to be speaking almost to herself. She flipped onto her back and scrunched down into the sheets. "Somebody probably still loves that girl. Even if she did do it."

"I'm sure somebody thinks they do," Eduardo said testily. "And she did do it."

"Somebody thought they knew her, too."

"That I don't doubt." Suddenly, Eduardo had the sensation that he had been in this moment for as long as he could remember—not this exact conversation, perhaps, but in some version thereof, some dialogue in which Maria wanted something from him that he could not, and would never be able to, discern. She knew—she must know—that he would have given her anything she needed. Not telling him what she needed was her way of forcing him to fail her, which she knew—she must know—was the most hurtful thing she could do to him. Eduardo could see this kind of moment stretch out forever around him. It was ahead of him and behind him. It was beyond him and within him. It was, perhaps, the dark matter of the universe, and all the astronomers could stop looking.

"You don't really love me," said Maria, blinking slowly. She said it as though it was a realization she had just made but did not really mind very much.

"My God." Eduardo shoved off the covers. He was blind with anger, shaken by the violence of its eruption. He had not even known how angry he could be about anything until now. "My every move, my every *thought,* is for you. This whole fucking case is for you. My whole life is for you. What more do you want from me?"

"It's not about what I want. It's not even about what you feel. It's about who I am. And you don't know that."

Eduardo threw the bedclothes on the floor, and then he hit the wall open-handed, with some force. Maria looked at the sheets in mild surprise. She never really had to register his physical strength, because Eduardo let her forget it; every time he touched her—every single time—it was with gentleness, restraint. But he was much, much stronger than she was, and he realized that in this moment he was reminding her of that—not because he was threatening her, but because he was demanding she take his proper measure.

Maria, however, did not seem troubled by this outburst. She just looked at the sheets, and then at him, with an expression of patient interest, as though she was an incredibly intelligent lamb. "I hate this about you, you know," she said.

Eduardo didn't know whether she meant his job, or his temper, or something else altogether, but he realized—finally, with great certainty and relief—that it did not matter. "Yes," he said. "I know." He got out of bed and stood. On the carpeting in front of him was a pale demilune, cast by the streetlight outside the window. "Why did you come back?" he said. "Really."

Maria rolled onto her back and put her hands over her eyes. "Because I had a dream."

"You had a dream."

"Yes."

"Really?"

"I dreamed you turned into a flower and I forgot to water you and you died."

Eduardo snorted. He was appalled.

"If you want the truth," Maria said from underneath the covers. "I think that poor girl is probably innocent."

Eduardo turned to the window. Outside, the sky was growing lighter and somehow pellucid, suggesting rain in its mood if not quite in its color. Soon it would be morning again. It was always almost morning again.

"What," he said. "Did you have a dream about that, too?"

At night, Sebastien kept up the anonymous donations. He gave money to Lily's parents' travel fund, and then he kept on giving. He gave money to Amnesty International, for Lily. He gave money to victims' advocacy groups, for Katy. He gave money to the Space Foundation for the stars (if ever there was a project that could swallow up any fortune, any lifetime). The Space Foundation sent him maps of constellations. He put them on the walls; he put them over the photo of his tapir. It wasn't actually his tapir: His father had shot it for him because he couldn't do it and had let him stand in the picture anyway. Now Sebastien's cowardly, adolescent feet poked out from underneath the purplish, smoky corona of a rotating galaxy. He put a map over the tapestry, partially obscuring it. Now the dogs chased streaky comets, the alluvial silt of the farthest stars. He put maps on the ceiling, making celestial clerestories. He realized he had never, in his entire life, slept outside.

He Googled "suicide" again and again, allowing himself each time to be moved anew by the automatic, impersonal concern of the Internet. It was so perfect in its abstraction, Sebastien thought. It was something like the Kantian categorical imperative, or the awesome callousness of nature, or the sort of nostalgic, flamboyant kindnesses that the United States very occasionally extended to its enemies: rebuilding postwar Germany, giving Osama bin Laden an Islamic ceremony before tossing his body into the sea.

In a way, Eduardo was surprised to find, losing Maria again turned out to feel almost natural. Eduardo had known that after the case was over he would have a feeling of having reached the peak of his life, of looking over its edge, of knowing that soon night would fall, and that even sooner it would be time to turn around. Now that Maria was gone again, he found himself heading back down already—and it seemed a less frightening journey, somehow, though he did have to marvel at its swiftness.

Her departure had been a catastrophe Eduardo had been drilling for most of his adult life. Her return had been, in the end, merely a kind of caesura between miseries. Or maybe not even that.

And yet it was true that Eduardo had been sure about her once—surer than he had ever been about anything else, before or since.

Over the months, Eduardo thought often of Lily Hayes's time in prison—of how difficult it must be to be there after a life as short and easy as hers. She'd have to recall memories that she'd barely been present for at the time; she'd have to turn them over and over again in her mind, looking for new details and complexities. It would be like scrambling for the crumbs of meals you'd consumed without knowing you'd need to ration them. It would be like craning your neck to try to see something beyond a picture's frame.

A year after the conviction, Eduardo read in the paper that Sebastien LeCompte was having an estate sale, and he hired a man to go to it and buy the Steinway. All told, the purchase was approximately what he'd made on Lily Hayes's conviction. He saw how this could be viewed as a kind of revenge, but really he meant it as a kind of penance—though not penance for the chance that he'd been wrong about Lily. Eduardo felt humility before that possibility, as before all other possibilities. He had done his best. He had made a good faith attempt at agency in this lifetime. This, and only this, was all that any of us could really do or know that we had done. Conceding the fallibility of your knowledge was only the first step: Given that, you had to proceed, you had to discern, you had to assess and evaluate and distinguish right from wrong, you had to sort out truth from falsehood (people might say they weren't doing this, but, of course, they were doing this; they were acting on many layers of unexamined belief with every breath they took, with every moment they lived). And then, whatever you decided you believed, you had to act as though you really believed it. If you did not do this, you weren't just a coward. If you did not do this, you were forfeiting something far bigger than bravery.

After Lily's sentencing, Sebastien was finally allowed to visit her in prison. He arrived to find her sitting at a table, smoking. Her hair was longer and seemed a different color—not just dirtier, but actually darker, somehow.

"They say that stuff will kill you," he said feebly.

"God," she said. "I hope something else gets to it first."

"Is your hair a different color?"

She shrugged. "I don't know. Maybe."

"They say Marie Antoinette's hair went white the night before she was executed."

Lily had once told Sebastien that he didn't know what he meant when he talked, but this was not an accurate diagnosis. Usually he just didn't care—he only wanted to sound clever, and there was a crystalline simplicity and directness in this, really, when you thought about it. But now he felt like he did care, he cared very much—he just didn't know what he was trying to say. Whatever that was was off in some other galaxy, the kind that was so far away that by the time you got there you'd be dead.

Lily shook her head. "That's not how it works. It's just that all her brown hair fell out." She took a puff of her cigarette. There was an intense agitation in her movements now that Sebastien hadn't noticed at the trial. "I can't believe they let you in here."

"Well, at this point it's the least they could do."

She gave him an unbelieving look. "I mean, I just can't believe they think I'm so dumb that I would say anything to you."

"What?"

"They're recording this, you realize?" she said. "They're trying to entrap me. They think you might help them do that."

Sebastien was not sure what his face was doing. Lily must understand that he'd lied for her, and been caught in that lie; she must understand that he had had no choice. But perhaps she loathed him for the lying anyway. Perhaps she thought he'd lied because he'd believed it was possible she had done it, or because he'd believed that other people would believe that it was possible. Perhaps she saw both of these things as betrayals. Or perhaps—and as soon as Sebastien thought of this possibility he felt its truth, like a truncheon to the soul—she really had no opinion on any of this.

"Well not, you know, intentionally," said Lily. There was a fluttery breathiness in her voice. "I don't mean that. I just mean they think I'll lose my head and forget where I am and suddenly remember I did things I didn't do."

She was afraid to even name those things, Sebastien saw. She didn't want to even give them a phrase, a recording of her voice stringing certain words together in a certain order, regardless of the context—such was the level of her distrust. Was this savviness (finally, belatedly)? Or just paranoia? Sebastien couldn't tell. But either way, who could blame her? He remembered his paranoia the day he'd flown back to Buenos Aires after his parents' death. His fear that day had not been limited to the plane ride; instead, his fear had extended nonsensically, ludicrously, both forward and backward in time, like some strange ivy that would climb toward either darkness or light. The fear had crept back into his trip's beginnings: It was waiting for him behind a newspaper in South Station, where the clean sheets of light falling through the window always felt somehow Atlantic, oceanic, and the ashen seagulls outside made smudges against the concrete and the sky. And the fear had crept forward to the rest of the day: If the fear did not crash his plane, then it would follow him through security—after he disembarked and hailed a taxi and rode through his streets, his former streets—and into his childhood home, and into the rest of his life. The fear could be patient, after all. The fear had all the time in the world.

"Are you losing it, Lily?" said Sebastien.

There was a flash of reactionary, automatic hostility on her face that faded into pensiveness. "How would I know?" she said.

"You don't have to worry about it," said Sebastien. "For obvious reasons, I'm not one to judge." He put his hand on the table, making it available for her to hold. Lily stared at it emptily, with an expression of incurious incomprehension, and made no move to take it. And suddenly Sebastien could see how Lily's sentence would go: how her previous life would turn to red, fetal memories; how her personality would liquidate. Twenty-five years. Twenty-five years. She would become obsessed with her cigarettes, with her minor grievances and feuds. Maureen and Andrew would keep coming, though less and less, and then they would die, one after another. Anna would keep coming, twice a year, at least; she would work for two years as an i-banker (there was no way that girl wasn't heading for an MBA, classics major or no) until she married another i-banker and they would produce two long-limbed children back-to-back. She would never give up distance running, and she would never give up sending Lily the necessaries—even as the necessaries changed, year to year, and even as there were less and less of them.

It would not matter. None of it would matter. Lily's spirit would not be able to stop its own decay any more than her body would one day.

"I'm sorry, you know," Sebastien said with feeling. "I'm so, so sorry."

Lily looked at him neutrally. "For what?"

. . .

It was two years before the appeal went to court. When the decision came, the murder conviction was overturned; the obstruction of justice conviction—resulting from Lily's lie about the marijuana—stood, with the sentence reduced to time served. On television, Andrew Hayes said, "Two years is a lifetime at her age. It's a lifetime." He looked drawn and aged. "She's already missed being an entire person she would have been. That person is dead, just like Katy Kellers."

He got shit for the comparison, of course. Yet Eduardo thought that it probably was true—though he did not know for sure, since he had not argued the case. In fact, he had taken an extended sabbatical from the law. He went to Ravenna, Italy, to see the early Christian mosaics there, in indigo and jade. He admired the vivid simplicity of their colors, their ethics. Afterward, he walked outside and the moon above him was like a single opal in the sky.

It was possible, of course, that Lily Hayes had been innocent. Of course it was possible; anything was possible. Embracing the chance of being right was incurring the risk of being wrong. Eduardo had accepted the same stakes as the soldier, the revolutionary, the reformer. He had known that any attempt at heroism may, in retrospect, be revealed to be villainous.

He had gambled on virtue. He was at peace. He went to the karstic caves of Slovenia. He stood in ancient churches and listened for what he might hear.

Sebastien began going outside.

First, he went down to the river to think about the stars. He tilted his head back to look at the sky. He tried to see it the way Lily might see it, or the way she might have seen it once.

We all had life sentences: You spent yours inside or out, but you had to spend it somewhere.

Above him, Sebastien could almost see the slit eyes of lenticular galaxies. That sense of being observed—it was why people invented their gods. It was why he'd invented the Carrizos. And maybe this was all he'd be allowed to keep from Lily: a sense of her gaze, a slightly softer, more sympathetic one, following him through the years, her lids lowering and lowering until, finally, they closed.

He would write her a letter one day, a long time from now, when everybody else had forgotten. *I still know you didn't do it,* it would say. *I know that. I know that. I know.*

And Lily would write back and say, *I'm glad you know it. But you should also know this: I did not do it, but I might have. I did not do it, but I could have. I did not do it, but perhaps, in another lifetime, I did.*

AUTHOR'S NOTE

In some of its themes, *Cartwheel* draws inspiration from the case of Amanda Knox, the American foreign exchange student accused, convicted, and acquitted of murdering her roommate in Italy. I was fascinated by the idea of writing about a fictional character who serves as a blank slate onto which an array of interpretations—often inflected by issues of class and privilege, gender and religion, American entitlement and anti-American resentment—tend to be projected. The fictional Lily Hayes shares these broad and nebulous qualities with Amanda Knox; their similarities lie in the contradictory but confident judgments they animate in others.

The eponymous cartwheel serves as a good example of the novel's intention, as well as its relationship to reality. In the book, some view Lily Hayes's interrogation room gymnastics as callous, others as benign, others as suspicious. These divided perceptions were initially inspired by the response to the cartwheel Amanda Knox was widely reported to have done during her interrogation—a cartwheel that, we now know, never actually occurred. This episode, I think, illustrates some of the central questions I wanted to explore in this novel—questions about how we decide what to believe, and what to keep believing—while also demonstrating part of why I needed a totally fictional realm to do this.

In contemplating the possibility that this book could be mistaken as a narrative about—and judgment on—real-life people and events, I've come to appreciate how entirely my view of writing and reading fiction is based on a single moral premise: that the act of imagining the experiences of fictional people develops our sense of empathy, as well as our sense of humility, in regarding the experiences of real ones. To me, the fictional barrier around the characters in this book isn't just a necessary prerequisite for trying (or even wanting) to write a novel about the fallibility of perception—it's also fundamental to my notion of fiction's ethical possibilities in the world. And so it is as a person, even more than as an author, that I ask readers to have no doubt as to whose story this is. In the real universe is a girl who never did a cartwheel. This novel is the story of a girl who did.

ACKNOWLEDGMENTS

Thanks to the Iowa Writers' Workshop and Stanford University's Stegner Fellowship program—for the time, the life-changing sense of possibility, and most of all, the people, I will be forever grateful. For their feedback on this book, I am particularly indebted to my incredible teachers at Stanford, Adam Johnson, Elizabeth Tallent, and Tobias Wolff, as well as my tireless comrades-in-workshop: Josh Foster, Jon Hickey, Dana Kletter, Ryan McIlvain, Nina Schloesser, Maggie Shipstead, Justin Torres, Kirstin Valdez Quade, and some other guy I can't remember. Many thanks also to Kate Sachs for the eventful early recon trip, as well as Adam Krause, Keija Kaarina Parssinen, and all of the terrifyingly smart members of the No-Name Writing Group for their incisive comments.

Thanks to my wonderful agent, Henry Dunow, who is as indefatigable as he is patient. Thanks also to everyone at Random House: Susan Kamil, Laura Goldin, Erika Greber, and Caitlin McKenna; confirmed publicity sorceress Maria Braeckel; and especially my editor, David Ebershoff, for his remarkable insight and dedication.

Most of all, thanks to Carolyn du Bois, for teaching me to see that truth is often complicated, and to Justin Perry, for making me believe that, once in a while, it is not.

CARTWHEEL

Jennifer duBois

A READER'S GUIDE

QUESTIONS AND TOPICS FOR DISCUSSION

1. The first paragraph of *Cartwheel* ends with a chilling statement: "The things that go wrong are rarely the things you've thought to worry about." Why do you think the author makes such a pronouncement at the beginning of the novel? What does she mean? Is this true in your life?

2. The story in *Cartwheel* is very much of our time. Lily's case becomes an international sensation because of Facebook, blogs, and the way shocking news and information can travel around the world within minutes. Social media plays a big role in *Cartwheel*. Does this change your view of social media? How do you use social media to share details of your life? What about your family members?

3. Why do you think Jennifer duBois chose to tell the story from four points of view? How does that affect the experience of reading it?

4. At one point, Lily's sister Anna says "everyone wants to love Lily," and that she's always played by different rules. Why does Anna think this?

5. Lily's father, Andrew, believes "everything vile about your children was to some degree vile about yourself." Is this a fair statement? Do Lily's parents fail her, or is this parental guilt?

6. What impact does her sister's ordeal have on Anna?

7. The title of the book comes from the cartwheel Lily turned between interrogation sessions. Why did the author choose this image as significant?

8. In what ways are Lily and Katy different? Why does Lily feel Katy's life was "easy"? Is she being fair?

9. Have you, or someone you know, studied abroad? Do you think it benefits college students to visit other countries? Why do you think Lily wanted to study abroad? What was she looking for?

10. Eduardo, attorney for the prosecution, believes Lily is guilty but that she doesn't understand why what she did was wrong. Do you agree?

11. Sebastien is an enigmatic character. What do you think Lily is attracted to about him? Where do you think his addiction for obscuring half-irony comes from? What consequences does it have for the unfolding of events?

12. The author uses ambiguity to tell this story. How does that affect your understanding of what happened? Which character do you trust the most?

13. Lily calls her family "repressed," saying they never learned how to mourn their first child, the sister who died before Lily and Anna were born. Why does she say she and Anna were treated like "replacement children"?

14. Do you believe the whole story comes out at Lily's trial?

TRAVELERS ABROAD—FIVE FAVORITE FICTIONAL JOURNEYS

by JENNIFER DUBOIS

PRAGUE, Arthur Phillips

Arthur Phillips's smart, sharply funny first novel follows a group of expats in post-Communist Budapest. Collectively, they are plagued by the creeping suspicion that real life is elsewhere—in the past, perhaps, or just possibly in Prague.

THE QUIET AMERICAN, Graham Greene

A prophetic critique of the folly of mapping simple theories onto complex realities, *The Quiet American* is also a broad reflection on the dangers of innocence itself; innocence, Greene writes, is "like a dumb leper who has lost his bell, wandering the world, meaning no harm."

DEATH IN VENICE, Thomas Mann

Thomas Mann's classic novella follows a German academic's consuming obsession with a young boy he spots while traveling in Venice. As his quest to attract the boy grows increasingly grotesque—and the threat of a looming cholera outbreak grows increasingly real—the story's surreal dreaminess becomes a nightmare's.

THE RELUCTANT FUNDAMENTALIST, Mohsin Hamid

This nuanced meditation on nationality, allegiance, and home is structured as a conversation between two travelers: a Pakistani speaker called Changez, and the unnamed (and possibly armed) American who listens to his story.

PALE FIRE, Vladimir Nabokov

Pale Fire is full of exiles: there is American writer John Shade, exiled from his own epic poem by the long-winded footnotes of academic Charles Kinbote, himself an exile from the mysterious land of Zembla, whose commentary increasingly concerns the story of Zembla's own exiled king. A prismatic exploration of narrative itself, *Pale Fire* is a book that somehow becomes a universe—making dazzled voyagers of us all.

Read on for an excerpt from

A PARTIAL HISTORY OF LOST CAUSES

by Jennifer duBois
Published by The Dial Press

CHAPTER ONE

ALEKSANDR

Leningrad, Russia, 1979

When Aleksandr finally arrived in Leningrad, he was stunned by the great gray span of the Neva. The river was a churning organ in the city's center—not its heart, surely, something more practical and less sentimental but just as necessary. The amygdala, maybe, or both kidneys. It had been six days from Okha—on a boat and then a train—and out the window he'd seen the entire country: first the teetering spires of Sakhalin's drilling rigs, as familiar to Aleksandr as his own dreams; then the abandoned green train at the port, melting into the sand ever since the war with the Japanese; then the ten thousand salmon rotting in the sun on the eastern shore, waiting for Moscow to telegram permission for their loading; then the curling stems of smoke above the villages that were impossibly far apart (he never knew he'd

been living in a country this enormous all along). He saw deconse-
crated cathedrals, miners with faces black and hard as their coal, great
shoals of stunted grass and bleached sky. By the time he arrived at
Moskovsky Vokzal, he thought he'd just about seen enough. He knew
he should be grateful. The trip to Leningrad had required months of
bureaucratic maneuvering, papers acquired and signed and lost, attempts and reattempts and bribes from Andronov, the man who would
be Aleksandr's trainer at the academy. Finally, one day, Aleksandr's
entry visa had arrived—with all the randomness of a June snowstorm
or a plague of falling frogs—and that was the bottom line, he often
thought: not that you could be sure that nothing would work, but that
you could be sure you would never, never know what would.

And on the tracks—amid the screeches of braking trains and de-
parting lovers, and the coiling smells of grease and cigarettes and
cooking oil and acrid cologne—he almost lost his nerve. He almost
wanted to drop his luggage on the track and ride the train all the way
back to the Pacific, although his only chess set was in his rucksack and
he was nearly out of bribe money. As the train had pulled into the station, the man next to him announced to the entire car that today was
Stalin's centenary. Everybody around looked quickly away. But here
was the evidence: Sinopskaya Naberezhnaya was overrun with police,
their uniforms striking red and gold against the horrible white sun.
They were there to make sure nobody got too mouthy or too festive.

"Papers?" A policeman was behind him; his tone suggested that
Aleksandr had already ruined his day. Aleksandr drew his hand against
his eyes, and delicate grains of soot fell from his eyebrows. Just over
one of the policeman's gargantuan shoulders, Aleksandr caught
snatches of the green-gray Neva. Its stark and sturdy arm put the city
in a headlock, he thought, or held it up like an osteoporotic backbone.

"Papers?" the policeman said again. His chinstrap was digging into
his prodigious neck, and his gilt cockade flashed in the sun. Aleksandr
rifled in his rucksack. When he produced his papers, the policeman
appraised them with a sour look and tapped his nightstick against his
thigh.

"Sakhalin?" he said. "Did you take the wrong train?"

And Aleksandr thought: It's a real possibility.

"No? Do you talk? Never mind. I don't care. Go on. I'm sure you know what day it is."

Aleksandr did know. And he was starting to decide about the Neva, too: really, it was the brain. Not the part of the brain that thinks up sonnets or show-offy chess moves; not the part that sighs sorrowfully in corners and reads Solzhenitsyn and wonders what it all can mean. It was the part that tells you to fuck, to run from things, to live, even when your better nature tells you not to.

Years later, after Aleksandr stopped playing chess and started playing politics, the city would become something altogether different. Bored women with absent eyebrows in Turkish silk bobbed in the lines outside nightclubs, pouring vodka of insane expense into the snow and laughing. Enormous billboards and neon signs made stamps of light against the sky, advertising dreams and attitudes and lifestyles of varying degrees of attainability. Leningrad became St. Petersburg, and St. Petersburg became a place to make and blow loads of cash—there were businesses and ladies enough for industrious men to conquer. Eventually, chess became something different also—once Aleksandr became the world champion and his brilliance was remarked upon so often that it became tedious. This was how somebody with some kind of unusual beauty—enchanting mismatched eyes, impossibly red hair— must feel: after a while, receiving extra credit for something so arbitrary becomes a burden. Chess was a part of him, no different from his poor posture or homely face. And chess became a humiliation and an indictment in the end—after he'd lost the title and his better moments were forgotten but his one best moment, that one best game, still hung over him, preceded him always, like a leper's bell. He was very good for a while, and then something else was better.

But when he was young, he'd had a whole life to imagine.

Stumbling out into the day from the train station felt like emerging from imprisonment only to be lined up against the wall and shot. Aleksandr made his way to his kommunalka first, picking through throngs of stern-looking people, and several small children tried to steal from him before he even made it out onto the street. He followed his careful directions to himself and kept a dumb, hyper-focused attention on his papers. The number of people here was staggering, and more people than lived in the entirety of Okha stepped on Aleksandr's feet before he made it to his new building.

The building was three stories tall and looked, from a distance, like a pile of cinders. In the packed brown snow of the front yard, a very young man stood next to an overturned trunk. The trunk's lid was unhinged like a half-open jaw, and its contents were splattered across the yard; clearly, it had recently been thrown down the blocky staircase. On the stoop stood a gray-curled old lady in a red housecoat. From the way she was shaking her fist at the young man, Aleksandr figured she was the steward. Up close, he could see that the front door—formerly red, he thought—was splintering. The windows above it were welded shut.

"Excuse me," said Aleksandr. "I'm moving in today."

The steward ignored him. "Go away," she said to the young man with the trunk. "Go away and never come back."

And Aleksandr thought: Maybe it's not too late.

The steward handed Aleksandr his keys. In the kitchen, the rusty communal sink smelled of urine. An older woman in a bathrobe, her hair piled implausibly into a towel, was making toast underneath the exposed piping. On the other side of the kitchen hung decadent skeins of ladies' panty hose. On the bathroom shower curtain, bright green frogs frolicked between patches of black mold. In the hallway, a sign admonished the tenants not to hang up their underwear outside.

Aleksandr's room contained a bed bolted to the floor, a chitinous desk, and an urn-shaped samovar, presumably left over from the previous tenant. Near the ceiling, the laths were showing through the plaster. Raggedy strips of light filtered through the tiny fortochka above the bed, and Aleksandr went to lie in them. The exposed mattress was vaguely moist against his skin. He stretched out his legs. In Okha, he'd shared a bed with his two kicking little sisters, and they'd thrashed all night like dying fish.

He stared at the crescent-shaped fungal smear on the wall; he gazed through the latticework of frost on the windowpane. He tried to sleep. At the end of the week on the train, he'd been so desperate for sleep that he'd tried briefly to sleep in the bathroom—balanced precariously above the hole that emptied onto the tracks—until someone had yelled at him to get the fuck out, idiot. But in bed, he found that he missed the oceanic rumble of the train. He found that he was restless with the energy of being somewhere new when, his whole life, he'd only ever been somewhere old. He found he didn't feel like taking off his shoes yet.

He thought of the policemen down at the train station. He wondered if, out in the city somewhere, anybody was dumb enough to be celebrating.

He wrestled his map from his pocket, picked up his rucksack, and headed down the stairs. In the kitchen, he passed a woman who was using a filthy spatula to scrape the remains of an egg off a pan. She looked at Aleksandr darkly and did not speak. Outside, the cold was settling into itself—announcing its scope, the way pain does after a moment or two—and the cold, along with the accumulated fatigue of six days on a train (two of them spent standing up), was making Aleksandr dizzy. All around him, buildings were painted blue only up to height level, and Aleksandr felt as though he were trapped in the mural of a child who had grown bored and wandered away. The wind kicked up.

Nevsky Prospekt was beautiful: the friezes and columns looked like ancient Rome, and the half-buried stores and bright orange signs and illuminated cinemas looked like the center of the very modern universe. Aleksandr recognized the rally by a beaming poster of Stalin, held high above the crowd like a grandfatherly, mustached god. The crowd was small—desultory and damp, ringed by nervous-looking police. As he approached, Aleksandr saw that the Stalins were everywhere: out of one photo, Stalin glowered menacingly; out of another, Stalin stared with an expression of stern benevolence. Into a microphone, a man droned dully about the Battle of Stalingrad. At the edge of the crowd lurked a small group of men with skunk-striped Mohawks and plaid shirts. Aleksandr leaned against a telephone pole and tried to listen. He was exhausted, he realized, and here—in this last pocket of stingy sun, with the wind breaking at the buildings behind him and the monotone buzz of military accomplishment in his ears— he thought he could probably fall asleep standing up. He pulled his cap tighter over his head. His gaze faltered. His head started to fall forward.

"Enjoying the show?" A man was talking to him. Aleksandr lifted his earflaps and looked. The man was tall and thin; when he moved, it looked like his joints were locking and unlocking and painfully rearranging themselves. He was holding a glass bottle of Pepsi and wearing no gloves. Next to him stood two other men. One was notably pale, even for here, and had eyes the color of kopecks. The other was short, scarred, and writing furiously in a notebook. His mouth moved as if he was chewing something, even though Aleksandr somehow felt sure that he was not. All three of them were dressed in striped sailor shirts and quilted jackets and sodden flapped hats. The tall one wore a small silver medallion around his neck.

"Indeed," said Aleksandr. "Quite a sight."

"To think Koba would be one hundred," said the tall man. His voice was flatter than irony. "What a pity he is not here to enjoy the party."

"True," said Aleksandr. "It's evidently true."

"His reforms were truly adequate to the task of modernization, am I right?"

"Very adequate. More than adequate."

"And that mustache," said the pale one. "That mustache was quite an achievement, yes? Koba had more hair in that mustache than some men have on their entire heads."

Aleksandr turned to look at him. There was something about this one's face that made Aleksandr not want to look at it straight: a haggardness underneath the eyes that raised uncomfortable questions about life in Leningrad. "Yes," said Aleksandr, staring balefully at the ground. "An impressive feat."

The tall man looked at Aleksandr with some amusement then. When he leaned in, his voice was lower. "Did you know he was five feet four?" he said. "He was. He was five feet four and had a bad arm. They never showed it in pictures. They never showed him standing next to anybody. He's sitting in all the pictures with other dignitaries."

"I didn't know that," said Aleksandr carefully. "I was given to believe that Comrade Stalin was a man of some stature."

Aleksandr did not understand how things had gone so wrong so fast, so he turned to the short man, whose scars looked as if they might have just as easily been from fights as from some debilitating skin disease, and stuck out his hand. "Hello," he said. "I'm Aleksandr Kimovich Bezetov. I just moved here." He cast a bright smile, because in Okha, old women had always responded well to his smile. The men shot glances at one another and seemed to experience some collective facial twitching. It wasn't eye-rolling, precisely, but Aleksandr was seized by a frozen feeling that it meant something similar. He looked at the men and squinted. He tried to see in them signs of trouble, but they just looked like everyone else he'd seen on his way from the train station—underslept and vaguely hostile. The tall one was thin, but the other two looked simultaneously chubby and wanly malnourished, as though they'd had enough to eat of only one kind of food. The shortest one crouched down to the ground, revealing the haunches of a mustelid.

"I'm Ivan Dmietrivich Bobrikov," said the thin one. "This is Nikolai Sergeyevich Chernov."

"A pleasure," said Nikolai from the ground.

"The sovok here is Mikhail Andreyevich Solovyov," said Ivan. "Where are you from?"

"Okha," said Aleksandr. "In the east."

"We know where Okha is," said Nikolai. "We're students of geography."

"Geography?" said Aleksandr politely.

"Well, history," said Ivan. He cracked his knuckles.

"Real history," said Mikhail.

"Shut up, Misha," said Ivan. He winked at Aleksandr as though they were adults looking over the head of a child. Aleksandr didn't know what would be communicated by winking back, so he didn't. "And why are you here, tovarish?" said Ivan.

In the center of the crowd, a man was offering a tender eulogy for Stalin. His voice buckled and his nose turned bright red with emotion.

"To play chess," said Aleksandr. "I have a place at the academy. I'm working with Andronov."

"Oh yes? And what is a boy from Okha doing at the academy with Andronov?"

Aleksandr scratched his nose. "I was in his correspondence course first."

"I see," said Ivan. "You have a favorite player, then? You like Spassky?"

"He's all right. He let himself be psychologically outmaneuvered by Fischer, though, in '72. All the nonsense with the money and the late arrival."

"That match was rigged by the Americans, though, am I right? They were controlling Spassky via chemical and electronic devices, yes?"

Aleksandr stared at Ivan. He had no idea what he was supposed to say to this. "No," he said slowly. "No, I don't think so."

"And Rusayev? You're an admirer, surely, of Rusayev?"

"He's a bore."

"A bore!"

"He would've lost to Fischer, too, if Fischer hadn't gone crazy."

"The Americans should still have the World Championship, you're saying?"

"Well, I don't know about should. I'm just saying they would."

"Hm," said Ivan. "Interesting ideas you have. Is that all you brought with you?" He eyed Aleksandr's bag. "Meager possessions. The sign of a strong commitment to the Party."

Aleksandr didn't like that Nikolai was still crouching; it made him look as if he was about to pounce.

"I have some other things in my building," said Aleksandr. "But I'm committed to the Party." It was nice to say a familiar phrase in a strange city.

"I'll bet," said Ivan, producing a piece of paper and a pen from somewhere inside his enormous black coat. He held the pen's cap between his teeth and wrote something down. "Here." He handed Aleksandr a piece of paper, and Aleksandr squinted at it. "Café Saigon," said Ivan. "Maybe you've heard of it?"

"No," said Aleksandr apologetically. He was forever having to confess to not having heard of things, not having known things, not having done things. It was tiresome.

"It's on the corner of Nevsky and Vladimirsky. It's the building that always looks like it's under construction. We're pretty much always there, since our flat really doesn't have heat. Stop by sometime, if you like. Everyone else there is always talking about music, but we can talk geography."

Aleksandr stared at him. "Isn't geography sort of a settled field?"

"Less than you might think, turns out."

"Well," said Aleksandr. "All right." He awkwardly held the paper in one hand and his small backpack in the other. In the square, a tinny recording of the national anthem was starting to play. Aleksandr tried to turn to face it, but Ivan caught him by the shoulder.

"By the way," said Ivan. "Are you any good? At chess, I mean."

"Oh. Yes. I'm maybe starting to be."

"You came to Leningrad to find out?" said Nikolai.

"Yes." This was embarrassing: something about admitting out loud that he'd moved across the continent to determine his skill level at a game seemed outlandishly childish, as though he'd told them that he'd run away to find something he saw in a dream.

"Good," Nikolai said. In the waning light, his spotted face looked like some sort of environmental catastrophe. "That's good. Leningrad is where you find out what you are made of, yes? What you can stand."

The men laughed. "Yes," said Misha. "That's true. Tell me, tovarish, what can you stand?"

Aleksandr twisted the paper in his hands. "I don't know." The anthem was reaching its bombastic conclusion now, and lyrics about scarlet banners and deathless ideals went sailing over Aleksandr's head.

"Don't worry," Ivan said, putting his pen back in his pocket. "You'll find out."

And Aleksandr did find out. He could stand, it turned out, quite a lot: he wasn't particularly bothered by the communal bathrooms, the thin walls, the lack of privacy. He had nothing to guard: no lovers, no secrets, no deviations from the politically acceptable. In Okha, he'd lived with a mother and little sisters who took no interest in him; here, he sometimes dreamed of having a dark, mysterious question at the center of his life. The kommunalki were designed to collapse families, flatten out intimacies, make everybody the keeper of each other's secrets until those secrets became shallow and harmless. Soon Aleksandr knew far more about his neighbors than he cared to—if the door handle was turned down, the neighbor was out; if the slippers were gone, he was in for the night; if a man came back to his wife after an absence, it was expected that the neighbors would take the children. Everybody walked around half dressed—the women with their pale legs slipping in and out of their bathrobes, the men wearing stained undershirts as they boiled potatoes. Everybody stole one another's food—gelid and anonymous items left on the stove would be quickly, quietly consumed—and during the month without hot water, the women took to setting pots to boil in the kitchen and bathing right there without closing the door. Aleksandr heard even more than he saw—the crying of infants and drunks and lovers and widows—and sometimes he wanted to make some noise back: make people stop their screaming for a moment and wonder at what was going on in *there*. But his evenings were silent. He drank tea and read his chess books and chopped time into little tolerable increments until he thought he might be able to sleep.

Days were not much better. He registered at the chess academy and started work with Andronov, the instructor who'd heard of Aleksandr from his eastern scouts and summoned him across the continent, making the trip possible through contacts and bribes and veiled threats. In the months before his departure, Aleksandr and his family had taken to regarding Andronov as a terrible destroying angel who'd capriciously chosen Aleksandr for an awesome, elevating, all-consuming challenge. So it was nearly heretical to admit that Andronov was a disappointment: he was a short man with a thick neck, as it turned out, and he spat involuntarily when he spoke. At registration, Andronov took a perfunctory glance at Aleksandr, a slightly longer look at his papers, and said, "You may go. You will play number eleven." Aleksandr took his damp papers and went where Andronov pointed. Number 11 was a surly, pimply-faced youth from Irkutsk. Number 11's pimples encouraged Aleksandr to think that he might also need a friend, but that was a mistake. Aleksandr's questions after their first match were met with withering thirty-second silences followed by monosyllabic answers. Aleksandr found he did not need friends so badly.

A few weeks into the term, Andronov stopped by to watch Aleksandr play. Aleksandr beat his opponent that day—in fact, he'd beaten everybody he'd played so far, and he would beat all of his opponents at the academy during his time there, and Andronov himself, eventually— but Andronov only sniffed and said, "Not bad, considering."

Aleksandr's days, then, were spent in chilly, high-ceilinged rooms, across tables from men and boys who seemed dreadfully unhappy to be there. At first they treated him with indifference; then, as his winning streak grew noticeable, they treated him with a simmering resentment so understated that it amounted, basically, to more indifference. After a while Andronov started treating Aleksandr a bit differently—never warmly, though he watched his matches with more interest and gave him extra gruff attention and advice. He seemed to regard Aleksandr as a prize horse who merited careful monitoring but would be shot like the others if his leg was broken.

Still, Aleksandr's days were bearable. The breaks were interminable and awkward, but the matches seemed to exist outside of time—he fell into them as though he'd been knocked unconscious, and he never grew accustomed to the strange feeling of coming out of them and realizing that hours had passed without him.

Nights were worse. His mother phoned him occasionally, and he would tramp down the hall in his slippers, trying to avoid the gray stains on the floor. His mother would warble about his sisters and their schooling and ask him when he might be able to send money. Other people would need the phone for more pressing concerns: illnesses, money transfers, semi-secret arrangements and negotiations. They would crowd Aleksandr off the phone with their scrutiny, their calculated proximity. "No, Mamenchka," he'd say. "I can't send any money yet." Then he would tramp back down the hall to his dark room, light a candle, turn on the samovar for tea, and close his eyes until he could almost hear his former Pacific Ocean out the window.

There weren't friends, exactly, at the kommunalka, but he did come to know the characters there with as much depth as he probably knew anyone. On one side of him lived a small family—a couple and their toddling, very dirty baby—and he began to understand that the man beat the woman, and that the woman pinched the baby, and that the baby had a different cry depending on who was being beaten or pinched. On another side was an old muttering woman who was in constant conversation with nobody, as far as Aleksandr could tell. There was a long-haired elfin man who brought home other men; he had a post at the university, and halfway through the year he was found out and fired and had to leave the city. Everybody watched while he left, picking up his matted fuzzy slippers and carefully banging them against the doorframe while the steward held his keys. There was a drunk who would drink your cologne or dandruff shampoo if you left any in the bathroom. There was a pair of young girls who slept days and took calls in the nights and disappeared. The rustlings and comings and goings of everybody around him made Aleksandr feel as though he lived at the center of a panting organism—an organism without an inner monologue, that ran through the forest in syncopated, unknowing movements, looking for something.

At night Aleksandr lay in bed and pressed his eyes closed so hard that he saw stark designs against his eyelids and imagined the lives of the people around him. He saw the night girls, Elizabeta and Sonya, reclining across their beds, legs tangled together with the unnatural ease women seemed to have with each other's bodies. Their room would have the faint smell of lilac, cold and mild. They would have a parakeet, and they would devote a tragic amount of attention to it. They would come home on winter nights and turn on the samovar, wipe off their eye makeup carefully, and laugh about the bodies and idiosyncrasies and preferences of their men. They were, as Aleksandr imagined them, not entirely unhappy.

The old woman, Aleksandr decided, was talking to her dead husband. In early versions, he imagined for them a love story so beautiful that he'd have to stop thinking about the old woman sometimes— when the wind sliced through the side of the building like razor through cotton, and the enormous coldness of his solitude made him somehow afraid, as though he'd been cast into outer space—and he'd have to go to his chess books to recover. The old woman and her husband had been the unusual kind of people who wanted more than anything to love somebody, and they'd been lucky enough to find each other, and once they did, they were happy together—not grudgingly so, not with resigned resentful contentment, but really, really happy— forever. He was arrested for anti-Soviet activities and sent to the gulag for ten years, and when amnesty came, the old woman waited and waited and worked to find him but couldn't. So she sat nights, looking out the north-facing window, talking to him, trying to lead him back to her, muttering to him her secrets and stories and permanent love.

This early version was too maudlin, thought Aleksandr—especially as the frost of October hardened into the deep ice of November, and the summer and Okha became a long time ago, and the chess institute yielded illumination and high praise and absolutely no friends—so he amended it: the old woman had hated her husband, who'd been a fat Party official with soft hands and pampered tastes and no loyalties to anybody. He'd sold out friends for almost nothing; he was motivated not by a genuine commitment to perfect social equity but by a shallow desire to be stroked and rewarded by superiors. She'd run away from him because the bitter indifference of the lonesome city was preferable to his petty attentions and cruelties. She cursed him all day long, every day, warding him away with her churning, self-sustaining hate. The hate rose from their building like steam and hardened into a charm that kept her safe—and she could never stop her muttering, no matter how crazy it made her look, no matter how the young people avoided her in the hallways.

Looking back, Aleksandr was embarrassed to admit, it wasn't the humiliations and the moral compromises and the general undermining of humanity that most bothered him. In those days, he followed the papers only as much as the papers followed chess—which was some—so big important lapses on other subjects did not concern him, though it was true that incompetence in running a city turned out to be several degrees worse than incompetence in running a village. The trash piled up in Leningrad as in Okha, but Leningrad produced more trash. In Okha the roads turned to lakes of mud that stuck so savagely that some trucks, every year, had to be left until things dried out in July, and the ice went unattended everywhere—but in Leningrad there was so much ice that the streets were impossible even for walking, forget driving, and Aleksandr quickly bent an ankle that turned black before it got better. But it was not terrible. He had a roof, at least, and there was always some kind of food at the market, even if it wasn't the kind you were looking for. He didn't care for the billboards and didn't believe in the slogans, but nobody else did, either. He regarded Communism as a kind of collective benign lie, like the universal agreement among human beings to rarely discuss the fact that everybody would one day die.

What bothered him most, actually, was the cold. The cold seeped into his bones in October and stayed there. His fingers and toes took on a deep reptilian blue that was difficult to shake, no matter how much he pinched them or stood covering himself in the lukewarm communal shower. It had been nearly this cold in Okha, he figured, but cold was different when you lived alone. His arms and neck ached from the tension of constant low-grade shivering; he slept fitfully, curling into himself and breathing into his pillow to catch snatches of warmth that soon turned moist and chilled. By January he almost could not remember what it felt like to be warm, to let his shoulders and jaw slacken, to take a breath in the fresh air that didn't nearly choke him with cold. This, he thought, this could drive a man crazy—it was like constant semi-starvation, or sleep deprivation, or whatever else they did to men in Siberia. If he had any secrets to reveal, he would confess them all for an hour by the summer sea, asleep in a ray of sun. He dreamed about warmth, he later thought, the way incarcerated men must dream about women.

And so it was not principle that finally drove him to the café on Nevsky and Vladimirsky. Later, journalists would want to know what impelled him to first start meeting with the other unsatisfied youth in Leningrad; what moral outrage finally pushed him over the edge and into the waiting arms of the dissident movement. And for a while he would tell them lies—about the constraints to his free and far-ranging ideas, to his literary appetites, to his pride—and they would nod appreciatively and respect him all the more. Until one day, long after his career in chess had peaked—he would always recall it was the year when he first lost to a computer, a much noted event that prompted worldwide speculation about the triumph of technology and the obsolescence of human beings, generally—he leaned in and told a writer from a small Azerbaijani newspaper the truth: that he'd started going to the cafés, at first, because they were the only place in that first forbidding winter where he could, for a moment, get warm. That was why he went the first time.

And for other reasons, he kept going.

JENNIFER DUBOIS's *A Partial History of Lost Causes* was one of the most acclaimed debuts of recent years. It was a finalist for the PEN/ Hemingway Award for Debut Fiction, winner of the California Book Award for First Fiction and the Northern California Book Award for Fiction, and *O: The Oprah Magazine* chose it as one of the ten best books of the year. DuBois was also a recipient of the Whiting Writers' Award and named one of the National Book Foundation's 5 Under 35 authors. A graduate of the Iowa Writers' Workshop, duBois recently completed a Stegner Fellowship at Stanford University. Originally from Massachusetts, she now lives in Texas.

jennifer-dubois.com
@jennifer_dubois

ABOUT THE TYPE

This book was set in Minion, a 1990 Adobe Originals typeface by Robert Slimbach (b. 1956). Minion is inspired by classical, old-style typefaces of the late Renaissance, a period of elegant, beautiful, and highly readable type designs. Created primarily for text setting, Minion combines the aesthetic and functional qualities that make text type highly readable with the versatility of digital technology.

Chat.
Comment.
Connect.

Visit our online book club community at
Facebook.com/RHReadersCircle

Chat
Meet fellow book lovers and discuss what you're reading.

Comment
Post reviews of books, ask—and answer—thought-provoking
questions, or give and receive book club ideas.

Connect
Find an author on tour, visit our author blog, or invite one of
our 150 available authors to chat with your group on the phone.

Explore
Also visit our site for discussion questions, excerpts, author
interviews, videos, free books, news on the latest releases,
and more.

Books are better with buddies.
Facebook.com/RHReadersCircle

RANDOM HOUSE READER'S CIRCLE ®

RANDOM HOUSE